KILLER IN THE DARK

KILLER IN THE DARK

Colin Foreman

Edited by Lillian King

The adventure continues.
Odin's secret agents arrive in Corfu
to kill the last Stone Keeper.
Alistair of Cadbol is under sentence of
death in the bowels of Berwick Castle and
Tella the Mac Mar forges a secret and terrible
alliance, to destroy the Younger and the
Celtic peoples of Scotland.
Only one man stands in Tella's way and he
is a young shepherd, and his name is
Dougie of Dunfermline.
The battle of the light iron is about to begin.

Killer in the Dark is the second part of a five book
series titled Keepers and Seekers.

This book is dedicated to the memory of Gordon Mead.
"Flash" was the biggest loony I ever knew and the
world is a poorer place without him.

A catalogue record for this book is
available from the British Library

Printed and bound in Poland by Polskabook

Published by Myroy Books Limited
Hillside House, Glenlomond, Kinross, KY13 9HF

ISBN 10 – 0-9548949-1-X
ISBN 13 – 978-0-9548949-1-7

Acknowledgements

I would like to thank the following people.

Lillian King (Editing)

Wayne Reynolds (Cover paintings)

Fiona Campbell (Black and white illustrations)

Lee Scammacca and Craig Williams at CREE8 in Kinross (Design and typesetting)

Rosie Crawford (Proof reading)

Ian Donaldson, Royal Bank of Scotland, Kinross (Overdraft)

George Grey and John Webb at Waterstones (Design and continued support)

Robert Snuggs at Bounce (Raw energy)

Martin West at Catnip (Super sourcing)

Abi and Jonny (Rave reviews)

I would like to say a very special thank you to everyone who bought a copy of the first book. All the profits from *To The End Of The World* are being gifted to the Children's Hospice Association of Scotland and, at the time of going to press with *Killer in the Dark*, you have raised over £10,000. CHAS do wonderful work and every penny will make a real difference.

CONTENTS

ABOUT BOOK ONE

Seven and a half thousand years ago, as the great ice sheets begin to thaw across Scotland, four brothers, Odin, Thor, Tirani and Myroy, survive a terrible accident to become Ancient Ones. The key to their eternal lives and extraordinary powers is a living ruby.

Fearing his brother's cruel ambitions, Myroy steals the stone from Thor and destroys his invasion fleet. Odin, who is driven by anger and greed, swears vengeance for Thor's death and vows to recover the ruby, and use its power to destroy the free peoples of Scotland.

There follows a cat-and-mouse game, through the long centuries. Myroy chooses the Donald family and their descendants to live a quiet life, and hide the stone from Odin and his followers, the Seekers.

In our time, three children visit their grandparents in Scotland and get lost in a snowstorm. When they take shelter in a cottage, Myroy tells them a story about a Celtic shepherd who lived centuries ago.

Dougie of Dunfermline faces the challenges of Mountain, Island and Castle to become the first Stone Keeper. Even though Dougie survives these challenges he knows little about the stone's power, or the danger it holds for his family. Certainly, he does not know that Gora and the souls of everyone who has ever tried to steal Amera's stone, remain trapped inside the ruby, waiting for someone to give the stone away, break Thor's curse, and release them.

Storm clouds gather for Dougie's king, Malcolm the Younger, and for his people, who are surrounded by enemies intent on their destruction. Norse warriors, led by Thorgood Firebrand, invade the north of the kingdom to escape famine in their own lands. At the same time, Tella the Mac Mar, eager for revenge after his defeat on Carn Liath, forges a secret and terrible alliance with the Welsh and the Angles.

When the old man's story is told, Peter Donald realises that he is to become the next Stone Keeper. The ruby is passed on to him, but he loses it, not to Odin's Seekers, but to Smith, a descendant of Tella the Mac Mar. Smith tricks Peter's sister into giving him the ruby and he uses its fantastic power to invade London. During the battle of Pinner High School, Peter recaptures the stone, but at an awful price, and he flees with his grandmother to Corfu.

In this book, in our time, Odin plans to hunt Peter down and use the stone to rule the world. In Celtic Scotland, Tella the Mac Mar plans his invasion. Only one man stands in his way and he is a young shepherd, and his name is Dougie of Dunfermline.

The battle of the light iron is about to begin.

PROLOGUE

THE MAP OF DENBARA THE SCRIBE : WINTER 676 AD

The ship lurched and the scribe lifted his quill from the parchment. Denbara was cold, very cold.

His fingers were white, and he cupped his hands together, trying to blow life back into them. He thought about his home and family, and wondered how things might have changed during his great journey. Few men, if any, would have seen all the places he had recorded over the last two years, but this was poor reward for the hardships he had endured in the name of his king.

He looked with pride at the map, with its headlands, bays and rivers, which marked the coast of Scotland. There was none like it in the world. Symbols told of the fast ways for travel and the areas that might be easily defended by an army.

The pathways north from Berwick were only thin lines of ink, but to the scribe they were the record of his every twist and turn. There was the mighty Forth and, above it, the Tay. These rivers formed the boundaries of rich lands, which would be highly prized by his master. Further north, hills rolled down to great plains, which reached out to a rocky coastline. These bleak shores marked the beginnings of the Cold Sea and Denbara shuddered as he thought about how its waters had nearly claimed him.

He felt lonely and tired, and troubled by the secret he kept.

"Not long now," mumbled Denbara as he remembered the promise made to him.

"Enough gold to complete your work and end your days in comfort," Tella had said.

The scribe looked around the inside of his shelter. It was small and makeshift, just sail cloth draped over a rope running from half way up the mast to the ship's rail, but at least he enjoyed more protection than the crew. They had to sleep out on the open deck. As it had done each day at this time, the canvas flap of his makeshift tent burst open, and a handsome, grinning face peeped in. Denbara hastily folded the parchment, tucked it into the pigskin wallet and smiled back.

Despite the need for caution and secrecy, he had grown to like and respect his young visitor. He was clever and helpful, and asked few questions. Denbara also owed him his life.

The storm had broken with little warning and the ship's master struggled to keep the ship head-on into the waves. A mighty wave crashed forward and Denbara felt the deck drop, then lift as it struck. The bow punched forward again and water covered the deck. The next punch threw up a shower and soaked him, salt stinging his eyes. He squinted and looked at the crew, huddling together, their backs pressed tightly against the ship's rail.

A lightning bolt lit the darkness and a thunderous boom followed a moment later. A warning cry sounded above the deafening wind. The wave hit the ship sideways-on and engulfed the deck completely. Barrels, boxes and ropes were thrown from one side of the deck to the other, and Denbara heard the crack crack crack of the edges of the poorly folded canvas. Then he was in the water, choking and struggling in the cold, boiling sea.

Denbara tried to drive these awful memories from his mind and smiled at the boy who had dived in to save him.

"And where do we go today?"

"We sail south and the skipper says we will soon be amongst many islands."

At noon, a mother tern watched two specks move slowly across her island and she tucked in her wings and dived at an incredible speed. The specks were men and moving towards her eggs.

"Is there any fresh water?" asked Denbara.

The deck hand shook his head and the scribe made a note. No water.

"And just the three sandy coves on the north side where ships can land safely and unseen?"

"Just the three," replied the young sailor and, anticipating the scribe's next question, "In a strong breeze, a day's sail at its longest and half that at its widest. It's a fair size."

"Is it named?"

"There are scores of islands like this one and my guess is few are named."

Denbara smiled. "Well, I named the last one."

He ducked as an angry tern swooped and screamed, inches from his ear.

"We must be near her nest."

The deck hand smiled and thought about the nest he had left to find adventure.

"Call it the Island of Lissy," he said.

Seven days later, the scribe sat with the boy in his shelter.

"Which wind has driven us?" Denbara asked.

"We continue to the south and the word is we are only three days from Skye."

"Three days," said Denbara. "Three days and then all is done."

Denbara walked out onto the deck and across to the ship's rail. He gazed at the coastline and thought about the words he would write on the map - *Dotted with many sandy coves. A small force could land here unseen.* High mountains rose up further inland and he guessed that far away, hidden by them, was Carn Liath. There were no cottages, or towers, and the map-maker's eyes searched for any detail he should include. The ship's master came to stand by his side and they talked about the distance and direction they had taken since the last sighting. The bitter wind was from the north and the land they had followed had remained on their left side. The master confirmed that the first of the Outer Islands was only half a day's sail to the west and Denbara made a mental note to check it was so on his parchment.

"I want to thank you," said Denbara, handing the skipper a small bag of coins.

"You have been the easiest of passengers to please and one of the best paying."

"Remember, my work is not to be spoken of to anyone."

The ship's master nodded. "I shall hold my tongue and so shall my crew."

They leant on the ship's rail and stared across the Great Sea. The bitter wind rose and the scribe shuddered again, but this time with fear.

On the final evening of the journey, the young sailor brought a bowl of steaming broth to Denbara's tent.

"Will I see you again?" he asked.

"Aye, I hope so, laddie," replied Denbara, "and how do you plan to spend the coins you have earned on the long voyage?"

"I thought I might visit the lands of the Franks and seek my fortune there."

The old scribe smiled. "Those lands are spoken of as warm and fair."

The sailor smiled too. "I have heard that said."

"Well, whatever you choose to do, may good fortune go with you, Alec of Dunfermline."

The friends shook hands.

In fair weather, and with a light heart, the ship's crew said their farewells on the sands by a small fishing village on Skye. Denbara was met by a warrior named Borak. He was dressed in the traditional black kilt of the Pictish people and led two horses.

"With a following wind we made good time," said Denbara.

Borak nodded and stared at the traveller's meagre possessions, as though searching for something important. He wrapped Denbara's shawl, writing box and cloth bag into the folds of a blanket and tied them securely to his own horse. The scribe's new companion remained silent for most of the short journey to the hill-fort at Deros. Denbara tried to make conversation by asking if there was any news from his home, on the other side of the island, but Borak said there was none and, with a growing feeling of unease, Denbara followed him up the grassy track. Many times Denbara reached inside his shirt to check that his wallet was safe.

5

Many times his guard thought back to the orders he had received from Tella the Mac Mar two summers ago.

"He may have spoken of our intentions to his family, Borak. Make sure they do not speak to others about it. Spare Aglan the Tongue Speaker. He will be useful."

Borak glanced at Denbara, taking no pleasure from knowing how he had earned his new position by killing every member of the scribe's family, except one.

A group of nine riders made haste towards them and Borak raised a hand. Denbara watched them stop, dismount and bow, and guessed, correctly, that his companion was high-ranking amongst them. Borak and one of the riders moved some way apart from the others and Denbara strained to hear their words. Their conversation sounded urgent and full of purpose. He thought Borak said, "But they *may* know," and the other man nodded in agreement.

The nine riders galloped away towards the fishing village and the two men were left to continue the last part of the journey alone.

Denbara had dreamt about his homecoming so many times on his travels. In strange lands he had wished for no more than to see the outline of familiar hills, the fine rooms of the royal court and the faces of his pupils. He remembered how he had been chosen as a boy and schooled in the ways of the written word. His own teacher was long dead and, now that his mission for Tella was complete, he could dedicate himself to the work he loved, the teaching of children.

He studied Borak and saw a sadness in the man's face. His stomach tightened and again that feeling of deep unease flooded through his veins.

The gate to the fort was menacing and well guarded. A single track curved up through a cutting made in the high earth banking and two great wooden doors opened to greet them. There seemed to be many more warriors than when he had left and they were going about their business in the wide open area, which led up to the inner walled circle. Here ancient stone walls protected the court of the Mac Mar.

Their arrival had not gone unnoticed and a young man raced over to greet Denbara.

"It is the master, the master scribe," he yelled.

Denbara looked down and smiled.

"Is that you, young Caricus? My, how you have grown."

"We have missed your teachings, master. Will you return to us?"

"Of course I will," replied Denbara. "As soon as my work is done."

"What work has kept you away from us for so long?"

"None that concerns you," said Denbara quickly, but he felt Borak's agitation at Caricus's question.

As they entered the king's chamber, Tella leapt out of his seat and, lifting the end of a wide table, sent goblets, plates, food and knives clattering to the floor.

"Place the map here."

A servant hurried into the chamber to clear up the mess and the king glared at him. The man went white with fear and retreated. He had seen that look before.

"Welcome home, Denbara," said Tella, "you have done me the greatest of services and you shall be richly rewarded."

The scribe took the pigskin wallet from his shirt and the king grabbed the map, and unfolded it upon the table. The three men talked for a long while about the symbols and their meanings. Tella asked many questions and thought long and hard about each detail, as if he needed to commit every single word to memory. Finally, the Mac Mar glanced at Borak and commanded Denbara to kneel before him.

"The map is the key to our ambitions as a people and without you, Denbara, the future would not be as clear to me as it is now."

From a heavy, wooden chest, the king took a bag of coins and handed it to Denbara.

"Take this as your reward."

"Thank you, Your Majesty," said Denbara meekly.

"Of course," continued Tella, "the real key to our ambitions is secrecy."

"And as you asked of me, I have kept our secret."

Tella spoke in a soft, cruel voice, "But can I be sure?"

Borak drove his dagger into the scribe's back.

As a pool of blood grew on the floor, Tella barked fresh orders at Borak.

"Ride with Tumora to Llewellyn, King of the Welsh peoples. Then go to Cuthbert. Ask them to gather their armies for the alliance."

Borak nodded.

Triumphantly, Tella held his map in the air.

"Tell them to wait for the Light Iron."

Borak nodded again.

"Tell them we are nearly ready. Scotland will be ours!"

CHAPTER ONE

ALISTAIR'S MESSAGE

It had been another long and hard winter. The tops of the hills surrounding Dougie's farm shone white with snow in the last rays of the sun. A cold wind blew and a small skein of geese flew overhead in a "v" formation and Dougie knew the weather would not begin to improve until these birds gathered together in great numbers and left to travel to the north. Each autumn they would arrive and signal the shortening of days, and each spring they would depart for unknown lands.

Dougie of Dunfermline cherished the seasons, lived by them and, like most of his people, he celebrated their passing with music, dancing and food. He was close to the land and noticed keenly the changes in weather and crops, and the habits of wild creatures. Warm winds were a time away yet, but Dougie smiled and thought of summer. He knelt to touch a snowdrop that had pushed its head up above the cold earth.

Then, as he often did, to remind himself of his friends, Dougie reached into his pocket and pulled out the brooch that the Younger had given him at Carn Liath. It was mysterious and beautiful. He stroked a finger over the deep red ruby at its heart.

"There is no more worth having than this."

The stranger on the hill had said that he would need to be ready to give the stone away gladly, but Dougie could not imagine doing so and once again he tried to understand what the man had meant and why his words seemed to have such a deep meaning. Dog danced around his master's legs and wagged his tail as though everything in the world depended on the affection of his master.

"Good boy," said Dougie as he bent to rub the sheepdog's ears.

"You're right, time to go back."

Taking a last look at the sheep, grazing contentedly in the fields, they set off for home. Having walked a short way, with Dog beside him, they stopped where the wild carrots grew. The ground was hard and bitten by frost, and Dougie knelt beside them and slowly scraped the earth away from a small clump of carrots with his dirk.

"More for the feast," he said and Dog raised his head and gave him a quizzical look.

The wind bit deep into Dougie's body and he shuddered with the cold. Glancing back over his shoulder, he saw the old stile where last spring the king's secret rider had brought a new adventure. It had taken him to the Great Palace and then to the very edge of the world. Dougie thought about the Outer Islands and the fleet of longships that had hidden there. He had nearly been killed by an arrow and it was only good fortune that had saved him.

His attention turned to his special supper. Mairi would be cooking the winter feast and he could just make out a thin trail of smoke rising from the smoke hole in the roof of his cottage.

Dougie dropped down onto the lower pastures and saw his children playing in a deep snow-bank, which was only a tiny fragment of the great white blanket that had once engulfed his land. Calum and Jock were throwing snowballs at each other and his little daughter was feeding the chickens. A snowball missed one of the boys and hit Tanny on the back as she bent to offer seed to one of the hens.

"I wish you would stop bloomin' fighting all the time," screamed Tanny.

The boys shouted back, "Mind your own bloomin' business," and pelted her with more snow.

"I wonder where they get such terrible language from?" thought Dougie, even though he already knew the answer.

Dougie's cottage was small, warm and cosy, and as he entered a rich smell of cooking hit him. Mairi was turning a spit on the wood fire and there was a wide variety of winter plants on the kitchen table. Dougie added the carrots and walked up to his wife and kissed her.

"How long before it is all ready?"

Mairi gave him a knowing look.

"A long while yet. Why don't you go and see your friends down at Arngask Farm whilst we are waiting?"

"Well, I had not thought of that, but it does sound like a fine idea." Dougie grinned.

Mairi gave him an, *I think that is exactly what you were thinking,* look and added, "Besides I do not want you here under my feet when there is so much to do."

Dog was already asleep on his blanket and Dougie moved quietly to the door, but as soon as he lifted the latch, the sheepdog leapt to his feet and bounded over to him.

"Aye, and you can take that dog, Dog, with you as well," scolded Mairi.

"Dog, Dog?"

"You know what I mean Douglas, take that bloomin' Dog with you."

"I wish you wouldn't say that word."

Dougie just made it through the door as a pig's trotter thudded into it.

It began to snow again as he set off for the meeting place. The wind swept into his face and he tucked his arms inside the fold of the thick plaid that trailed up from his waist and over his shoulder. Head down and determined, he was soon in sight of familiar lights.

"Greetings, young man," grunted Grant, the owner of Arngask.

"Greetings to you," replied Dougie.

Grant was one of the grumpiest men that Dougie knew. He had a face that looked as though it had spent many years being beaten by rough weather, and much of its character came from the deep lines running down it. But as Dougie would point out to his friends, Grant always kept an ample supply of heather ale and encouraged good company. His cottage, like everyone else's, was small and did not need many of the local shepherds to create a warm and friendly atmosphere.

Conversation always seemed to turn to either the problems of being a farmer, which Dougie would readily join in, or gossip about who was doing what. Dougie would avoid these discussions remembering what his grandmother had always told him.

"Dougie, if you do not have something nice to say about someone, then do not say anything."

He drank a few wee drams with his thirsty friend, Stewart of Glenbowmond, and the evening passed swiftly as they talked about barley, oats and the do's and don'ts of lambing.

After a while Dougie made his excuses and stood to leave. As he did, the door burst open and two strangers, one small and one very large, entered the cottage with thick snow billowing in behind them. Their faces were hidden by their plaids, which were crisp and white. The men walked straight towards Dougie and stood in front of him, steam rising from their cold garments.

They looked as though they had travelled a long way through the bad weather and shared an important purpose. Few strangers called on Grant and, in these dangerous times, people were wary of anyone they did not know. Stewart leant back on his stool and reached down into his belt for his dirk. Dog gave a low growl. Dougie stared at them and put his hand onto Stewart's arm as if to reassure him.

"It is a cold night for the men of Tain to be so far from home."

The two warriors pulled the frozen cloth from their faces.

"Aye, it is that, laddie," replied the big man.

"It is good to see you again, Hamish," smiled Dougie, "and you too, Donald."

The men shook hands. It had been nearly a year since the friends had shared an adventure, and Dougie thought again about their terrible journey, aboard the *Pride of Tiree*, to the islands beyond Oban.

"What brings you here?" asked Dougie.

"Grave business," said Hamish, the biggest and strongest warrior in Scotland.

"Aye, grave business," added wee Donald, shaking his head slowly.

"And business that we cannot discuss in front of others," continued Hamish.

"Are you sure about that?" questioned Donald, glancing hopefully at the heather ale.

Dougie looked at his friends. "Have you eaten?"

Dog raised a hopeful ear.

"Not since breakfast," lamented Hamish rubbing his empty belly.

"Well, you shall stay with me and join our winter feast," invited Dougie.

The sheepdog bounded around them in the snow and the shepherd was surprised to see that there were three horses tied to the branches of a tree.

"Can you ride?" asked Donald.

"I have only tried it once before," replied Dougie truthfully, "and a lot depends on the horse."

"Well up you get, laddie, you are about to get plenty of practice," warned Hamish.

On the short journey to the cottage, Dougie of Dunfermline worried about his friends' words and wondered what he should say to Mairi about their unexpected guests. She would probably be very welcoming, and later he'd get a scolding for dumping travellers on the household without warning. Dougie shuddered and not from the cold. Secretly, he would rather face the Picts, or the Norsemen, than Mairi when there was a "telling off," to be had. But, Mairi took it all very much in her stride and greeted Hamish and Donald warmly. Then she hurried them in front of the fire.

"You must be frozen through."

The children were desperate to hear their stories. Of course they included the battle on Carn Liath and the adventures on the far islands, but they also told of strange lands across the sea in Ireland, and south to the borders with the Angles. The feast was a merry one and, soon after the last dish was finished, the wee ones were put to bed where they lay together, curled up in a large shawl.

The friends sat together, staring at the burning logs that gave the room its only light.

"Well Hamish, you have not come all this way to pay us your compliments," said Dougie.

"No, laddie," replied Hamish. "Alistair is missing."

"Wise words," said Donald.

Dougie sat back on his stool and Dog raised his head and looked up at them as if to say, "Who is missing? We are all here."

Mairi put her arms around Dougie's shoulders and, knowing something bad was coming, gave him a comforting squeeze.

"For some time now, Alistair has been working for the king. Malcolm has nearly been killed on three occasions and we do not know who is behind it."

"And Alistair was given the task of finding out," added Donald. "The last we heard was that he journeyed to the south."

"The south?" asked Dougie, remembering the words of the stranger on the hill, who had warned him that he would face another adventure to the south.

"Aye laddie, he went to the lands held by the Angles. We think he found out that someone there wants to unseat the king and put a new ruler in his place."

Hamish passed Dougie a parchment.

"Malcolm has given us horses and asked us to discover what is going on. Our only clue is a note written by Alistair and handed to us by a messenger ten days ago."

Dougie and Mairi stared down at a single, torn page and a message that had been written in great haste. Neither could understand it and so Donald read it aloud for them.

Please pass this letter to Hamish of Tain.
Hamish, I have reached the Old Toll House in Melrose.

There is business here that is darker and more secret than we ever imagined. If you do not hear from me again within seven days then I beg you, get word to Malcolm the Younger to seek out the shield with the Saxon cross.
I remain forever, your friend and in your debt.
Alistair of Cadbol.

"Where is Melrose?" asked Mairi.

"Two days' hard ride to the south," said Hamish, "and close to the border with the Angles."

"Tough border country, at the end of the world," added Donald grimly.

"Have you ever seen a shield with a Saxon cross?" asked Mairi.

"Never on my travels," replied Hamish, "and I am familiar with most of the signs of the clans."

Donald nodded. "Aye, this is not a Scottish shield we are looking for."

Mairi stood.

"You will need a good night's sleep and food for the journey."

Her words were brave and yet the manner in which she spoke them told of other feelings.

Later, Dougie kissed her lovingly.

"Thank you. Will you be alright?"

"Dougie of Dunfermline, just you be back for the spring planting," she said and for some time they sat together, holding hands and staring deep into the dying embers of the fire.

The morning was bright and fresh. Mairi rose first and gave the children the leftovers from the winter feast. Hamish opened one eye sleepily to the noise of the squabbling children.

"There is no sleeping in with that lot."

Dog jumped on him and licked his beard.

"Or with you," he growled.

An hour after sunrise the three riders stopped to take a last look back at Dougie's farm. A long trail of disturbed snow snaked behind them, down the hill towards the white cottage where little Tanny chased the chickens.

"A fine family, Dougie," said Hamish in a kind voice.

"Noisy bloomin' children," added Donald.

"Don't say bloomin'," snapped Dougie crossly.

"I can't imagine where I picked it up," said Donald.

The friends pushed on southwards and made good progress. When the sun was at the highest point in its low winter arc, they reached the great river. Dougie thought that it must be over a thousand paces from shore to shore and that crossing these dangerous waters should not be attempted without an experienced guide. He glanced at Hamish.

"What is the river called?"

"This is the Forth."

"What happened to the third?" asked Donald.

"This is the Forth," continued Hamish, "and we need to find the ferry crossing from the village of Culross."

They rode east along a ridge that followed the line of the river and in less than an hour they saw, below them, a close-knit group of houses that huddled around a small pier.

"Have you been here before?" asked Dougie.

"Aye, once as a boy," confirmed Hamish, "you pay a coin and the ferryman takes you over."

"For a coin I would expect the Younger himself to row us over," said Donald.

A rough track led down to a pier where a small boat, with a single brown sail, bobbed up and down beside it.

"We will never get the horses on that thing," warned Dougie.

"It's not the *Pride of Tiree,* is it?" replied Donald.

"And it is not the sea we are crossing," growled Hamish.

The friends rode down into the hamlet. It seemed deserted and they tied their horses to a small, weather-worn fence that ran along the bank by the pier. A brass bell stood at one end of

the fence and Donald went over to it. A sign read *Ring the bell.*
He rang the bell. It gave out a sad clang that carried a great
distance in the still air. They all stood looking at the ferry and
stamped their feet on the cold ground to keep warm. As they
spoke, their breath came out in white shadows.

After some time they thought they could hear someone
laughing. Down the track from Culross came an old woman,
bent in two with age and supporting herself with a crooked staff
that was as gnarled as her face.

"I hope the ferry goes quicker than she does," said Donald
cheekily.

"I heard that," croaked the old woman, "I fought at Carn
Liath."

"Sorry," apologised Dougie, trying to win her over, "we wish
to travel across the river."

"Ten coins," cackled the woman.

"Ten coins!" gasped Hamish in disbelief, "I once paid a single
coin."

"The great Arkinew, the king's alchemist himself, passed
here last moon. He says it is *infation*."

"In what?" asked Donald.

"*Infation*. Costs go up, boats need repairing and I need to
make my living."

"You could buy a boat for ten coins," bellowed Hamish.

"Then buy yourself a boat," snapped the old woman harshly.

Dougie smiled at her. "Five coins for all of us."

"You look like a nice young man," cackled the woman, "six
coins."

"Agreed," agreed Dougie.

"Six coins," exclaimed Donald, and Dougie kicked him.

"Remember why we are here. Is Alistair not worth six
coins?"

Hamish and Donald glanced at each other as if to say, "It's a
close thing."

Dougie would never forget the ferry crossing. The horses

were nervous and reluctant to go on board. They pulled hard against their reins and shook their heads in fear.

"Untie the ropes," cackled the ancient crone.

As the sail was raised and the boat drifted wearily away from the pier, Dougie thought about Kenneth of Blacklock. They quickly picked up speed and a broad white wake marked their uneasy passage. Forty paces from the shore, Hamish and Donald were amused to see an old man hobbling out of one of the cottages. He was clearly upset about something and shouted angrily, and waved a stick in the air.

"Just ignore him," chuckled the old woman.

"Why so?" asked Dougie.

She gave Dougie a cheeky wink.

"The old fool has been chasing me for years."

"I think she likes you," teased Donald.

"I heard that," said the old woman, "I don't show my favour to anyone you know."

The small craft rose and fell with each wave, and made slow progress against the strong current. The woman threw her head back, gave out a raucous laugh, and revealed a mouth without teeth and two rows of black gums.

"Good job you are not paying by the day."

Water began to spill on board as they met the rougher waves, which mark the deepest parts of the river. Hamish and Donald worked frantically with their hands to throw it back out and the old woman, bent double at the tiller, watched them and cackled joyfully.

With great relief the friends finally reached the far shore and disembarked. The horses too seemed to welcome solid ground beneath their feet and stamped their hooves to show it.

"Have a safe journey," said the woman.

"Thank you," said Dougie.

"All part of the service."

Donald lifted his eyes to the sky.

"You robbed us of our coins," added Hamish rudely, as the

ferry slipped away from the shore.

"I like coins and I have not enjoyed myself so much for many a year."

"You handle the ferry wonderfully," called back Dougie, his hands cupped around his mouth.

She tossed her head back at the old man on the far shore. He was still dancing with rage.

"Bet he is as mad as a Pict without a mountain."

"How so?" called Dougie.

"It is his boat and I've not done this before."

Her wild laughter grew fainter and fainter as the wind carried her back across the cold waters of the Forth.

Apart from the ferry crossing, the rest of the journey to Melrose was uneventful. Dougie noticed that the hills of the borders were white, low lying and rounded.

"Good country for sheep," he thought, and then, like his friends, his mind went out to Alistair.

"I wonder how he is," said Dougie, more to himself than to the others.

"Aye," replied Hamish and Donald together.

***

The cell in the bowels of Berwick Castle was no more than five paces square. It stank of death and decay, little light troubled it and water froze on its walls. The chains round Alistair's ankles bound him to a great iron ring that was buried in the centre of the cell and he cursed as he realised they could not be broken.

He peered through the gloom at his companion. It was almost as if the man had no face, for his white hair and beard seemed to be as one, reaching down to the belt of the torn and filthy plaid he wore. In the gloom, Alistair couldn't guess how old the prisoner was, but he could see that he was very thin. The man's arms and legs were like twigs and his ribs showed through his wheezing chest.

"What are you doing here?" asked Alistair.

"Having a rest and a nice change," wheezed the man in a Scottish accent.

"A nice change?"

"Aye, I spent five years in the cell next door and the guards put me in here for a bit of a change."

Alistair felt his spirits falling.

"It's a wee bit warmer in this one and it has running water."

The bearded man ran his hand down an icicle that hung above his head and licked his finger.

"Lovely," he said.

Alistair thought about the events that had led to his capture, totally alert to all the sounds of his new home. The shallow and regular wheezing of his cellmate, the occasional scuttling of a large black rat and the constant dripping of water. The rhythm of his friend's wheezing was shattered by the opening of a grille at the base of the thick oak door. It snapped open loudly and then shut again in a second. Alistair could just make out that two tin bowls had been thrust into the cell by a gloved hand.

"Supper time," shrieked the man excitedly, and he dragged his chains across the floor to reach the food. "Excellent. Extra maggots."

Alistair looked at the hunk of bread in his dish. It seemed to be moving. He lifted it to his nose and his head leapt backwards with the smell of rotting flesh. In the darkness, Alistair watched his cellmate pick out small worms from the bread. Many were long dead, but it was the wiggly ones he seemed to enjoy the most. The man made sounds of hungry pleasure as he lowered them, one by one, into his mouth.

"Quite the best I've had for ages," he wheezed.

"Quite the most disgusting thing I have ever seen."

"Don't you want yours?"

Alistair shivered with the cold.

"I'm not hungry."

The prisoner grabbed Alistair's bowl and devoured its contents.

"Two bowls. Just like a winter feast."

"Why have you been imprisoned?" asked Alistair politely.

"Stole a pig."

"And how long have you been here?"

"Don't know exactly, about seven years."

"Seven years for a pig?"

"It was a big pig," said the man proudly.

"And what's your name?"

"They call me Bob the Pig Stealer."

"Doesn't sound very fair to me."

"It isn't fair," added the man indignantly. "My name is Mackey."

"Well Mackey, it is a pleasure to meet you. My name is Alistair of Cadbol."

"And what did you steal?"

"I didn't steal anything," replied Alistair in a hurt voice, "I was on a mission for my king."

"Treason, eh? Lucky devil, you will probably get out in a week."

"I do not think so," continued Alistair darkly, "for if I am judged guilty then I will be beheaded in one moon."

"Still, it could be a lot worse."

Alistair struggled to see how it could be worse and sat in silence for a good while.

"Got any good stories?" wheezed Mackey.

"Would you like to hear how I came to this place? It is a story of high intrigue, desperate doings, honour and deep friendship."

"Not really. Got any jokes?"

"No I don't," snapped Alistair.

"Only fooling. Get on with it, I haven't got all day."

Alistair rested his head in his hands, deep in concentration, and wondered where to begin. It had all happened so quickly and the order of events was not fully clear to him. He carefully felt the back of his head. It was tender and the two egg-sized lumps still throbbed. Peering through the gloom, at the shape that was his cellmate, he told his story.

One moon before the shortest day of the year, Alistair had been invited to join the Younger at the palace and he found him in good spirits for there were few problems across the kingdom. On the afternoon of his arrival, he joined a party of nine riders and they hunted deep within the royal forest. The king speared one wild boar and his men another three. Satisfied with the bounty, they set off for the palace talking freely, happily, and looking forward to a fine supper. But, on a narrow path that skirted a deep loch, they were attacked by twenty soldiers on horseback. The king's bodyguard fought bravely and six men fell, but only after they had won the time needed for Alistair and Malcolm to escape to safety.

Despite being shaken, the king raised his men and set off back to the scene of the battle. The dead Scots lay undisturbed on the field, but the enemy had long gone, and in sadness the party returned to the palace. It had been a mournful evening, with Malcolm sitting alone, deep in thought. Later, Alistair joined him and discovered that this was not the first time he had escaped an attack on his life.

"Did you see their shields?" asked Alistair.

"Aye, they bore a Saxon cross, the same as before," replied Malcolm darkly, as he remembered Helden's bloodstained body.

"If they have tried before, they will try again."

"And next time I might not be so lucky. Will you do something for me?"

"I am at your service, my lord."

They discussed a plan in which the king's riders would seek out the fortress of the enemy and, next morning, men were despatched to the north and to the far west. Alistair headed south with strict orders to report back every seven days. He talked to farmers and clan leaders, and listened to many conversations in the meeting places throughout the borders. Nobody had seen or heard of soldiers bearing the sign of the Saxon cross and Alistair began to lose heart.

On the path to Melrose, he stopped to water his steed at a small stream that gurgled its way down a grass-covered hill, broken by birch and small copses of willow. He looked up at the grey clouds and guessed the first snow of winter would arrive before nightfall. As he stood to leave he noticed a line of horsemen, like dark shadows, silhouetted against the skyline.

"I wonder what they are up to?" he thought.

He decided to follow them at a distance and his cautious approach was helped by their fresh tracks, obvious in the snow that now fell. The weather worsened and though he could still make out the direction they took from their tracks on the path, he couldn't see more than a few paces ahead. Several times he stopped to listen for the sound of horses, or men, but nothing came to him on the wind. Worse still, the heavy snow was beginning to obscure any sign of his quarry on the path. Alistair patted his horse to give it encouragement and decided to risk moving on more quickly.

They travelled as fast as the conditions allowed and Alistair's body became masked in white. He peered ahead intently for any sign. But, without warning, they rode straight into the riders, who had settled on making camp in the foul weather. Two of them pulled Alistair from his horse and dragged him to a makeshift tent that had been hastily erected beside the path.

"What have we here?" demanded a well-built soldier.

"I am Alistair of Cadbol and I travel to Melrose on honest business."

"You are not on the road to Melrose," snapped the man angrily.

Alistair gestured out at the falling snow.

"I lost my way. Do you have any food?"

It was the last thing he remembered for the hilt of a sword came down upon his head and he crashed to the floor. When he came to, Alistair felt sick. His body lurched from side to side and he opened an eye and blinked with pain. He was lying face down on the back of a wicker cart with his hands and feet tightly bound. To his left was a heavily armed warrior, on a brown steed, riding alongside. The man carried a shield and it bore the sign of a cross.

"Not good," said Alistair.

The cart lurched violently, his head hit the wooden floor and he was sick.

"I am not even on the Great Sea."

After what seemed like an eternity, the party stopped. One of the riders hauled Alistair roughly from the cart and kicked him towards his leader.

"Hungry now?" snapped the big soldier and he spat on his prisoner.

"Why are you doing this?" asked Alistair, with all the courage he could muster.

"That's my business."

Alistair was tied to a great stone and, tilting his head back, he saw that it was a tall cross like those painted on the enemy's shields.

"Not good," he mumbled again.

Alistair surveyed the camp that was built around the cross. The four wooden huts did not seem to have been there long and they were hidden from the main track by a thick pine wood. Tied to the lower branches of the trees were twenty-three horses, his own amongst them.

"If only I can get to them," he thought and he began the long and painful struggle to free himself from his bonds.

He guessed the huts contained stores of food for the soldiers' long journey north into the Scottish kingdom. They were Angles and mostly spoke in an unfamiliar tongue. Alistair had heard stories about them. For many years there had been an uneasy truce and the border lands had enjoyed prosperity. But they had a fierce reputation and before the Long Peace they had tried to conquer Scottish lands.

It was beginning to get dark when a guard came over to check on him. The man pulled hard on the ropes, sneered and kicked Alistair in the ribs.

"Not hungry yet?" he mocked, and laughed as he walked back to one of the huts.

Alistair began to feel the biting cold. His hands were numb and turning blue, but he kept on rubbing the rope against the hard edge of the stone. Eventually it frayed and broke. He sat still for a long time, checking for signs of the enemy. When it was dark, he took one last look at the firelight that shone through the cracks in the huts. Then he rose and ran to the horses. He released them from the trees and mounted his steed. With a loud shout, that bolted them in all directions, he galloped from the camp. The angry cries of the Angles grew distant and a huge wave of relief swept over him. Even the leather bag he kept tied to his saddle was still there.

"Good. I would have been really angry if they had taken my coins."

Alistair decided to find Melrose and send a message to Hamish before riding north to report to Malcolm. He travelled through the night and as a weak, yellow sun broke over the hills he finally reached the small market town.

Alistair chose a small meeting house, on the edge of Melrose, called the Old Toll House, and made his acquaintance with the owner, a round, red-faced man named Jamie. The man seemed courteous and attentive, despite the early hour of his arrival, and Alistair put this down to the coins in his purse. But his instincts told him not to trust this man.

Hastily, Alistair wrote a note to Hamish and secured its despatch with three coins and a solemn promise from a stable boy for its safe arrival. The boy was dressed in rags and had sad, dark and deep-set eyes, but there was an honest look about him. Hungrily, Alistair ate porridge and oatcake, and eased his sore head with a dram of warming heather ale. Sleep overcame him and he retired to his room and fell, utterly exhausted, onto a straw bed.

Half in dream, half in nagging doubt, Alistair opened his eyes. He was still exhausted and yet something had compelled him to wake. Bright winter sunshine streamed through the room's small window and he seemed to be alone. It was noon and Alistair sat up and yawned. What a night it had been and he hoped it would never be repeated. He stood and went over to the window. Below in the courtyard were many horses. He stiffened and guessed too late that they belonged to the Angles.

"Not again," said Alistair feebly, as the hilt of a sword came down again upon his head.

Alistair tugged at his chains.

"I was carried down a stone staircase to the dungeon. I must have been in a daze, but the last thing I remember is hearing two men talking. One was richly dressed and called Cuthbert. The other man had his face hidden in darkness and all I could make out was that he had a very dark beard. They laughed when they saw me and spoke about the way being clear for the next attack on the Younger."

A grunt came from the other side of the cell.

"And that is my tale," concluded Alistair.

He peered through the gloom again at his friend who was breathing slowly and deeply.

"Exciting isn't it?"

There was another tired grunt.

"What do you think, Mackey?" persisted Alistair, but his new companion was sound asleep.

***

In the brightest room of the castle, graced with fine furniture and colourful tapestries, Cuthbert the Cautious, Baron of Berwick, pawed greedily over his copy of Denbara's map. His thin fingers ran eagerly over a large area of Scotland. He picked up a quill and drew a small cross in the centre of the lands he planned to conquer once Malcolm was dead. He smiled and thought of the money he would earn from taxing the people there. Then the smile turned cruel as he lifted a parchment and lay it on top of the map. A servant walked quietly into the room with a jug of water and bowed.

"Get out, you dog," growled Cuthbert and the man fled to the door, scuttling like an insect.

The baron raised his quill and signed Alistair's death warrant.

CHAPTER TWO

MELROSE

 Dougie was hungry. His stomach complained noisily and his thoughts drifted from Alistair to his children and to Mairi's lamb and barley broth. Hamish sighed.

"Half a day's ride to Melrose, half a day to supper."

"Wise words," said Donald.

They pressed on as fast as the weather and the will of the horses would allow. Cold water dripped down Dougie's neck and the distant rumble of thunder spoke of more rain to come. Several times, the outline of the hills in front of them lit up like stone giants and with each flash of lightning they struggled to keep control of their frightened steeds. It was early evening when three wet, tired and hungry travellers rode into Melrose. Donald pulled Alistair's parchment from his purse and read it.

"Look for the Old Toll."

But it was difficult to see anything through the torrential rain and on reaching the far outer edge of the market town they decided to dismount, go back and ask for help. Help came in the form of a young boy who sat in rags at the side of the street. His head was bowed and when he glanced up at their horses, Dougie looked into two tired, sad and empty eyes.

"Excuse me," asked Dougie, "do you know of a meeting house called the Old Toll?"

"Aye, I do," replied the boy softly.

Dougie sensed a loneliness about him and said in a kind voice, "You know it."

"It's not far, but I would never go there."

"Not far then, they are glad words for tired travellers."

The boy stood, sending a wave shooting down a puddle that ran the length of the lane.

"Where are you from?"

"From north of the Forth," said Hamish, "and what is one so young doing out so late and in such foul weather?"

The boy clasped the bridle of Dougie's horse and eagerly led him through an alleyway to a cottage with a small bed painted on its door.

"That is often the way for an orphan, sir."

"This is not the Old Toll," said Dougie.

The boy tried to lead him to the door and gave him a warning.

"I see many things living on the street and the Toll is a bad place."

"But we must go to the Old Toll."

"Jamie lives there and he has no time, or kind words, for the likes of me."

Dougie pointed at his companion.

"Do you see Hamish, my big friend? He will make sure Jamie welcomes you."

The orphan considered this for some time and with an earnest look, that sought only the truth, he spoke to Hamish.

"Do you promise?"

"Aye, I do," and much to his embarrassment, Hamish had his giant hand clasped by the boy who pulled him towards another house, just fifty paces away. It might have been on the other side of Carn Liath for all they could make out of it through the rain.

The Old Toll was really two white cottages joined together to form a long house. Smoke rose up into the rain from holes in the thatch. The orphan seemed reluctant to cross the threshold and so it was Donald who knocked on the door. A small red-faced man opened it and his face lit up at the thought of paying guests.

"My name is Jamie," smiled the innkeeper, "and welcome to the Toll."

He ushered them out of the rain and, as Hamish entered, Jamie slammed the door shut on their guide.

"He is with us," said Dougie.

"That scrounger is not with anyone," hissed the innkeeper angrily, and as he spoke the friends detected another side to this man. Donald pulled out a coin and tossed it to Jamie.

31

"That is the cost of entry for our friend."

The man looked at the money greedily. "Of course, of course, any friend of yours is welcome here."

"Of course," added Dougie wryly, and he nodded at Hamish to open the door.

The boy was walking away with his head down and his bare feet ankle-high in water. The poor soul looked thoroughly dejected.

"It's alright to come in," called Hamish, in a reassuring voice.

The boy looked at him through sad eyes and marched into the tavern with a brave dignity that came from knowing how to accept small victories, after so many of life's hard defeats. But on seeing Jamie, the orphan kept as far from the innkeeper as he could and settled himself down in a corner by the fire. Water dripped off his sodden rags and he held out two cold hands towards the flames.

"Are you hungry, laddie?" asked Hamish.

"Food?" and there was such hope in his voice that Dougie could not help but smile too and offer to pay.

A bowl of hot broth and thick chunks of bread were quickly placed before him and he clumsily clasped a spoon, and ate eagerly.

"Wonderful," he said, and it was soon gone.

"Have another?" offered Donald, "but make it last for the sake of my shrinking purse."

He considered this with wide eyes and, as if in slow motion, moved more steaming broth to his lips.

"Jamie," asked Dougie, "we seek news of our friend, Alistair of Cadbol."

"Not a name I remember," admitted Jamie, "and I am very good with names."

"He would have stayed here around twenty days ago."

"No, not a name that comes to mind. He definitely did not stay here."

Donald took out the crumpled parchment.

"This says differently," and he passed it to Jamie.

He seemed worried by the note and his voice faltered.

"I think someone has been tricking you. I have not seen this before."

"I have," yelled the boy in an excited voice.

"You have seen this note?" exclaimed Dougie.

"I was working for a meal in the stables and a stranger gave it to me. He also gave me three coins for my trouble."

"And what did you do with it?" asked Donald quietly.

"I gave it to a farmer, who had business to the north, with a promise to pass it onwards."

Out of the corner of his eye, Dougie saw Jamie backing away towards a door. He nodded at Hamish who strode over and grabbed his shirt. Jamie gave a frightened squeal as he was lifted off the ground and thrown without ceremony on the floor.

"Shall we start again?" asked Hamish.

"I do not know anything," cried Jamie.

"The stranger did stay here," said the boy excitedly.

Dougie's voice was quiet. "We only wish to find our friend,"

"I would like to help, but I cannot," mumbled Jamie in a frightened voice.

Hamish raised his claymore so its tip touched his throat.

"I cannot tell you."

"I do not believe you," growled Hamish menacingly.

A determined look flashed across the innkeeper's red face.

"I will not tell."

"Fire!" cried Donald.

"Where?" asked Dougie, glancing around anxiously.

"A lovely fire," shouted Donald and he shot across the room and picked up a torch from the wall.

"Burn it all," yelped Donald as if madness had taken him.

He danced wildly around the room waving the flaming torch above his head. The impact on Jamie was immediate.

"You can't burn my home. It's all I have."

"Then tell us all you know," said Hamish harshly.

"They will kill me."

The sacking that covered the windows caught fire.

"If you want somewhere to live, you will need to chance that," said Hamish coolly. "Do you know of Alistair?"

"Burn it all," yelped Donald with a look of great pleasure on his face.

"Stop that madman," screamed Jamie.

Dougie and Hamish looked at each other, not quite knowing what had come over Donald either.

"Your friend was taken by Angles to Berwick Castle, that's all I know. Now please stop him."

"How long ago?" asked Dougie.

"Fifteen, maybe sixteen days."

The effect of this on Donald was immediate. He stopped dancing around the room and went to join the orphan by the fire. They grinned at each other as Hamish dragged the burning sacks from the wall and stamped on them.

"Where is Berwick?" asked Dougie.

"It is in the lands called Northumbria," said Donald gravely, "and a fair ride from here."

"Well the sooner we start, the sooner we shall arrive," added Hamish, who kicked Jamie as he spoke. "We will need food for the journey, so go get it now!"

Jamie shot him a look full of hatred and disappeared into a back room. After five minutes, in which the boy stuffed as much bread in his mouth as he could, Jamie returned with a bag of provisions. Unnoticed, he also brought in a dirk.

"Thank you for all your help," said Donald sarcastically.

"Aye, the perfect host," added Hamish in a voice as cold as ice.

The friends left the tavern, Dougie first, then Donald and then the orphan smiling contentedly with every step he made to the door.

"I told you it is a bad place," he said.

As Hamish strode to the door, Jamie called out to him.

"Hey, big man."

Hamish turned and his heart stopped as a dirk flashed through the air. Suddenly, the boy dived in front of him and took the full force of the sharp blade. He fell to the floor and blood spurted around the hilt of the dagger. Hamish dropped to his knees and cradled the orphan's head in his giant hands.

"Bad place," he coughed.

"Aye, you're right there, laddie," said Hamish quietly.

Dougie watched them and then glanced around for Jamie, but he had gone.

"I hope you find your friend," whispered the boy.

Hamish gave the boy a kind smile.

The orphan smiled up at him and as a long, last breath came from his lips, he shut his eyes.

It was some while before the friends left the Toll. Hamish was very quiet and kept his own company as arrangements were made for the resting of the body. Eventually, Dougie's thoughts returned to their quest and he realised there would be little point going to Berwick Castle without an army. But Alistair was a prisoner and his heart told him that he must attempt some kind of rescue. Despite his protests, Donald agreed to leave them and go back to the palace to tell Malcolm about the Angles, and bring help.

South of Melrose, Dougie looked at his big friend. His cheeks might have been wet from the rain and he thought that he heard Hamish say something, but he kept his silence and, with heads bowed against the foul weather, they rode on into the darkness.

With another hour to daybreak, Donald's horse retraced its steps back to the Forth. As cold rain lashed against his face, Donald tried to work out how long it would take to reach Malcolm, raise soldiers and get to Berwick. Certainly, Dougie and Hamish would reach the castle first and he hoped they wouldn't do anything reckless before he arrived with help.

By late morning the rain had stopped and the low-lying hills around him were transformed in the bright sunshine. With the change in weather, and as his plaid dried, Donald's spirits rose and he began to believe that perhaps he had fallen lucky with the easier task. However, he would rather have been with his friends in danger, than carrying a message on the lonely road.

Donald stopped to rest where the path crossed a small stream and ate oat bread, cheese and apples. He gave an apple to his horse and she devoured it gratefully before going back to drink the water. They began again and made good time to the banks of the Forth. The path that came up from the south simply stopped at the sand by the water's edge. It was nearly nightfall and Donald guessed that the ferry would only run in the hours of daylight. He peered across at Culross and could just make out the mast of the ferry and the lights that shone out through the windows of the cottages. There was no bell on this side of the river to attract the attention of the old ferryman, and so Donald tied his horse to a small tree and settled down for the night.

The light faded, the wind eased and a feeling of calm fell over him as he sat and watched the great river. To pass the time he tried to think how the Angles had crossed it. Not by the ferry, for they had many soldiers and horses. The people of Culross would also know about them and word would have been sent to Malcolm. Donald could hear crows cawing to signal the closing of the day and he began to doze. Then he sat up.

"They must have a ship."

He ran to his horse. Determined to use whatever light that was left to find it, he rode silently along the sand towards the sinking sun. The bank edged in and out, and Donald searched for any sign of men, horses or boats. He struck lucky. Ten minutes' canter from the path, the sand disappeared and large rocks barred the way. Donald dismounted and climbed up to see over them.

A small river poured its waters into the Forth and had cut a channel some fifty paces wide into the bank. Moored on the other side of the channel was a long, narrow ship with two masts and a flag bearing a cross. A soldier walked on deck.

Donald crouched and looked at the dark, cloudy sky. He took his clothes off, wrapped them into a neat parcel and placed his claymore on top. He put his belt back on, tucked his dirk into it, then slowly climbed down the other side of the rock and lowered himself into the water. He gasped at the cold.

Silently, he swam across to the side of the Angle ship. Only his head showed above the water and on the deck above, he heard the man moving things around. Donald inched his way around the hull until he found the anchor rope. He pulled himself up and gingerly lifted his head so that he could see inside the boat. Still only one soldier, with his back turned, and busying himself with wooden boxes.

"How did I get myself into this?" thought Donald.

He raised himself some more and straddled the rail that ran around the ship, and took the dirk in his hand. Like drum beats, water dripped off his chest onto the deck. He crept forward and the ship's timbers creaked under his weight, but still the man did not turn.

Donald sprang and knocked him down. He raised his dirk, but strong hands grabbed his and they rolled from side to side in a desperate struggle. The Angle arched his body and Donald found himself pinned on his back, with the bigger man trying to turn his blade. The tip of the sharp dirk shook above his face. The enemy started to put more of his weight behind his arm and Donald's strength began to fail. Slowly, it edged nearer. Donald threw his head to one side and let go of the man's arms. The blade shot down, sliced through Donald's ear and embedded itself in the wooden deck. He ignored the pain as he kneed the man away. The Angle pulled at the dagger. Donald grabbed a wooden box and brought it down squarely onto the man's head. He slumped to the floor and the box broke open. Swords of all kinds spilled out.

Donald sat down, exhausted, and glanced around. The boat was full of boxes and he guessed they all contained weapons. It would take him all night to throw them overboard and so he decided to sink the ship. He dragged the man from the ship and laid him on the bank, before going back to build a fire in the centre of the deck. It caught quickly and Donald fed the flames with boxes, ropes and sail cloth. He cut the anchor ropes and kicked the blazing ship away from the bank. It was quickly grasped by the fast current and glided away towards the great river.

Donald watched it go and felt his ear. Half of it was gone.

At the palace, Malcolm and Archie, the king's eccentric alchemist, listened intently to Donald's story and asked many questions. Archie faced the wall with Gangly, the last of the Ghilly Dhus, sitting on his shoulder. He was the cheekiest of creatures and no more than an arm's length long. Donald looked at his long, thin legs and bright red waistcoat. The imp stared back at his ear and stuck his tongue out.

"I cannot raise an army in so short a time," said Malcolm, "but we can leave with my bodyguards at once."

"Only thirty men?" asked Donald.

Gangly moved his elbows in and out like a chicken.

"Thirty of my best warriors," replied Malcolm, "and a small force can move more quickly than a large one."

"And we may not need an army," added Archie mysteriously, "for I have looked into the Oracle of the Ancient Ones."

"Grumf," grunted Gangly.

"I am not an old fool," replied Archie crossly, "for who would not want an understanding of what might be."

Malcolm groaned.

"Grumf."

"Doubters, I am surrounded by doubters, just you wait until you see my latest *experident*."

With Gangly telling him which way to go, the old alchemist walked backwards from the chamber.

The decision was made to ride south and give whatever help they could to Dougie and Hamish. Donald ate a hurried meal whilst preparations were made for the long journey to Berwick.

The courtyard of the palace was a hive of activity. Children passed weapons and provisions up to the soldiers on their horses. Women kissed their menfolk goodbye, and the king gave instructions to his advisers for the running of the kingdom in his absence.

Staring down on them from a high window, the young Prince Ranald smiled to himself. Anyone who saw him might have said that his face showed relief at not being asked to join his father on the journey. Secretly, Ranald was wondering what life would be like if his father did not return.

Malcolm mounted his white horse and ordered the opening of the main gate. As he did, a large four-wheeled cart drawn by six horses trundled across the Palace Green. Archie held the reins and sat facing backwards. Gangly shouted instructions at him.

"Grumf. Grumf."

"Yes, right turn," replied Archie, "you will tell me when to stop, won't you?"

"Grumf," shouted Gangly.

They stopped in front of the king who stared at the back of the cart. Its contents were hidden by a large cloth. The children pointed at Archie and started to giggle, and a small boy walked backwards into a wall and fell over.

"What are you up to?" asked Malcolm.

"It is my latest *experident* and it might come in useful," replied Archie.

Malcolm the Younger, King of the Scots and Protector of the Stone of Destiny, raised his eyes to the sky.

CHAPTER THREE

BERWICK CASTLE

Dougie and Hamish rested after a day's ride south of Melrose and made camp just off the path in a horseshoe of tall gorse, which provided some shelter from the wind and rain. Dougie peered out and wondered if it was possible for anyone to be wetter than he was.

Something made him glance at the horses. Their heads were up and alert, their ears pricked forward and their bodies like statues, tense and still. He walked over and patted their necks, talking to them in a soothing voice. It was lucky he calmed them for the thunder of hooves rose quickly. Then the thunder was gone. Dougie ran to the top of a small rise to look down on the path that curved around its base. He lay flat, crawled forward and counted eighteen horses. All but two had riders and all riders carried shields marked with the sign of a cross. They rode south. He ran back down the slope and kicked a sodden, tartan mound. It moaned and moved a little.

"Get up, Hamish."

A large, tired and irritable face looked up at him.

"Where is breakfast?"

"Get up and get going."

The mound tried to stand and fell over.

"I must weigh more than my horse," moaned Hamish.

Dougie pulled himself up into his saddle.

"Riders, heading south at the gallop. This is our first piece of good fortune."

"It doesn't feel like good fortune," said Hamish, trying to stand again. "I hope the day gets better."

It did. After an hour the rain gave way to sunshine and the friends began to dry out. Their quarry could only just be seen in the distance, but the land changed from rolling hill to flat moorland and there was only one path by which they could move through it. This was a barren and lonely place, and the bogs looked wet, rank and deadly.

All day, they kept their distance, sometimes galloping when

they lost sight of the soldiers over the horizon, or slowing to a trot, so as not to be seen.

"Do they never stop to eat?" lamented Hamish.

"They will not stop," replied Dougie.

"How so?"

"My guess is that Jamie has told them of our visit and intention to find Alistair. They rode by us at dawn and believe we are still ahead of them. They want to kill us before we reach Berwick."

"Nice thought."

"But they will lead us straight to Alistair."

"If he is still alive," said Hamish and there was silence again for a good while.

***

Alistair was alive, but not enjoying himself. The cell was still dark, cold and smelly, and Mackey, Bob the Pig Stealer, was getting on his nerves.

"Got any more stories?" he asked for the tenth time.

"Not if you keep falling asleep I don't," said Alistair bitterly.

"I fell asleep because it had been an exciting day."

"An exciting day?"

"Aye, extra maggots and two bowls of supper," he croaked eagerly, "it doesn't happen every day you know."

Alistair looked grimly at the lines he had scored on the wall since he had arrived. Day was as night, night was as day in the cell, but guessing that they were fed once each evening he made it twenty seven days. That meant there were only three days to his execution.

"Three days," he said grimly.

"Three days, I don't know that story. Is it a good one?" said Mackey.

"Three days and then I will be beheaded."

43

"Could be worse."

"Don't start that again."

Alistair lowered his head onto his knees, shut his eyes and tried to sleep. The cell door shuddered and two mighty bolts cracked open. Two soldiers walked into the room.

"Time's up," ordered one loudly.

Alistair, in deep despair, felt sick again.

"I must have miscounted."

***

Berwick Castle was the biggest thing built by man that Dougie had ever seen. As they peered out of a small wood, some way from its great fortifications, the friends could clearly see an outer wall, a higher inner wall and a central tower that was the highest point for miles around. A flag with a cross flew from the top of the tower.

"No disrespect to the Younger," said Hamish, "but that must be the most magnificent castle in the world."

Dougie nodded.

"The outer walls could be twice as high as those at the palace."

"Twice as high and twice as wide."

"I wonder what that thing at the gate is?" asked Dougie.

The friends watched as a cart drawn by oxen rolled up to the castle. A guard came out to meet it and four more men appeared above them, alert and ready with spears, looking down from battlements overhanging the gate. The soldier walked around the cart and prodded the bags it carried. He talked for some time to the woman who drove it and then waved her forward. Hamish hadn't eaten for an age and he wondered if the bags contained the garrison's supper. His stomach rumbled.

Then something else was moving, slowly, at an even pace, and they heard a loud grinding noise. Iron spikes rose from the ground and above them a thick iron trellis disappeared upwards into the wall.

"That thing could hold back an army," whispered Dougie.

"Don't worry," said Hamish, "all we have to do is get in and get out."

"And get Alistair," added Dougie.

Hamish stared blankly at the ground.

"Aye, that's all."

As the cart disappeared, a thin, long-haired and nearly naked man was thrown out of the castle.

"Let me back in," the man demanded, as he picked himself off the ground. "I have a year to do yet."

"Get lost," replied a guard angrily, "and don't steal any more pigs."

"I like pigs."

"What on earth is that?" asked Hamish.

"That, my friend," smiled Dougie, "is more good fortune."

The stranger walked, reluctantly, away from the castle along a lane towards a nearby village. The friends watched him go and retraced their steps through the wood to a point where it met the lane. The thin, long-haired man spoke bitterly to himself and kicked stones as he approached them. Hamish hid behind some bushes and sat on a cold, fallen tree.

"A fine day now that the rain has eased," said Dougie in a friendly voice.

"A bad day for me," replied Mackey, in his wheezy Scottish accent.

"How so?" asked Dougie seeking conversation.

"The rain never bothered me in my lovely cell and now I have been thrown out."

"Lovely cell?"

"And a change of cell every few years, a companion and two bowls of supper, yes two bowls, not one."

"A companion you say, that was lucky."

"Well, he was a bit boring, still it could have been worse."

"Is it worse for him?" asked Dougie, "After all, he is still a prisoner."

45

"Aye, but not for long, he is to be beheaded in three days."

Dougie looked anxiously over the man's shoulder at a bush where a large and attentive face peered through the leaves.

"May I ask you the name of this unfortunate creature?" asked Dougie gently.

"It is Alistair the Tadpole, or something like that. A nice man but just not appreciative of a good cell."

Dougie's heart sank at these words.

"Could he be Alistair of Cadbol?"

"Aye, that's him. He told me some story about being on a mission for his king."

"And who is your king?"

"Don't know. Haven't had much news for a long time. Who is on the throne at the moment?"

"In Scotland it is Malcolm the Younger," replied Dougie.

"It makes little difference to me," croaked Mackey, "but I bet he's better than Tella. I never liked the Picts."

"And what is your name?"

"The guards had lots of names for me, but you can call me Mackey."

"Mackey, would you be our guest at supper? I am afraid that we have journeyed far and carried little, but you are welcome to share what we have."

"Can I have two bowls?" asked Mackey.

"If not one morsel touches my lips, you shall have two bowls," smiled Dougie, and he gestured to Hamish to join them.

In the heart of the wood, night was broken by a log fire and the smell of hare stew raised the spirits of the rescuers. Dougie cut his plaid into two pieces and graciously gave half to Mackey.

"Not sure about the colour," said their new friend.

"It is the king's own tartan and the symbol of the Scottish people," said Dougie in a hurt voice.

"Got one with a nice bit of yellow in it? I like yellow."

"No, but I have a third bowl of stew."

"It has been a long time since I had three bowls," said Mackey, edging nearer to the warmth of the fire.

"So, time is running out," said Hamish quietly.

"Still, it could be worse," wheezed Mackey.

"Does anyone have any ideas about how to rescue Alistair?" asked Dougie.

"We could dress up as merchants and bluff our way in," suggested Mackey eagerly.

"I could tie myself to the underside of that old woman's cart and, once inside, wait until dark," added Hamish, "then I could lower a rope down the wall and then you could climb up."

"Or we could wait for Donald to bring Malcolm's army and pray that they arrive in less than three days," said Dougie, but he and Hamish knew there was no chance of that.

"Or we could capture some of the riders and dress up in their uniforms," continued Hamish, but as they discussed the ideas, each seemed to be more and more impossible.

Dougie thought long and hard.

"The ideas might just get us in Hamish, but they won't help us release Alistair unharmed. There could be scores of soldiers inside the castle."

"Three hundred," wheezed Mackey.

The friends fell silent and stared at the embers of the fire for some time.

"Of course, you could always use the secret passage," said Mackey.

***

As much as Alistair had been driven mad by Mackey, he now missed him. His cell door opened and torchlight blinded him. A guard thrust the tip of his sword onto Alistair's chest and Cuthbert walked in. He smiled cruelly.

"How does it feel to spend your last day alone and forgotten? How does it feel to know that after the rising of the sun, your head will rest on a spike above my gates?" Cuthbert walked back to the door. "How does it feel to know your people will soon pay tribute to me? How long will it be before they, like you, are completely forgotten?"

***

The friends sat in stunned silence and stared at Mackey, who was clearly enjoying the stew. His face was buried deep inside his bowl, like a boar rooting for acorns, and he licked noisily at every last drop of gravy.

"Secret passage?" asked Dougie.

"Aye, it runs from the river on the other side of the castle. Goes right into the dungeon it does," exclaimed Mackey, a big grin on his face.

"Mackey," said Hamish, "may I ask how you know of it?"

"You don't spend half of your life in the cells without knowing about things like secret passages. I even used it the last time I was thrown out for good behaviour. I got free bed and breakfast for weeks."

Hamish looked at Dougie and Dougie looked at Hamish.

"Mind you," he continued, "it is dangerous after a lot of rain because the river rises and floods the entrance. I wouldn't like to be caught in there I can tell you. Any more stew?"

"Would you show us, Mackey?" beseeched Dougie.

"Only if you let me stay inside."

"He's mad," thought Hamish, as the rescuers rose for the difficult walk to the other side of the castle.

With little moonlight they made slow progress and it wasn't until dawn that they finally reached the banks of a river, swollen by the rain that had fallen on the high ground in the last few days.

"Can you remember where the entrance is?" asked Dougie.

"Of course I can," snapped Mackey, "I am not an idiot you know."

Hamish raised an eyebrow and Dougie had to hide his face.

"Do you see the roots of the big oak?" continued Mackey, who pointed at the bank twenty paces from them. "Mind you, it is small and you will need to wriggle through the first part." He looked at Hamish and added, "and you might need to cut yourself in two to get in."

Hamish sucked in his great stomach.

They agreed that there was no point waiting and that the big man would watch from the woods, and have the horses ready. Mackey would lead, and Dougie would follow. They would have no torch, for everything they might use for tinder was sodden.

"I wish I was coming with you," lamented Hamish.

"Old friend," said Dougie in a kind voice, "keep watch for us, we will not stay in the castle a moment longer than we need to."

Mackey walked slowly into the river and shivered. With the water up to his waist he turned to face the bank and disappeared into the roots of the tree. Dougie noticed that in the short time they had stood there a stone that had at first been visible was now covered by the rising torrent. He said nothing and followed Mackey.

The first few feet were the hardest as the tunnel was narrow and partly submerged. Following only five paces behind, Dougie could just make out the shape of Mackey's body pushing forward slowly. It was cold, damp and smelled of unmentionable things.

"What was the tunnel built for?" asked Dougie quietly, his nose twitching with disgust.

"To take unmentionable things out of the castle," replied Mackey, chuckling.

"You didn't mention the unmentionables before."

Any light that had come from the entrance was soon gone. It was pitch black and Dougie reached a hand forward and rested it on Mackey's shoulder, one blind man leading another. Dougie hit his head on a rock and cursed.

"Mind your head," warned Mackey.

"Thanks a lot," moaned Dougie and they inched forward nervously.

The walls were cold and covered in slime and they waded through foul water that reached up to their knees. Dougie could not see a thing and so he shut his eyes to comfort himself. They seemed to be going upwards and gradually the water level fell. The floor became dry in places, but their progress remained agonisingly slow. The passage here was so narrow that Dougie's shoulders scraped against both walls and they stumbled forward, feeling their way with outstretched hands. They heard a scuttling noise and something brushed their bare legs. Dougie froze and lost his grip on Mackey. He stepped forward quickly and his face was covered in a silky sheet. In that moment of sheer terror, Dougie screamed.

"Keep quiet," hissed Mackey, "remember it could be worse."

"How can it get worse?" snapped Dougie.

"If I can't find the torch."

Dougie strained his eyes to see his companion. He heard a sound like stone being struck on stone. In the dark, the noise could have been a mile away, or two paces. Then he saw sparks and, at last, a tiny flame as Mackey placed tinder against dry wood. They were standing in a twisting corridor of rock and torchlight danced around its walls. Around them, many pairs of red eyes stared at the intruders, and Mackey waved the flame across the floor. Rats ran in all directions and Dougie brushed the cobwebs from his face.

Mackey pointed triumphantly forward.

"I knew it was around here somewhere."

The tunnel became a small black hole just wide enough for them to squeeze through. The last of the rats were scampering through it and Dougie noticed that the walls, on the other side of the hole, were green. In times of flood, everything here would be under water.

"That's odd," squealed Mackey.

"What is?"

Mackey looked at Dougie, "I'm sure that the last time I was here there were two torches on this ledge."

Dougie wanted to turn back, then thought about Alistair.

"Let's go."

Further on there was less water and more headroom. At one point, Mackey's torch lit up a tall ceiling twenty paces above their heads, a natural crack in the rock that made Dougie feel as though he were standing at the bottom of a great chimney. Except this chimney did not have the comforting smell of burning logs.

"Not far now," encouraged Mackey.

"I'm glad about that. There isn't much life left in the torch."

A growing gurgling and splashing behind them made them turn, and Mackey held the torch out in front of him. The small black hole they had crawled through was completely submerged. A stream of rising water raced after them, lapping at their heels.

"We may get in, but I do not think we can get out, not back this way."

With danger behind them and a lessening light to see by, the rescuers quickened their pace. At last, they came to a roughly hewn wall that blocked their way. About an arm's length above the floor a single stone was missing and out of it came a small trickle of unmentionable things. There was a dim light behind it.

"That's a nuisance," said Mackey, "that wasn't there last time."

"It will be more than a nuisance if we cannot move it," gasped Dougie in a scared voice.

Water splashed above their ankles and the torch began to fade. Desperately, they threw their weight at the wall. It seemed impenetrable. The flood rose to their waists.

"Still, it could be worse," encouraged Mackey.

Dougie was cold and scared, and could not see how things

could be any worse than they were right now. As the torrent reached his chest, Dougie forced his claymore into the gap in the stones and leant against it. There was a mighty crack as the blade broke, but a single brick had come loose. He plunged his head into the water and picked up a stone that lay by his feet, and desperately used it to strike the weak point in the wall.

"Quiet," hissed Mackey, "you will wake the guards."

"Show me a quiet way to break down a wall," said Dougie angrily and he choked as he swallowed a mouthful of foul water. "Start hitting the top of the wall!"

Mackey's head disappeared under the water and he resurfaced with a rock, and smashed it against the wall. A crack appeared like a lightning bolt, zig-zagging through the mortar. The rising torrent suddenly overcame the blockage. There was a roar as rocks tumbled and the wave shot forward, and they were carried head first into the torch-lit dungeon of Berwick Castle.

"Piece of cake," spluttered Mackey as he was swept along the floor.

"Quickly, Mackey," whispered Dougie, "show me Alistair's cell."

"It's my cell."

"Show me your cell!"

"Touchy, aren't you?" said Mackey, and he stood up, brushed himself down and walked over to a heavy oak door, with a small iron grille at its base and two black bolts. Dougie grabbed a torch from the wall, slipped the bolts, bent his head and walked in.

"Hello Dougie," said a familiar voice.

"Hello Alistair, how are you?"

"Glad in my heart to see you, old friend."

"Well the plan was to take you along a passage to the river," said Dougie as he knelt to look at Alistair's chains, "but that way is flooded."

Dougie put his foot onto a link that seemed most worn, took his dirk from his belt, put it into the chain and lifted. There was a loud crack as the bonds and blade were broken.

52

"I don't know why I bother with claymores and dirks," said Dougie ruefully. "They never last long."

"I hope the new perfume you are wearing won't last long either," sniffed Alistair and the two friends shook hands.

"Give me your sword Dougie, it may be broken, but it would give me great comfort to hold it."

"You should get going," said Mackey at the door. "Before you go, you couldn't lock me into the cell next door could you?"

"Nothing would give me greater pleasure," grinned Alistair, and with a ceremonial bow, he ushered the prisoner into his new cell. Through the small grille Mackey shouted out.

"If you are ever in the castle, remember to drop in for a chat."

Alistair and Dougie grabbed torches and rushed to the far end of the dungeon, and went up a steep, narrow stone staircase. Dougie counted thirty steps, and was first to reach an arch with another oak door.

"What's beyond the door?" asked Dougie.

"No idea," panted Alistair, "when I came down I was carried."

They listened for any sound of the enemy with their ears pressed against the wood and heard nothing. No voices, no horses, nothing.

"Well we can't stay here," said Dougie. "Hamish is waiting with two horses if we can just get out."

Cautiously, he opened the door and put his head out into bright morning sunshine. It immediately popped back in.

"The enemy?" asked Alistair.

"I don't know, I was blinded by the daylight."

"Open it slowly and give our eyes time to adjust."

After a few minutes of worrying and listening, Dougie put his head out again. Fifty paces in front of them, across grass, was the main gate to the castle. It was open and one guard stood by it.

Slowly, Dougie moved back behind the door and told his friend what he had seen.

"It could be worse," said Alistair.

"Don't you start," snapped Dougie, and they decided that their only chance of escape was to charge the gate.

"On the count of three," counted Alistair softly, "one, two, three."

Dougie ran as fast as he could through the oak door and straight into an Angle warrior. He knocked the man clean off his feet, but even with the element of surprise, strong hands held him tightly by the throat. Alistair dived onto the soldier and plunged the broken claymore into his back. The man screamed.

Alistair ran towards the guard by the gate who took out his sword and then, when they were twenty paces apart, he brought it down onto a thick rope that ran from a great wheel to a hole at the top of the wall. Immediately, the morning air was cut by a loud grinding noise and thick iron spikes began to descend to block their escape.

Alistair shouted, "Let's get out of here."

Dougie pushed the man off his body and felt something tear from around his neck. He got ready to run too, but something compelled him to look back at the dead soldier. He held a leather cord in his outstretched hand. At its end, shining deep red in the sunlight was the brooch Malcolm had given him, his ruby.

"Come on!" yelled Alistair.

Dougie saw with horror that iron spikes now covered half the gateway. Alistair had killed the guard and was outside the castle waving frantically at the wood to get Hamish's attention. The grinding of iron on stone seemed to grow louder.

"Come back," pleaded a deep voice.

Dougie stopped in his tracks. He turned again and saw a man in furs, with a stone spear, sitting next to the brooch. Dougie's mind told him that he had never seen the stranger before. Dougie's heart told him that he had known Gora for a thousand years.

Gora beckoned him and lifted the ruby to the sky with a skeletal hand. A rich, blood-red light made all around them strange and ghostly.

"Come back," he urged again and his eyes bore deep into Dougie's soul.

Dougie felt his legs walk, uncontrollably, back towards the stone. It was as though he was a part of someone else's dream.

"Come back, come back to us," Gora repeated.

"Leave it, Dougie," came a soft voice, "let it go."

Dougie turned to look into the face of Alistair. He was smiling gently and his eyes conveyed such genuine friendship.

"Let it go, young Dougie," he said again.

"Join us," demanded the man in furs, but the spell was broken.

"You can have it," said Dougie, and they sprinted to the gate and dived under the spikes as they crashed to the ground.

***

In another time and in another place, a great stone rolled across another doorway. A man driven by greed and starved of hope, started to shake uncontrollably. Gora's torch flickered and went out.

CHAPTER FOUR

FIRE IN THE SKY

Everything was in complete chaos. Men shouted from behind the iron grid and tried to lift its great weight. A spear flew past Dougie's shoulder and right ear. Alistair grabbed it.

"Over here," boomed Hamish and they ran for their lives.

Ahead of them on the castle path was a wagon and a blue gypsy caravan. The wagon carried food for the garrison and Hamish, with a loaf of bread under each arm, was being hit with a stick by a woman in a long shawl.

"Thief," she cried, and hit him again.

Inside the castle walls, the rope must have been retied, for the loud grating noise began once more. Alistair smacked the leading oxen on its flank with the shaft of his spear and the wagon bolted forward at the gateway. Soldiers, who crawled under the rising spikes, saw the cart rushing towards them and dived back inside.

The Scots mounted their horses with Dougie sitting behind Alistair. Their steed would be the slowest with its extra burden.

"We can't outrun them like this," warned Dougie.

They rode to the woods where the path cut through on its long journey north and Alistair slowed.

Hamish pulled back on his reins to stay with them.

"Hamish," said Alistair, "Give Dougie your horse, hide in the woods until the soldiers pass by and then make your way as best you can to Melrose."

"But ..." complained Hamish.

"No buts, old friend, one strong man on foot and two men on two horses may have a chance."

Big Hamish looked distraught, but dismounted, wished them, "Good speed," and watched them gallop out of sight along the shaded woodland path. He did not have to wait long for the Angle warriors. Hiding in the trees, he heard the riders of the Saxon cross thunder past. Their noise seemed to go on forever, but at last it faded into the distance and Hamish lay hidden for some while listening. The winter forest was tranquil, with few birds to break the peace with song. He sniffed the air and smelled fresh bread. Hamish reached inside his shirt and pulled out a large round loaf. It was still warm.

"Good speed," he said again, and smiled as he bit off a great chunk.

***

Dougie's horse was enjoying the chase immensely. It threw him up and down, and took the bends at a terrific speed. Alistair glanced over his shoulder.

"I thought you couldn't ride."

"I can't," panted Dougie, "but I can hold on as well as anyone."

Alistair chuckled to himself and peered ahead onto barren moorland. It stretched out as far as he could see. The sandy path cut a yellow ribbon through the green and brown landscape. There were no trees, no cover and still a whole day's sunlight for their pursuers to keep them in view.

"So, it's just a race," he thought.

A short while later, an armoured snake emerged from the trees. It was long and menacing, and Dougie sensed its presence, but did not risk turning his head when he needed all his concentration just to go forward. Like Alistair, he began to worry about the fate of his big friend.

***

Hamish was sleeping like a baby. The crumbs of two loaves lay over and around him, and not a care in the world showed upon his face. Somewhere, deep in the wood, a crow cawed noisily and he opened an eye lazily. Shafts of bright sunshine shot down through the canopy of leaves and a robin busied itself by marking out its territory. He opened the other eye and patted his stomach.

Thinking things through, he decided that he would need a change of clothes for the journey.

"In a plaid I will stand out like a sore thumb."

He made his way back to the path and waited for something to happen. The something that happened was a blue gypsy caravan. Like the thunder of the soldiers' horses, he did not see it at first, but heard it. The sound of pans, swaying on large hooks, and softly chiming with each turn of the wheel. There was a gentle rhythm to it, and a sweet harmony accompanied by strange words …

> Lords and thieves, rich and poor,
> Prince and pauper seek my door.
> Bright sun, star and cool, blue moon,
> Show the secret of man's fortune.
> Tell me thy name and I'll tell you the line,
> Tell me thy birth and I'll tell you the sign.
> The mists of time show me the way,
> Is five coins too much to pay?

"I would say it was," thought Hamish and he decided to keep his money safe in his purse.

As the caravan came closer, he saw that it was driven by a dark-skinned, wide-eyed woman, with jet black hair that fell to her waist. She could have been plain and she could have been beautiful, she could have been eighteen, or fifty. She was everything and, at the same time, nothing.

"Hello," said Hamish smiling, "I mean you no harm."

"I know that," said the Romany, "would you like me to tell your fortune?"

"Not for five coins I wouldn't."

"Keep your money safe in your purse," she answered in a faraway voice. "Hear my words first and then decide if you wish to cross my palm with silver."

"Don't get your hopes up," thought Hamish.

"I always live in hope," continued the woman and she threw a cloak to him. "Quickly, put this over your tartan. You will not get very far looking like that."

"You really can tell fortunes," gasped Hamish, staring up into her large, brown eyes.

"I have that gift, but I was outside the castle when you brought the horses to your friends."

"Ah," said Hamish, "why do you help me?"

"Because I know that your intentions are good and more riders are coming."

Hamish pulled the cloak over his body and sat next to the gypsy.

"What's your name?"

"The Great Barbarini," she replied proudly.

"That's a bit of a mouthful."

She urged the oxen forward. "Call me Babs."

They had not journeyed far when the sound of hooves came up fast behind them.

"Ten riders," whispered Babs, "one, a man who walks with death."

"Lovely," thought Hamish, and he raised the hood of his cloak.

The men were dressed like the castle guards and carried the same shields. They stopped and a lean, bearded man asked if they had seen strangers on the road. Babs said that she had not, but that many riders had gone by her, at great speed close to daybreak, and that they went north. Hamish looked at the soldiers. One of them was a round, red-faced man. It was Jamie, and Hamish felt his blood boil. Babs quietly put her hand on his and spoke softly.

"Let's get on, husband."

The men rode away.

"You know the fat one," said Babs after a while.

"He killed a friend of mine."

"Remember, husband, revenge is a dish that is best served cold."

"What is all this husband stuff?" asked Hamish, edging slightly away from her.

But the mysterious woman gave no reply, she simply smiled and he thought that her dark skin had turned a little pink.

***

"Poor Hamish," panted Dougie for the tenth time, "I bet he's dodging soldiers in the forest."

Alistair glanced back to see their pursuers menacingly outlined against the horizon about two miles away.

"They are gaining. We must keep a safe distance, at least until nightfall."

But nightfall seemed an age away. Dougie's back and arms ached, and his horse was starting to tire. In front of them, under bright sun, the bleak moor stretched out like a brown cloth, smooth, still and lifeless. He urged his steed forward and, rounding a bend, it stumbled. Dougie flew through the air and crashed, heavily, into tall grass that lined the sides of the pathway. Cautiously, he sat up and felt for broken bones. His ribs hurt, but everything seemed to be working, so he stood up. There was no sign of the horse and then he heard the terrible sound of wild neighing. It was a noise he had never heard any beast make before.

Behind a clump of reeds, half buried in slime, a writhing mass kicked and threw its head desperately from side to side. The horse sank deeper. Dougie dived for the reins and pulled. Slowly, he was dragged forward on his stomach into the bog. He pulled harder and found himself looking into large, haunted eyes. They were full of terror.

The pool had the steed fully in its grip now and only the head was visible. The horse snorted and black mud came out of its flared nostrils. Dougie let go of the reins and, with a last shake of its mane, the poor beast was lost. Large bubbles formed a ring upon the ooze and the reins slipped down between them.

Then they too, were gone forever.

"Where's your horse?" shouted Alistair.

Dougie pulled himself backwards and pointed at the bubbles on the surface of the mud. He felt dazed and sad.

"Come on, Dougie, get up here, we must keep going."

After a hundred strides a thin sheep track verged off the main path. Alistair took it and Dougie was nearly thrown again as the horse veered sharply right.

"Where are we going?"

"No idea," called back Alistair, "but we cannot go on as we are."

Dougie stared anxiously forward for reeds marking the edges of the bogs, but saw none. They seemed to rise uphill for a short while and below them, some way to their left, was the main pathway.

"They will not be fooled," shouted Alistair, "our horse is leaving deep prints in the sand."

"Bit of an old worrier, aren't you."

The track rose and fell, then rose again, and Alistair's horse began to slow. In front of them a great wall loomed up from the moor. It seemed ancient and ran west as far as the eye could see. The fallen remains of a stone tower, now derelict and overgrown, lay four hundred paces to their right. Before them the wall stood high and menacing for a good distance on both sides, blocking their way completely. Dougie wondered who had built it and why it was here in such a desolate and lonely place. Alistair guessed what he was thinking.

"Stories tell that this wall was once built as the northern boundary of a great empire many generations ago."

The friends dismounted and walked up to its base. The wall was three times the height of a man and, from the fallen rubble, had probably once been even higher.

"Well, we can't go forward, there are no paths along its edge and we cannot go back."

Alistair pointed back at the path. Enemy riders were less than a mile away.

"Well, let's see how many of them we can take with us," said Dougie bravely.

Alistair raised his spear in defiance and Dougie held aloft the handle of his wee, broken dirk. They smiled nervously and sat down to wait for the attack.

"Are you still hungry?" called a voice. It was the big soldier whom Alistair had met at the camp of the Saxon cross. "I shall enjoy killing you," he jeered.

"I don't like the look of him," said Dougie.

"He is very good to his Mum though," replied Alistair.

"Aye," agreed Dougie and together the friends said, "because he never goes home."

To the astonishment of the Angles, the two Scottish warriors began to laugh. But it was the hollow laugh of men who expected to die.

Their astonishment did not last long. A man in rich robes, mounted on a fine white stallion, rode forward. Cuthbert smiled cruelly.

"Kill the Scots slowly."

Over a hundred riders dismounted, raised their swords and began to walk towards them.

"Well, this is it," admitted Dougie.

"Aye," replied Alistair.

Dougie noticed that he had a look about him that he had seen before. There was no laughter there now, only a hard look, shaped by anger and determination. Dougie felt embarrassed.

"I just wanted to say it is a bad way to end, but I wouldn't have missed our adventures for the world."

The friends shook hands for the last time and stood together, ready to meet their doom. They edged backwards towards the wall. Dougie felt sick, but if Alistair was afraid then there was no sign of it. The shepherd thought about his children and wondered how Mairi would cope without him. As the enemy approached, step by step, he tried to raise his dirk, but his body didn't seem to work anymore. He was frozen with fear.

Something hit Dougie on the head and he cried out in pain, and looked up. Sliding down a rope from the top of the wall was Donald.

"Thought you might like a bit of a hand," he said brightly.

Ropes tumbled down all around them. The Angles stood and watched. They had been expecting an easy kill and now they wondered if a great army lay in wait for them on the other side of the wall.

"Donald," gasped Dougie in a disbelieving voice, "how on earth …"

"I'm with Malcolm and his bodyguard. We saw you being chased across the moor and rode across to join in the fun."

Alistair shook Donald's hand warmly.

"I promise never to ask Hamish to tell jokes about you ever again, old friend."

"What happened to your ear?" asked Dougie in a concerned voice.

Donald softly touched the side of his head.

"Time enough for tales when our work is done here."

"Did I not tell you, Dougie, that I saw Donald at the tavern a wee while ago?" asked Alistair in a cheeky voice.

Dougie shook his head.

"Aye, and I said, 'would you like a dram of the ale?' And do you know what Donald said?"

Dougie shook his head again and grinned.

"He said, 'No thanks, I've got one ear.'"

Donald groaned and handed Dougie a new claymore. In moments they stood alongside thirty of the best warriors in Scotland with the Angles watching them. Cuthbert was counting, weighing up the odds and he quickly realised that they were still very much in his favour. He glanced at the top of the wall and Dougie's eyes followed the baron's. Looking down on them, with his long grey hair swept back by the wind, was Malcolm. His eyes greeted Alistair and Dougie, and then he spoke in an impressive voice.

"So, Cuthbert, it is you who has been trying to kill me."

Cuthbert remained silent, and his horse tossed its head impatiently.

"There is nothing for you to gain here, go back to your own lands and avoid a war that would surely lead to your own destruction."

"My destruction," sneered Cuthbert, and his men jeered at the Scots.

Malcolm's reply was as cold as ice.

"I make you a promise, you will never rule any part of my kingdom. Not as long as the High Table exists."

"Then we had better kill the High Table as well," shouted Cuthbert cruelly, and he ordered his men to attack.

The Angles came at them quickly. Dougie was attacked by two soldiers. He was no warrior and he tried desperately to wield off their blows. Alistair came to his aid and then fought bravely against the giant soldier who had taken him prisoner. But the man's greater strength was no match for Alistair's experience and as the Angle raised his sword, Alistair brought his claymore down, with all his might, onto the enemy's shoulder. The sharp blade severed the man's arm and he cried out in agony.

Donald fought bravely and killed a soldier with an almighty blow. But the king's bodyguard were falling around them in the bloody fighting. There were simply too many Angles and even if two were killed to every Scot, then still more were ready to join the attack.

Malcolm felt helpless. The years were against him and he knew that if he joined his men in combat and fell, then Cuthbert would have achieved his aim cheaply. The whole kingdom would be at his mercy, leaderless and vulnerable.

As the friends were forced back to the wall, Dougie glanced up and saw Malcolm, his face lined with age and worry. In contrast, Cuthbert was grinning as he urged his men on from a safe distance. The Younger shouted down desperately to Cuthbert.

"What is it you want?"

"Your death," sneered Cuthbert.

The fighting was furious and exhausting. Donald felt the muscles in his arms ache with pain as he raised the heavy claymore, time and time again, to block the blows aimed at him. But the enemy were tiring too and eventually the two sides broke apart to recover and renew their strength. Alistair stared at the enemy and then at the bloody field of battle. There were bodies everywhere. Some crawled away like animals, some moaned in pain and some lay still.

Not for the first time, Dougie was to do something he might regret later. Yelling, "For the High Table," and holding aloft his claymore, he charged. The Angles laughed at him, stepped forward and then stopped in their tracks. A jet of fire flew noisily from behind the great wall and over Dougie's head. He looked up and counted five red streaks, cutting the air like a knife. The streaks landed amongst the enemy and exploded. Great plumes of smoke shot earth, men and weapons high into the air. Those horses that were not tethered bolted, those with riders reared up on their hind legs in sheer terror. More streaks shot from behind the wall, this time screaming and leaving green tails of fire in the sky. They exploded amongst the Angles who ran for their lives. Many were caught in their deadly explosions.

Dougie saw Cuthbert abandon his men and gallop away. He thought that through the smoke he could also see a richly dressed warrior, heavily built, with black hair and a thick black beard, going with him. For a moment, Dougie thought he might have been the Mac Mar.

Donald opened his eyes and took his hands away from his one and a half ears.

"What was that?"

Dougie looked at Alistair and grinned.

"It is the future," he said.

Tella kicked the flanks of his horse to catch up with Cuthbert.

"We must still press on with the alliance."

"But what was it?" asked Cuthbert.

"My guess is a trick of a fool of an alchemist and nothing that can stop us if we fight together."

"But how can we be sure?"

"You will be sure when you get your first delivery of the Light Iron."

***

"What on earth do you call it?" asked Malcolm, ruler of all the Scottish people and Protector of the Stone of Destiny.

"Grumf."

Archie walked backwards towards his king and sponsor.

"Quite right, Gangly" answered the alchemist, "it is called *bartillery*."

Malcolm stared in wonder as he ran his hands along the pipes that were strapped at an angle on the back of the wagon.

"Bartillery?"

"I thought it might come in useful," continued Archie. "Of course it's not perfected yet, it is still an *experident*."

Now the king had a glazed look in his eyes.

"An *experident*."

"But a few more looks into the Oracle of the Ancient Ones and we'll get there," said Archie in a matter-of-fact voice.

Gangly the Ghilly Dhu ran his hands up and down his red waistcoat.

"Grumf."

"No it is not time for lunch," replied Archie.

One of the king's bodyguard ran to join them and fell onto one knee.

"Shall we chase the Angles, Sire?"

Malcolm regained control of his thoughts.

"No, let them flee and tell others our lands are not to be troubled."

Dougie, Donald and Alistair dropped down from ropes off the wall.

"Welcome home," said Malcolm and he shook their hands.

"Your Majesty," said Alistair, "Berwick Castle flies the flag of the Saxon cross."

"Cuthbert is indeed cruel and greedy, but I never believed he would be brave enough to attack us on his own."

Dougie's mind went back to the warrior with the black beard who had ridden from the battle. But he might be wrong and he decided not to say anything about it. Then he felt sick with worry as he realised he had lost the brooch.

"I am sorry, Sire, but I have lost the brooch you gave me."

"Worry not, Dougie, we did not lose you, or Alistair, and men with good hearts are worth more than rubies." Malcolm looked straight at Dougie and spoke again, "Indeed men with good hearts are more powerful than stones."

A strange look came over his face and it was as if he wanted to say more, but couldn't.

Dougie felt his mind wander back to the courtyard of the castle and the strange man who had pleaded with him to return to the ruby. Then he sensed they were all staring at him and felt embarrassed.

Alistair realised this and broke the silence.

"We all have tales to tell over supper and I, for one, could eat a whole boar."

At the word boar, the thoughts of three warriors went out to their missing friend.

"I wonder how Hamish is doing?" asked Donald.

Hamish had enjoyed a wonderful lunch. Babs had stopped the caravan and cooked meat with barley, in herbs picked from the roadside. Beginning their journey again, Hamish felt his eyes close with the gentle rhythm of the oxen, the wheels and the pans. Babs smiled at him and gestured to the inside of the caravan. Gratefully, Hamish lay on a soft bed. His body moved contentedly with the motion of the small room, and within seconds he was fast asleep. Hamish dreamed of heather ale and friends, and places visited long ago. He smiled to himself in his sleep and a small brown face, that occasionally glanced back from the front seat, smiled with him.

"My wee Hami," whispered Babs.

But wherever Hamish's mind went in his dreams, the face of a boy, a small orphan boy, was with him too. Perhaps it was the silent pans that woke him. He sat up with a start and realised the caravan had stopped. He sensed danger, pulled the hood of the cloak over his face and left by the back door. A black stallion was tied to a wheel and he moved silently past the horse, running his hand soothingly down his neck as he went. Ahead of him was the back of a round man, who wore the same uniform as Cuthbert's soldiers.

The man was shouting at Babs.

"Where is he?"

"He has gone."

"He was one of the Scotsmen, the big one," screeched Jamie, "tell me where he is."

"He has gone to find a dish that is best served cold."

"I will kill you if you do not tell me."

"I am not scared," said Babs bravely.

Jamie moved his face close to hers and Babs did not turn a hair as she smelled his disgusting breath.

"You will be."

"I am not scared."

"And why is that?"

"Because I am destined to win the heart of a wee Hami," said Babs.

"A wee Hami?" sneered Jamie.

A great hand went around his neck and his short legs began to swing above the ground.

CHAPTER FIVE

A GOOD TELLING OFF

Dougie of Dunfermline, farmer, hero of battles and the friend of royalty, was a worried man.

He would gladly face the Picts, Norsemen and Angles together, rather than get a good telling off from Mairi.

He glanced back at his friends, shrugged his shoulders, climbed over a stile and crossed the lower pastures that rolled down to his beloved home. The path was still visible in the twilight and a fire, that glowed through the cracks in his door, spoke of a warmer welcome than he could expect or probably deserved. He took a deep breath, knocked and walked in. Dog barked and ran around in excited circles.

Little Tanny shouted, "Pappa," and threw her arms around him.

The boys charged forward and asked if he had killed anyone, or stolen any bloomin' treasure. Dougie smiled, hugged them and glanced across at Mairi. She continued to cut meat into strips, with her back to him. A knot tightened deep in his stomach.

"We need to talk."

"Oh, you disappear for months on end and now you want to talk to me," snapped Mairi.

"Not good," thought Dougie. "I had better not mention the brooch."

She turned and glared at him. It was a look that had taken twenty thousand years to develop and it could freeze a man in his tracks at a hundred paces. Blood drained from Dougie's body and his mouth didn't seem to work any more.

"I, er, wanted to say, er, that I am sorry," he burbled.

The children made a silent retreat to their bed.

"Oh, sorry now is it? You bring all your friends round here at feast time, without a moment's notice, and you expect me to provide for them."

"Yes," said Dougie. That was a mistake.

"Yes is it, I'll give you yes," and she threw a pot at him.

72

Outside the cottage, a group of hardened warriors doubled over laughing. Another thud came as something else hit the wall and Alistair shook his head with tears in his eyes.

"A fine woman," whispered Donald.

"None finer," said Hamish.

"Never mind that," giggled Alistair, "go and give the others a hand."

Dougie retreated behind the children.

"Listen to me, Mairi. I wanted to say that I am sorry."

"You said that before," shouted Mairi who armed herself with a sheep's head.

"And I wanted to say that I will make amends."

Mairi had a look of thunder on her face.

"Too right you will."

"In fact, I am going to make up for it right now."

Determined to put things right, Dougie bravely went over to Mairi, took her arm and walked her to the door. There was a light tap on it and the children glanced up from their bed.

"If that's your friends come to scrounge more food, you are for it, Douglas," she said bitterly.

Dougie opened the door and there stood the Younger, with crown and finery, ruler of all the land.

"You'll have had your supper then," barked Mairi sharply, and then she went scarlet as she realised who he was.

"Ah, you must be Mairi," said Malcolm kindly.

Mairi bobbed in a fashion that was something like a curtsey.

A voice behind them muttered, "It must be the bloomin' king!"

Malcolm smiled and spoke in a commanding voice.

"I have never had the chance to thank you for your help."

"My help?" spluttered Mairi.

"Without you, Dougie would never have been able to do the things he has done for the kingdom. You must be very proud of him."

Mairi glanced at her husband.

"Oh yes, very proud," but there was something in her voice that made Dougie doubt it.

"It is only a small gesture compared to all that you have given up in the name of the Scottish people. I would like you to join me for a feast."

"A feast?" gasped Mairi.

The king stepped aside to reveal the royal tent, tall and splendid, outside the gate to their garden.

"And, of course, the children are welcome too."

There was a shriek of delight from the back of the room and Dougie took hold of Mairi's hand.

"You wait until I get you on your own," she hissed out of the corner of her mouth.

Dougie smiled at her lovingly.

The feast was one to remember amongst a lifetime of feasts. Mairi and Dougie sat on the top table with Malcolm. Archie entertained the children with magic tricks, much to the annoyance of Gangly who tried to kick them with his long legs, grunting, "Grumf," in what was clearly a very rude way.

After the roast boar, Malcolm turned to Dougie with a stern look on his face.

"So you lost the ruby then."

Mairi looked at him sternly too and the party hushed.

"I'm for it now," thought Dougie.

"I have no others like it to give you," and then Malcolm smiled. "Alistair has told me about the brave rescue." He paused solemnly. "And so, Dougie of Dunfermline, I bestow upon you the position of Knight of the High Table."

The room cheered, including Mairi, who did indeed look very proud now.

"You must now choose your title. Do you wish to be known as Dougie, Conqueror of Carn Liath?"

Dougie shook his head, it sounded too grand for him.

"Do you wish to be spoken of as Dougie, the Norse Slayer?"

"Not really," muttered Dougie meekly.

"How about, Dougie … Dungeon Master?" urged Malcolm.
Dougie looked at his feet.

"Well what do you like?"

"Sheep."

"Very well Dougie of Dunfermline, from this day you shall be known by my subjects as the Shepherd Warrior."

There was another huge cheer.

Alistair turned to Hamish, "You know, Dougie and Mairi make a fine couple."

"Aye," and Hamish's thoughts went out to Babs.

Alistair nudged him.

"You know, Donald and his wife are just the same," said Hamish.

"How so?" asked Dougie.

"Well, only last summer I went to their cottage and Senga opened the door."

"Did she now?"

Alistair and Malcolm were already grinning and Donald was getting out of his seat.

"I said, 'how is Donald?' and she said, 'he went to the bottom of the garden to pick a cabbage and he fell terribly ill.' I said, 'that is terrible, what are you going to do?' and she said she was going to boil some beans."

A shield crashed down upon Hamish's head as the tent erupted with laughter.

***

As the men of Tain and the king's bodyguard returned to the palace after the feast, the Younger pulled Alistair to one side.

"You are absolutely sure?"

"I am," said Alistair.

"Dougie gave Amera's stone away and told Gora he could have it."

"It is as Myroy predicted. Dougie is now the first Keeper."

Malcolm nodded. "Then all we have to do is wait."

Alistair nodded too. "Mountain, island and castle is over, and our greatest test is coming."

***

Dougie whistled and Dog bolted across the field to chase the sheep into the lower pasture. It was a beautiful summer's day and the far hills were purple as the sun lit the heather. He sat down for his lunch and whispered, "There is no more worth having than this."

Dog bounded across the grass and jumped onto his chest to lick his master's cheek. He shook his head in disbelief.

"Dougie, the Shepherd Warrior."

The sun warmed him and he took one last look at his flock and fell asleep contentedly. Dougie dreamt of many things; his family, and the people and lands he had seen on his travels. A broad smile appeared on his face, as he thought about Donald and Hamish, and then grew sad as he remembered the orphan boy and the poor horse that had lost its life in the bog. But his slumber grew more restless as his mind wandered to the brooch given to him by the Younger. Suddenly his dream became so clear that it was as though he was living in another place and another time. He was standing outside the dark entrance of a cairn framed by three stones. There were strange people all around him, angry people, but they could not see Dougie. Some beat drums, some waved spears above their heads. Others rolled a huge stone across the entrance.

Dougie ran to the entrance, looked down the passage and saw the animal panic on Gora's face. The man was twenty paces from the open air and, if he reached it, there might just be a chance for him to escape.

But stone grated across stone and Gora stopped to stare at the disappearing line of torchlight, confused, not understanding at first what was happening. The Sea People began to chant, a drum thudded and all sounds became muffled, as though they struggled to even enter the cairn. This time Gora did not hesitate and, desperately, threw himself forward. He reached an arm through the opening and forced the ruby into Dougie's hand.

Dougie woke up. Sweat poured out of every pore in his body and he blinked in the sunshine. For a long while he sat and relived the dream. Eventually, he tried to stand and as he put his hand down to support his weight, he felt something between his fingers. It was the Younger's brooch. Dougie stared at it. He was drawn to the ruby. It was almost as though the stone called to him and he dropped it on the ground, and felt scared. The sheepdog licked his face and the spell was broken.

"Come on, old friend," he said kindly to Dog, "there is something I have to do."

They made their way towards the stile. It was a long walk to the loch, which fed the stream that watered Dougie's farm. But it was a fine day, Dog was good company, and so the time passed quickly. Standing on the shore, Dougie took one last look at his ruby. It shone blood red and was quite beautiful. A feeling of great reluctance came over him and he hesitated for a moment. Then thinking how it had nearly cost him his life, and Alistair's, at the gate of Berwick Castle, he drew back his arm and threw it into the deep water.

He was frightened by the stone and it was fear of its power that allowed him to overcome any desire he had to keep it. He remembered Malcolm's words at the great wall.

"Worry not, Dougie, we did not lose you, or Alistair, and men with good hearts are worth more than rubies."

He stood by the loch and closed his eyes as a warm breeze blew over him. In his mind, Dougie thought that he could hear strange words and one of them might have been "Myroy." He stared at the slopes, on the far side of the loch, and saw two men staring back at him. Both were smiling and the cloaked stranger, whom Dougie had seen on the hills since he was a boy, waved. The other man was thin and dressed in furs.

"You gave the stone up gladly, Dougie," said Myroy.

Dougie nodded and wondered how his voice could travel so far. In his heart he knew that after two thousand years, a soul imprisoned in the stone, was now free. At last he shouted back across the water.

"But there is so much I do not know."

"There is much you must not know yet, young Dougie," replied Myroy, "except perhaps that the stone is ancient and powerful, and was once held by your father's line."

These words hit Dougie like a falling tree and he felt numb. He had no memories of his parents and would treasure anything that might have belonged to them.

"I would not have thrown the stone away if I had known that."

Myroy replied in a slow and deliberate voice,

"For a small time the stone must be hidden. You are now the Keeper, but we have more terrible adventures to face before the kingdom is truly free."

Dougie raised an eyebrow at the awful thought of more adventures. The man in furs seemed to be getting smaller and fading away. Even from this distance Dougie could see that a white glow, that had been the warrior, was reforming slowly into a bird-like figure. Myroy pointed to the loch and the osprey spread its wings. Like a slave released from his chains it soared high above them. Then it dived at incredible speed into the rippling waters.

"I am truly proud of what you have become," continued Myroy, "so keep safe until you are asked to seek the Light Iron."

Dougie lowered his head as he tried to understand the stranger's words. It seemed as though every time they met he was left with more questions than answers and a feeling that each question would shape his very future.

He lifted his face. "Will Alistair be with me?"

The Ancient One ignored him and began to draw a circle on the ground with his staff.

"And the stone shall return to be held by your line."

"My children?"

Then Myroy was gone and on the wind Dougie thought that he heard him say, "Be ready."

Dougie stood for ages watching the cold waters of the loch. Then the light faded quickly as though an immense shadow had been thrown across the land. He looked up at the sun. It was hidden by a cloud that moved faster than any he had ever seen. The great flock of birds swooped together, as though they were one creature, and the loch lit up once more. Hundreds of majestic ospreys, the lost souls of the stone, hovered above the grey water and then dived into its depths. It was a wondrous sight and it enchanted him. The air seemed to be charged with a great power, a natural power, like that of a breaking storm. And then all was still.

He smiled at the far hills and bent down to tickle Dog's ear.

"Let's go home," he said.

***

One moon later, Dougie entered the cottage and felt that something was different. The children were talking excitedly, in whispers, and Mairi was skipping between the table and the fire.

"Anything exciting happened to you lately?" she asked.

Dougie thought about the dream, Myroy and the ospreys.

"Not really, what's for supper?"

Mairi placed a bowl of steaming lamb and barley broth in front of him and Tanny ran over to sit on his knee.

"You won't go away again, will you Pappa? Well not without us, anyway."

"Not if I can help it."

"We will all be going away for a wee while," said Mairi.

Dougie's spoon hovered in front of his mouth.

"A rider came whilst you were up on the pastures. Hamish of Tain has invited us to his Union of Souls."

"Hamish, getting married?"

"In ten days, so you had better ask Stewart of Balgedie if he can keep an eye on things for us."

"But how will we get to Tain? I don't even know where it is."

"The Younger will send an escort for us," said Mairi proudly. "Being a knight of the High Table seems to have its benefits. I thought I might make myself a new shawl."

"I'd rather stay here."

"And miss out. Not a chance. Besides, I've told all my friends about it. Douglas, you just make the arrangements and tidy yourself up a bit."

Dougie groaned.

"Can we go?" asked Calum and Jock together.

"We will all go," said Mairi, sternly.

Dougie gave in, as he always did, and bounced Tanny up and down on his knee. She giggled and kissed him on the cheek. The shepherd looked into her wide, excited brown eyes. A little bit of Mairi was behind those eyes. A little bit of him too and, most of all, a lot of Tanny herself. He kissed her back and wondered if one day she would keep the stone.

"There is no more worth having than this," he said and finished his broth.

CHAPTER SIX

CORFU TOWN

As Grandma walked down the steps onto the tarmac at Corfu airport, the brilliant sunshine made her blink. Warm air enveloped her and it was like standing in her airing cupboard back in Glenbowmond.

Peter had wept openly and then stayed silent during the flight and now she watched him walk, head down, towards the terminal building. She moved beside him and put her arm through his, and without any sign that he had noticed her, they followed the other passengers through passport control.

Outside the terminal, a bright yellow taxi broke ranks and drew up quickly beside them. Bernard was out of the car in a flash, taking their bags and ushering them onto the hot rear seats. They drove in silence, northeast towards Kassiopi, and after half an hour were past the hotel complexes and tavernas that hugged the beaches. They turned off the main road and rose up the lower slopes of Pantokrator, the highest mountain on the island. The air was cooler here and the narrow lane twisted through olive, orange and lime groves.

Bernard swivelled round.

"Not far now, Maggie."

She nodded and squeezed Peter's hand. He didn't move and sat like a statue until they turned through large, black metal gates which closed automatically behind them. Bernard's house was white with a red tiled roof and green shutters framing large picture windows. A veranda ran all the way around the house and its garden boasted some of the most colourful and beautiful flowers Grandma had ever seen. Within the high walls that completely encircled the garden, it was a peaceful, perfumed sanctuary. She smiled at Bernard and thought that if Peter could recover anywhere, it would be here.

Bernard introduced them to Mr and Mrs Agnedes. Old Mr Agnedes tended the garden and his wife kept house. Their dark, wrinkled skin, warm smiles and busy manner helped Grandma feel more at home. Bernard ordered tea and led them through large, simply furnished rooms with bare white walls, and out through glass patio doors to a huge swimming pool. They sat and stared down the mountainside towards the sea. A huge red sun was falling behind the distant hills that marked the shores of Albania.

"How did you know we were coming? I couldn't get through on the phone."

"Myroy told me."

Grandma glanced at Peter. "What should we do?"

"Stay safe. Stay together. Give you and Peter time."

"Will the Seekers come?"

"They will."

"How will we know when they are here?"

Bernard took an old, dog-eared card from his pocket and flicked it with his finger.

"We have friends here, Maggie, good friends." He stood up. "Will you excuse me? I won't be long. I ought to go and speak to one now. Might be best if you two try and get some sleep. It's like the desert. Gets dark quickly on Corfu."

Spiros Theopoulis, Commissioner of Police, had a stern face and a dark, stern-looking uniform. He sat behind a huge, neat desk and studied his friend as he entered his office. Bernard sat down and placed a small, round pebble on the desk.

"Do you need men?" asked Spiros.

"I need eyes and ears," replied Bernard. "The Keeper is here."

He took back his pebble and, as he walked back to the door, he heard Spiros lift a phone.

"We have received intelligence of a large drugs shipment arriving on the island soon. Double surveillance teams at all ports of entry. They may have blond hair and blue eyes. Report back to me each hour."

***

83

Next day, Bernard left the house early and Grandma made friends with Mrs Agnedes who seemed to spend her entire life in the kitchen. They had first met after the war, and now they talked, as best they could, about recipes, Grandpa's friendship with Mr Agnedes and the lands around Glenbowmond village. But the conversation always came back to Peter.

"He still sleeps?"

Grandma looked at her watch.

"Best to leave him. He's had a bad time of it."

Mrs Agnedes smiled and placed a skinned rabbit in a large pot and surrounded it with chopped onions and garlic cloves.

"Who is his favourite food?"

"Oh, Peter will eat just about anything. Loves ice-cream."

The old lady skilfully stripped a stem of rosemary and tossed the leaves in the pot, and poured in a wine glass of olive oil.

"Last, salt and pepper," she said proudly.

"Is that all?"

"Simple cooking and wonderful, er, how do you say?"

"Flavours?"

"Yes, flavours. He is one of Bernard's favourite dishes."

She put the pot into the belly of a huge cooker and set the timer for two hours.

"Shall we make Peter some breakfast?" asked Grandma.

"Why not take tray to him?"

Peter yawned and opened an eye, and shut it again. He rolled over to escape the bright sunshine and thought about Dougie's journey to the Outer Islands. But even though he could remember every word of Myroy's story, live each part of the adventure, his mind always went back to Mr Smith's exploding body and James's grinning face as they had raced up the motorway to Luton Airport. Then he saw the picture of his family and their car exploding. That picture, framed by the plane's window, haunted him. He began to cry again.

Outside in the garden, someone was using a lawnmower. He thought he heard whistling. He rolled back over and through the

84

window, in a light blue sky, he watched swallows dart around as they hunted for flies. He felt hunted too.

Perhaps his family weren't really dead. Yes, that was it. Myroy would be able to take him back through time to the moment he had been dropped outside the terminal building. He could warn them. Tell them to get out of the car and into a taxi. The bedroom floor began to shimmer and Peter leapt out of bed.

"I am ready to go."

"Go?" asked Myroy.

"Back to Luton. Back to yesterday."

The Ancient One's eyes flashed.

"Do you think history is a game? Do you think being a Stone Keeper is a game?"

"But we can save them."

"They are gone."

Peter felt his voice rising. He began to shake and pointed his finger at Myroy.

"They are not gone."

Myroy's face became lined and full of concern.

"They are gone."

"But they don't deserve to die."

"They did not deserve to die."

Peter burst into tears and sat on the bed. Myroy watched him and stayed silent. After a while Peter took his head out of his hands.

"Why are you here?"

"To help you."

"Help me. Help me lose more of the ones I love?"

"Help you move on."

"I do not want to move on. I want to go back."

"Peter, you must move on and be ready, and hold the memory of your family in your heart."

"I don't think I will ever be ready."

Myroy sighed. "To understand the future you must understand the past."

"I don't want to be a Keeper any more. I don't want to hear any more stories and I don't want this bloody stone."

He threw Amera's stone at the wall. It pulsed blood red and rolled across the floor. Myroy ignored it. Peter put his head back into his hands. After a long silence, he lifted his face up, eyes red with tears.

"I am sorry I said that," he whispered.

Myroy nodded and sat on the bed beside him.

"I want you to listen to me. Alistair has sent a message north. The alliance is forged and Dougie faces his third test before becoming the first Keeper."

"I am not sure I am ready."

"Together we are stronger."

"I feel so weak. So tired."

"Listen to me," said Myroy kindly.

Peter got up and walked to the window. Below him a boy was walking beside the pool with a black bin liner. He turned and nodded.

Myroy smiled.

"It had been another long and hard winter. The tops of the hills surrounding Dougie's farm shone white with snow in the last rays of the sun. A cold wind blew and a small skein of geese flew overhead in a "v" formation and Dougie knew the weather would not begin to improve until these birds gathered together in great numbers and left to travel to the north. Each autumn they would arrive and signal the shortening of days, and each spring they would depart for unknown lands.

Dougie of Dunfermline cherished the seasons, lived by them and, like most of his people, he celebrated their passing with music, dancing and food. He was close to the land and noticed keenly the changes in weather and crops, and the habits of wild creatures. Warm winds were a time away yet, but Dougie smiled and thought of summer. He knelt to touch a snowdrop that had pushed its head up above the cold earth."

The Ancient One spoke about the Winter Feast and the journey to Melrose. Peter even managed a small smile when he learnt about Bob the Pig Stealer and how Malcolm the Younger had appointed Dougie to the High Table of Scotland. Then Dougie wondered if Tanny would one day carry Amera's stone and the story was told. Myroy disappeared into the floor.

"Has he eaten anything?" asked Grandma.

Mrs Agnedes shook her head.

"Trays three outside room. All full."

"Do you think we ought to check on him?"

"No."

"But what should we do?"

Grandma felt tears well up and Mrs Agnedes put an arm around her.

"Do nothing," she said.

Three days later, Mrs Agnedes woke Peter by quietly opening the shutters and placing a huge glass of fresh orange juice on his bedside table. He blinked. Mrs Agnedes gave him a broad smile, wiped her hands on her apron, said something he couldn't understand and went out.

Peter lay still and listened to the sounds out in the garden. Mr Agnedes was cutting the lawn again and birds sang. Water tinkled as the sprinklers were turned on. He still felt sick in his stomach and sipped his juice. It tasted different to the cartoned orange he was used to. Thicker too. He liked it. Outside, someone started to whistle a tune with only four notes and the tune repeated itself, over and over again.

Peter kicked his sheet away, wrapped a towel around his waist and walked onto his balcony. A boy, about the same age as him, dressed only in red swim shorts, trailed a net on a long pole, up and down the length of the pool. Every now and then he stopped whistling and emptied the contents of his net into a bin bag.

Peter called down. "Hello."

The boy grinned up at him and shouted back in broken English.

"Good morning, Peter. How is you tomorrow?"

Peter smiled back at the handsome tanned face and the mop of thick, black hair that rested above it. He pointed at the pool and moved his arms like swimming strokes.

The boy laughed, said something in Greek and pointed down the hill.

"Katerina's kitchen."

Peter shrugged his shoulders.

"Katerina's kitchen," the boy repeated.

Peter grabbed a tee-shirt from his holdall and dressed. He pushed Amera's stone deep inside the zipped pocket in his shorts, dashed out and met Grandma on the stairs.

"Morning, Peter. Isn't it a lovely day? Bernard has offered to take us into Corfu Town this afternoon. Says there is a lot of good history there."

"That would be nice. Who's the boy by the pool?"

"That's Mr and Mrs Agnedes's grandson, Stefanos. Want any breakfast?"

"Love some. See you in a minute." He ran down to the pool.

"Hi, Stefanos."

"Herete." Stefanos thumped his chest and beamed. "Me Stefanos Agnedes."

They shook hands.

"Why did you point down the hill?"

A bell rang out and Mrs Agnedes called out.

"Stefanos."

Stefanos winked at Peter , dropped his net and ran off.

On the veranda, Bernard stopped spooning strawberry jam onto a croissant, wiped his hands on a napkin and tossed Peter a small book.

"Thought you might find it useful."

Peter looked at the photo of a white windmill on the cover and the words, *Greek Dictionary and Phrase Book.*

"I met Stefanos this morning. He seems very nice."

"He is nice. But I think Mrs Agnedes finds him a bit of a handful. He will be off now to Katerina's kitchen."

"Down the hill?"

"About a mile down the lane that leads to the beach. His mother runs a small taverna that old Mr Agnedes bought her when her husband died. One of his many jobs is to wash the breakfast dishes."

"Doesn't Stefanos go to school?" asked Grandma.

"Of course he does, Maggie. Although I'm not too sure how well he's doing. Besides it's a holiday on the island at the moment."

Mrs Agnedes bustled over and placed another tray on the table. It was full of coffee, breads, pastries and freshly baked biscuits. She smiled at Bernard, gathered together the used plates and then made the shape of a pot with her hands.

"Tomorrow, Kotopoulo Xoriatikos?"

Bernard smiled back and glanced at Peter.

"Village chicken with potatoes and oregano. Quite delicious. I forgot to mention, we are going to eat out tonight as a bit of a treat."

"Would you mind if I helped you make it?" asked Grandma.

Mrs Agnedes enthusiastically nodded at Grandma. Then she left.

"Extraordinary woman," said Bernard.

Peter bit into a pastry.

"Great cook."

"And one of the bravest women I have ever known."

Grandma nodded at Bernard in agreement.

"After the war they came to stay for a week with us in Glenbowmond. It was Grandpa's way of saying thank you."

"The people on the island are very generous, Maggie, and without Mr and Mrs Agnedes I might not be here now."

Peter watched Mr Agnedes move his wheelbarrow between beds. He stooped to tend some geraniums. They were so much bigger, so much brighter, than the geraniums his mum had grown in the conservatory at home. Suddenly, he burst into tears.

Grandma sniffed disapprovingly. The inside of the taxi smelled of sweat and disinfectant, and Mr Minolas glanced back at her.

"The best cab on the island, yes?"

He swerved to avoid a pot-hole in the road.

Grandma grabbed Bernard's arm and stared at the back of the driver's bald head.

"Wonderful."

"You English?"

"Scots," corrected Grandma.

"Ah, Scotland. A beautiful place, Scotland. With such beautiful ladies."

He winked.

Grandma tightened her grip on Bernard's arm and watched a lorry thunder around the bend in the coast road. It seemed to be coming straight at them. Mr Minolas swerved again.

"Damn lorry drivers. They should learn how to drive," he moaned.

Peter stared out of the window at the sugar cube houses perched on the hillside and the people on the beach on their left hand side. The blue sea looked gorgeous.

"Can we go to the beach sometime, Bernard?"

"Of course. Although I want you to avoid the busy beaches where I can't keep an eye on you. I'll ask Stefanos to take you to the Secret Cove. Great place for snorkelling and very private."

The cab's brakes slammed on and they all lurched forward.

"Best cab on the island," repeated Mr Minolas.

The market, inside the walls of Corfu Town, bustled with fast scooters and tourists, even though it was early in the tourist season. Bernard led them down narrow twisting lanes lined with shops selling postcards, tee-shirts and leather bags. Peter stopped to look at a stand covered in sunglasses and thought that Kylie might like them. Grandma started to haggle with a lady for a cotton shawl.

After a while they were walking through a cooler area with alleyways protected from the sun by the four-storey houses on both sides. High above the alleyways, lines of washing showed that this was a place for locals, rather than visitors. As they walked, several men called out to Bernard, respectfully, and he waved back at them. Then they were out into bright sunshine again, in a square surrounded by cafés and neat rows of tables and chairs where men sat in small groups drinking coffee. Some played chess.

"Let's take the weight off our feet shall we?" suggested Bernard and he gestured towards a café near a small fountain. "You like ice-cream, don't you Peter?"

"Love it."

"Well, they make wonderful ice-cream here. Big portions too."

"Can I get a cup of tea?" asked Grandma.

Bernard nodded and placed their order, in perfect Greek. Peter sat, enjoying the sun, and watching the people in the square. Everything seemed to be done at a slow, leisurely pace, and he guessed that life here hadn't changed much for centuries.

On the other side of the square, Mr Minolas sat down and ordered something. Then he too watched the people in the square. But most of all Peter felt as though he was looking at him.

"Do you know Mr Minolas?" asked Peter.

"He used to do the odd job for me. Still does."

Mr Minolas began to read a paper and occasionally lowered it to peer over the top at them.

"He seems very interested in us," thought Peter.

A waiter brought a tray and placed a huge bowl of ice-cream in front of him.

"Wow," said Peter as he lifted his spoon.

Inside Peter's pocket, the stone pulsed red. In a side lane an engine roared. Mr Minolas stood and waved frantically at Bernard. A black car swerved into the square and shot towards them. Bernard grabbed Grandma and pulled her out of her chair. Then he grabbed Peter as the car smashed into their table. Chairs and ice-cream flew up into the air. Then the car was gone.

Bernard ran over to Mr Minolas.

"Did you see the driver?"

"Blond hair," he said.

***

Peter spent the afternoon by the pool hoping to see Stefanos again. To pass the time he read the dictionary Bernard had given him. After an hour he could speak Greek. Maybe not like a local, but enough to get by on.

"Being a Keeper has some advantages," he thought.

"Although you will be alone," said Grandpa's voice.

Peter froze.

"Is that you, Grandpa?" he stammered.

"It is, laddie."

"I thought you were dead?"

Grandpa ignored his question.

"Myroy says that more of Odin's people are on the way. Tell Bernard tonight and ask him about Alex."

"Alex?"

"Alexandria. To understand the future you must understand the past."

"That's what Myroy told me," said Peter. "Why can't you tell me?"

But Grandpa did not reply and he was left to his own thoughts beside the pool. He picked up a small plastic bag and took out the sunglasses he had bought for Kylie.

"Well, Grandpa, I am not totally alone," he whispered and went inside.

Bernard's office was crammed with antique furniture that once had cost a lot of money. A computer rested on a solid mahogany desk and Peter felt drawn to it. He booted it up and

92

connected to the internet.

Hi Kylie! Miss you lots. When things have settled down a bit I will come back to see you. Miss you so much. Got you a present too. xxx

He pushed send.

The office door opened and Bernard stared at him.

"You bloody fool."

***

Thorgood Firebrand passed a sign that read, "Constantis and Andreous Advertising," and, ignoring a secretary, walked straight into Miltos Constantinis's office. It smelled of stale cigar smoke. Miltos glanced up from his laptop. His visitor was sleek, elegant and ageless and, as he wondered how much the man's suit cost, his secretary burst in.

"Sorry, Mr Constantinis, I …"

Miltos turned the palms of his fat hands up in an apologetic gesture.

"No problem. I have been expecting this gentleman." He fixed his eyes on Thorgood. "You are Mr Brand from Oslo, are you not?"

Thorgood smiled politely and placed his briefcase onto Miltos's desk, and flicked its catches. The secretary shut the door behind her.

As Miltos spoke, a cigar butt in the corner of his mouth moved up and down.

"I hope you understand that what you ask is impossible. Our poster sites are booked by clients months in advance."

Thorgood ignored him and handed over a CD and a single A4 picture, showing the photo of a teenage girl. Her outstretched hands handcuffed together. At the bottom of the poster design was a slogan.

Coming soon – RELEASE ME – the new fragrance from OASV Europe.

"Your fees are twenty thousand US dollars for four weeks on all billboards on Corfu."

Miltos nodded.

"And you will have to spend a lot of time and effort managing clients when their advertisements do not appear on schedule."

"I told you, Mr Brand, what you ask is simply impossible."

Thorgood took a cheque from his pocket and handed it over.

"Half a million dollars," spluttered Miltos.

"And here is a little something for you."

Thorgood turned the briefcase around so the businessman could see inside. It was full of American dollars.

"Another half a million. Do we have a deal?"

Constantinis stood and shook his hand.

***

Beside the swimming pool, in the grounds of the most expensive hotel on Corfu, Thorgood stripped off to his boxer shorts. He undid the strap of his Rolex watch and placed it in a bin liner with his suit, and dumped the lot in a bin beside the pool bar. He dived into the cool water and relaxed as his submersed body shot forward. Then Thorgood Firebrand surfaced in Odin's underground chamber and, without hesitation, pulled himself up onto a rock and wrapped a towelling robe around his body.

"Is it done?" asked Odin.

"The advert will appear all over the island in one moon. Our ship will land at Corfu Town at the same time. Our men are briefed and ready."

"And the new gun?"

"To be tested during the voyage."

Odin tapped a number into his mobile phone.

"Olaf. Meet Thorgood at the quay immediately."

"I obey, master."

Thorgood walked through the rock wall and emerged inside

the long office. He dressed quickly in a dark blue suit and called the lift.

Ingrid Hellergren smiled up at him from the reception desk. "Off anywhere nice?"

Thorgood smiled back. "I thought I might get myself a bit of a tan."

***

Katerina's kitchen was two hundred metres from the sea and shaded by gnarled trees that looked as old as the tea towels Stefanos was washing. Plastic tables and chairs waited for the first of the lunchtime tourists to arrive. A Greek pop song came on the radio, which Stefanos turned up, and he grabbed a tray covered with bottles of olive oil, and salt and pepper pots. He sang along and Peter smiled as he danced between tables and put the pots out.

"You like dancing?"

Peter replied, in Greek, "I too embarrassed."

Stefanos stopped dancing and said in Greek.

"You can speak our language?"

"This morning. Learned."

"How can you learn Greek in a morning?"

Peter smiled. "Story long."

"Stefanos!" yelled a voice from inside the kitchen.

Stefanos shrugged his shoulders and quickly finished laying out the tables.

"That's my mother. Hates loud music. How about a swim? I'm just about done here."

"Love to," beamed Peter. "What is Secret Cove?"

Stefanos knocked a salt pot over and poured salt into his hand and threw it over his shoulder for good luck.

"Wait and see," he said.

The soles of Peter's feet flinched with each step across the hot sand. He glanced back at Katerina's kitchen now half full with visitors.

"We are busier every year," said Stefanos. "Do you have any snorkelling things?"

"Left London in hurry. Not got much."

The boy grinned.

"On Corfu, you don't need much to have a great time, but you are going to need a mask at the very least. Come on, let's get you sorted out."

He led Peter off the beach and up to a ramshackle store that had a weather-beaten sign above it. The sign read SUPER SUPER MARKET. Peter looked at the buckets and spades, postcards and hats as Stefanos talked to the owner. The man studied Peter's feet and smiled, and handed over a plastic bag containing the large flippers, mask and snorkel.

"How much owe you?" asked Peter as they continued towards the end of the beach.

"I didn't pay for them. I haven't got any money," beamed Stefanos.

"How get them?"

"Half a day. I offered to look after the shop for half a day. It's how I get everything I want."

"How many jobs got?"

"About thirty. On Corfu we have a saying for it. 'To bake bread is to be close to God.' It means that if you work and live a simple life, and you will be happy."

Peter thought about Dougie and his life as a shepherd.

"I agree."

Stefanos stopped and looked round.

"Ok. No one about. Follow me."

They walked to a line of rocks where the sand ended suddenly. Then they were scrambling up and over the rocks to a thin steep path that headed inland. The path was edged with speedwell, mallow and orchids. Higher up the wild flowers gave way to broom and gorse. Then they left the path, with Stefanos leading, and came out onto a flat rock pavement with a steep drop on one side. Stefanos walked towards the edge of the cliff and disappeared.

Peter ran to the edge and stared down at a small cove. A tiny beach lay on one side and the cliffs formed a protective three quarter circle around an emerald blue pool.

"Perfect example of coastal erosion," thought Peter.

Stefanos must have dived about ten metres into the sea and a ring of bubbles showed where he had hit the water. But he wasn't there now. Worried, Peter stared down and waited for his friend to surface. A minute passed and he wondered if he should run back to the beach and get help. Then a masked, grinning face broke the surface.

Stefanos cried out, "Come on in."

Peter tossed his bag into the sea and jumped. Seconds later his grinning face appeared beside his friend.

"Sea warm."

Stefanos nodded. "Come on, get your mask on."

Peter pointed at Stefanos's mask. "Where you get mask?"

"I'll show you. Take a deep breath and follow me."

Peter trod water and, clumsily, pulled his flippers on.

"Make sure it is a deep breath," repeated Stefanos and then he dived.

Peter followed into a fantastic world. The water was so clear that he could see all the way down to the sandy sea bed. Small shoals of brightly coloured fish darted around and four larger grey fish swam lazily just above the sand. Stefanos's flippers moved up and down rhythmically and then he turned and headed straight to a hole in the cliff, and swam right into it. Panic ran through Peter's body. He needed air and he surfaced and gasped, and trod water. He looked at the cliff and the small waves that ran up to it. Then he sucked in a huge lungful of air and dived again. The hole in the cliff was a black forbidding circle as wide as Peter's outstretched hands. Summoning up his courage, he swam in and found himself rising up a straight passage. At last his head broke water.

"You took your time, didn't you?" said Stefanos.

Peter pulled his mask off and looked around the underwater

cave. A rather grand candlestick with three burning candles gave off a dim, spooky light and the walls seemed to dance with shadows.

"What great place," replied Peter.

"My Grandfather found it when he was a boy and the entrance is always covered by the sea. I sleep here sometimes. Great fun when you want to disappear for a while."

Peter pulled himself out of the pool and onto the wide rocky ledge where his friend sat. As the candles flickered, he saw cracks running across the walls. In some of the cracks, Stefanos had placed spare flippers, masks and books. Blankets and beach towels filled one large crack.

"How you get books here?"

"In plastic bags. Fancy some chocolate?" He broke off a chunk and tossed it to Peter, and grinned. "It is a great place and I've never brought anyone here before. When you have got your breath back, let's go for a proper swim around the cove."

"Love to," said Peter.

A few minutes later, Stefanos disappeared down into the pool and Peter got ready to follow. He thought about the stone in his pocket. It was too dangerous to just carry about with him and he stood on tip toes, and felt about for a high ledge. He found a good one and hid Amera's stone.

"Oh, Peter, your back is very red," Grandma said later.

"How did you get it?" asked Bernard.

"Snorkelling with Stefanos. I had a wonderful time."

"When were you swimming?"

"Lunchtime."

"Well we've caught it early enough, but don't underestimate how strong the sun is. Most people avoid noon till two and swim early in the morning. Here, Maggie, rub this on his back."

Grandma took the tub of natural Greek yoghurt and raised an eyebrow.

Bernard smiled. "An old remedy from Grandpa in the desert."

"Oh, I spoke to Grandpa this morning," said Peter. "He said to ask you about Alex."

"Did he now. Well let's go to supper first."

"Did he lose the stone in Cairo?"

"No, not in Cairo, but he did lose it."

Outside, Mr Minolas piped his horn.

"Come on, let's go and get fed," suggested Bernard and they rose.

The taxi still smelled of sweat and swerved to avoid the potholes on the coast road northeast towards Kassiopi. Peter felt a little light headed and turned green.

"You are dehydrated. When we get to Estonis I want you to drink lots of water," said Bernard.

"Is it a good restaurant?" asked Grandma.

"Best on the island, Maggie."

"And best taxi on the island," said Mr Minolas.

She put her arm through Bernard's again and Peter watched the road ahead, and the sun fall to touch the ocean. Then he sat bolt upright.

"Stop the car," he shouted.

"Why shall I stop?" asked Mr Minolas.

"Stop the car!"

The taxi screeched into a narrow lay-by and Peter was out the door in a flash, and running.

Bernard followed and watched the Keeper. Peter was standing like a statue in front of a huge advertising poster. The poster had a picture of a sad girl in handcuffs. Its caption read, RELEASE ME.

Peter swayed and before he fell, Bernard thought he said six words.

"Oh, Kylie, what have I done?"

CHAPTER SEVEN

BALADO TO SIWAH

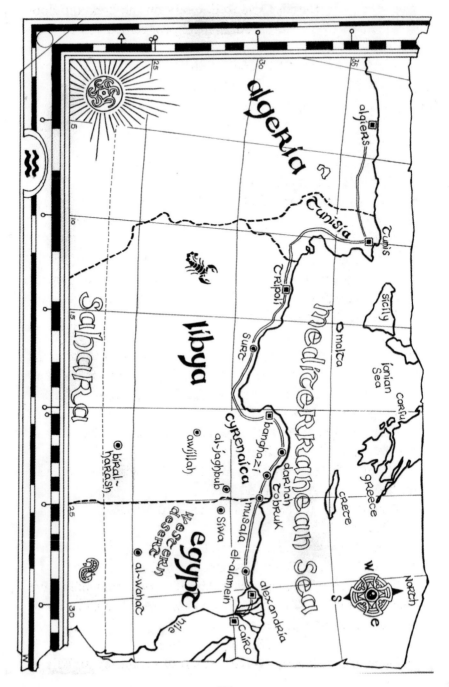

Bernard knocked gently on the bedroom door and called out in a soft, concerned voice.

"Peter. Peter."

No reply.

"Peter. It's Bernard."

"Go away."

"We have to talk. I have something that might help you."

"Go away."

"Something that happened a long time ago."

Peter sighed, swung his legs off the bed and put his head in his hands.

"What have I done?"

"Peter, please."

"Give me a moment, won't you," he said angrily, but instantly he regretted saying it and walked across to open the door.

Bernard smiled kindly at him.

"I pieced the whole story together, about what happened to the stone in North Africa, with Chalky and your Grandfather after the war. Of course, I was a young man then. Young and very much in love with Maggie, but, as you will hear, some things are meant to be and some things aren't."

Peter thought about Kylie and he walked back to the bed and covered himself in his sheet.

"It might help. Myroy's stories helped us when we believed we had been beaten in the desert."

A muffled reply came out from under the sheet.

"Desert?"

"Grandpa asked me to tell you the story."

"Didn't Grandpa lose the stone, like me?"

"He did. Now, rest and listen. My life, your life, would have been very different if I had married Maggie. The story really begins in August nineteen forty two."

18th August 1942

General Montgomery gave Bernard a reassuring smile and

103

spoke in his eager, clipped voice. "There is no need to worry. I will give you my full backing."

"What if they say no?"

"Then they say no and we do it anyway."

Two great oak doors opened, together, and a pretty lady, with an eager face and dressed in the dark blue uniform of the Women's Auxiliary Air Force, asked them to come in and stand in front of a long table. A huge map of Europe covered one wall of the War Room in the basement of Whitehall. A large, menacing shaded area covered most of it.

Bernard looked at the faces of the uniformed War Cabinet and at a podgy, balding man, dressed in a civilian suit, who sat quietly at one end of the table puffing on a thick cigar. He was older than the others by a good twenty years.

Montgomery stepped forward.

"Gentlemen. Thank you for seeing me at short notice."

The sombre faces of the Cabinet nodded.

"As you know, two weeks ago you appointed me to head up the British Expeditionary Forces in North Africa and I need to give you an immediate and frank update. Our men are in poor shape, with low morale, and tanks that lack the fire power to face up to the German Tigers. I can improve morale, but I need two things from you. Firstly, I need large numbers of desert-ready battle tanks. The American Sherman tanks would do the job if you can get them. Secondly, I need to give you a quick history lesson."

He strode over to the map of North Africa on the wall opposite the map of Europe.

"In the early stages of the war, the Italians drove east from their base at Tripoli."

He tapped Tripoli with his stick.

"They entered Egypt and dug in, and were eventually chased back along the coast road by the Eighth Army, past Darnah."

His stick went into action again.

"We divided our forces so that half continued to chase them

along the coast road. The others cut across the desert of Cyranaica to head them off at Benghazi. They surrendered and Tripoli fell soon afterwards."

A dark-haired man coughed apologetically.

"Yes, we know all this," said Major Nick Trevellyn.

"You do. But my question to you all is, 'Have we learned from it?'"

The bald man at the end nodded at Montgomery to continue.

"Fearing total defeat in the desert, Hitler sent one of his best men, Field Marshall Erwin Rommel, to Tunis. He was reinforced with seasoned troops and the highly effective Panzer Divisions of the newly formed Afrika Corps. They recaptured Tripoli, Benghazi and Darnah. The last twelve months have been like a game of chess played by armoured divisions across the Western Desert.

Tobruk fell to the Germans in June and they captured thirty five thousand British troops. We recaptured Tobruk and today it holds out, but only just. Australian, Polish and Indian forces are under siege and suffer day and night air attacks. Most of our Eighth Army has dug in around El Alamein to halt the next German advance."

"But what is your point?" asked a good looking man in a Naval uniform.

"My point is that that if the line at El Alamein fails, Rommel will be in Alexandria in a week and then walking the streets of Cairo."

The man at the end stood up and cigar smoke trailed after him.

"We must take the pressure off Tobruk and reinforce the Eighth Army." He smiled at Bernard. "And that is why you are here, isn't it."

Bernard stood to attention.

"Yes, sir."

"Stand easy," said Montgomery. "Tell them your idea."

"For all their victories, the Afrika Corps is vulnerable. It is over a thousand miles to Cairo from its main base at Tunis. They have one, maybe two, long and vulnerable supply chains. Their tanks cannot run for more than thirty miles without fuel. My idea is to strengthen the Hurricane fighter-bomber squadrons at Alexandria and focus them on the main German supply bases at Tripoli and Benghazi. At the same time, we need to start to fight a different kind of war. A dirty war. I want your approval to form a new attack force capable of deep-penetration raids across the desert. If we can destroy just one of Rommel's big fuel dumps, we can stop his tanks almost immediately."

"What do you need?" asked the bald man in a deep, gravelly voice.

"Brave men, luck, explosives, jeeps and nights without a moon."

"Anything else?"

"Complete independence from the normal chain of command. For absolute secrecy, I must report directly to General Montgomery."

"Monty, make sure he gets what he wants."

Montgomery saluted and as they were shown out. Winston Churchill called after them.

"Tell your men. Tobruk must not fall again."

Outside the war room, Major Trevellyn caught up with Bernard.

"I wonder if I might have a quick word with you?"

Less than three weeks later, Bernard stared out of his office window, across the grassy parade ground, at the hastily erected huts that made up Balado training camp. On one side of the parade ground, soldiers jumped out of the back of a Bedford lorry and kit bags were tossed out after them. Someone knocked on the door.

"Come."

Sergeant Sturgess marched in.

"That's the last of the trainees, sir."

Bernard nodded and hoped they were better than the last lot.

"So far we have sent one hundred and fifty men back to their regiments and the Long Range Desert Group is only half full. We are running out of time."

"Yes, sir."

"Get them fed and into hard training right away."

"Yes, sir."

When the door closed, Bernard thought about the hundreds of meetings with senior people in the regiments, to find the pick of the men in the British army. He opened a brown folder and read again the notes he had had made on the new arrivals.

Sandy Turner

Five foot, seven inches tall.

Age 19.

Born Birmingham.

Commended for bravery in France.

Ginger hair.

Midlands boxing champion 1937.

Speaks German fluently.

No pre-war employment record.

Tough.

Lofty Simpson

Six foot, two inches tall.

Age 23.

Born Oxford.

Commended for bravery in France.

Chemistry teacher.

Good thinker – top grades at university, etc.

First class radio operator.

Duncan Donald

Six foot tall.

Age 19 (seems very mature for his age).
Born Glenbowmond.
Commended for bravery in France.
Shepherd.
Very fit and level headed.
Almost perfect photographic memory.
Quiet.

Dick Chalk
Five foot, five inches tall.
Age 22.
Born Camden Town.
Thief. Served three years in Brixton prison.
Cool nerve.
Looks at things in a different way.
Hates authority – may clash with Sergeant Sturgess who in the police force before the war.

Based upon these training records, Bernard might be lucky to get only one new recruit out of the four. Then he thought about the pretty girl in the canteen and decided to ask her to go to the pictures.

***

Private Dick Chalk picked up four trays and passed three behind him to Duncan Donald who, in turn, passed two trays back to his friends, Lofty Simpson and Sandy Turner. Chalky looked at their different uniforms.

"When did you lads arrive?"
"Just got here," said Lofty.
"Call me Chalky. First time to Balado?"
Duncan smiled.
"I was born less than five miles from here."
"Blimey, you've come home the long way round, ain't yer?"

Duncan nodded. He had joined up at the start of the war and was sent across to France, only to be shipped back to Dover when the Germans kicked them out.

"What's for supper?"

"Loop the loop and steak and kidney pud. Food's not bad on the base."

"Loop the loop?"

"Blimey. You Jocks ain't that educated, are yer? It's soup."

Duncan lifted his tray and an old woman ladled something green into his bowl, and tossed a slice of bread next to it.

"Heads up," warned Chalky. "SS on the prowl."

"SS?"

"Sergeant Sturgess. Ex London Bobby. Bossy geezer. He's got it in for me, because of my job before the war."

"What did you do?" asked Sandy.

"Best burglar in the East End."

Duncan held up his tray again and a lump, that looked a bit like steak and kidney pudding, was dumped onto it. He glanced up at the server. She was the prettiest girl he had ever seen. His mouth fell open and she smiled at him.

"What you looking at, son?" said a loud, officious voice.

Duncan continued to smile at Maggie.

"I said, 'What are you looking at, son?'" repeated the sergeant.

"Leave it out, Sarge," said Chalky. "He's just off the boat and probably 'asn't seen a woman for months."

"You stay out of this, Private Chalk, or you will be on fatigues quicker than you can shin up a drainpipe and nick an old lady's handbag."

Sergeant Sturgess walked up behind Duncan and prodded his shoulder.

"You after trouble, Jock?"

Duncan turned, smiled and placed a hand on his breast pocket.

"None of us want any trouble."

"None of us want any trouble" repeated SS.

"Together we are stronger."

"Together we are stronger."

"A sergeant must have lots to do."

"I have lots to do," the sergeant said and left.

***

In the canteen food-queue, Lofty was talking to Chalky, and Duncan was staring at Maggie, trying to summon up the courage to ask her to go to the pictures.

"This queue gets shorter every day," said Lofty. "The training's too tough for most of the men and they are soon sent back to their regiments."

"Great, init. More grub than I've 'ad in ages."

"Excuse me," said Bernard politely, "privileges of rank." He pushed past them to stand in front of Maggie. "I wondered if you would like to come to the pictures again. I could pick you up about seven."

"That would be just fine."

She glanced at Duncan and his sad face told her what she wanted to know. Later, the friends lay on their bunks.

"Ask her at lunchtime tomorrow," said Lofty.

"Och, what chance have I got? He's the Camp Commander and he's got a car."

"Ask her anyway," said Sandy.

"Give 'er the old charm, boy," suggested Chalky. "Say she's really pretty, girls like that."

"She really is very pretty," said Duncan and he made his mind up.

***

A weak dawn sun burst over the Lomond Hills and lit the sixteen long wooden huts and orderly lines of Balado training camp. Behind the huts, a dozen army-green Bedford lorries stood neatly parked. In front of the huts, a square grassed parade ground contained a high parachute training tower on one side. The entire camp was surrounded by a ten-foot high barbed wire fence broken only by a guard post manned by four military policemen.

On the square, at morning parade, Bernard addressed the remaining sixty men. There had been over three hundred, drawn from nearly every regiment and now he had less than two weeks to select the last thirty men. He stared at the faces along the ranks. Every one of the men here was fit and brave. But fitness and bravery alone wouldn't be any good where they were going. He needed men who could think.

"Over the next two weeks, you will all be tested. Pushed to the limit. One in two of you will join me for special duties vital to the war effort."

"Another bossy geezer," whispered Chalky.

"Your observations are basically correct," whispered Lofty.

Bernard raised his voice.

"Yesterday's forty mile route march and machine gun practice will seem like a picnic compared to today's objective. In a moment, I want you to open the envelopes given to you by Sergeant Sturgess. You were given strict orders not to open them until instructed to do so. Has anyone opened their envelopes?"

No one said anything.

"Right, open them now."

Chalky, Duncan, Sandy and Lofty reopened theirs.

"The map inside," continued Bernard, "shows the location of a remote farmhouse near Perth, about fifteen miles away. We will break into units of four men. Each unit must collect their new uniforms from the farm. You are not allowed to use any type of vehicle. So no hitching a lift. Return here in four hours."

"Sod that," said Chalky.

"Quiet in the ranks," shouted SS.

"Dismiss the men, Sergeant."

"Squad ….. dismissed," roared SS and men ran off in all directions.

Lofty led his friends behind the huts and over to a Bedford.

"Got the keys Chalky?"

"Easiest job in the world. There ain't a lock on the base I can't open."

Sandy took the wheel, the engine roared into life and the lorry lurched onto the track which went out to the guard post. From nowhere, SS stepped onto the track and raised a hand that looked as though it was slowing traffic.

"I might have known it would be you lot. Stealing army property. I'm going to throw the book at you."

Sandy jumped down and hit the sergeant in the face.

"You are for it now. We are all for it," warned Lofty. "Assaulting an officer. SS really will really throw the book at us."

At the camp's exit, four military policemen raised their rifles at the Bedford and Duncan touched his breast pocket.

***

"When the war's over, I'm goin' to Sandy's ruddy house to nick the silver."

"SS is ok. One of the nurses says he came out of the hospital hut this morning," said Lofty.

Duncan looked at the four wheelbarrow loads of potatoes and groaned as another was wheeled in by Sandy. Everyone groaned.

"Plenty more where that came from."

"Did you 'ave to hit him so 'ard?" asked Chalky.

"I didn't. He must have a weak chin."

Duncan peeled another potato, with his bayonet, and tossed it into a tin tub half filled with water.

"One hundred and eighty."

He peeled another.

"One hundred and eighty one."

SS walked into the shed at the back of the canteen. He stared disapprovingly at their sand-coloured shirts and shorts, that they had taken from the lonely farmhouse near Perth. Gingerly, he touched the bruise on his chin.

"Right, get your things, lads. Something's up. Everyone is to report on the parade ground in ten minutes."

Duncan stood and sheathed his bayonet.

"Aye, Sergeant."

"The last time I heard, Private Duncan, in the British Army we say, 'Yes, Sergeant."

"Yes, Sergeant."

"What's your name? I'm going to write it in my notebook."

"Duncan Donald."

"And are you a thief like Chalky?"

"No, I'm a shepherd."

"Do you think you're tough?"

"No, sir. But my friend is."

Sandy came to stand beside Duncan and SS marched out. As he crossed the parade ground he muttered, "I'll fix you, Private Duncan."

***

At supper, Duncan shuffled nervously along the food queue with his friends willing him on.

Maggie dumped roly poly pudding on his plate.

"Maggie, I was wondering if you would like to go to the pictures tonight?"

Her face lit up like a beacon.

"I'm sorry, but Bernard has asked me out for a drive tonight."

Duncan's heart sank and Lofty nudged him.

"What about tomorrow night?"

"Lovely. Tomorrow would be just fine."

"Lovely," repeated Duncan and across at one of the tables SS heard him.

***

"Good evening, Mr McGregor. I think you went to school with my father, Duncan Donald," lied Duncan.

Maggie's father looked into the same face he had known as a young man.

"My word, you are the spitting image of your father. Welcome. He was a great man."

Duncan shuffled his feet.

"I wanted to do things properly and ask your permission to take Maggie to the pictures tonight, sir."

"A Donald needs no permission from me and I know she's looking forward to it. Hasn't talked about anything else all day."

***

Duncan was polishing his boots when SS walked into the hut. He stood, smartly, and saluted.

"Private Duncan, I've put you onto guard duty tonight."

"But I've …"

"No buts, son. Report to me at 1800 hours. I heard you were due to take a young lady out and Captain King has offered to stand-in for you. Can't have her disappointed now, can we."

"But I've …"

"Like I said, son, no buts. We've all got to make sacrifices. There's a war on."

Chalky, Duncan, Lofty and Sandy slung their rifles over their shoulders and walked the length of the perimeter fence. As they approached the guard post, a staff car stopped before the barrier. A pass was handed out of the window to a Military Policeman. The barrier rose and Bernard drove out.

Next morning, Duncan received orders to go to Captain King's office in hut twelve. He smartened himself up and, nervously, knocked on his door.

"Come in."

"Thank you, sir."

"Stand easy."

"Thank you, sir."

Bernard handed Duncan a brown envelope.

"You are a very lucky man."

"I am, sir? I don't feel very lucky."

"A very lucky man. I took Maggie to the pictures last night and I think she was expecting you."

"Sergeant Sturgess put me onto guard duty."

Bernard nodded at the envelope.

"That's a twenty four hour pass. Use it wisely."

"I still don't understand, sir."

"When a beautiful woman goes out with you and all she does is talk about the kind smile of one of your men, you know it is time to surrender."

Duncan's heart leapt.

"She said she would be ready to go for a picnic up to the waterfall in an hour, if that's ok with you?"

"Ok with me?" he mumbled.

"And by the way, I will be speaking to Sergeant Sturgess. You call him SS, don't you?"

"Aye, sir. I mean no, sir. I mean thank you, sir."

***

Bernard looked at the thirty men he had chosen and prayed that he had chosen the right ones.

"In one hour, we leave for Glasgow to board HMS *Ulysses*. We will arrive in Alexandria in three weeks. During the voyage Sergeant Sturgess and myself will take you through advanced weapon training, explosives, radio and night patrol tactics. We must work together to succeed and, from now on, we will operate informally."

Chalky put his hand up.

"Does that mean I can call Sergeant Sturgess, Sidney?"

"Call him what you like. But remember, in the desert, your life might depend on him."

Chalky grinned at SS, whose face was a picture.

"Is there anyone here who cannot drive?"

Duncan raised his hand.

"Come and see me when we reach Alex," said Bernard.

"Yes, sir."

"Yes, *Bernard*. Right, everyone, collect your things and load the Bedfords."

SS got ready to roar, "Squad, dismissed," and Bernard raised his hand.

"Off you go, everyone."

***

Everyone found it hard to sleep during the hot, stifling nights in cramped quarters aboard HMS *Ulysses*. They had steamed at full speed through the dangerous waters of the Mediterranean, not stopping for supplies and certainly not stopping for the light-show as enemy planes bombed the poor souls on Malta.

Now Duncan stood by the ship's rail, staring down on the quay at Alexandria. Sherman tanks were being off-loaded by huge cranes from freighters. A line of ambulances was surrounded by busy men and women in white coats, getting ready to replace the tanks with the wounded. If they made it back past the enemy submarines, the sick would be recovering in hospitals across Britain in weeks.

Despite the frantic activity on the quay, Duncan thought about kissing Maggie at the waterfall and promising to meet up again as soon as he got some leave. He knew that at some point he would need to tell her the truth about his age. He was old enough to be her father, but he felt young, looked young. The stone saw to that. But how would she react?

Bernard joined him and wiped sweat out of his eyes with his sleeve, and smiled.

"She loves you, Duncan."

"Girls can be funny though."

"Not Maggie. She's made up her mind."

"That's a very scary thought."

"I still think you are the luckiest man I know."

Duncan watched as a steep gangplank was lowered onto Egyptian soil.

"It's so hot and it's not ten o'clock yet."

"We must get used to the desert quickly," said Bernard. "I've arranged for us to set up a forward operations camp at an oasis called Siwah to the south west."

"Any Germans down there?"

Bernard took a roughly drawn map of North Africa from his belt pocket and unfolded it.

"Not the last time I heard. Have a look at the map."

"The distances are huge," said Duncan as he memorized it.

"And in between the oasis where we will be operating, there isn't anything, except burning desert."

Bernard ran a finger along the coastal road from Alexandria, through Musala, Tobruk, Benghazi and all the way west to Tunis.

"That's where most of the fighting is going to be. Tobruk is under siege again and the RAF are planning to mount night time raids on Rommel's supply bases around Benghazi."

"But you think the Tiger tanks are getting fuel by another route."

"They must be. I suspect they are holding huge quantities of supplies at Al-Jaghbub, so we will attack there first."

Chalky came running over to them.

"SS says the Bedfords are ready, with enough tinned food to feed a ruddy army."

Bernard flicked the map.

"Have you got it, Duncan?"

"Got it."

Bernard laughed.

"Suppose I can throw it away now."

But he folded it up carefully and put it back in his pocket.

"Chalky, tell the men to get their things down to the lorries. Make sure they treat the explosives with the respect they deserve. Duncan, you can learn to drive with me."

In thirty minutes, five fully laden trucks were parked in a line at the side of the road outside of the heavily guarded dock gates. In the first Bedford, Bernard gave Duncan his first driving lesson.

"That's it. Clutch down twice. Into first gear. Bit more revs. Handbrake off."

Behind them, Lofty and Sandy heard the engine of the lorry in front scream and the gears give off an agonizing crunch.

"How much explosive are we carrying?" asked Sandy.

"About five hundred pounds. Enough to blow the pyramids into outer space."

Duncan's lorry hopped forward and stalled. Bernard smiled encouragingly.

"No problem. Have another go. Clutch down twice. Into first gear. Bit more revs. That's it. Handbrake off."

Duncan's Bedford leapt backwards and smashed into the truck behind.

After about fifty miles, Duncan began to relax a bit and enjoy himself. There was no obvious road and the convoy snaked past rocks and pot-holes, and held a steady south-westerly course from Bernard's compass. Later, in the blistering noon heat, some of the Bedfords overheated and steam blasted out of their radiators. Whenever this happened, they stopped, brewed tea and ate eggs that they fried on the bonnets.

"How much further, sir?" asked Sandy. "The men are packed in like sardines and melting."

"About a hundred and fifty miles," said Lofty. "We are making about fifteen miles an hour, so that's ten hours."

"Hope it's cooler in Siwah."

Bernard shook his head.

"Don't get your hopes up. There are trees for shade and not much else. It gets hotter the further you move away from the coast."

"No shops?" asked Chalky.

"No."

"What a way to fight a ruddy war."

Duncan joined them.

"Sandy says his radiator's cooled down now. Might be best to travel when it's dark."

"We'll be doing a lot of that," warned Bernard.

They watched the sun go down below a distant line of hills and, almost as if a switch had been thrown, it went dark.

After hours of hard driving, Duncan began to tire and his concentration wavered.

"I've never seen so many stars."

"Keep your eyes on the ground. The headlights don't give us much warning of trouble."

Duncan stared ahead.

"The others still with us?"

Bernard glanced in the big, square, shaking mirror that was bolted to his door. Four pairs of headlights snaked behind them.

"Better slow down a bit. Sandy's truck has fallen behind a bit."

"I'm only doing ten miles an hour."

"Slow down anyway."

"We still on course?"

"As best as I can tell. We can't be too far away."

Duncan's head began to nod.

"OK, Duncan. Let's stop. I had better take the wheel for a while."

Later, a huge orange sun burst over the horizon and the shadows of the trucks grew into long black fingers. Now the convoy began to plough through deeper sand, and struggled up and down small dunes that took them in and out of the brilliant sunshine. Duncan was back at the wheel and, in half an hour, his back was drenched in sweat again. He dropped down a gear and the truck laboured up across a rock pavement.

"Stop the truck," ordered Bernard.

Duncan applied the brakes and the other Bedfords caught up with them. Below them, in an unbroken and vast desert, was an almost perfect circle of palm trees.

"Let's go an' 'ave some brekky," said Chalky.

Within the oasis something metallic flashed in the sun.

"Let's go cautiously," said Bernard. "Sergeant."

"Yes, sir."

"Take Chalky and find out who's there."

"Yes, sir."

"Take a Bedford and be ready for trouble."

They all watched as their friends drove down towards Siwah and stopped about four hundred yards from the trees. A man in uniform came out to meet them. Bernard ran to get his binoculars.

"They are wearing overalls and I can't make out their uniforms. Don't think they are German or Italian though. Hold up. SS is waving at us to join him. Sense any trouble, Duncan?"

"No. I think we're alright."

"Right, start the engines."

By the time they reached the oasis, SS and Chalky had taken their lorry into the trees and the convoy followed in their tracks into dark, cool shade. It took their eyes a few moments to adjust.

"Welcome to Siwah, Captain King. Corporal Buchan and Private Moffat, of the Royal Electrical and Mechanical Engineers, reporting for duty, sir."

"Blimey, the REME out 'ere," said Chalky.

"Out here for two weeks. Special orders from General Montgomery. Said you might need a bit of a hand."

"Thank you, Corporal. Any sealed orders?"

"Yes, sir. By dispatch rider from Alex two days ago."

Bernard tore open the envelope with TOP SECRET written on it. Corporal Buchan coughed politely.

"Not sure you should open that in front of the men, sir."

"Out here, we are all in this together. Looking at the date on this, the RAF bombed the petrol dumps at Benghazi five days ago, but the Tigers are still advancing, which means they still have fuel."

Lofty nodded.

"So your theory about a desert supply route is right."

"Anything else?" asked Duncan.

"We are to attack the oasis at Al-Jaghbub as a matter of urgency. It's signed by Monty himself."

"Permission to speak, sir," said Moffat.

"Speak whenever you have something to say. We can't work with too much discipline."

"The desert to the west is more rock than sand and we thought the Bedfords would suffer in the heat."

"Too right, son," said Chalky.

Moffat turned.

"Would you like to follow me?"

They followed him past a pond of disgusting looking water, into a darker area under the trees, and bent under camouflage netting suspended from the top branches. Makeshift tents had been erected under the nets between the palms and beyond them stood six new American jeeps.

"We painted them black and sand, reinforced the chassis for rough ground, cut the roofs off, enlarged the fuel tanks, fixed two ten gallon water tanks on the bonnet and mounted a Vicker's heavy machine gun on the back."

Buchan tapped it.

"This baby will fire over a hundred rounds a minute. You have brought plenty of explosives, but the intelligence people told us that if there is a petrol dump, it will be heavily guarded. You may not get close enough to lay any charges."

"What else have you got for us?" asked Sandy.

"Mortars. Two per vehicle. With practice you can fire ten shells onto a sixpence in less than a minute."

Moffat cut in.

"And for the journey to Al-Jaghbub, you are going to need a detailed map of the Western Desert. It's in your tent, sir."

"I'm impressed," said Bernard. "You two have been busy. Now, show the men where to bunk down and get the kettle on. We need to think up a cunning plan."

CHAPTER EIGHT

AL-JAGHBUB

"Who the hell are they?" asked Bernard.

Lofty lowered the binoculars.

"They are Bedouin, the wandering tribespeople of the desert, and they are probably thinking exactly the same thing about us."

"What do they want?"

"What they have wanted for thousands of years. Shade, water and somewhere to graze their animals."

"Will they fight?"

"They may do. They have a fierce reputation."

"We don't want 'em 'ere," said Chalky.

Duncan looked at the line of five horsemen who sat like statues on the top of a sandy ridge about a quarter of a mile away. Then, as they emerged from behind the ridge, he counted nineteen camels walking single-file past the riders and towards the oasis.

"They may have information."

"Think of them as a large family," said Lofty.

"Well, does anyone have any ideas?" asked Bernard.

"Take them a gift to show our intentions are not evil," Duncan suggested.

"Right-oh," said Chalky and he walked out to meet them.

"What's he up to?" asked SS.

Bernard took the binoculars from Lofty.

"I think he's giving the children something. Hello, he's waving."

As the tribespeople approached, they saw how tough, how hardened the men were. They wore white robes and black headdresses tied with white cord, and carried long rifles. Chalky picked up a young girl and carried her on his shoulders. The girl laughed.

"What are they saying, Chalky?"

"Not much, Sarge, and anything they do say is double-Dutch to me."

Bernard stood up.

"What did you give the children?"

"Sergeant Sturgess's tinned chocolate bars. Bit melty, but the kids loved 'em. Nicked 'em out his rucksack last night in case of such an emergency."

SS reached into his breast pocket.

"You tea leaf. I'm going to write your name in my notebook again."

Chalky gave him his notebook back.

"Why you ..."

"Ask nicely and you can 'ave yer pencil back an' all."

"That's my police issue pencil. I'm going to ..."

Bernard raised his hand and smiled.

"Both of you, go and tell Moffat and Buchan to prepare a meal for our guests."

Everyone else watched the Bedouin bring their camels into the oasis and skilfully pitch their tents around the pool. They kept their distance and lit a fire, and something about the way they acted told Duncan that this was an important, almost sacred, place for them. A woman pointed an accusing finger at some empty tin cans under a palm.

"Sandy, let's tidy the place up a bit."

Sandy bowed politely at the woman and collected up the rubbish with the Bedouin men watching in amusement. One said something and the woman giggled. Later, as the sun went down, trays of food were taken over to the Bedouin tents and their guests shared small cups of tea with them, no one understanding a word the other was saying. At times it was a bit awkward and Duncan told Sandy about his farm and sheep to fill in the gaps in the conversation.

Next morning, he was the first to wake and he thought he heard a voice on the other side of the oasis, where the Bedouins camped. Grabbing a rifle, he stepped quietly over Bernard, slipped out of the tent and ran to the edge of the palms. The camels were walking away, in a line, beginning another long trek across the desert. A large, bearded rider pointed his long rifle at him and smiled.

"You are a shepherd like us and you have many sheep."

Duncan nodded.

"And you have lots of water."

"In Scotland, laddie, we have more water than we know what to do with."

"And the grass?"

Duncan thought of home.

"The hills are green and I miss them. Where did you learn to speak English?"

"We may choose to live a simple life, but we are not a stupid people."

"How do I say thank you?"

"Say, 'May you always find water and your people enjoy peace.'"

"May you always find water and …"

The Bedouin raised his hand.

"My people will, but I do not think yours will. Tell the one you call Bernard that the Germans hold Al-Jaghbub. There is much fuel there. That is what you wanted to know, is it not?"

Duncan smiled back and stood alone for a long time, watching the tribespeople get smaller and smaller, thinking about Maggie and what they would find at Al-Jaghbub.

Apart from an enemy spotter plane circling above the oasis, nothing much happened that day. They gave the jeeps another check and practised firing the mortars. For most of the time they sat, drank mugs of tea and chatted until Bernard called them together at dusk. He stared at the faces of the men he had selected at Balado. They were getting browner by the day. A small black cloud of flies, constant companions here, hovered above each of them and their scruffy, sweat-drenched uniforms stank. They looked more like a band of pirates than a disciplined fighting force.

"Lofty and SS will take the lead jeep. Chalky and Sandy jeep two and Duncan will be with me in jeep three. The rest of you will stay here. If we don't come back in four days, Corporal Buchan will organize a second attack on Al-Jaghbub."

"Yes, sir," they said together.

"We will travel at night and sleep rough under the camouflage netting during the day. Any questions?"

"More men could give more fire-power. Why can't we all go?" asked one of the men.

"More fire-power, yes, but the key to this mission is speed and evasion. That means a small force. Any other questions?"

No one had.

"Right, we leave in ten minutes."

After six hours hard driving, they were cold, exhausted and totally covered in dust. It was difficult keeping a true westerly course when the headlights lit such a short distance ahead. The intense concentration for obstacles on the ground and enemy patrols left their nerves frayed. With total relief, they felt the sun break behind them even though it made their skin itch. The beginning of another day in an arid oven.

As they had done in training, they searched for a rock formation, a dry river bed or the edge of rare scrub. Anything that would form a line if seen from the air. They parked their jeeps in a line too and ran the netting from the first to last. Remaining invisible to German planes was going to be their best form of defence.

They sat in shade under the netting, sipped water and dozed. By noon it was unbearably hot and Chalky opened some tins, and they ate melted, salty corned beef and warm peach slices.

"I wonder if the German advance has been stopped yet," said Sandy.

***

A massive cloud of black, acrid exhaust fumes shot out the back of the Tiger tank as its engines revved one last time before shutting down. Gruber's deep voice called up from inside.

"Ten kilometers."

General Georg Grau glanced back at the classic "V" formation of his Panzer division and knew they could drive for ten kilometers more without refuelling. He jumped down and banged the thick armour plating as a sign for the crew to come out and cool down.

Hans Luberman watched Georg study his map and wondered when he ate. Their crew, all the Tiger Crews, had lived in each other's pockets since the victory in France, the sea voyage to Tunis and the hard-fought advance here to Musala on the Libyan and Egyptian border. In all that time he couldn't remember his General eating anything and yet he had so much energy, such attention to detail, such courage. In fact, after all their adventures, he realised he didn't know anything important about him at all. Georg raised his tanned, clean-shaven face from the map and fixed his light blue eyes on him.

"Hans, get the men together. We must talk about what to do next."

In minutes, the tank commanders of SPZ ABT 100 Panzers sat in a respectful ring around him.

"The British have dug in along a north-south line at El Alamein. We have enough fuel to attack them, but need more if we are to smash through and attack Alexandria."

"How far are the fuel tankers behind us?" asked Hans.

"With the Benghazi dump destroyed, there may be a few tankers that reach us in the next forty eight hours. After that we must rely on any that make it through the desert from the supplies in the south."

A commander in the ring raised his hand.

"Yes, Pieter."

"Do you want some of the Tigers to return to Tobruk and help the second siege?"

"No, we stay together. Tobruk will fall to our ground troops anyway. I am sure you agree, Pieter, that the power and manoeuvrability of our armour is needed here on the front-line."

"What does Rommel say?" asked Hans.

Georg thought about his last, hurried, radio conversation with his Field Marshall.

"Don't know. He has been called back to Berlin for a special briefing."

"Then we must decide ourselves."

"If we break into Allied territory and run out of fuel, we will be in real trouble."

Hans smiled.

"But we will lose the momentum we've built up. The British are on the back foot."

"You would risk the lives of the men for the sake of a few days?"

"We have risked our lives many times and won through."

"I agree, Hans, but this time I sense trouble. I do not think the British are just digging in. What are they up to?"

Pieter nodded.

"They may be planning an attack. Do you remember the Sherman tanks we fought ten days ago? We hadn't seen them before. Who knows how many they have now."

The other commanders nodded.

"Then it is decided," said Georg, "we wait to see how much fuel reaches us in the next few days. If there is enough to see us to Cairo, we attack. Meanwhile, I want the Eighty Eight artillery guns to set up a defensive line here. If the British tanks advance, tell them to blow them back into Egypt. We must also lay mines from the sea to the desert."

Hans watched the commanders rush away with their orders.

"You do that very well."

Georg studied him in the same intense way he had studied his map.

"Do what very well?"

His polite voice contained a hint of agitation.

"Have a conference, ask for suggestions and then everyone goes away agreeing with what you wanted in the first place."

Georg nodded at their Tiger.

"Private Luberman, our tank is a disgrace to the German army."

Hans grinned at him and knew what was coming.

"Same thing happens every time we go for a quiet drive in the desert, sir."

"Make sure it is armed, refuelled and ready for action in one hour. Tell Gruber to prepare a meal for the crew."

"Will you be joining us, sir?"

Georg unscrewed the cap of his water bottle and took a sip.

"I've already eaten. By the way, Private Luberman, if you weren't my best driver you would be on the Russian Front by now."

***

Before sundown, they heard the sound of aircraft. Three bombers, high up in the cloudless blue sky, were flying North East. Chalky scrambled under the netting to Bernard's jeep.

"Three Stukas. I fink they're goin' to Siwah. Not much else round here."

Bernard looked worried.

"Sure they were Stukas?"

"Funny shaped wings. No doubt."

"What's up?" asked Duncan.

"Stukas are short-range bombers. When we get to Al-Jaghbub, we might find an airfield."

Lofty joined them.

"Time to go, sir?"

The next five hours were easy going despite the dark, as the land became sandier and flatter, a good surface to drive on. At one point, Duncan topped twenty miles an hour and the other jeeps began to fall behind them, but always driving in the tramlines of their wheel tracks. Land mines would be a constant danger from here on in.

Chalky took one hand off the wheel and blew onto his numb fingers.

"I didn't expect it to be this cold in a desert."

Sandy looked up at the stars and the sliver of a crescent moon. It was black and eerie, and a bitter wind lifted dust which felt like sandpaper on his cheeks.

"Slow down," said Sandy. Bernard and Duncan have stopped."

They parked close to the other two jeeps and Bernard was beside them in a flash.

"Get the netting up right away, lads. We're in for a rough time of it."

As the wind grew in strength, they struggled to pull the camouflage netting over the jeeps and peg it down. Duncan tied a scarf around his face and felt as though he was suffocating as the sand swirled around them. He couldn't see more than an arm's length in any direction.

"Get under the net, Lofty," he shouted, but his warning was lost in the howling storm.

Lofty's tall figure continued to struggle with the net on his jeep and Duncan grabbed him and forced him back to his own jeep. As they ducked under the netting the wind rose to a deafening roar and the netting flew off into space. They crawled to the next jeep and dived under its net.

"'Ello lads. Fancy a brew?" asked Chalky.

By late afternoon on the following day, the sandstorm ended as suddenly as it had begun. They crawled out from under the netting to find one jeep completely buried with only the barrel of the Vickers showing out of the sand. The shadow of a huge dune, that hadn't been there when they had stopped, cloaked them from the sun and Bernard ordered SS and Chalky to climb it and take a look round. As they rose, their feet slipped back almost as far as they had climbed and soft sand filled their boots. Exhausted in the heat, they crawled the last bit and peered out.

"Ruddy hell," said Chalky.

"For once, Private Chalk, I agree with you."

Below them about a mile away was the cigar shaped oasis of Al-Jaghbub. Bulldozers laboured to clear a runway and hundreds of German soldiers efficiently dug sand away from aircraft. A convoy of nine fuel tankers came out of the palms and headed north. The long barrels of two Eighty Eight guns stuck out of the shade. To the West, beyond the oasis, rose the dark silhouette of a line of hills.

"Ruddy hell," repeated Chalky.

When they had run back down the dune, Bernard gave them new orders.

"Keep the nets up till nightfall and leave Jeep Two buried. We have no choice but to hide here."

They all nodded and knew that the easiest way to get caught would be to start the engines in daylight.

"How long till dusk?" asked Sandy.

"Looking at the sun I'd say about ten hours," said SS, "any chance of some food, Lofty?"

"No time for food," interrupted Bernard. "I want every weapon checked and cleaned. Sandy, unbolt the Vickers and give it a thorough going over. We'll dig Jeep Two out when it gets dark."

***

At the base in Alexandria, General Montgomery stepped out of his tent to speak to his men.

"What a stroke of luck. The RAF says that the Panzer Divisions have stopped east of Musala. Tell the Royal Navy to land as many Shermans as they can. I don't care where they get them from, but I want them here in two days. We were lost if they had gone on, and now we have a real chance. Funny though, not like Rommel to press home an advantage. Sergeant Major."

"Sir."

"They are laying a corridor of mines to defend their positions. It's like a devil's kitchen. Find out how to punch a hole through them. In ten days we need a door opened to Tunis. Corporal Higgins."

"Sir."

"Get the jeep. I want to speak to the men. The war in the desert has turned," then Monty added, "as long as Captain King can starve the Tigers of fuel."

***

Chalky and SS's faces were as black as coal and they crawled down the dune towards a dark scar that marked the entrance to a wadi which ran down into the oasis. Neither spoke. Both thought about Bernard's orders.

"Have a good look round. Find out where the fuel tankers are parked. Count the big guns. Be back in an hour."

"Easier said than done," thought Chalky.

SS tapped him on the shoulder and he nearly jumped out of his skin. The sergeant put a finger to his lips, gestured for him to stay put, then was gone, crawling slowly along the shadows in the dry river bed. Chalky glanced at his watch, but the dial wasn't clear enough to read. Then SS was back with him and pointing ahead. It seemed like an age before they made the cover of the palms. Looking back, they saw armed guards at about four hundred yard intervals around the oasis. One lit a cigarette. The guards hadn't seen them.

They dashed from tree to tree, stopping to listen, nervously, before moving on. Chalky spotted the fire, with men moving around it. They crawled forward and heard voices and skirted around the fire and counted four Eighty Eight big guns on this side of the oasis three more on the other side, but no tankers. SS took a torch from his pocket, cupped his hands around the bulb and for a brief moment shone the beam onto his compass. He pointed north and Chalky followed, crawling again in shadow.

More voices. Someone laughed. A generator was switched on and huge spotlights lit up a clearing that was full of petrol tankers.

SS and Chalky lay perfectly still as someone shouted something, angrily, in German, and the lights were turned out. Then they made their way back to the wadi.

"So, seven big guns and the tankers are parked by the northern edge of Al-Jaghbub. Well done, both of you," said Bernard.

"It's probably three times as big as Siwah," said SS.

"And ruddy guards every four hundred yards all the way round it," added Chalky.

Lofty nodded.

"We shouldn't be too surprised that it is well guarded."

"But they aren't expecting any trouble," said Duncan, "who would be out here?"

Bernard lifted the netting and stared out into the darkness.

"Any problems with Jeep Two?"

Sandy shook his head.

"Mortars ready?"

Duncan nodded.

"Right, check your watches. It's now 0002. We attack at 0030."

As they went to take their positions, one man driving and one standing, holding the Vickers on the back of the jeep, SS whispered to Chalky.

"The boot polish you lent me. It was mine, wasn't it."

A huge white toothed grin appeared on Chalky's black face.

They started the engines and drove away from the oasis for about a mile before turning north to circle right around Al-Jaghbub. Then they split up and each jeep took its own position overlooking the palms at the northern edge of the cigar. Duncan could just make out a guard running along the edge of the trees. He turned the engine off.

"They know we are here."

Bernard pointed the barrel of the Vickers at the trees.

"But they don't know where we are. Get the mortar."

Duncan spread the tripod out on the ground and placed a heavy box of shells beside it, and tore the wooden lid off.

"Ready."

"Don't forget. Fire one shot long, then one short. That'll give you the range."

Duncan cupped his hand around his torch and checked his watch. 0029. Off to their left they heard a thud. Five seconds later another thud.

"Lofty's keen, isn't he?"

Two explosions followed, one about a hundred yards from the oasis, the other right inside it.

"Ok, Duncan. Let's destroy some fuel."

Bernard's machine gun roared into life, sending streaks of yellow flame into the oasis. Two other streaks copied it and the trees were cut to pieces. Duncan dropped a shell down the barrel of the mortar. It thudded and shot out, and landed long. He raised the pin in the forward leg three notches. He fired again. Seconds later, a fireball erupted up out of the trees as the burning carcass of a fuel tanker rose fifty feet into the air. Inside his breast pocket Amera's stone pulsed.

Bernard yelled out.

"You've got the range. Let them have it."

Duncan dropped one shell after another into the barrel. In ninety seconds he was out of ammunition. The thuds from the other mortars stopped too, but it didn't matter. Al-Jaghbub was an inferno.

He grabbed the mortar, threw it onto the passenger seat and started the engine. They drove at speed towards the western edge of the oasis where the others joined them. Shapes waved at them from the jeeps to show they were alright. Duncan cut across the sand onto the runway. One after another, they drove straight down it, Vickers guns spitting flames at the Stukas. One blew up and crashed back to earth. Then they were away, back into darkness, and they drove west towards the distant line of hills.

"Clever," thought Duncan, "they are bound to think we would head northeast back to Siwah. Better cover in the hills too."

After three hours they made camp in the bottom of a twisting ravine and stretched the two remaining nets across the jeeps. They stared at each other.

"Not bad," said Bernard. "The whole thing didn't take more than five minutes. Get on the radio, Chalky. Tell the boys at Siwah that the job is done."

***

Hans looked at Georg and pointed south.

"Well, something must have happened. No radio contact for twenty four hours and no fuel tankers at all."

"We've had problems with the radios before."

"Not for twenty four hours."

Georg nodded.

"Order a plane to fly down to Al-Jaghbub. Tell the pilot to report to me as soon as he gets back."

At first light next morning, Georg Grau led a formation of five Tigers and a fully laden fuel tanker south across the desert. At top speed they made the oasis in sixteen hours and stared in horror at the charred remains of the supply dump. About a hundred armed soldiers ran out to meet them. One stepped forward.

"Ah, Franz, had a little trouble?"

"Good to see you, Georg. The airfield is fine. One plane can be repaired when we get the parts, all the fuel is destroyed and the Eighty Eights are untouched."

"Was it an air attack?"

"No. We think it was British commandos."

"Out here?"

"According to the map the closest oasis is Siwah, just inside Egyptian territory. They may have driven out from there."

"Get on the radio, tell Von Spere to bomb Siwah."

136

"Yes, Herr General."

"I have sent orders to the commander at Surt. Fuel, arms and supplies are on the way. I want this base up and running tomorrow."

Georg looked around at the flat, featureless landscape and at the hills to the west.

"Are you sure they went back to Siwah?"

"I am not sure. Their tracks went west and then disappeared, where the sand gives way to rock, but I think they pretended to go west to throw us off the scent. There isn't a single drop of water that way and Awijllah is one hundred and fifty kilometers to the south west. They might just make it, but they wouldn't have enough fuel to get back."

"How far away are those hills?"

"About ten kilometers."

"I want them checked out. Hans, make sure the tanks are ready to conduct a search. We will leave one hour before nightfall."

Ten minutes later Hans ran over to join them.

"Siwah will be attacked tonight."

"When they attacked here, they attacked the tankers and not the whole oasis?"

"They did. Most of the northern edge of Al-Jaghbub is burned to a cinder. The rest is OK."

"Clever, they know we can't fight without fuel." Georg looked at the far hills. "Let's hope someone is at home."

***

Chalky and Duncan sat on watch on a rock high above the ravine where the jeeps were hidden.

"Fink we'll make a run for it tonight?"

"I'm not sure, laddie. Bernard will tell us when he's ready."

They stared across the rock and sand at a thin trail of black smoke that still rose out of the oasis. Duncan sat up.

"I think we've got company."

"Chuck us the bins will yer."

Chalky peered through the binoculars at a dust cloud that moved quickly towards them.

"Blimey, Tigers. Four of 'em."

"Stay here. I'll tell Bernard."

Soon everyone joined Chalky on the rock and Lofty said what they were all thinking.

"To get here so quickly they must have broken away from the main Panzer Divisions near the coast to the north."

"What do we do now?" asked SS.

"We can't fight Tigers," said Sandy, "we would be dead in minutes."

Bernard looked down into the ravine.

"The hills are pretty rugged. They can't follow us up here. I think we should hide and wait it out."

"But they might find the entrance to the ravine. I'm sure that lower down it's wide enough for a tank to squeeze through," said Duncan.

Bernard stood.

"Lofty, you and SS go down the ravine. Make sure there aren't any tyre tracks to give the game away. Duncan, you hide here and watch them. Let me know if they drive up the ravine."

"What do we do?" asked Chalky and Sandy together.

"Get the Vickers ready. If push comes to shove, we're not going without a fight."

Duncan watched the Tigers skirt around the edge of the hills, whilst down in the ravine the others listened to the incredible noise of their engines. One tank stopped at the entrance to the ravine only to move on again after a soldier got out to look at the ground. Duncan let out a huge sigh of relief, but the Tiger stopped, its gun turret rotated and the barrel lifted. It seemed to be pointing right at him. He sat like a statue and his shirt became drenched in cold sweat. Then the tank drove away.

***

"You are quite sure?" Georg asked.

Hans nodded.

"Quite sure. There was a boot print in the sand near to a ravine. It is too narrow for tanks to get up. We will need men to get at them."

"I want everyone armed and ready. We will get them, when they least expect us."

An hour later Georg crept forward through the darkness, lifted the edge of the camouflage netting and sat down beside Chalky who dropped his mug of tea.

"Good evening, gentlemen."

Bernard grabbed his revolver and Georg raised his hands as if surrendering.

"Please do not do anything, how do you British say, too hastily. I have over one hundred men around your jeeps with orders to shoot anyone who does not do what I say."

"You get it first," said SS.

"I may do. But I have taken the risk because killing soldiers in cold blood is not my way of doing things. War is war, but we do not have to behave like animals."

"What have you done with Lofty?" asked Sandy.

"Lofty?"

"Tall man. On guard."

Georg held out an open hand towards Bernard's gun.

"Please. Give me the gun. Lofty will have a sore head in the morning. That is all."

Bernard turned the revolver around and placed the handle into Georg's waiting hand.

"Gentlemen, I think your war is over."

139

CHAPTER NINE

THE CAMP WITH NO NAME

They sat together, legs crossed and hands on their heads with four guards sitting comfortably in the corners pointing machine guns at them. Duncan glanced out of the back of the lorry at the disappearing palms of Al-Jaghbub and guessed they were being taken west. After two hours of bone crunching lurches, his bottom was completely numb and his arms ached from the effort of holding them up. He dropped them for a second to rub life back into them and a guard kicked him in the ribs, and said something harsh in German. Duncan put his hands back on his head and thought about General Grau who now held Amera's stone.

Around noon the heat became unbearable, even for the guards, and they stopped and ordered the prisoners to take the lorry's tarpaulin cover off. They were given water before setting off again and blessed cooler air blew through their hair. Before sundown, they stopped again, the guards shouted at them to get out and herded them towards a wood and wire gate about twenty feet high.

Beyond this was another gate and beyond that hundreds of Allied prisoners, who stopped milling around to watch them enter. As they passed through the two gates an Italian soldier pointed down the corridor of land between the barbed wire fencing that surrounded the entire camp. A sign read ACHTUNG MINEN and had a skull and crossbones on it. They nodded to show they understood.

Bernard had never seen so many different uniforms in one place. Canadian, Polish, French, Indian, British, New Zealand and Australian troops talked in small groups in the shade of long huts that were laid out in evenly spaced rows. Each hut was numbered with red paint and they were escorted to number sixty eight. Their Italian guide smiled and spoke in English with a mild, educated Italian accent.

"Welcome to our little camp, like Butlins no?"

They looked around hut sixty eight, at the bunk beds,

corrugated iron roof and old, thick brown curtains framing small, barred windows. It was soulless.

"I am General Maximillio Morentis and I run an efficient camp. Follow the orders of my men at all times."

"Where are we?" asked Lofty.

"In the desert a long way from anywhere."

"It must have a name," said Duncan as he pictured every detail of Bernard's map in his mind.

In an elaborate, apologetic gesture, Max lifted his hands.

"There are no parades, no inspections. You can come and go in the camp as you please."

"Can we go outside?" asked Sandy.

"Unfortunately, no. If you are thinking of planning an escape do not bother. If you get past the mine-field the desert will claim you. The sun does terrible things to the body and mind."

Bernard nodded.

"Apart from that I have nothing to tell you, except that meals are served twice a day. The times vary, as does the quality of the food. In my home city of Milano, the food is, em, exceptional. Here we survive on what the Germans give us, but please, do not blame my men. We eat the same as you."

He bowed politely and left.

Over the next few hours they walked around the perimeter fence, searching for any sign of weakness, and counted the Italian guards; about forty. Then they talked to the other prisoners and found out that some of them had been there for nearly a year. At supper they ate a kind of stew with chunks of black bread. It wasn't bad. It wasn't good either. Then they settled on their bunks in hut sixty eight and talked until they were bored.

"If I stay 'ere, I'm gonna go bonkers," said Chalky. "If every ruddy day is like this I fink I'd chance the desert."

Lofty sighed.

"Not without water. Did you see how the guards at dinner gave everyone as much water as they wanted, but were careful not to let anyone take any cups away with them?"

143

Bernard stood up and lifted the edge of a curtain to watch the sun set. A lorry was collecting the guards from around the inside of the camp, after they had locked the prisoners into their huts for the night, and he knew this lorry would then take the guards outside through the double gates.

"They know we won't get far without water."

Duncan joined him.

"One of the Polish soldiers told me an Australian got out about a month ago. The guards didn't even go looking for him. Three days later he wandered back into camp like a madman. Still hasn't fully recovered."

The hut went quiet and Duncan thought about General Grau. Did he know about the stone's power? Was he using the stone right now to destroy his enemies? Was he a Seeker? What would Myroy say? A bolt was thrown on the door by a guard outside, a lorry's engine revved and the hut fell into darkness. Then the floor began to shimmer like moonlight on water and Myroy rose, and spoke to Duncan.

"You have lost the stone."

"I have. When we were captured, all our possessions were taken."

"You took it into a war when it must be held in the keeping."

"Who's that geezer?" asked Chalky.

"He is an Ancient One," said Duncan.

"Oh."

Everyone stared at Duncan and Myroy.

"I did bring it here, although I did not have any choice. Have you not taught me that if hidden it cries out to its master."

Myroy's face became fierce.

"This war is nothing compared to the war that will follow if Odin holds the stone."

"Who is Odin?" asked Bernard.

Myroy ignored him.

"Even now, Georg Grau gathers his tankers, his fuel, and prepares

144

to go north. With the stone to aid him his army will be victorious. Then it will not be long before the Seekers hear the stone's call."

Lofty felt frozen to the bunk. SS's mouth was wide open. Myroy put his arm around Duncan.

"Now, in another time, in Pinner, the Keeper has also lost the stone. Your help is needed."

They disappeared down into the earth.

A second later they came back up and Duncan looked as though he had been in a fight.

"You still have time," continued Myroy, "you must get the stone back."

SS wondered how old this man was? Who he was to talk to them in such a commanding way? If he knew how to get them out of the camp, why didn't he tell them?

Myroy rounded on him.

"This is not a game. For thousands of years we have protected your families. Brave men have died doing it."

Sergeant Sturgess felt himself shrink and Myroy's face softened.

"But we are stronger together," and in the timeless dark of Hut 68, he told them the story he had told every new Keeper. All of it, up until their time, and when he finished, the men came out of a dreamlike adventure. Bernard stood and stretched.

"We must catch up with General Grau before he reaches Musala."

Myroy nodded.

"You are now Keepers. Carry a round pebble, the size of the ruby, with you always. It is how we identify ourselves to each other when we need help. Never forget that our people are all over the world."

"Blimey. Yer don't get many pebbles in the desert," said Chalky.

SS looked sheepish.

"So all we have to do is get through the mines, cross a desert without water and take back the stone from a German General who is surrounded by Tiger tanks."

"That's right," said Duncan.

As Myroy descended down through the floor, he pointed at Bernard.

"Use your new knowledge wisely."

Then he was gone and they sat in complete silence until Lofty glanced over at Chalky.

"How would you steal it?"

"Easy," said Chalky, "I'd wait till he goes to the bog."

***

For the last few days, everything had gone really well at Al-Jaghbub, unexpectedly well at times, and Georg Grau stared with satisfaction at the ninety fully laden fuel tankers, now ready to re-supply his Tigers to the north.

"The commanders say they are ready for escort duty," said Hans.

"Where is Gruber?"

"On the radio to Surt. They may send more tankers here. I thought it best to order them to wait here in the oasis until called for. They are vulnerable if they travel across the desert unprotected."

Georg considered this.

"Good work, Hans. Do the Panzers at Musala know we are coming?"

"No. Intelligence believes the British may be listening in to our radio frequencies. It's a risk we shouldn't take. There will be time enough to brief them of your plan when we arrive."

Georg felt a flood of unnatural optimism.

"In less than a week, the war in North Africa could be over."

Suddenly, he felt very hungry and took the ruby from his pocket and stroked it.

***

General Montgomery was briefing his team just behind the front line at El-Alamein.

"The RAF say that after their last bombing raid, the road east out of Benghazi is impassable. They have flown many times across the desert, to the south of Musala, and have seen no fuel convoys. That means the enemy Tigers stand with only the fuel they have in their tanks. They cannot attack us. They can only defend their own positions. Sergeant Major."

"Yes, sir."

"Tell us about their positions."

"The Germans are in a line fifty miles north-south from Musala. They wait in three lines, with mines at the front supported by machine gun emplacements. About two hundred tanks form the second line and behind them are batteries of heavy guns. The Eighty Eights have a range of two miles and are, probably, the most accurate and deadly field-guns in the world."

"Thank you, Sergeant Major. Anyone got any thoughts?"

A short plumpish man with spectacles and a dark tan stood.

"If we can punch through this line at any point, drive our main force through and destroy their supply chain they are lost. Their tanks can't chase us, not far anyway, and we can leave them to sit in the desert until they run out of water."

"What if they don't follow? What if they attack Alex?"

"They can't drive through their own mines, can they?"

"They are bound to have left secret pathways through the minefield, but I still like your plan, Captain Nichol."

Another man stood.

"We need to balance attack and defence. If we send all our mobile forces through the enemy line, the Royal Artillery could provide a barrage of cover. If they were properly dug-in the twenty five pounders could also stop a possible attack by the Panzers, particularly if their Tigers were short of fuel." He nodded at a man in an RAF uniform. "The Hurricanes could play an important role too."

"Very well, gentlemen, work out the finer details. Make sure the Shermans, ground troops and artillery are ready. I want every last Hurricane in the Mediterranean flown here."

An hour later, a corporal brought Monty a decoded radio message from London.

> *If the Germans are refuelled, they will*
> *cut your men to shreds.*
> *Attack anyway. It's a good plan.*
> *Winston Churchill.*

***

"Thank you for seeing us, sir," said Duncan.

General Maximillio Morentis smiled impatiently.

"What is it you want?"

"To make everyone's life a little easier, sir," said Bernard. "We would like to volunteer."

"Volunteer?"

"We know we haven't been here very long, but we noticed that the sanitary provision is poor, for your men and ours."

"Sanitary provision?"

"The toilets, sir. A hole in the ground, whether you are a General or a private. It's not right, sir."

Max eyed Bernard suspiciously.

"Under the close supervision of your guards, we could make life a lot easier for everyone."

"What do you need?"

"A spade to dig a bigger hole, wood for toilet seats, old newspapers that we can cut into squares, some canvas and rope to make a private tent."

"Ha! So, everything you need to dig an escape tunnel."

"May I respectfully remind you, sir. The fence and mines are not our prison. We are all prisoners of the desert."

Max slowly nodded.

"We suggest enough materials for five toilets for the men and two for officers. Generals, of course, will have one for themselves."

***

As Lofty wrote in German on a piece of wood, *Officers Only,* Duncan tore strips of newspaper into squares and SS sewed two edges of canvas together.

"This is the most stupid plan I have ever heard of, Private Chalk."

Chalky grinned and SS continued to moan at him.

"If I had a notebook, which I don't because you have nicked it again, I would write your name in it. Stupid plan."

"Why? The Germans always obey orders and General Grau is like anyone else. He has to go from time to time."

"And all we do is wait inside until he comes in, bash him on the head and pinch the stone back."

Chalky glanced at the guard who sat lazily with his rifle across his lap.

"That's right."

"But what if he hasn't got it with him?" asked Lofty.

"Do you fink he would give a beautiful fing like that to someone else? Bet it's worth a bob or two."

"Well, here we are, in a prison camp in the middle of the Sahara and I am sewing bits of canvas together to make a gentleman's toilet."

"By the way, Sarge," said Lofty, "you've stitched that too high up. Got to leave a gap for the General to squeeze through."

SS sighed.

"The boys at the station will never believe this."

***

"Off you go, Lofty," said Duncan. "Sun's going down."

His friend left the hut and hid behind it. A few minutes later an Italian guard slid the bolt on their door and ambled off to board the lorry. Lofty came back round and unbolted it. Staying in shadow they crept from hut to hut, carrying strange shapes, to a point where they could see the gates being opened. The lorry passed

149

through and Sandy could just make out Bernard's boots, dragging along the ground, as he clung to the underside of the truck.

"Thomas Goodfellow," whispered Duncan.

As it had done the night before, the lorry parked beside three huts used by the Italians. The guards jumped out, went inside one of the huts and the sound of a gramophone record wafted through the open door.

"Never liked opera," thought Bernard and he waited for the driver to join the others.

The man jumped down from the cab and ambled over to a guard who stood by the gate. They lit cigarettes and talked. Bernard crawled to the other side of the lorry and, after an age, the driver came back and rounded the edge of the truck. Bernard hit him and he fell. Bernard checked the man's pockets, took the lorry keys and a pistol, put on the man's hat and ambled towards the gate.

The guard said something and Bernard waved his hands in an apologetic gesture, just like Max had done. Six feet away, he raised his pistol. Shadowy figures ran to stand on the other side of the wire and Bernard nodded at the guard to unlock the gates. As they passed the man, Sandy delivered a perfect right hook and carried him back inside, before locking the gates again.

As he ran to the lorry, Sandy saw Chalky go into a hut. Then he came out carrying two water drums. He grinned and passed them to Sandy. Then he dived back inside and emerged with an armful of rifles. Bernard started the engine and checked the fuel gauge, three quarters full. They roared away into the cold desert night.

An hour later, General Maximillio Morentis stared at the driver and guard, who stood with their heads bowed, trying not to smile.

"What did they steal?"

The driver took one step forward.

"A lorry, six rifles, two cans of water, a radio set and, er …"

The driver and guard glanced at each other.

"Out with it."

"The General's new toilet."

They drove as fast as they dared through the darkness and headed northeast towards Musala, hoping to intercept the German fuel tankers, who had probably already left Al-Jaghbub.

"It's a long shot," said Bernard, "there could be hundreds of miles of sand between us and the coast."

"And they will travel quickly," added Duncan.

A grille in the wall behind their seats snapped open and Chalky's grinning face appeared.

"We've opened the boxes we found in the back here. Two were empty and one's got a ruddy radio in it."

"Right. Get Lofty onto it right away. Send a message to the RAF at Alex. Tell them to bomb the convoy heading north out of Al-Jaghbub."

"Right-oh." The grille shut.

Five minutes later it snapped open again.

"Lofty says it's knackered. Something to do with the set's crystals being damaged."

"Fix it," said Bernard and the grille snapped shut.

"If only we could get a message through," said Duncan.

"If the convoy is bombed, we might be able to get the stone back."

They stared across a vast, desolate and empty landscape lit by a fierce high sun. A heat haze shimmered above the sand. Bernard slammed the brakes on.

"Quick, the binoculars."

Duncan handed them over as the grille snapped open.

"Are we nearly there yet?" asked Chalky.

Bernard scanned the horizon off to their left. Another metallic flash came from a long way off.

"It's them," he said.

***

151

Hans shouted up from the belly of the Tiger.

"How far to Musala?"

Georg shouted down.

"Ten hours."

"We have half a tank of fuel, sir," added Gruber.

"We keep going until nightfall. Then we rest. At this speed we will refuel all our forces at noon tomorrow." He felt the stone in his pocket. "And then we attack."

***

Duncan kept the lorry about a mile behind the last tanker in the convoy and, in the back, Bernard wondered if Georg Grau would order his men to stop and rest.

Reading his thoughts, Lofty said, "They may not. They fear being caught in open desert in daylight and we are probably in range of the Hurricanes now. Even the Tigers can't stop them."

"What do we do if they don't stop?" asked Bernard.

The lorry lurched violently and a wooden toilet seat fell down and hit SS on the head.

"I see Duncan's driving isn't getting any better."

Chalky grinned.

"If they don't stop we'll put plan B into operation."

"What's plan B, Private Chalk?"

"Nick a German radio. Call the RAF and grab Amera's stone out of the wreckage."

"Doesn't sound like a very good plan," said Lofty.

"It's a better ruddy plan than this toilet caper," said SS.

"You're just jealous 'cos you didn't fink of it."

The grille snapped open and Sandy's face appeared.

"Duncan says turn it down. I had better brush up on my German. The convoy's stopped."

At the head of the convoy, General Grau sighed and spoke to Hans.

"And what are you grinning at, Private Luberman?"

Hans remembered Georg eating sausage and brown bread for breakfast. It was more than he had ever seen him eat and now he had ordered Gruber to make stew.

"Getting a bit of an appetite, aren't we?"

Georg did feel very hungry and it had been like that since he had taken the brooch from the British soldiers. He nodded at their Tiger.

"I know," said Hans, "our tank is a disgrace to the German army."

"Make sure it is refuelled and ready to go immediately. Tell the commanders to leave one machine gunner on guard beside each tanker until dawn."

"Yes, sir."

"And Private Luberman."

"Sir."

"You can take the first watch."

Georg turned away to inspect the camp.

"Oh, sir," said Hans.

Georg groaned.

"Yes?"

"Seeing as you are now eating as much as everyone else, would you ask Gruber to save me some stew?"

***

In darkness, Sandy and Chalky crept towards the German convoy, carrying boxes containing ropes, canvas, spades, the sign and a toilet seat. Two guards sat with their backs to them and Sandy moved silently behind the men and smashed their heads together. Chalky joined him and they dragged the two limp bodies into the desert and away from the tanker that had foolishly parked furthest from the centre of the camp. They stripped the Germans, put their uniforms on and collected their boxes. Heavily laden, they marched past a massive Tiger and down rows and rows of tankers.

General Grau entered a tent and Chalky nudged Sandy. More

Germans in smart uniforms entered the same tent.

"It's a kitchen," said Sandy.

Chalky nodded and they dropped their boxes, in full view of the enemy, and began to dig.

Peering over the top of a sand dune, with the Italian lorry hidden below them, Bernard, Duncan and SS waited for their friends to return.

"They've been gone ages," said Duncan anxiously.

"They have been gone twenty minutes," corrected Bernard.

"Is there anything we can do?"

"No."

"But what if they are caught?" asked SS.

"Then the world will be in real trouble."

***

Sandy placed the wooden seat with a hole in it above the pit and Chalky popped outside, and hung up a sign that read, OFFICERS ONLY. Then they waited in silence with Chalky peering out of a gap in the canvas at the tent General Grau had entered. Every few minutes he glanced back at his friend and shook his head.

Inside the kitchen tent, Georg patted his full stomach.

"That was quite the best goulash I have ever eaten, Gruber."

"Thank you, sir. I thought that after the war I might become a chef."

The other tank commanders in the tent nodded in agreement.

"When you do, you must tell me where you set up shop."

"I will, sir, and it won't be in the Sahara."

The men laughed and Georg rose to make one last inspection of the camp.

"We have an early start tomorrow, gentlemen. I think I will turn in."

It was a clear signal that dinner was over .

Gruber left instructions with his men in the kitchen to tidy things away and stepped out of the tent. A new tent had appeared from nowhere and he glanced around, like a naughty schoolboy deciding whether he should be naughty or not.

"Ruddy hell," warned Chalky, "he's coming in 'ere."

"Is it the General?"

"No."

"Right, get in the pit."

"I'm not goin' down there."

Sandy held the toilet seat up, jumped in and crouched down.

"Come on."

They replaced the seat as the canvas door opened.

Five minutes later, Chalky's head popped out the hole in the warm seat, a square of newspaper stuck to his hair. He breathed out and sucked in clean air. Outside the tent, two men began to argue.

"Is there something you want to tell me, Gruber?" asked Georg.

Gruber stood to attention and said nothing.

"It seems that you have been promoted. What does the sign say?"

"Officers only, sir."

"Are you an officer, Gruber?"

"No, sir."

"Gruber, tell me why we have rules in the German army."

"To stay a highly effective fighting force, sir."

"That's right, Gruber."

Gruber smiled and Georg frowned.

"Did you put this tent here?"

"No, sir."

"Who did?"

"Don't know, sir."

"If this is one of Private Luberman's little jokes, tell him I will be speaking to him."

"Yes, sir."

"Now don't let me catch you using the officers' toilet again."

"No, sir."

Gruber dashed away and Georg opened the canvas flap of the tent, and four strong arms grabbed him.

"Here they come," said Lofty.

"Can you see them?" asked Bernard anxiously. "Have they got the stone?"

"Can't see them. I can hear them." Lofty's nose twitched. "And smell them."

Two dark shapes sprinted past them towards the lorry. Sandy shouted out.

"Right, we've got it. Let's get out of here before they find out."

"All aboard," said Chalky and he gave the stone to Duncan, who gave it quickly to Lofty.

"Hook this up to the radio. Might work, laddie."

Bernard drove east for an hour, when the grille snapped open. SS's face peered through.

"Excuse me, sir, but Lofty says he's through to Alex, but is having a bit of a problem convincing them of our story."

Bernard slammed the brakes on and ran around the lorry. Duncan followed and they found the back bathed in a red glow. Lofty looked up.

"Got a Major Trevellyn on the radio, sir, says he knows you."

Bernard took the microphone.

"Hello, Mike."

A cautious voice answered.

"Hello, Captain King. Understand you've had a spot of bother."

"That's right, sir. We've got a good signal here. How about you?"

"Weak at first until we switched to Long Wave. Strong now."

"You must send the Hurricanes to intercept the German fuel convoy. About ninety tankers heading north. They must not reach Musala."

There was a pause.

"Do you remember, outside the War Room, I asked you for a codename for the mission."

"That's right, sir. Operation Hit and Run."

"OK Bernard, tell your lads to keep their heads down. The planes will scramble in five minutes."

As the sun rose and bathed the Western Desert in orange light, Chalky and Sandy stripped off their stinking uniforms and put on their clean ones, and joined the others who sat on the roof of the Italian lorry with their legs dangling over the side. They stared north and counted the distant plumes of black smoke as the Hurricane bombers went to work. Dull booms followed each flash, like a faraway thunderstorm, and many more black plumes rose up into the air. No one spoke and no one felt proud of what they had done. Men were dying in a place with no name.

***

Bernard smiled at Peter.

"After that, things were pretty straightforward. We drove all day, occasionally swapping drivers so we could all grab a few hours' sleep. Fearing an attack from our own side, we dumped the enemy lorry about five miles south of Alexandria and walked with our pants on our heads to protect us from the sun. I saw Duncan feel his breast pocket many times to check the stone was safe. Eventually, we arrived at the British Expeditionary Forces headquarters and were fed, watered, and showered. In my mind, everything is so clear. I remember that as we dressed into clean uniforms, a messenger came in and handed me sealed orders."

"Major Trevellyn's compliments, sir."

"Thanks. What's the news?" I said.

"We broke through the German lines last night. Tobruk has been relieved and what's left of the Afrika Corps is retreating west along the coast road."

Duncan looked at the orders and said what everyone was thinking.

"Is it leave?"

I tore the envelope open and smiled.

"No rest for the wicked. We have to report to the quayside in an hour. We'll be boarding HMS *Invincible*."

"Where are we going this time?" asked Lofty.

"Seems that Monty wants us to go and cause a bit of mischief on an island."

"An island?" asked Duncan.

"Called Corfu."

CHAPTER TEN

MAID OF NORWAY

In darkness, with wispy clouds covering a Gora moon, the *Maid Of Norway* cruised at thirty knots into the Mediterranean with the twinkling lights of Gibraltar off the port bow and the shadowy outline of the hills of North Africa to starboard. Thorgood Firebrand joined Mick Roberts at the stern rail and handed him a rifle.

"Try this."

Mick took it and studied the short barrel, long telescopic sight and square ammunition cartridge.

"The CAR is light," he said as he pulled it to his shoulder.

Contact between the butt and his shoulder automatically lit the green night sight, and he scanned the waters behind the ship. The sensors identified a target over one and a half kilometers away, and small red letters appeared on the screen.

TARGET?

Mick squeezed the trigger and two hair thin lines, one vertical and one horizontal, came in from the edges of the screen and centered on the target. More red words.

ADJUSTING FOR BREATHING

The information disappeared instantly and new words appeared.

ADJUSTING FOR WIND SPEED

Then –

READY TO FIRE

Mick squeezed the trigger some more, the gun spat and over a mile away a gull exploded, and dropped into the sea.

NO FURTHER SHOT REQUIRED appeared and disappeared.

Mick lowered the rifle and the display went black.

"How many rounds does it hold?"

"A hundred."

"How much?"

"It is still experimental. About one hundred thousand US dollars."

"Quite deadly. Better than anything we have."

"I shall recommend that all the Valkyrie be armed with the Computer Aided Rifle," said Thorgood and left to talk with Odin.

At the same moment at Secret Cove on Corfu, the stone pulsed blood red and cried out. Peter sat on the veranda of Bernard's house, sipping pineapple juice and staring up at a Gora moon. It was full, silver and bright. Suddenly the hairs on his neck stood up as he sensed its incredible power.

Five hours later, as the *Maid Of Norway* passed between Malta and Sicily into the Ionian Sea, a helicopter landed on its helipad and Mick helped the co-pilot unload twelve wooden boxes. Each box had "Mackenzie Industries" burnt in black on the side and contained ten CARs, and enough ammunition to destroy an army.

On the bridge, Odin, Thorfinn and Thorgood watched the helicopter rise and turn west. Olaf Adanson, dressed in a crisp white captain's uniform, stood motionless at a state of the art wheel that would have been more at home in a sports car than in the most luxurious motor cruiser ever built.

"It is the best infantry weapon in the world," said Thorgood.

His Grandfather, Thorfinn Firebrand, nodded.

"Where are Mackenzie Industries based?"

"Miami."

Odin looked at Thorfinn.

"Too far south for the coming war."

"Yes, master."

"Go to Miami and buy them. Relocate the best people and machines to OASV Armaments in Canada. Begin full-scale production in ten days."

"I obey, master."

Thorgood watched Thorfinn leave the bridge and reappear a deck below them by the ship's rail. He stood on the rail and dived into the sea, and Thorgood knew he had already surfaced at the quay on the banks of Lake Ontario to make the arrangements.

Odin turned his back on the banks of computer screens below the long curved window of the Bridge and looked at Thorgood.

"How many arms companies have we moved north?"

"Twenty."

"I wish to inspect the *Black Slug*."

"Yes, master."

They stepped inside a canister set into a white pipe which ran from the bridge down through every one of the *Maid Of Norway's* five decks. Thorgood placed a key into a panel containing buttons for decks one to five and pushed another button hidden behind the panel. The lift descended to the bottom of the ship and when the doors opened they stepped out into another world. Lit by red lights, the submarine's interior was like a spaceship.

The detachable body of the *Black Slug* ran the entire two hundred metres length of the *Maid Of Norway*, with the tail about half the width of the head. Under the waves, the *Slug's* two huge eye-like windows shone red.

"Detach," said Odin.

Crew members, dressed in black T-shirts and shorts, ran to their positions in reclining seats and pulled cordless flat LCD screens off the walls and placed them on their laps. Two of the crew pulled down what looked like full-visor motorbike helmets out of the roof and put them on. Curled, spring-like wires linked the helmets to more flashing panels on the ceiling. The *Black Slug* dropped silently away from the hull of the mother ship and the rhythmic heartbeat of the engines started up.

"Fifty knots," said Thorgood.

Mick Johnson pressed a button on his control pad and the sub raced forward at an incredible speed. Two powerful red beams shot ahead and lit up a fantastic underwater world. A school of silver fish darted downwards to avoid them.

"Head north," commanded Odin.

The *Slug* veered, turning in less than its own length, and accelerated. Thorgood watched a changing LCD display.

100 KPH. 120 KPH. 140 KPH. 160 KPH.

"Load the missiles."

A mechanical cranking noise came from the back of the sub.

"Target, Master?" asked Mick.

"All surface vessels on-screen."

A detailed underwater chart of the Ionian Sea was replaced by a grid covered in dots with small flags beside them.

One flag read –

Fishing Vessel, 30 metre hull, 5.22 Kilometers NE.

Another read –

Passenger Ferry, 121 metre hull, 7.7 Kilometers NNE.

"Destroy the ferry," said Odin.

Two darts shot out from either side of the *Black Slug* and, seconds later, a blinding flash and deadly explosion ripped open the hull of the SS *Andropolinos*.

"Target destroyed," said Thorgood.

Odin stared out of the windows at his kingdom.

"Satisfactory. Return to the *Maid Of Norway*."

After docking, Odin stepped out of the lift cubicle onto the bridge.

"Olaf, when do we arrive?"

"We dock at Corfu Town in one hour."

"Instruct Johnson to take the girl and guard her aboard the *Slug*. Tell him we will be boarded by the local police and to be ready."

"I obey, Master."

***

Bernard sat with Spiros Theopoulis, Commissioner of Police, at a round plastic table, drinking black coffee and watching the *Maid Of Norway* dock.

"It is them, isn't it?"

Bernard nodded.

"Are your men ready?"

"They come now."

As a covered gangplank was lowered onto the dock, four police cars drove along the quay to meet the ship.

"The Athens Police do not know how they got the authorization through so quickly. Their papers will, of course, be in order."

Bernard made a sign, like writing on a small piece of paper, at a waiter. The waiter brought him the bill and left.

"Like most countries, the Greek Government will contain Seekers, or ministers in their pay."

"With the right papers I cannot stop them."

"But you can make it difficult. Search the ship and delay them for a day."

"We won't find anything. They never make mistakes."

"One day they will."

They stood and shook hands.

"Give me a day. I need to speak with Peter."

On board the *Maid Of Norway*, one of Spiros's men questioned Thorgood Firebrand.

"Papers, please."

Thorgood handed the policeman a small brown satchel containing the crew's passports and an envelope marked *Ministry of Archaeology and Culture*.

"Purpose of visit?"

"We are underwater archaeologists undertaking research of special scientific interest to your government."

"Duration of research?"

"Not less than ten days. Not more than sixty." Thorgood smiled. "A lot depends on luck."

"I want your permission to search the ship. It will not take long."

"Please, come aboard. We have nothing to hide."

As the police walked up the covered gangplank, Odin entered the lift and dropped down into the *Slug*. As he stepped out, the pipe rose up into the hull of the mother ship.

"Detach."

Johnson pressed a button and the *Black Slug* sank down to rest on the sandy seabed of Corfu Bay.

Thorgood led Kylie out of her cell at the back of the *Slug* and escorted her to a raised platform in front of one of the eyes. They were submerged in shallow water and the sea was well lit, and emerald shafts rippled on the walls around her. Odin joined them.

"Where is Peter?"

"I don't know."

His intense blue eyes studied her and he knew she was telling the truth.

"Why do you want his stone?" she asked.

"Do you remember what happened at Pinner High School?"

"I remember living a kind of dream and doing things I didn't want to do."

"A man named Smith held the stone and in a few days the United Kingdom was brought to its knees. When I hold it, the world as you know it will cease to exist."

Kylie raised her handcuffs and pointed at him.

"I think you are horrible."

Odin gave her a small smile.

"Thorgood, take her to Doctor Picnic."

"I obey, Master."

As he led her towards the back of the sub, Kylie turned on him.

"Why do you obey him? Why don't you stand up to him?"

"He is my master. He is your master now."

Thorgood Firebrand pushed her through an oval metal door into a cabin with a single couch in its centre. A bald man, in a white coat, held a needle. He held it up and stared at a small jet of dirty brown liquid squirting out of its tip.

"This isn't going to hurt a bit," he said.

Later, Odin walked into the cell where Kylie was sleeping.

"Is it visible?"

Thorgood held Kylie's face, turned it gently to one side and pulled her ear forward.

"There is a tiny scar, here," he pointed.

"Is the tracker working?"

"Thorgood turned the screen of a laptop to face Odin. Every five seconds a red dot flashed and a noise like a saucepan lid being hit with a wooden spoon sounded out.

"Accurate within a distance of two thousand kilometres."

Odin nodded.

"The scar is small. Will she know she has been operated on?"

"Doctor Picnic does not think so, but she will feel sick after the anaesthetic."

As Odin left he gave Thorgood new orders.

"Kill the Doctor. Time his death in the *Explorer*."

***

Kylie awoke with a thumping pain behind her eyes. She tried to sit up and felt sick. The room spun around her and she fell off the bed onto her hands and knees and vomited. She stared around. She was back in her featureless cell with its single round underwater window and she crawled to the door, and hit it with her shoe. It opened immediately.

"Can I have a towel and a glass of water, please. I've been sick."

The guard, in a black T-shirt and shorts, shut the door and Kylie pulled herself up onto the bed, sitting with her head in her hands. The door opened and the man placed a towel beside her, and gave her a plastic cup.

"Thank you."

The man nodded and closed the door behind him. Kylie thought about how a car had screeched to a halt next to her as she walked to school. She hadn't even had a chance to cry for help. She had been driven for about an hour with two blond haired men either side of her and then ordered out, and marched to a small jet which flew to another deserted airfield that she guessed was on the west coast of France. By the time she was aboard the *Maid Of Norway*, the class register would have been taken and her teacher would have thought that she was late, or unwell. She felt very unwell now.

A gloved hand tapped on her window and she stumbled over to look out. A diver in a black wet suit, stared back at her and then swam away. Two metres away, a round diving bell with a large glass porthole, hung beneath the *Maid Of Norway* on a chain. Bubbles rose in a swirling chimney above the diving bell which had, OASV DEEP SEA EXPLORER written on it. Standing at the porthole, a bald man in a white coat clawed like an animal at the glass. Then he was writhing on the floor, with a purple face and horrific bulging eyes. His silent screams were broken by rapid gasps for air.

Kylie left the window, sat back on the bed and was sick again.

***

Stefanos went over to the radio, turned it up and danced between the tables in Katerina's Kitchen.

"You must have got away with sending the email and, as for the poster, anyone can get a photo of Kylie and change it on the computer. Bet she's at school now."

Now that ten days had passed without anything bad happening, Peter began to feel happier. He couldn't contact Kylie because Bernard kept his office locked and had changed his email address, and upgraded his security software.

Peter copied his friend, arms out like plane wings and, in time with the music, he bent his knees to place mustard and ketchup bottles onto the tables on either side of him.

"Stephanos!" yelled his mother.

He ignored her and squatted to dress the last two tables with sauces. Peter grinned and turned the Greek pop song down.

"Fancy swim? Let's go Secret Cove."

Thirty minutes later, Peter watched his friend's feet disappear into the black hole and followed. The underwater passage didn't seem as long, as threatening, now that he had swum up it a few times. Then his head broke water and he went to sit beside his friend on the rocky ledge in the cave. Stephanos gave him some chocolate.

"My Grandma and Grandpa seem very worried about something."

"Worried?"

"Yes, something's up. Even Bernard wasn't his normal self this morning. When I cleaned out the pool, he sat on the veranda staring out to sea and fiddling with his mobile."

"Could be anything," said Peter.

"Could be. Don't think so though. Have they said anything to you?"

Peter shook his head and took another bite of chocolate. Grandma had given him a funny look at breakfast and he hadn't thought anything of it, but now he decided to keep the stone with him. When Stephanos dived into the pool, he felt around in the high rock crevice. His fingers curled around Amera's stone and it pulsed, and the cave became the colour of blood.

Suddenly, Odin sat bolt upright and shouted at Olaf Adanson.

"The stone cries out. Bring the girl to the aft deck now."

"I obey, Master."

Kylie was rushed from her cell and soon stood beside Odin, who took her hand and held it tightly.

"Do not be frightened," he said in a cold voice.

Then he pulled her off the side of the ship and they plunged into the sea. In less than a second, they rose to stand on the water in the centre of a round cove with a small beach on one side. Two boys were climbing up a narrow path to the top of the cliffs.

Kylie called out.

"Peter."

Peter turned and saw her, and his jaw dropped when he saw

168

Odin holding her hand. Then they were sinking down into an erupting sea of bubbles.

***

"But I did see her," insisted Peter.

Bernard ignored his plea for help.

"Is the stone safe?" he asked.

Peter took it from his pocket and placed it on the table.

"If you give Odin this stone, he will kill Kylie anyway, and you."

"Can't we do anything?"

The old man thought in silence and finally nodded.

"Come on. If she is a prisoner of the Seekers, she will be held aboard the *Maid Of Norway* docked in Corfu Town. Let's ask Spiros to search her again."

But, later, Spiros refused.

"Their papers are in order and I need a reason to search their ship."

"If you check with the British Police you will find that a girl has gone missing on her way to Pinner High School."

"I have already checked and what link can there be? A girl goes missing in London and a legitimate archaeological survey team docks in Corfu Town."

Someone tapped politely on the Commissioner of Police's door and a uniformed officer walked in, and placed a file on his desk.

"Can't this wait?" asked Spiros.

"I think you should read it now, sir."

Inside the file were photographs of a bald, naked man's body. A yellow post-it note read, *Body washed up on Nissaki Beach.* Spiros raised an eyebrow and reached behind his chair for a small brown satchel. As Bernard and Peter watched, he thumbed through the crew's passports and stopped at the face of Doctor Marius Picnic.

"We have our reason," he said.

As the police boarded the *Maid Of Norway*, Kylie felt the *Black Slug* sink again. Small bubbles rose up past her window and she wondered what was going on. She knocked on the door and it opened.

"I'm afraid I've been sick again. Could I have another towel and glass of water?"

The door shut and she sat back on the bed. The guard came in, placed the towel on the bed and handed her the water. Kylie threw it into his face and dashed out the door, and slammed it shut. She turned to face Olaf Adanson who was pointing a gun at her.

"Back inside," he said.

***

Peter sat with Bernard in the back of Mr Minolas's taxi, watching the search party walk out of the end of the covered gangplank and knew, from their expressions, that they hadn't found anything.

Peter turned his face away and saw a group of beautiful ladies, in bright yellow dresses, giving out leaflets to tourists along the quay. One lady saw him and skipped over, and knocked on his window. Peter wound it down and she handed him a leaflet.

"It's going to be the biggest promotion event on the island in years," she said. "Bring your girlfriend. She could win a free bottle of fantastic perfume."

Peter stared at the girl's face on the leaflet. A caption underneath read –

RELEASE ME. The new fragrance from OASV Europe.
Be on the beach at 3.00 pm today.

As Mr Minolas drove away along the quay, a car started its engine and tailed them.

"Black Mercedes," said Bernard.

The taxi turned quickly into the narrow streets of Corfu Town and Mr Minolas spoke into his radio. As they passed an alley, an old van drove out and blocked the way behind them. Men jumped out of the Mercedes and began to argue with the driver. Mr Minolas snaked his way through the lunchtime traffic and then they were out on the Kassioppi road.

"It was a trap wasn't it? This whole thing is a trap." said Peter, but no one said anything.

As they drove through the gates of Bernard's villa, Grandma hurried out to meet them. She held a leaflet in her hand and called out.

"Peter, you mustn't go. Promise me you will not go. Odin will kill us all."

CHAPTER ELEVEN

A UNION OF SOULS : SUMMER 677 AD

Peter had cried during lunch and Mrs Agnedes looked critically at the full plates returned to her kitchen.

"The food was lovely," reassured Grandma, "but I'm afraid no one is very hungry at the moment."

"Will he go?"

"I don't know. I really don't know."

In his room, Peter thought about Kylie and half made up his mind to try and rescue her. The floor began to shimmer and Myroy's body rose up.

"What do I do?"

The Ancient One ignored him.

"The next part of the story begins with what was once called a Union of Souls. In your time you call it a wedding."

Peter put his head in his hands and pictured Kylie's face.

"I am about to lose my girlfriend and you want to tell me about a bloody wedding," he hissed.

"What did grandma say to you when you came back to the villa?"

"You are torturing me."

Myroy became fierce.

"What did she say?"

"She said that Odin will kill us all."

Myroy came to sit next to him and put an arm around his shoulders.

"What did you ask of me?"

"I asked, 'What do I do?'"

"And what is the answer?"

"I must listen to the story. To understand what is to be, I must understand what has been."

Myroy nodded.

"Dougie was the first Keeper and you will be the last. We cannot hide the stone from the Seekers forever. In some time they will hold it."

"And we cannot destroy it."

"What does history tell you?"

"The Younger tried to destroy it and nothing even put a scratch on the ruby."

"So, if you are ready, I must tell you about Dougie's next challenge. You have heard about his adventures in Mountain, Island and Castle. Now you must learn about the slaves of the foundry and the Younger's plan to make Patrick Three Eggs his ally. He knew his people could not fight Tella's alliance alone."

Peter stared out of the window. The swifts were back again and darting around in a beautiful clear blue sky. He tried to remember everything Myroy had told him so far and couldn't. Kylie's face filled his mind and he knew he was going to lose her as well as his family. Grandpa had said that he would be alone as a Keeper.

"She is the next part of my terrible price, isn't she," he whispered, but Myroy had already begun his story.

Three friends, a king and an alchemist tried to console the biggest warrior in Scotland. They had shared many adventures, defending their lands, and now they sat in awkward silence and stared at the shields on the walls of the Great Hall. Even Malcolm the Younger was lost for words. He fiddled with his empty goblet and stroked his grey beard. This was supposed to be a celebration.

Hamish of Tain, fearless defender of the kingdom, was wondering how he had fallen in love so quickly with the gypsy girl. True, she was beautiful and mysterious, and true, Barbarini the Traveller had helped him escape from the Angles.

"How on earth did I get myself into this?" he said.

It was the eve of his wedding, a Union of Souls that Babs had accurately foretold, at their very first meeting after the turn of the year, and Hamish was dreading it. His stomach was in knots. As the tension, the expectation, had grown over the last few days, he had thought of leaving. Run away from the course set for him.

Like his friends, Hamish wore his best plaid. Everyone was neat and clean, unrecognisable.

"It is destiny," grumbled Hamish, and his head sank into his hands.

"Cheer up, Hamish," chirped Donald, his short and loyal friend.

"Aye," replied Hamish, but he didn't cheer up.

"The Union is a fine thing," continued Donald.

"I would rather face an army than make a fool of myself in front of you lot. Besides, I am too young to marry."

"How old are you?" asked Dougie.

Hamish took a sip of heather ale.

"Not sure."

Dougie smiled at his friend. "I am younger than you and have been happily married for many summers."

Hamish growled at him like a bear.

"Perhaps Your Majesty could send me on an urgent and secret mission?" asked Hamish hopefully, but Malcolm shook his head.

"Hamish, everyone is nervous the night before their wedding, it is a natural thing," said Dougie.

"Getting dressed up in finery and having the bath is no natural way to behave. I smell like heather."

"Not old Heather of Strathmiglo?" chirped Donald, "better keep that quiet from Babs."

Malcolm groaned and nodded at a servant to bring them more ale.

"Marriage is all about caring deeply for someone," said Alistair, "why, Donald and his loving wife Senga are a fine example of that. Are they not Hamish?"

"Aye, they are," replied the big man.

Alistair grinned at Dougie.

"Why, two people can show their true love for each other, despite anything," continued Hamish.

"Aye, despite anything," agreed Dougie who noticed that

Donald, who was often the butt of Hamish's jokes, was looking apprehensive. The others just grinned.

"And do you know what, young Dougie?" asked Hamish.

"I do not," replied Dougie truthfully.

"The love in a union like theirs will overcome even the biggest of problems."

Dougie glanced across the table to see Donald rising to his feet.

"Would you like a small example?"

"Aye, I would," replied Dougie, not really knowing where all this was going.

"Well, only the other day Donald told me that Senga had said that she would leave him if he went off on another adventure."

"Leave him. That's terrible," said Dougie.

"Aye," added Hamish, "and do you know what Donald said?"

"I do not."

"That he was going to really miss her."

The room burst into fits of uncontrollable laughter as Donald's shield came crashing down onto the big man's head.

"I suppose there is nothing to worry about," conceded Hamish after a while.

"I suppose your new-found bravery has nothing to do with the ale?" asked Donald cheekily.

Hamish shot him a look.

"Grumf."

"No, Gangly, you cannot have any ale," replied Archie, "don't you remember the last time you tried it and the disastrous results?"

"Grumf."

"No, I am not an old fool you rude imp. I am the king's alchemist and don't you forget it."

Archie was sitting facing the wall as he always did. He would even walk backwards with the Ghilly Dhu sitting on his shoulders, telling him which way to go. In fact he was now so used to looking where he had been that, without the cheeky imp, he couldn't go anywhere without bumping into things. Gangly crossed his long dangly legs and adjusted a button on his bright red waistcoat. He glanced at Dougie and stuck his tongue out.

"Did I mention that I have looked into the Oracle of the Ancient Ones and seen the wedding? It will be a rainy day, but everything will go ahead peacefully."

"The Oracle is an important piece of alchemy," said Dougie.

Archie seemed encouraged by this.

"Yes indeed, and who would not want to see the things which will be? Why only yesterday I saw an image of a man flying in the sky. One day man will fly!"

"Grumf."

"No, they will not have tired arms," continued Archie, "for they will use great machines with whirly things called *wet engines.*"

"Grumf," said Gangly in a rude tone.

"It will catch on," replied Archie, "it is the future."

Dougie noticed that every time Archie spoke, Gangly took a long, thin wooden pipe from his pocket and sucked up the heather ale from his master's goblet.

"It is time for the toast," commanded Malcolm royally.

"I am not hungry," replied Donald.

"The toast of good wishes for the Union," continued Malcolm, "please raise your goblets."

Dougie passed Archie his empty goblet and the alchemist said, "I am sorry, Your Majesty, but I seem to have got ahead of everyone else."

"Well order some more," barked the king with a note of annoyance in his voice.

Gangly gave Dougie a wicked look, waved the little pipe at him and stuck his tongue out again.

"And so it is with great pleasure," said Malcolm to the

circle of friends, "that we pass on our blessings to Hamish and Babs. May their time together be long and happy and may their children be strong and many."

"Hamish and Babs," cheered everyone and they emptied their goblets.

Hamish looked embarrassed by the attention and the thought of children. He hadn't considered this possibility and began to look miserable again.

As if sensing his friend's unease Alistair said, "How about a story to fill the hours?" and as it always did, the thought of retelling the tales of the past lifted their spirits.

The servant returned to their table and Dougie noticed Gangly getting his pipe out. As was the custom, the king began his story first and he talked long about the great battle on Carn Liath, when the Picts had raided the villages of the northern glens and provoked a war that Tella the Mac Mar had hoped would result in the Scots retreating from their lands. In fact the Black Kilts, despite superior numbers, had been defeated and driven off to live on the Island of Skye.

"Tella is mighty bitter about it all," continued Malcolm, "and he is an evil and scheming enemy. I would not be surprised if we hear from him again at some time."

Everyone nodded and Gangly made a sound that was somewhere between a "Grumf," and a hiccup.

"Your turn, Alistair," said Dougie eagerly, and his friend told them about being held as a prisoner of the Angles, in the bowels of the great castle at Berwick.

"It was the most miserable time of my life," he said, "and I cannot tell you the joy and thankfulness I felt towards Dougie when he rescued me."

Dougie went bright red with embarrassment and Gangly moved his elbows in and out like a chicken.

"The cells are cold and smell of death," continued Alistair, "and there is no sense of the passage of time for the gloom is unchanging. Night and day are as one."

It was Donald's turn next and he spoke of the Norsemen and standing on the cliffs at Oban, looking down upon the fleet of longboats as they drifted towards them.

"I must admit to being mighty relieved when they chose to sail south and fight somewhere else," he said, and the party nodded once more.

Malcolm called over to the servant for more refreshment and Gangly got his pipe ready again. The king stood and solemnly introduced the next storyteller.

"We are here the night before Hamish's wedding and the knight before us is a Warrior Shepherd."

Alistair smiled at his nervous friend, and the king continued.

"Of all my loyal subjects, I think most kindly of Dougie for he has shown much courage in his adventures, despite the fact that he is not a person who possesses the natural daring of a warrior."

Malcolm looked at Dougie who was feeling more and more uncomfortable.

"I do not know what to say," said Dougie.

"None of us do at times like this," replied Malcolm, and then he sat down as an instruction for the shepherd to begin his tale.

Dougie felt dumbstruck. He was not one to lead, or to command an audience, particularly when that audience included so many of the strong and good. He felt the eyes of his friends staring at him and Gangly raised an open hand to cover his mouth, and yawned cheekily.

"Well, we have had a good harvest," mumbled Dougie.

Gangly threw his head back in disgust.

"Aye laddie," said Alistair in an encouraging voice, "tell us about the farm."

"It is a beautiful place. The land is rich and the crops do well from it. The hills are wonderful this time of year, and even though they have none of the rugged splendour of the great mountains, like Carn Liath, they are a place of quiet and do provide some protection from the worst of the weather that comes from the north."

Gangly had his pipe in Archie's goblet and was making a rude slurping noise. Archie tried to turn his head to see what was happening and the imp shoved the tube back into his pocket, and started to whistle innocently.

"Very ….. nice," said Malcolm, and he turned to Hamish to rescue Dougie.

"I remember the time when we saw Archie's new experident," continued Dougie. "I have never seen anything fly into the sky like the *bartillery*."

"Aye," encouraged Alistair sitting forward, "what else do you remember about it?"

"Well, that's it really," admitted Dougie, and Alistair sat back in his chair.

"What about you, brave Hamish? You must have many a fine tale to tell," chirped Donald.

"Aye, laddie," replied the big man, "I remember meeting Babs for the first time on the road, in the forest outside Berwick Castle. It was a lovely day, the birds were singing and, of course, she called me husband. Can you imagine that. Calling me husband. Why, I had not spoken to her for more than a moment."

"See the future can she? Good, good."

Archie nodding in a way that showed it clearly meant something. But Hamish's thoughts were now back on the wedding and he growled miserably again.

Suddenly, there was a thump on the table as Gangly fell off Archie's shoulder.

"No wonder you are the last of the Ghilly Dhus," yelled the alchemist in an exasperated voice.

"There goes your imp," smiled Alistair.

"There goes my lift home," replied Archie sadly.

***

A thin line of gold burst over the crest of a hill to reveal the black silhouette of a cloaked man. Outstretched in his right hand was a staff, upright and unwavering. In the other was something that looked to Dougie like a bunch of flowers. The sun rose slowly until half of it showed through the cold morning air. The Druid was like a statue. At the base of the hill, grass, bracken and tree shone yellow and orange, and the shadows shortened. It was going to be a beautiful day.

A small hand slipped into Dougie's. It was his young daughter, Tanny.

"I wish they would bloomin' well get on with it," she said.

Mairi shot her a scolding look and the little girl buried her face into Dougie's plaid to escape her mother's stare.

The sun rose higher and, eventually, the whole of its fiery surface was revealed. Two more figures could now be seen. A woman walking slowly towards the Druid from one side, and a giant of a man walked towards him from the other side. They reached the point at the base of the sun together. The woman took hold of the flowers and the man took the staff.

There was a great cheer and the crowd, who waited patiently at the foot of the hill, began to run up the slope. The children were dressed in bright colours and carried handfuls of flowers. The womenfolk talked eagerly to each other and some sang songs of celebration. The men, in their finest clothes, followed last of all and, as was the tradition, they wore a sprig of heather in their bonnets.

"Have you ever seen anyone more nervous on the eve of his Union?" asked Alistair.

"No," and Dougie smiled at his closest friend.

"Hamish will be glad to have his friends around him," added Donald.

"Aye," laughed Dougie, remembering the ale and stories shared the night before.

"Is Babs not a fine woman?" continued Alistair.

Donald nodded. "None finer."

"Except maybe for one," said Dougie in a louder than normal voice, and behind them someone added, "That was the right answer, Dougie of Dunfermline," and Mairi put her arm into her husband's.

On the summit, the guests formed a large ring around the Druid. He was tall, old and elegant in manner and wore a long white robe, which matched the colour of his beard. He spoke softly and clearly.

"As the sun brings a new day, and as spring marks the beginning of new life, we join together to celebrate the Union of Souls."

The Druid spoke for a long time about plants and animals, seasons and weather, and how all life depends above all else on Mother Earth. Hamish shuffled his feet, and Dougie's two boys, Calum and Jock, started to poke each other.

The old man looked at the couple and moved them together so they could embrace.

"With love for each other and with respect for the world in which we live, I call upon you, Hamish of Tain, to make thy promise."

He paused and smiled.

"Will you care for and protect this woman, and love her for all time?"

"Aye, I will," mumbled Hamish nervously.

"I now call upon you Barbarini the Traveller, to take thy promise. Will you care for and cherish this man, and love him for all time?"

"I will," replied Babs and she looked into the eyes of her husband.

The Druid took the staff and flowers, and stepped back. The couple kissed as the crowd cheered again.

With Babs and Hamish leading the way, the long procession snaked its way down the hill towards the Great Hall. They forded a stream and passed a line of brightly coloured caravans, which were the homes of the gypsy people.

One hundred paces long, forty wide and with white walls and thatched roof, the Great Hall was the meeting place for Hamish's clan. Inside it was dark and warm, and on a great trestle the food was laid out. A whole roast boar, many roast lambs and chickens, and bowls full of peas were surrounded by smaller dishes of all kinds of cooked meat and fish. Children slipped in and sat with their parents. Hamish and Babs, and the Druid walked to a raised platform at the far end.

Joyful music struck up and people danced, slowly and gracefully at first, and then wildly as the rhythm quickened. When the musicians were bade to stop by the Druid, Hamish and Babs were ushered to the floor and, alone, in front of their kith and kin, they danced to the sound of lyre, pipe and drum. Dougie thought Hamish looked a little awkward, moving his great body around and around. But whatever he may have lacked was more than made up for by the beauty and skill of his partner. The music stopped and the room hushed as two men entered the hall. The children nudged each other.

Tanny said, "It's the bloomin' king again."

Malcolm walked, regally, down one side of the hall and an old man, with a Ghilly Dhu on his shoulder, walked backwards down the other. With much ceremony, they sat at the ends of the raised table. The Druid stood and spoke the words everyone wanted to hear.

"Let the feasting begin."

With that, the crowd dived for the food and there was chaos. A roast chicken flew through the air, a jug of heather ale smashed and an old woman cried out in pain as she was crushed underfoot by the unruly mob. The top table had the privilege of going second, when things had calmed down, and Archie turned to Babs.

"I have seen the future and one day people will do something called *gooing*."

"*Gooing*?" asked Babs.

"Aye, they will form an orderly line and wait, peacefully, for their turn to get their food."

"I don't like the sound of *gooing*," thought Hamish, who could fight his way to the front of any *goo*.

"Grumf," said Gangly, as a young girl was carried from the hall screaming.

"You are right, old friend," replied Archie, "it is difficult to see how 'gooing,' might catch on."

"I have seen the future too," said Babs darkly.

"And what did you see, my dear?" replied Archie.

"Five armies," she whispered.

A slice of ham landed on their table and Hamish took a huge, grateful mouthful.

"A good do this," he said, food flying in all directions.

"Yes indeed," replied the old druid as he picked a chunk of fat out of his beard.

As was the tradition at a Celtic wedding, when the guests had taken their fill, more food was brought to the trestles for the important guests. Babs took a plate of fruit and vegetables, and Hamish two plates, piled high with all kinds of meat.

"They will get on well together," said Donald to Alistair in a mischievous voice.

His wife Senga kicked him under the table.

Dougie noticed the gypsies sat together. Many of their menfolk wore brightly coloured silks and had rings in their ears. Stories told that, as a people, they had travelled far across the sea from the east and had become so used to travelling that the wandering itself had become central to their way of life.

During the eating, three of the gypsies drifted around the hall playing stringed instruments and singing beautifully in a strange tongue. When the song ended the Scots applauded, but the gypsies were quick to note that no coins came flying their way, as might happen in other lands.

The most difficult part of any Scottish wedding is when the parents of the two "souls of union" are introduced and it was to be particularly difficult on this occasion. Hamish was an only son and, much to the amusement of his friends, his mother doted and fussed over him. In her mind, wee Hamish should never marry. He was far too young for anything like that. The fact that he had worked since he was a boy and was now a great warrior had no place in Shona's thinking.

So, after the feast, and after the drinking of much heather ale, a large, timid man, with fear in his heart, led his small mother across the hall. The conversation, with Babs' mother, Benita, began courteously enough.

Hamish introduced them and Shona said, "Greetings to you and all your friends."

"Thank you many times, kind lady," and Hamish saw her husband's chair edge away from them. "You have prepared a magnificent feast," continued Benita.

"Thank you," said Shona.

Their eyes locked together like wrestlers.

"Could you spare a moment to see the caravan we have made as a gift for the lucky couple?" asked Benita.

"What caravan is that?" questioned Shona, who seemed to be standing taller than she normally did.

"Your son is a big, strong boy and we have made the caravan larger and more comfortable than any made before."

"It sounds lovely," said Shona, "but I do not think they will be needing it."

"How so?" asked Benita, with what could have been a smile, or a snarl, on her face.

"Well, of course," added Shona, who looked at Hamish for agreement, "they shall come and stay with me."

Sensing danger, Hamish cut in quickly.

"We have not yet decided where we are going to live, Ma."

"Don't be silly, dear, I cannot have you sleeping in a draughty caravan," replied Shona.

"A draughty caravan," snapped Benita angrily, "I did not come here to be insulted."

"Oh," said Shona, "where do you normally go?"

The scene which followed needs little description, except

to say that the mayhem of the feast was like a quiet picnic compared to the pitch battle that erupted. As was normal in these circumstances, the women retreated out of the hall to talk about the shortcomings of their men.

The children got behind tables to cheer and throw plates and goblets at the other side. Hamish and Babs were ushered to safety by Malcolm and Archie. Horses awaited them. They were to honeymoon at the royal palace as honoured guests. Hamish glanced back at the Great Hall. It seemed to be shaking.

Inside, Dougie was being spun around on the shoulders of a large gypsy. Donald dived bravely into two of them, and Alistair grabbed a side of pork and wrapped it around the head of an opponent. A group of Scots lifted a long bench and charged the Romanies.

Dougie felt himself flying through the air and out of a window. The Druid, his face full of horror at the fighting, stood up and shouted.

"Think of the example you are setting the wee ones."

Everyone ignored him.

"Remember why we are here."

The fight went on.

"Peace, love and respect for others."

He was knocked senseless by a leg of lamb.

***

Dougie awoke next to Donald and Alistair. His head hurt and his mouth was very dry. He sat up and looked at his friends. Their eyes were open, but nobody seemed to be at home.

"I must have eaten something that disagreed with me," he muttered.

"Wise words," groaned Donald.

"What a fine wedding," continued Dougie.

"None finer," grunted Alistair.

Dougie stood, wobbled and stumbled towards the bathing

pool. He stared down into still water and, in the reflection, saw a black eye. Once, through a deadly mist and with a Black Kilt's hands around his throat, he had seen a shiner just like it. He went cold.

"I wonder what Mairi will say?" he said.

CHAPTER TWELVE

THE MIGHTY BLADE

Malcolm the Younger, King of the Scots and Protector of the Stone of Destiny, ran for his life. Great tongues of fire shot out the door and chased him across the Palace Green. Black smoke spewed out from every crack in the wooden hut and a mighty, mechanical *boom* echoed around the palace walls.

"There must be an easier way of finding the answer," thought Malcolm.

Archie walked backwards out of the inferno that was his *experident*. Gangly looked as though he had slept in an oven. His jacket was singed and smoking, and he shook his head as if to say, "Not again."

"I think we were nearly there this time," stated Archie in a calm voice.

"Grumf!"

"What do you mean I am not nearly all there?"

"Grumf," continued Gangly, who nodded at the king.

Archie walked backwards towards him.

"Ah, Your Majesty."

Malcolm stamped out the last of the flames, which threatened his fine robes.

"It is something to do with the variation of heat in the furnace and the small addition of a complex mix of different compounds at key points in the production process."

"What?" asked Malcolm.

"I'm not sure yet, but a few more looks into the Oracle of the Ancient Ones and we will get there."

"Grumf," grunted Gangly.

"No it is not time for supper yet," snapped Archie crossly, "and this is too important to stop for a mere trifle."

"Grumf, grumf," said Gangly.

"How can you like trifle? It hasn't been invented yet and it certainly doesn't help us solve the mystery of the mighty blade."

Gangly rolled his eyes skyward as if to say, "We could be here for months trying to solve this one."

Seven days had passed since the Union of Souls and it was four days since the new iron had been brought to the palace. It had been known for some time that someone was arming the king's enemies with sword and spear, but it was only when soldiers had set upon a band of Black Kilts, near Stranraer, that the weapons themselves had been captured.

The Picts were increasingly bold and dared to travel, without permission, on Scottish lands. The king's secret riders were disappearing again as they went about their business in the High Glens. Now this. The new blades were lighter and stronger than any blades made before. Andrew of Ayr had laid a shining sword in front of the court. A child could have lifted it, and all other weapons shattered on its hard edge.

The Younger, like Myroy, knew this meant trouble. Any army who faced an enemy armed with the light iron was sure to be slaughtered and their lands taken. In these uncertain times, there was a constant threat of invasion and many peoples looked jealously at the Scottish kingdom. The prosperity of the Long Peace had a price.

Now, the mighty blade was sure to change the balance of power and threaten the nation the loyal clans had taken so long to knit together.

Archie was given the task of finding out the secret of how to make it and Malcolm called for a council of the Knights of the High Table. The secret riders went to every part of the kingdom to fetch them and, in two days' time, forty of the bravest and most loyal of his warriors would gather at the palace to decide on the best course of action.

Malcolm sat alone in his royal chamber. The deep lines on his face showed the worry he felt in his heart and he ran a hand slowly, deliberately, down the edge of a captured sword. The thin line of a cut formed on the tip of his finger and round beads grew larger, joined together and dripped onto the stone floor.

One by one, each drop added to a small, red pool, and, in the silence of his lonely room, Malcolm stared down at his blood, and thought about the future of his people.

***

Dougie of Dunfermline was counting his sheep. It had been a fine summer and the crops had grown quickly. During the spring, only three lambs had been lost to foxes and now Dougie's flock numbered over a hundred. He enjoyed being a farmer, indeed he believed he was born to it, and felt deeply content as he watched his stock graze peacefully on the high pastures. The far hills shone purple as the last rays of sun lit the heather and, in the distance, a light mist grew above the loch where he had thrown his ruby away.

Dog ran along the line of a stone wall, like a mad thing, and wagged his tail as he hunted out unusual smells and noises. Dougie sat and ran a hand through his long brown hair. He shut his eyes and listened to a bee buzzing between wild flowers and wondered what drove it to work so hard. The base of the sun rested on the western hills and Dougie whistled to Dog. He stood and peered down at his farm. It looked like a small box with a yellow thatch crown and, inside, Mairi would be making lamb and barley broth.

"There is no more worth having than this," he said and the sheepdog glanced up and cocked his head to one side as if to say, "Time for supper yet?"

Someone called out his name and Dougie's eyes searched the high pastures for a cloaked figure. The old watcher stood alone by the stone cairn, which marked Lissy's resting place. Myroy bent, placed a flower upon her grave and remembered the love Lissy had given to the twins as they grew up. No one in the world could have done more. Then he looked over at the heir of Donald and smiled. Dougie felt as though he had known the stranger all his life, but wasn't even sure of his name.

"The time is near to seek the light iron," said the man.

Dougie's stomach tightened. Every time he talked to him he was dragged away from his beloved farm. Dougie strained to get a better view of him.

"How might I call you?"

"Some call me Myroy."

"But why must I go?" asked Dougie.

"I made a promise a long time ago, to your mother, and there is much left for you to do."

"To seek the light iron," said the shepherd.

"Aye, to the west," said Myroy softly and his words came to Dougie as though he was standing right beside him.

"Can I not stay here and tend the sheep?"

The stranger ignored him.

"The map is the key and you must stay close to Alistair. He will protect you."

Dougie stared at the ground.

"Why me?" he asked.

But the cloaked figure had vanished and Dougie thought he heard the words, "Because it is your destiny," spoken in a soft voice carried along by the breeze.

The troubled shepherd and his dog made their way down a steep path to the stile. They crossed the stream and walked, side by side, through the lower fields. Dougie stopped to look at his prized herbs and beans, and smiled as he remembered the honour gifted to him by the king.

"Me, a member of the High Table."

He shook his head. He was a shepherd, not a warrior.

Outside the cottage, Dougie's boys fought over a fallen log. When Calum stood on it, Jock pushed him off, and when Jock stood on it, Calum pushed him off. Wee Tanny yelled at the chickens and threw seeds onto the grass.

"Come and have your bloomin' food,"

Dougie smiled and wondered what light iron was.

In the dead of night, Dog raised his head and growled at the cottage door. In a tired voice Mairi mumbled, "What's up, laddie?" and immediately went back to sleep.

Outside, a rider dismounted and tied two horses to the farm gate. He wore the Younger's tartan and marched, with purpose, to deliver his message. The sheepdog barked and Dougie sat up as the rider knocked quickly on the door. The children glanced nervously at each other and Mairi pushed her husband from the bed.

"If that is one of your thirsty friends you are in big trouble, Douglas of Dunfermline."

Dougie urged Dog to stop barking, took his dirk from his sock and cautiously opened the door.

Mairi thought she heard the stranger ask, "Can you ride?" and Dougie say, "No, but I can hang on."

"More bloomin' trouble," Mairi groaned.

The children were very excited and wanted to hear any scrap of news the king's messenger would tell them. He ate a large bowl of steaming porridge, which Mairi made for him, and it was agreed that he and Dougie would travel to the Palace at first light. Calum, Jock and Tanny were told to calm down and their guest settled into a corner, and wrapped himself up in his plaid, and in no time his breathing became gentle in sleep. Dougie knew Mairi was not happy and kissed her.

They talked in whispers about the children and what she would need to do to keep the farm going without him.

"We have done it before and I have no doubt we shall have to do it again."

"I will come home as soon as the king's work is done," replied Dougie soothingly.

Mairi gave him a brave smile.

"You better had, husband."

"Will you get the chance to bloomin' kill someone?" chirped a small voice from under a blanket.

"I certainly hope not," answered Dougie truthfully.

"Or bring back some treasure?" added another voice.

"Go to sleep, my wee ones," said Mairi.

Dougie put his arm around her and for some time they sat close together, in silence, watching the dying embers of the fire and praying that whatever lay ahead would be over quickly.

The gathering of the Knights of the High Table was already underway in the great banqueting hall of the palace when Dougie arrived. Malcolm looked stern and grave as the light iron was passed around the long table, but his face brightened and he smiled, as the most timid of all his warriors made his way nervously to the last empty chair.

Prince Ranald watched Dougie's every step. He wondered why his father thought so highly of this common farmer. He also wondered why he had been gifted the Elder's brooch. Like the crown and the power it brought, the great jewel was a part of his inheritance and now he remembered the words he had overheard when Arkinew had spoken to his father.

"The stone has been hidden and as long as it remains beneath the water, no enemy can hear its call," the alchemist had said.

"And Myroy believes it to be true?"

"Dougie gave it away gladly. He threw it without question into the loch by his farm and the souls it imprisoned are free. But remember, the stone came to him, he did not steal it."

"Grumf," grunted Gangly.

"Yes I agree, Gangly," continued Arkinew, *"the stone can never be completely destroyed, only held in the keeping, if the old stories are true."*

"Is it as powerful as Myroy foretold?" asked Malcolm.

Arkinew thought long about this.

"Even Myroy, the wisest amongst us, does not know its full power. But he does fear the stone."

"And if an enemy marched before it then they would surely destroy us," said the king, *"if it was held by a man who was driven by anger and greed."*

Ranald stared at Dougie and his eyes searched his clothes for the gold brooch, and the ruby which lay at its heart, but there was no sign of it.

"One day it will be mine," the young prince whispered under his breath,

Dougie glanced around at the fine carvings and colourful tapestries of mythical beasts and scenes from battles fought long ago. A huge painting of a thistle ran across the high ceiling. The hall was bright and charged with excitement, and Dougie wished, above all else, that he would not have to speak in front of so many strangers.

Malcolm stood to address the High Table. He paused and took a long, grey sword in his hand. Deliberately, he raised it above his head and thrust the iron downwards into the oak table. Slicing down through the air it bit into the hard wood and was buried deep. He let go of the hilt and the mighty blade swayed back and forth like a tree in the wind.

"You have all seen the new iron," said the king.

Even though he had once held Torik Benn's axe, Dougie thought he hadn't and wondered if he should raise his hand.

"The army that carries these swords will destroy their enemies," he continued. "That is why we are here."

Malcolm looked at his Knights through worried eyes.

"We now know the Black Kilts have them."

His warriors gave a low murmur.

"We know the Mac Mar seeks revenge. We know that, given even half a chance, he would use them against us."

There was an even bigger murmur from around the hall.

"But we do not yet know how to make the light iron, or who else knows its secrets."

Malcolm's gaze fixed upon the swinging hilt of the sword. Dougie thought the king looked tired.

Then the Younger's eyes flashed and any sadness or worry they held disappeared. They became hard and determined.

"We must stand together," he said. "I know there is a terrible secret behind all this. Great danger threatens our people."

Malcolm sat down again, at the head of the High Table, and stared at the point where the blade cut into the oak.

"We must discover where and how the iron is made. If we can, then much of what is unknown to us may become clear."

"Your Majesty, is it true that you believe the threat comes from the west?" asked Robert of Inverness.

The Younger nodded. "These weapons were captured near Stranraer, but I do not believe the Picts are making the light iron on Skye. It is much more likely that they are buying them from someone who sees it in their interests to arm our enemies."

"And has the alchemist found the secret?" asked Robert.

Malcolm reached up and ran his little finger along a singed eyebrow.

"No, not yet."

The room fell silent again and eventually the king rose to speak.

"I need your help. Andrew of Ayr, will you take nine knights south, to beyond the borders?"

"Aye, Your Majesty," replied Andrew gravely.

"Robert, will you take the same number over the sea to the north, and Findlay will you lead the Knights of Fife and search the eastern lands?"

"Aye," they said together.

"And Alistair," continued the king, "will you lead the Men of Tain to Stranraer?"

"Gladly, Your Majesty," promised Alistair.

"So, it is done," concluded Malcolm, "we meet again in forty days."

And not for the first time Dougie was to do something he would come to regret later. Slowly, he raised his hand and felt as if the whole world was looking at him. The Knights of the High Table fell silent. The Younger smiled, and nodded in a way that invited him to speak.

"Can I go west too?" he asked.

CHAPTER THIRTEEN

ROAD TO STRANRAER

Dougie and Alistair were walking along the line of the palace walls and catching up on old times.

It was as if they had never been apart, for their conversation flowed eagerly. Alistair told of his journey across the Great Sea, and Malcolm's hope of building on the good relations he enjoyed with Patrick Three Eggs, King of all the Irish peoples. Patrick had even agreed to consider bringing the two nations together through a royal marriage. In return, the Younger had agreed to build a church on the small Island of Iona where Patrick's envoys could claim royal protection.

Dougie talked about the fine summer, his crops and livestock and, of course, about Mairi and the children. He always felt like a pauper at a rich man's table when talking to Alistair, for his life had little of the excitement which his friend so obviously enjoyed, but Alistair listened intently to his stories.

As Donald and Hamish went to collect the horses from the stables on the other side of the palace, the friends went to see how Archie was getting on with the light iron. Crossing the Palace Green, Dougie saw Archie walking backwards out of his shack, cloaked in soot and smoke, with Gangly coughing and saying, "Grumf," in a very rude way into his master's ear.

"Hello, Archie," said Dougie politely.

"Grumf," coughed Gangly.

"Ah, my young friends, how are you?" replied Archie.

"In fine spirits," replied Alistair, "and we are on another mission for the king."

Dougie wasn't looking forward to the mission one bit, but didn't say anything and smiled at the imp on Archie's shoulder. Gangly stuck his neck out and moved his elbows in and out, like a chicken.

"Grumf."

"No we are not having chicken for supper," said Archie.

Gangly stuck his tongue out at Dougie.

"Do you have any of the *bartillery* left, for us to take on our adventure?" asked Alistair.

"I'm afraid not," replied Archie sadly, "the next delivery of sulphur will not be in Scotland for hundreds of years, and it is sulphur which gives the *bartillery* its whizzing noise and awesome power."

Dougie looked worried by this and Gangly started moving his elbows in and out again.

"How are you getting on with the new iron?" asked Alistair, to change the subject.

"Not so well," admitted Archie, "if only I could see for myself how it is made."

"Can you not use the Oracle of the Ancient Ones?" asked Dougie innocently, and at this Gangly threw his eyes to the sky as if to say, "Don't encourage the old fool."

"Ah, how very clever of you, young man. The Oracle does allow the learned to see into the future but, alas, not into the present," replied Archie, who seemed pleased that, at last, someone was taking an interest in his work.

"Well, we hope to see it," said Alistair, and he told Archie about their mission to the west to seek out the makers of new iron.

Archie listened to the details of Malcolm's plan and Gangly stared at Dougie, and drew his finger along his throat.

"Your end is nigh!" screeched Archie. "Your flesh shall be cut to pieces, and your blood and skin returned to the earth."

He ran backwards into his hut.

"Cheerful as ever," laughed Alistair.

"Aye," said Dougie, but the alchemist's words troubled him.

Ten knights mounted fresh horses in the cobbled courtyard of the palace. Alistair was to lead the party through lonely places for three days until they reached the shelter of the old fort at Kilmarnock. Stranraer, one of the most important ports of trade with Ireland, was two days' ride from there. Most nights they would sleep beside the path they followed.

Much to the Men of Tain's amusement, Hamish was saying goodbye to Babs.

"I will hurry home to you soon my love," said the big man in a sheepish voice, hoping that none of his friends could hear what they were saying.

"It will not be soon," replied Babs in a soft voice, "but you *will* keep safe."

"I'm mighty glad about that."

He kissed her. The soldiers made a soft cooing noise, like a dove, and Hamish went bright red. As he mounted a large and strong bay stallion, Babs looked up into her husband's eyes and gave him a warning.

"Beware the man of fire."

"I'll watch for him, sweetheart," said Hamish and the Men of Tain started cooing again.

It was a lovely day as the children cheered the party through the palace gates and Dougie glanced back at more knights who were preparing for their own quest to another part of the kingdom and, most likely, beyond its safe borders.

The sun shone and spirits were high, even though the importance of the task weighed heavily on their shoulders. Standing amongst the crowd, Babs watched them go. Despite the presence of so many people she felt alone, but something in her heart told her that Hamish would return. She prayed that her instincts, which she could not explain, would be right.

"Stay safe, my wee Hami," she said softly.

Dougie rode next to Alistair, Donald rode by Hamish's side and six knights from Tain followed. They made good progress and when the sun was at its highest point, they stopped for food and water. Dougie rested and ate a meat pie. Hamish ate three. Alistair guessed they would reach the old fort at Kilmarnock by nightfall. By late afternoon, the land ahead was green and broken by rolling hills that were crowned with clumps of willow and birch. Dougie dismounted and rubbed the black soil between his fingers.

"Rich earth for farming."

His thoughts went out to his own land and family, and Alistair smiled at him and nodded mischievously at Hamish.

"You know, young Dougie," said Hamish, "Donald was put in charge of a farm once."

"I did not," replied Dougie, and Donald's one and a half ears pricked up.

"And did you know he was the rudest and worst farmer there has ever been?"

"I did not," admitted Dougie.

The Men of Tain were grinning.

"Aye laddie, and when his father came home all the sheep had gone and Donald's mouth was full of chicken feathers," continued Hamish. "Now do you know why Donald got into trouble?"

"Was it for losing the sheep?" asked Dougie.

"No, it was for being so fowl-mouthed."

A shield came crashing down on his head, and everyone laughed.

***

Rain lashed against Hamish's face.

"I knew it couldn't last," he said.

It was still many miles to the fort. The sun could hardly be seen through the rain and an orange tinge to the clouds told them that it was now low in the sky. The horses slipped on the muddy path and seemed reluctant to press on. Alistair's horse looked thoroughly miserable. The mare's head was down, and her light step, that had brought him this far, was now tired and forlorn.

Dougie's plaid was wet through and his back itched as water dripped, like a burn, down his neck. Through the gathering gloom he saw the path wind in and out of the valley for many miles ahead. There was no sign of house, or man, or fire.

"This is the worst part of adventures," he muttered miserably.

"No laddie," replied Alistair, "we have faced worse than this."

"And I would bet your last coin that there is worse to come," added Hamish.

203

"Aye, like a man of fire," said Donald.

The Men of Tain started to coo again.

For some time, Dougie had felt uneasy and put this down to his nervousness and imagination. He kept glancing back, over his shoulder, and yet they seemed to be alone on the hills. As the party forded a fast-flowing stream, Dougie's horse stopped to drink. He was joined by one of the men from the Black Isle, a bright lad named Robbie. As they rested, the others moved on ahead of them, and Dougie glanced back again.

"What's the matter?" asked Robbie.

"Oh, nothing. Just a feeling."

"You should listen to those feelings," warned Robbie, and they cantered to rejoin the others.

In the half-light of dusk, the weary travellers sighted shelter. Surrounded by a circular ditch and wall, was a single round-house. From the bottom of the outer ditch to the top of the wall was the height of three men. Its roughly hewn stones looked ancient and in places the defences were missing.

They rode in silence through a fallen gateway and tied their horses to posts, which seemed to be the last things holding up the wall. Dougie stood and looked at his new home. The round-house was thatched from a tall central point, down on all sides to waist height and it did not seem to have an entrance. The old fort felt lonely, abandoned long ago. Dougie felt lonely too and decided to find a way in. He walked around its sides and, after twenty paces, came to a small opening, which might have been made for a child. He went in. It was dark and smelled of sheep.

"Just like home," said a voice behind him.

Dougie turned to see Robbie's smiling face. He was about the same height as Dougie, but stockier and distinguished by an unruly red beard. Something about him made you want to smile.

"Soon have the fire going," he promised and cheerfully went about collecting wood.

Later, Robbie disappeared, whilst the warriors settled down

inside the round-house, and then he came back with two plump hares, netted on the grassy slopes around the fort. Soon, they were enjoying steaming broth and bread with cheese, and Dougie felt much better.

He was also pleased to have made such a good new friend. Robbie was a farmer too and seemed to share the same problems that Dougie had with his children. He was the kind of person who smiled when others felt down, and his stories made the evening pass quickly. Wrapped in his plaid, Dougie watched the firelight dance across the roof timbers and wondered who had built it, so many summers ago.

"They say the early Scots lived here and that, in the lowlands, there were many families who lived in small forts like this. They must have felt a great need to protect themselves and their animals," said Alistair.

"They must have been very cold in the winter."

Dougie's voice was tired and he was soon fast asleep. Whatever woke him left the others snoring and mumbling as tired men often do. He rolled on his side and listened to the wind as it swept around the thatch of the round-house and began to think an animal had startled one of the horses.

"You should listen to those feelings," said a voice like Robbie's in his mind, and he got up.

Outside, the night air was cold and there was little moonlight to see by. He walked around the walls and the hairs on his neck bristled. Was he being watched? But nothing moved and the horses seemed calm enough. Yawning, and not too pleased with himself, Dougie went back to bed.

It rained again all next day and Alistair saw no reason to stop. They rode for mile after mile in silence, and hoped to find a safe and dry place to rest in the evening. In the far distance, Dougie thought he saw the sky meet a grey sheet of flat land. As they got nearer to it, the rain stopped and the sun broke through the clouds. In front of them the Great Sea shone like gold and the riders smelled salt. For Dougie, it brought back the memories of the voyage to the far islands, aboard the *Pride of Tiree*. He glanced at Alistair and his friend nodded back, as if he was thinking exactly the same thing.

A day's ride from Stranraer, the party shared out their food and slept on the beach. Robbie had quickly built a fire from driftwood and cooked porridge from the last of the oats. Hamish had eaten most of it and, if they were tired the night before, they were now exhausted.

Despite the fact that there were ten of them, brave, hardy and well armed, Alistair ordered a watch to be kept at all times. Out here, in the open, they would be an easy target for robbers. They agreed to share the burden and, when the moon reached a set point in the sky, one watch-keeper would hand over to the next.

Typically, Robbie asked to go first and Dougie sat with him as the others settled down to rest.

"Are you still getting those feelings, laddie?" asked Robbie.

"Aye, I am, and yet I have seen nothing to make me think I should have them."

They talked for a long time about their farms and Dougie discovered that Robbie's wife was heavy with child.

"And you left her?"

"Aye laddie, the king's work is the king's work and there is still thirty days before the baby comes," stated Robbie in a matter of fact voice.

"You will be counting the days then."

Behind the red beard, Robbie smiled.

"What else is there to do?"

Dougie's watch would follow Robbie's so he wrapped himself up against the sea breeze and listened to the waves crash onto the shingle beach. When he finally slept, he saw himself walking along a path. He kept glancing back over his shoulder and quickening his pace for no reason at all. His dream darkened and as he walked, pairs of eyes watched him from a distance and seemed to follow his every move. It was as though he should be somewhere else, but no matter which way he turned, the eyes were there and a soft voice was saying, "Dougie, Dougie." The voice grew louder and called his name. Hands grabbed at him and one shook his shoulder. He woke with a start and looked up into Hamish's face.

"Dougie, you didn't wake me for the watch."

Dougie sat up, yawned and blinked in bright morning sunshine.

"Nobody woke me."

Alistair was running along the beach and calling out, "Robbie, Robbie," and, suddenly, Dougie realised that his friend was missing. He leapt to his feet and joined the others. With claymores ready they walked in all directions from the camp, their cries growing fainter as the search widened. Dougie thought back to his dream and glanced around for an enemy, for he now felt sure someone *had* been watching them as they journeyed from the palace.

The beach changed from shingle to sand and, after a few paces, Dougie saw many footprints leading back towards the path. He called to the others and started to run up the slope of a dune. Near the top, he caught his foot on a clump of coarse grass and found himself peering down into a sandy hollow. It was full of black flies and smelled of death.

At its base was Robbie. He was lying on his back with unblinking eyes, which stared fearfully skywards. He was cold and still as stone, and the blade of a great axe was buried in his bloody chest.

CHAPTER FOURTEEN

LEGEND OF THE WATCHTOWER

With its cottages forming a ring around a small stone harbour, Stranraer looked like a horseshoe, standing defiant against the Great Sea. Four fishing boats were tied to a quay and many others were returning from their work in the far distance.

It was late and they did not expect to see many folk on the road, but a long line of people was moving slowly towards the beach. The party watched them in silence. On the sea breeze, they heard crying and a mournful song that spoke of tragedy.

The wind blew through Alistair's hair and he glanced across at Dougie.

"Something has happened," he said. "This will not be a good time to introduce ourselves."

The line of mourners stopped and formed a circle around a small boat, which was pulled up onto the shingle. They were too far away to hear exactly what was going on, but they could guess. After some time, the craft was pushed, by many hands, into the sea and tongues of flame leapt up inside it. Eventually, the waves began to overwhelm the listing boat and the ocean claimed it. Then, as slowly as they had arrived, the crowd walked slowly back to the village.

"A funeral," said Donald, and their thoughts went back to poor Robbie.

"Aye," replied Hamish in a sad voice.

"We will need to be careful as we go down," warned Alistair.

"Aye," agreed Dougie, for strangers could never expect a warm welcome, especially when a death had occurred. Still, they were tired and hungry, and no one saw the point of spending another night under open skies.

The horses made their way down the sandy path and, as the light faded, cottage fires shone out through tiny windows.

"Is there a tavern?" asked Dougie.

"There was," replied Alistair, "but it is many summers since I was here."

They tied up their horses and walked around the harbour. Two men sat behind the shelter of a roughly hewn sea wall and mended nets. Dougie and his friends stopped to watch them and the fishermen ignored them, preferring work to conversation. Even their boats looked as though they would rather be left to their own company and, like the men, they had a tough, weathered appearance. All the woodwork was bleached grey by the attack of wind and sun and storm.

The *Leather Bottle* was a white, stone building and not unpleasant to the eye. Its small door faced the sea and a trail of smoke puffed out of a stumpy chimney. The sound of merrymaking could just be heard though its thick walls.

Alistair called his men together and asked for two volunteers to enter first.

"We shall appear less threatening if we go in dribs and drabs."

Donald and Hamish went off to pave the way. The others waited quietly for their signal to follow.

The evening sea breeze was bitter and Dougie pulled his plaid round his neck. He looked up the lane at the cottages, and still saw nothing to confirm his suspicions about an unknown enemy.

One of the Men of Tain pointed back at the harbour. The last of the fishing boats were coming home to unload their catch and Dougie decided that tending the flock was far easier than winning anything from the ocean. One of the boats was called *The Cormorant* and it was steered by a giant of a man who was at least as tall and broad as Hamish. He also had a thick black beard.

Alistair saw Dougie's stare.

"Many of the peoples of the west have black beards. They may still be loyal Scots and it is not a sign that they are of the Pictish people."

Dougie nodded, shivered and settled himself to wait for his friends.

As Donald entered the tavern, the full flow of conversation stopped. Men sitting on low stools eyed him suspiciously, particularly when Big Hamish stooped through the door and raised himself to his true height. After an awkward pause, the locals continued their stories as if they were not there at all. An old man, with a wrinkly brown face, stared at Donald and finally gave him a smile.

"You will be strangers then," he said.

"Aye, tired and hungry strangers who seek the comfort of the tavern," replied Donald.

"And what is your business?"

"We are on honest business and may only stay a short while," growled Hamish.

"And where are you from?"

"We are Men of Tain," said Donald honestly.

The old man looked at them and went to the other side of the bar.

"If you are from Tain you will like your heather ale."

He poured them a goblet each.

Donald and Hamish sipped the golden liquid and Hamish said, "This is not from Tain. Must be a Lowland ale."

The innkeeper smiled, nodded approvingly and added, "Excuse my caution, but we get few visitors from the outside and many strange things have been happening around here lately. My name is Calder and may I welcome you to the *Leather Bottle*, the finest inn in all Stranraer."

A local man coughed.

"And ….. true, the only inn in Stranraer."

He smiled again and his face became creased.

"You said strange things have been happening?" growled Hamish.

Calder glanced around anxiously and caught the eye of a surly looking man in a black cloak, who sat alone in a corner.

"Oh, nothing really. Would you like a room for the night?"

"We all would," said Donald.

Calder's eyebrow lifted a full inch.

"*All* would?"

"We have travelled far and the roads are too dangerous for two alone," added Hamish.

Calder watched the top of Hamish's head scrape against the ceiling.

"You look as though you are big enough to look after yourself. Still, do not let them wait outside. Fetch them in. Fetch them in."

Donald went to the door and beckoned the others to join him.

"Nine. So many!" exclaimed Calder, but he welcomed them and arranged benches in a half circle around the fireplace.

Soon the party was fed and watered, and they settled down to a pleasant night under cover. Dougie noticed that at first the fishermen were reluctant to involve them in their conversation, but after an hour the mood of the inn relaxed and the travellers were treated to stories about fierce storms and giant fish, which had got away.

Wee Andy, who seemed to be able to tell a fine story, entertained them for a long time. He asked if they had seen the funeral and they said they had, but from a distance.

"Aye, aye, it is a bad business," he drawled, "and so young too."

"So young?" asked Dougie.

"Aye, aye, och aye," drawled the fisherman, "a boy, only fourteen summers young. Dared by his friends to go to the watchtower after dark. Aye, a great tragedy for the village and the third not to heed the warnings given to us."

"The warnings?" asked Dougie nervously.

"Aye, aye, och aye, if only I could remember them."

Andy stared down at his empty goblet and Dougie smiled, and nodded at Calder to recharge the man's memory.

"It all started when my father was a boy," continued Andy. "The greatest fisherman in those days was One Arm Mac. It was said he could *smell* the fish beneath the waves and brave any storm, even when others would cower in their beds as they listened to the screaming winds."

He paused and sipped his ale. The audience, including the locals who had obviously heard this one before, sat in respectful silence.

"Then on the night of a great storm, One Arm Mac was begged by his wife not to set out for the fishing grounds off Watchtower Point. He laughed at her and went off to find a willing crew. But no one would join him. No man who respects the power of wind and wave would. But Mac respected nothing and he left the safety of the harbour, under quarter sail, grinning as he battled against the gale."

Andy paused and looked sadly down at his last drops of heather ale.

"It is a shame for the last part is the best part and I am not sure if I can remember how it goes."

Calder raised an eyebrow again and Donald, who was clearly enjoying the story, offered to stand another round of drinks.

"Aye, it was perhaps the most terrible storm these coasts have ever seen," mumbled Andy and he stared into the fire, as if remembering all the dark nights that had been sent to test the fisher folk of Stranraer.

"Aye, aye, och aye," drawled Andy, "and so it was that on that terrible night, One Arm Mac braved the storm. He held the ropes from the sail in his teeth and steered for the open sea with his one arm on the tiller. True, he had done it before, but as any man who makes his living from the sea will tell you, the ocean has its own moods and desires and will not be cheated by those who laugh in its very face."

Several of the Men of Tain, themselves fishermen, nodded gravely in agreement.

"And so it was that as the village slept, a ghostly bell sounded on the wind. It tolled and tolled for hours, and no sign of it could be found. It was as though some phantom of the sea had decided it was time for Mac to leave this world."

He stared up at the ceiling and Dougie was alarmed to see that Andy's ale was going the same way as poor Old Mac.

"The wind roared and waves crashed across the harbour wall onto this very inn. No soul had ever known a night like it and, to this day, no storm has ever been as fierce."

Andy paused again and the only sound came from the logs, which hissed and cracked in the fire.

"Aye, aye, och aye, a terrible way to die," and he raised his voice and rolled his eyes, "a terrible way to die."

A shiver went down Dougie's spine.

"The bell tolls for anyone who dares to defy the Great Ocean, dares to sail near the old watchtower, and to this day only fools brave the curse of One Arm Mac. Those who do are found washed up on the beach at high tide. Mac's boat was never seen again, and of Mac, only his hand, his bloody severed hand, was ever found."

Dougie shuddered again.

"And so my advice to any stranger is, beware the storm, beware the watchtower in the hours of darkness and heed the warning of the phantom bell."

"Cheery isn't he?" said Alistair, as Andy was rewarded with another dram.

Donald looked up at Hamish.

"Does old Mac scare you?"

"No laddie, he seems 'armless enough to me."

Listening to the stories and warmed by the fire, Dougie became slightly more relaxed than perhaps he should have been. When asked by a local why they had travelled to Stranraer, he said, "We are on the king's business," and Alistair kicked his shin.

Out of the corner of his eye, Dougie noticed the man with the black cloak make his way to the tavern door. He cursed himself for being so stupid and decided to go to bed early. In one of the back rooms of the inn, he lay wrapped in his plaid, and remembered the events of the day. In a place halfway towards sleep, Dougie began to believe he was not alone and became uneasy, even though there was no sound, or movement. A cold chill ran down his spine as darkness changed to silvery moonlight and then back to darkness again.

He turned to look at the window and thought he saw the outline of an old man, sitting in the half light of the deep sill. Dougie froze with fear and could only manage a single, nervous, whispered word.

"Hello."

"Hello," replied the man in a deep, rough voice, "you are not from these parts."

"No," said Dougie.

"Are you a sailor?"

"I am a farmer and these are indeed strange lands to me."

"Aye," agreed the shadow, "will you be needing a boat to aid your search?"

Dougie tried to turn his head to get a better look at the window, but no part of his body seemed to want to move.

"I do ….. not know."

"Sailing around these waters is a dangerous business."

"I know that," replied Dougie and he thought about the terrible storm that had once carried them to the island of Mull.

The man smiled as if he was grinning into the wind.

"Well if you ever need a boat, seek me out and I will be *pleased* to help you."

"Thank you, and how shall I call you?" asked Dougie, fearfully.

The man rose and walked slowly to the door. Dougie thought he only had one arm.

"Call me Mac," he said, and he left the room.

With visions of ghosts in his mind, Dougie tried to settle down for the night and by the time Alistair joined him, he was fast asleep. Outside the inn, a cold wind picked up and the slender branches of a fir tree brushed against their window. Somewhere, in a distant field, an owl hooted as she searched her territory for food and, despite it all, the friends enjoyed a deep and peaceful slumber.

Whilst they slept, a mournful *clang* sounded in the dark hours and many of the villagers listened, afraid of what they could not see, or truly understand. The phantom bell rang out across land and sea, and those who listened to its dreadful toll checked the bolts on their doors and cowered, wide eyed, in their beds.

Dougie awoke to a stream of bright sunshine. As he lay in his warm plaid, he looked at the window and remembered the strange man who had sat there. Any fears he might have had about meeting the ghost of One Arm Mac, seemed to dissolve in the daylight and he decided not to mention anything about it to his friends. They were bound to make fun of him and his imagination.

Breakfast was fine and hearty. Fried haddock, warm bread and jugs of cool milk were brought before them. As they finished one plate, the busy innkeeper would cheerfully bring another, and even Hamish ate his fill.

"Will you be leaving today?" asked Calder.

"No, we need to stay for a while longer," replied Alistair.

"Did you not hear the bells?" asked Calder in a grave voice.

"No, what bells?"

The others shook their heads at Alistair to show that they too had not heard them.

"It was a warning, a terrible warning," cried Calder and he glanced around the room as if some phantom might be listening, and Dougie's thoughts went back to the funeral for the young boy the day before. For him, that was warning enough.

As they mounted their horses, Donald asked, "Well, we are in Stranraer, so what is to be done?"

"I don't know," admitted Alistair, "does anyone have any ideas?"

"We need to have a good look around and that's for sure," added one of the Men of Tain.

"Wise words," said Donald, "and it would be quicker if we split up to do it."

217

They decided to divide themselves up into three groups. One group to head back north along the coast road, another to explore the lands to the south, and the last to try to find if there was anything suspicious in the area around Stranraer itself.

"We meet again at the tavern at sunset," ordered Alistair, and the riders went about their work.

It was a beautiful day and, if anything, a bit boring at first. Alistair, Hamish and Dougie rode for many miles through the fields and lanes around the village. They tried to speak to the local people, but they would lower their heads and usher their children away, as if being near them might bring some terrible tragedy.

"Friendly lot," moaned Hamish, but Dougie thought they looked scared of something.

"I think this business with old Mac and the bells is just a load of nonsense, brought about to scare the local people," said Alistair.

"It scares me," muttered Dougie.

"Why would anyone want to scare them?" asked Hamish.

"So they stay away from the old watchtower," replied Alistair grimly, "and that is why we need to go there."

"I don't like the sound of that," thought Dougie, but he turned his horse to follow the others along a sandy track, which snaked its way towards the far headland.

As they got closer, they saw that the tower was perched upon a high cliff. It looked ancient and desolate and, to Dougie, just the sort of place where a phantom might live. It didn't seem to have any windows or doors and the walls were made of large slabs of grey stone. Some of the stones had fallen down and, despite their strength, the years had worn them smooth.

The sandy path narrowed and great clumps of gorse grew right across it. This path had long been abandoned to the will of nature. The horses couldn't go any further and so they tethered them on long reins to enjoy the sunshine, and whatever grass they could find.

The climb to the top of the headland was steep and difficult, and Dougie had to stop many times to catch his breath. When he finally reached the top, Alistair was already walking around the base of the tower, searching for a way inside. He found a small door, on the seaward side, made of thick oak panels. It had seen better days and hung on a single rusted hinge. Hamish tossed it aside as if it was a chair and, nervously, Dougie followed his friends into the gloom.

They stood at the bottom of a spiral staircase, which rose up inside the tower. As they climbed, any light from the doorway deserted them and Dougie groped his way forward, placing one tentative foot in front of the other. He counted ten steps and lost his balance on a loose stone, and fell forward and cursed. His hand came down onto something that felt like thin pebbles, all strung together. He kept hold of it, and tried to guess what it was.

Hamish lifted him back onto his feet.

"Are you alright?"

"Aye," replied Dougie, "but I will be mighty glad to get back into sunshine."

"Me too," admitted Hamish, and the friends moved on.

At the top of the old watchtower, Alistair stared out across the Great Sea.

"I can understand why they built the tower here," he said, "this must be the highest point of land in these parts."

He glanced down. Burnt logs lay amongst a charred circle of grey ash.

"So even ghosts need a fire to keep warm," he thought.

As Dougie reached his side, he saw Stranraer and its harbour, like a toy, below them. But the ocean dominated the view. It really was a beautiful day and Dougie imagined that from up here your eyes could reach out to the very end of the world. They stood together, in awed silence, and watched the sea.

"What are you are holding, laddie?" asked Hamish.

Dougie opened his fingers and fainted. The skeleton of a man's hand, held together by decaying gristle, fell to the floor.

After his friend's shock, Alistair decided they should return to the horses and have food. They ate happily enough and Dougie was glad to be out in the fresh air for the place scared him even in daylight.

When the sun was at its high point, they decided to go back to the harbour and take a boat out, and study the coast in a different way. They gathered the horses together and Hamish asked Dougie if he needed a *hand*. This greatly amused Alistair, and Dougie suffered a long line of comments, such as, "Could you *hand* me that?" and, "Is this view not *hand*some?"

The fishermen on the quay seemed as reluctant to talk to them as everyone else in the village. One by one they were refused the loan of a ship and their money made no difference at all. Finally, they came across the *Cormorant* and Dougie recognised the owner; a giant of a man with a thick black beard.

"Will you take us upon the sea?" asked Alistair.

The man looked them over and seemed to be turning something over in his mind.

"I am Gordon. Are the nine of you to go?"

"No, just we three," replied Alistair and he wondered how he knew there were nine of them.

"Ten coins," he smiled.

"Ten coins," complained Hamish, "you don't know an old woman at Culross, do you?"

The man shrugged his shoulders.

"Ten coins is agreed," agreed Alistair, "*hand* it over, Dougie."

Dougie still felt unsure about Gordon, but as the afternoon wore on, it became clear that the skipper knew his boat and the moods of the ocean. They speared sea bass and, in the sunshine, the visit to the watchtower and their quest to find the makers of light iron, were soon forgotten.

Gordon proved his knowledge about the currents, tides and habits of the fish. But he never sailed anywhere near the watchtower. The waves were small, even a good way from the shore, and Dougie felt mighty relieved. The sun was low in the sky and turning a bright orange, to celebrate the end of a fine day. But Gordon stared at a line of dark clouds on the far horizon.

"Bad weather coming. It will not take the clouds long to get here."

As he said the words, a strong breeze ran across the deck.

"Can we go across to the cliff below the old watchtower?" asked Alistair.

The skipper seemed taken aback by this, but he managed a smile.

"I would like to. This time of year the fishing is good, in the shallows around Tower Point. But the rocks beneath the cliff are sharp and dangerous."

Alistair nodded and Gordon turned the *Cormorant* towards the safe waters of Stranraer harbour. With the breeze on their backs, the boat sped shoreward and it was just before dusk when they tied up at the quay. Donald was there to greet them.

"Catch anything?" he asked.

"Supper," said Hamish cheerfully, "did you?"

"Not a thing," and they all knew he meant he hadn't found any trace of the enemy either.

Back at the *Leather Bottle* they talked about their adventures and waited for the others, the party who had gone south, to return. By the end of supper, Dougie sensed Alistair was worried.

"Still no sign?" he asked.

"No," replied Hamish, "I think I might take a wee wander up to the main path to see where they are."

Donald went with him and they returned with no news, and it was decided that nothing could be done until morning, and they went to their beds. Tucked in against the cold, Dougie watched Alistair. He was staring up at the ceiling, deep in thought, and Dougie decided to leave his friend to his thoughts, and dozed off.

"Wake up," whispered Alistair.

"Huh," mumbled Dougie.

"Get Hamish and Donald."

"Why?"

"Because we have the king's work to do."

A few minutes later, four sleepy Scots sat, with claymores in their hands, on the harbour wall.

"What are we waiting for?" asked Donald.

"The signal," said Alistair.

"What signal?" yawned Hamish.

On the wind, from far away, a bell slowly rang out. *Clang Clang Clang.* They all stood up, fearful of the noise.

Alistair said, "That signal," and he walked towards the edge of the village.

"Where are we going?" asked Donald.

"Don't ask that," thought Dougie.

"To the watchtower," replied Alistair.

"I knew it," said Dougie and, with his head down, he followed the others on the long journey to the base of the headland.

Everything seemed different at night and Dougie noticed that the bright, sand-coloured hill path, which they had climbed that morning, was now like a black snake. It twisted up to a terrible stone head at the very top of the cliff. In the darkness, there was a strong and heady smell as broom, stock and sea campion competed together to scent the air. Many times he stumbled and once he cursed loudly, as his hand clasped around sharp gorse for support.

Alistair grabbed him and thrust a hand across his mouth.

"Keep quiet, or all will be lost."

With the tower in sight across open grass, the friends watched for any sign of an enemy. The wind whipped across the cliff and the first drops of rain began to fall. The bell continued to toll, mournfully, and was definitely louder here. It seemed to come from the very bowels of the Earth.

They stood like statues, but no light shone out of the doorway, or from the top of the tower. Dougie looked across to the clifftop and, for a moment, a cloud moved away from the moon, and the headland was bathed in silvery moonlight. He thought he saw an old man, with one arm, studying him. Dougie tried to get his friends' attention, but they were staring at the tower. He glanced back, and the man had disappeared into darkness.

Eventually, Alistair dashed to the entrance and waited, motionless, with his back pressed up against the outer wall beside the door. He waved at them to follow and Donald went inside first. Dougie followed him and could barely make out Donald's shadow at the base of the spiral staircase.

"I cannot see a thing," boomed a deep voice behind them.

Dougie turned to see Hamish's huge outline. When he turned back, Donald had gone.

"Donald has disappeared," whispered Dougie urgently, "he was here, right in front of me, and now he has gone."

Secretly, he wondered if Donald had gone the same way as the shadowy figure on the cliff.

Alistair spoke in a calm voice.

"He cannot just disappear. Listen."

The friends stood in silence and Dougie thought that he heard a terrible, phantom-like moaning,

"Aaaah, aaaah, aaaah."

"It is One Arm Mac," warned Dougie in a scared voice.

Then a warm glow rose up through the floor. It was dim and ghostly at first, and then it grew brighter.

"Aaaaah, aaaaah," moaned a weak voice.

"It is Mac rising from the underworld," whispered Dougie.

Alistair gripped his arm to reassure him and Hamish raised his claymore. Suddenly, Donald's head popped up through a hole in the ground.

"Hello. Guess what I've found."

"It looks like a hole," said Hamish.

"Not just a hole, come and see."

A man's height below a trap door in the floor, at the base of the watchtower, was a small room. There were wooden steps leading down to it and, once inside, Donald's torch revealed a tunnel. The tunnel disappeared into the earth and seemed to go on forever. Every hundred paces, a torch was held to the side of the wall by an iron spike. Dougie tried to count them and stopped at fifteen.

"So that's how they do it," whispered Alistair.

"Do what?" asked Donald.

"We will talk about that later," continued Alistair. "Hamish, go to the top of the tower with Donald. If you see a man warming his one hand on a fire, throw him to the fishes."

In the firelight, Dougie saw Hamish raise his eyebrows and then nod in agreement.

"When you are done, wait by the entrance of the tower and keep it free from the enemy. That's our escape route."

"And where are you two going?" asked Donald.

Alistair grabbed Donald's torch and pointed it down the tunnel. Dougie felt the hairs on his neck stand up.

The friends split up and Dougie followed Alistair. The way was well lit and they only stopped in the half-light, between torches, to listen out for strange sounds. But all they heard was the mournful toll of a bell. The friends made steady progress and, gradually, the bell was accompanied by the sound of waves.

Sometimes they had to duck, as the ceiling lowered and Dougie noticed the tunnel floor changed from hard rock to sand. The sand was dry for a good way and then became damp.

"The sea must come up here at high tide," said Alistair.

Dougie wasn't comforted by this, but pushed on to be with his friend. Eventually, the tunnel widened out and they froze. Loud banging noises and the voices of men echoed towards them.

Alistair placed his torch on the ground and beckoned at Dougie to follow him. They inched forward and the tunnel ended in a rocky, high-sided inlet. To their right was the open sea. To their left a large ship. A rope ran from the ship's rail, by the bow, to a great bell, which was chained below a rocky overhang. As the waves raced into the channel, the boat rose and fell and the bell tolled out its terrible warning.

The far side of the inlet was covered in wooden boxes, stacked high by a line of men who worked from the deck of the ship to the shore. Many of the warriors had black beards. They all wore black kilts.

"Picts," whispered Dougie.

"Aye, Picts, and look what they are doing," replied Alistair.

Dougie watched as each man passed a box to the next. On the small dock, beside the ship, stood Gordon, directing the soldiers as they unloaded the cargo. One man dropped a crate and many iron swords fell noisily to the floor.

Gordon's face went red with anger.

"Be careful, you fool, these swords are worth more than gold."

"I've seen enough," whispered Alistair, "let's go back."

"Hold on," urged Dougie and he pointed at the ship.

The water seemed to be ebbing slowly back out into the ocean and several of the Picts were ordered to leave the chain of box-carriers and go to the ship's mast. A sail was unfurled and it carried a sign. Three legs, joined together at the hip.

Alistair's voice became grim.

"That is the symbol of the people of Man."

They listened as Gordon barked orders at his men.

"Borak and Tumora. Throw them into the sea."

The Black Kilts lifted up long, heavy bundles and balanced them, one by one, on top of the ship's rail. Then the tartan packages were dumped, without respect, into the cold, cruel sea. Three lifeless splashes.

Dougie fell to his knees as the bodies of their missing friends floated away on the tide.

CHAPTER FIFTEEN

ACROSS THE SEA TO MAN

There had been a lot of discussion until the small hours, and Donald and Hamish had wanted to know everything about the ship, the bell and the secret inlet. Duncan and Dougal, the remaining members of the party, were brought in too and Alistair took them into his confidence.

"As I see it, Black Kilts have been landing arms, many arms, made of the new light iron, right here in Stranraer. The locals are kept away from the watchtower by the story of old Mac and his ghostly bells. The bells are used to guide boats into the secret inlet, in the dark hours, when there is no moon. They also build a fire on the top of the tower. At sea, you must be able to see it from miles away and yet nobody looking from the village would ever know it was there."

"But why are they doing it?" asked Donald, who put words to what everyone was thinking.

"I don't know," replied Alistair truthfully, "but the answer lies across the sea."

Dougie remembered the tolling bell and the three legs on the ship's sail.

"On the Island of Man," he said in a quiet voice.

"Aye, on Man," replied Alistair.

"And what shall we do next?" asked Hamish.

"Two things," said Alistair. "Firstly, Duncan and Dougal must ride to the palace, with all speed, and tell Malcolm about the Picts in Stranraer. He will decide what to do about them. Secondly, the rest of us must sail to Man and we cannot leave from anywhere near here. In fact, I know just the person to help us." He paused mysteriously.

"But how can we leave Stranraer without raising suspicion?" asked Dougal.

"In the morning, I have no doubt we shall be brought bad news. If I'm right, the bodies of our friends that were dumped into the channel will be washed up on the beach, adding to the fear that Mac walks the cliffs at night. When we are told, we shall pretend to fear for our own lives and then flee, promising never to return."

"Shall we not stay to build a cairn to their memory?" asked Dougie.

"No, we go at the first opportunity," said Alistair.

It was raining again when the tired Scots rose and ate. It was not long before a fisherman came running into the inn, and the friends played out their story, paid Calder his due and rode towards the coastal path. After half a day's ride, Duncan and Dougal left them and headed east towards the old fort at Kilmarnock. The rest continued north to seek out an old friend. Three days later, four horsemen rode into view of a grey and angry sea. They were tired, hungry and soaked to the skin. Tall waves crashed onto the harbour wall and the small port of Oban looked as though it clung helplessly to the shore.

Alistair led them down narrow lanes to a small cottage on the edge of the village. The window shone with a warm glow and, once again, Dougie saw the model of a ship on the sill.

Kenneth of Blacklock was as grumpy and welcoming as ever. He bade them in with a grunt and then made sure they were warm, dry and fed. Soon they were discussing the events at Stranraer and the task ahead.

"I sailed to Man five summers ago, seeking the fish with my brother, Helden" said Kenneth, "and at that time they were loyal to the Welsh King, Llewellyn."

"The Welsh King?" asked Dougie.

Kenneth gave him a rare smile. "Aye, laddie, Man is, and always has been, at the very centre of trade and war. Generations ago it was held by the Irish and then the Angles. Even the Scots ruled over it once, and its people have become fierce and independent by nature."

"What are the people like?" asked Hamish, as he bit into a thick piece of crust, the last remnants of a fish pie.

"Much like you, or me," replied Kenneth, "and certainly they have no love for the Picts, who they see as greedy and dishonourable."

"They don't seem too bad," said Dougie.

Kenneth scowled and the small room went quiet.

"Not too bad until they decide they do not like you. If the weather turns, we can leave on the morning tide."

He left them to prepare for the long journey.

They spent a pleasant evening drying out and talking about their last voyage across the Great Sea. The wind eased and the rain did not seem to be falling with the same ferocity, and Dougie wondered how Duncan and Dougal were getting on. As if sensing his thoughts, Alistair said,

"They should be at the Younger's Palace by now."

In fact, Duncan and Dougal were surrounded by Black Kilts and fighting for their lives. As the Picts charged the gate at the Old Fort at Kilmarnock, the two brave Scots drove them back again. Borak and Tumora urged their horses into a gallop and charged. Borak swung his axe and it sliced into Dougal's shoulder, and he fell in pain to the ground. Loyally, Duncan stood over him, circling a claymore above his head, and watching helplessly as ten of the enemy advanced towards them.

Gordon, one of Tella's most trusted warriors and the man chosen to replace Torik Ben, smiled.

"Where are the others?" he demanded.

"At the palace of the true king," lied Duncan.

"You are not telling me the truth." Gordon spat on the ground. "No matter, we will find them."

He laughed and waved Borak and Tumora, and the foot-soldiers, forward for the kill.

***

Kenneth woke them at daybreak with mugs of a wonderful fish broth and told them to hurry down to the quay. The *Pride of Tiree* was in fine condition and her polished brass shone in the morning light. The skipper had obviously been busy, for supplies of all kinds were tied to the deck. These included a huge barrel of fresh water and half a carcass of salted mutton, roped to the barrel's side.

"Let go aft," demanded Kenneth, and Dougie ran to the back of the ship and threw the rope ashore. The old sailor smiled at him, approvingly.

"You could make a fine hand."

"Don't mention *hands*," said Dougie as he raced to let go forward, but the others soon started on the *hand* jokes again.

They all knew that in the safe waters of Oban Sound the trip would be calm and pleasant. But beyond the Sound was deep water and Dougie was dreading it. He just had time to warn Hamish as the last point of land passed by.

"Hold on to your breakfast."

The ship began to rise and fall as it drove through bigger waves. Dougie occupied himself with ropes, with anything, anything at all, and even took over the tiller from Kenneth. But, keeping busy was no defence against the return of the sickness and when Donald was sick over the side, he had no choice but to make a dash for the ship's rail.

"A farmer's place …… is definitely ….. in the fields," groaned Dougie, as his fish broth rose up inside him like an erupting volcano.

Dougie felt completely at the mercy of the cruel sea and suffered ridicule from those who escaped it. Alistair and Kenneth seemed to take great amusement from the shade of green of their faces, and laughed heartily at the miserable state of their friends. Dougie prayed for the passage to end, but they had only been sailing for an hour and the journey to Man would take two days and nights.

Big Hamish cried, "Oh no!" and then, "hueeey," as he was sick over the side.

It was like a chain reaction and poor Donald and Dougie pointed their mouths again at the waiting sea.

"Better out than in," encouraged Alistair.

"When I …… get the use of my ….. body back …. hueeey!

…. I am going ….. hueeey! ….. to brain you," gasped Donald.

"See what I told you, Kenneth," continued Alistair, "you cannot get the same quality of warrior as you used to."

"I'll give you …… the ….. hueeey! …. 'the same quality of warrior,'" gasped Donald.

"Will you? Will you really?" asked Alistair. "Good, good." He grinned at Kenneth.

But even the terrible curse of the oceans does not last forever. By sunset, on the first day, the waves had calmed and, refreshed with drinking water, the friends settled down to recover from their ordeal. Dougie took over the tiller from Kenneth and the Men of Tain decided to fish for their supper.

Donald's line caught first, but from the easy way he could pull it towards the ship, they knew it was a poor reward for the effort. Hamish did not seem to be having any luck either, and sat, bored, staring at the waves. Then his line tightened too and it bit deep into his skin.

"Tie the line to this," shouted Alistair, and frantically Hamish wrapped the cord to a stout wooden pole.

A long battle followed. Hamish pulled and his mighty arms gained a small advantage. Then the line slackened and suddenly tightened, as the fish turned and used its full weight against him.

Dougie noticed Kenneth's face. It was lined with concern.

"What's the matter?" he asked.

"I have seen a fish behaving on the line like this before," he replied grimly, "keep the tiller."

He took a dirk from his sock.

"This will feed us for days," said Donald.

"Donald, help him bring the fish to the side of the ship," ordered Kenneth.

Struggling together and risking a snapped line, the two friends made slow progress and at last a thrashing body hit wood.

"Tie it here," ordered Kenneth, "and do NOT put your hands over the side."

Hamish and Donald looked at each other, but they did as they were told and were mighty glad they did.

Standing someway back from the rail, the crew got a brief glimpse of a long, thin tail. Its dull brown skin glistened as it broke the surface. Hamish leant further forward to get a closer look and Kenneth grabbed him, and pulled him back.

"Fool," yelled Kenneth.

Suddenly, a giant head leapt up and rows of sharp teeth, like spines, bit deep into the ship's rail. The devilfish hung there, studying them through small, evil, black eyes. Its head was the size of a man's chest and its coiling body many times that in length.

"Conger!" warned Kenneth, and he cut through the line with his knife.

The great eel went back into the deep, as quickly as it had leapt up, and the friends stared at each other and decided they had had enough fishing for one day.

Before dusk, the sky turned black and Kenneth ordered them to lash anything which could move to the deck. The waves began to rise and a thin drizzle dampened their spirits. The wind stopped. The *Pride of Tiree* floated in calm waters and Dougie watched the skipper. He looked like he had when the devilfish had leapt up at them.

"Get the sail down now," he shouted.

They untied the ropes, the brown cloth fell and it was rolled up quickly, and lashed to the deck.

"What's the hurry?" asked Donald.

The skipper ignored him. The answer to his question was screaming across the sea like another devil. With a deafening scream, the storm broke upon them and the ship was thrown, madly, from side to side, like a cork in a stream. The air howled and the rigging sang as ropes were hit by ferocious winds.

Dougie had never been so scared. He was helpless. All he could do was hang on for dear life and watch Kenneth steer into each towering wave. Waves like mountains. Water poured onboard and, as each deluge threatened to sink them, they filled canvas buckets and emptied them over the rail.

This went on for an eternity, and many times they believed they would drown. The storm showed no sign of easing and if the ship was ever to face a wave, sideways on, it would surely be swamped and lost.

Kenneth had a look of incredible determination on his face, but even he was having trouble steering a safe course. Most of the time he couldn't even see where he was heading. The rain lashed out at them and seemed to be fired, like an arrow, across the deck. Their eyes stung as it hit them.

Dougie was exhausted. He knelt and filled his bucket, and threw the heavy water overboard. But, time and time again, the boat leant over and cold sea rushed in to replace anything he managed to toss out.

"Keep bailing," shouted Kenneth.

Dougie kept bailing.

Then Kenneth's manner changed. For an age, he had struggled with the tiller and looked as though nothing could sway him from that single, vital task. But now he stood upright, still, alert. Listening intently for any sounds other than those of the mighty gale. His eyes widened and he stared ahead. Dougie followed his gaze, but couldn't see anything except white foam on angry waves.

"Land!" yelled Kenneth.

Donald thought he could hear a distant rumbling noise, cutting through the screaming wind. He tried to stand, to get a better view, and was thrown, roughly, back onto the deck as the ship lurched skyward. Dougie tried to stand and fell over too.

"There," shouted Hamish, and his outstretched arm pointed towards the bow.

The wind was now squarely behind them and it drove them, without mercy, towards a line of dark cliffs, where they would surely be smashed to pieces. Angry lightning lit the sky. Seconds later, a huge clap of thunder deafened them. Another white streak shot down from the heavens and struck the mast. It burst into flames like a torch. Kenneth battled to keep the ship from capsizing and plumes of water crashed over the sides, and drenched them.

Dougie grasped the ship's rail as though his life depended on it. It did. He peered forward, towards the land, and saw enormous waves battering a line of cliffs. The cliffs seemed to form an impenetrable wall of rock and, in his heart, he knew they had no chance of avoiding them. The wind increased its fury and they shot forward at an unbelievable speed. There was a ripping sound, as the hull scraped its way over the submerged teeth of the shallows. The ship lurched violently, onto its side, and splinters of wood flew up into the air.

"This is it," thought Dougie, but he hung on.

Now everyone was exhausted and only Kenneth worked to hold some kind of a course. Suddenly, he raised his arm and shouted.

"There," and they all looked.

But when the lightning flashed again, they could only make out the profile of the cliffs. As tall as twenty men.

"Donald, what's he on about?" yelled Hamish.

"No idea," cried Donald, but no one heard him.

"There," shouted Kenneth again.

Alistair leapt up to help him push the shaking tiller to one side. The boat lurched.

Kenneth shouted, "Keep your hands in the boat."

"Where else would I put them?" cried Donald and, for a second time, no one heard him.

Dougie stared ahead and prayed. A bolt of forked lightning attacked the land at the top of the cliffs and, for a single second, he thought he saw a gap in the hills to their left. Jagged rocks lined both sides of what might be a thin channel. Behind him, two dark shapes wrestled with the tiller to steer a course towards it.

A huge wave lifted the boat and tipped it forward. They raced ahead and sliced the boiling sea in two. The rail above Dougie's head snapped off, like a twig from a tree, as it hit an overhanging rock. The boat lurched and there was a mighty *crash* as wood was ripped apart by stone. Then they fell as the wave retreated. Another wave picked them up and threw everyone forward. The noise was incredible, deafening, and cold spray drenched them.

"Hang on," shouted Kenneth.

Tall rocks, on both sides of the ship, tore at the planks without mercy. Another monstrous wave raised the boat and, like a cork popping out of a bottle, they were spat down the narrow inlet. As they fell again, a rock burst through the deck by Dougie's feet. Then the rock was gone, as the broken and battered carcass of the *Pride of Tiree* was dumped, ungraciously, onto a small shingle beach.

They all jumped down onto land and Donald knelt to kiss it. Kenneth ordered them to tie the ship to rocks and, in torrential rain, it was finally secured.

"Welcome to Man," laughed Alistair, but Kenneth was in no mood for laughing.

He stared at the wreck of his boat. Great open gashes ran down both sides of the hull, the mast was burnt away and a complete corner of the stern was missing.

"She has had her day," muttered Kenneth, and Dougie was left to wonder if they might ever get home.

They worked until daylight, unloading what was left of their provisions. The water barrel and mutton were gone, but they still had their claymores, apples and some oat cakes. The beach led up to a steep cliff and at its base was an overhang of rock, which provided some shelter. As the first rays of sun shone beneath the black clouds, they huddled together to sleep.

Dougie saw Kenneth sitting apart from the others. He was staring down at a piece of wood. It was broken in two and bore a single word. *Pride*. He decided to ask his friend about the island, in part to learn about its land and people, and partly to take Kenneth's mind away from the ship he had loved and lost.

The sailor *was* thinking about his ship, but for a reason. He was saying a last goodbye to Helden.

"Man is one of the larger islands and has often suffered from its location," he said at last and Kenneth managed a weak smile. "On a clear day from the summit of Snaefell, its tallest mountain, you can see the lands of four Peoples. To the west, the Irish, and if you were to look to the north east and then turn your head to the south east, you would also see cliffs that mark the edge of the kingdoms of the Scots, Angles and Welsh."

Dougie thought about this.

"And that is why they are independent, fierce and untrusting of strangers."

"Aye, laddie."

"What is Man like?"

"The best natural harbours are on the eastern shores and that is where most of the people live. They seek the fish around the island and these seas are prone to terrible storms."

Dougie nodded and glanced at the broken piece of wood Kenneth held in his hand.

"Apart from the high moorland, it is good farming country and between the twisting lanes, small fields are divided by low stone walls, and these are home to fine examples of sheep and cow."

Dougie thought he might feel at home here and, without meaning to, suddenly yawned.

"Am I boring you, laddie?" asked Kenneth, and then he yawned too.

When they woke, the storm had moved on to trouble other lands and the rain had stopped. They were still wet through and needed to build a fire, but the driftwood, which littered the beach, was sodden and useless. Alistair shivered and stared along the inlet. He thought he saw men, on the summit of a far cliff, pointing down at the wreck. They disappeared and Alistair raced down to the water's edge, and cut the lines to the ship. Tied ropes would warn an enemy of their safe arrival.

Dougie opened his eyes, slowly. He ached all over and rubbed his shoulders, as much to check that they were still there as to bring some comfort to his sore muscles. He watched Alistair cut the lines and wondered what his friend was up to. Then Alistair ran back to them.

"We cannot stay here," he said quickly. "People are coming and we don't know what kind of a welcome we might get."

He was right to be cautious. The men who came down the cliff path wore black kilts. From their hiding place, behind damp, sea-weedy rocks, they watched the enemy approach the ship. There were four of them and they climbed aboard, and no doubt discussed the chances of anyone getting ashore alive. One of the Picts searched the beach, for any sign of strangers, but the shingle leaves no trace of footprints and, after a while, they all left to report what they had found.

The Scots decided to follow them, at a distance, and hurriedly gathered their meagre belongings together. They climbed a steep cliff path and Dougie glanced down onto the inlet that had saved them from the storm. It was hopelessly narrow and he realised just how lucky they had been. Along this coast, there was no other refuge like it.

Waves still raced up the rocky channel and the hulk of the ship rose and fell with each one. Without lines to the shore, it was dragged backwards and by the time they reached the summit, the *Pride of Tiree* had gone forever.

The land ahead was pleasant and blessed with low, rounded hills. Sheep grazed on lush grassland and there were few trees. The sun was now high in the sky and it warmed them. So did the effort of keeping up with the enemy. The Picts half walked, half ran, up and down the small hills, and seemed intent on reaching their destination as quickly as they could.

Several times they fell behind and nearly lost them. Once, they got too close and had to hide behind a stone wall to remain unseen. The path was well worn and led them towards a small hamlet of white cottages. Alistair told them to slow down, as the enemy walked through it, but no one came out of the cottages to greet them. The Picts did not stop and marched out of the hamlet, and the friends had to decide whether to follow, and risk being seen, or to skirt around the fields at its edges.

"If we go around," warned Alistair, "we may lose sight of them."

"Wise words," said Donald.

Hamish munched on an apple.

"If we go through, we are bound to be seen."

Dougie stared at the houses. There were nine and they all seemed deserted. He stared harder and asked, "Are they not strange roofs?"

They all looked and Kenneth said gravely, "They have no roofs."

The friends ran down the slope to the first cottage and stood with their backs against its wall. Donald pushed his head around the corner and then beckoned them to follow.

"What has happened here?" he asked.

Every building was a ruin. Many of the whitewashed stones were blackened by fire and timbers were burnt away. Dougie and Alistair entered a doorway, which had no door, and found the bodies of a family sprawled on the floor. Decayed and horrible. Birds had pecked out their eyes. One of them had a spear, still upright, sticking up through the bones of the ribcage. Dougie felt sick and ran out to the path.

Suddenly, Kenneth called out to them and they hurried to his side. The enemy were disappearing over the crest of a far hill.

"We need to get going," he urged, and he pointed at the disappearing Picts.

Tall clouds of black smoke rose up on the far side of the hill and Dougie feared they might discover the horrors of another torched village. They hurried on and, this time, Alistair led them away from the path.

"If we meet anyone when we climb, we'll be in real trouble."

They made their way past granite outcrops, which were home

to coarse grasses, blaeberry and heather. Many trees had been felled, recently, for their stumps still showed the mark of the axe on fresh wood. There was little cover and so they crouched, ready to fall flat if an enemy approached. But none did and, as they crawled the last few paces, to a point where they could see into the next valley, an amazing sight came into view.

Below them, the land ran down to the sea and on its slopes sprawled a huge fortified camp. None of them had ever seen anything like it before. It was laid out like the three leaves of a clover. The camp was protected on all sides by towering stakes with their tops sharpened to terrible points. They stared at it in awe. It was huge.

One of the three circles of the clover leaf was full of tents. Perhaps fifty in all, and one of them was of great size and splendour. The second circle contained makeshift huts, and here women and children washed and cooked. But it was the third fortified circle that held their attention. Ten tall stone chimneys bellowed out thick smoke. Soldiers in black kilts carried long whips, which cracked if any of their prisoners slowed in their work. Carts full of a black rock were being driven by horses away from a dark hole in the ground. More rock was being brought from a ship that lay beside a busy quay, just outside of the camp. There were hundreds and hundreds of busy people in the third circle.

Dougie ignored the slaves and tried to count the Picts, and gave up at eighty. At least half their true number. Below them a poor soul carried black rock, in a large wicker basket, to the mouth of a fire, which burnt fiercely at the base of one of the chimneys. He dropped his load and they watched as he was beaten, wickedly, by two of the guards.

White steam hissed as it was released from the furnace and, as it came to rest in long, thin channels, it cooled into iron.

The friends edged their way backwards below the crest of the hill and looked at each other.

"So that's how they do it," said Alistair.

CHAPTER SIXTEEN

SLAVES OF THE FOUNDRY

There were few places to hide on the hillside and so they retraced their steps to the deserted and ruined village. They chose a cottage that stood alone and some way off the main path to hide in and huddled together inside its charred walls. Donald suggested stealing a Pictish ship and returning to Oban, but Alistair was determined to learn more about the fortress.

"We must find out how they make the iron."

"It is what the Younger asked of us," agreed Kenneth.

Donald and Dougie glanced at each other and even Hamish's face showed concern.

"The Picts might be more alert now they have found our ship. If we do go, it had best be under the cover of darkness," he suggested.

As the sun fell, they shared the food they had saved from the wreck. There wasn't much of it. Some cheese, an apple and two oatcakes each. Dougie stared at it and remembered Mairi's hot broth. Home seemed a very long way away. Sensing his friend's falling spirits, Alistair gave him a smile and winked at Hamish.

"You know, Dougie," growled Hamish, "this supper reminds me of Donald."

"It does?"

"Aye, it does. Why, only last summer, Donald went home to his good lady and asked her what was for supper."

Dougie sensed Donald standing.

"And Senga brought him a crab."

"A crab," muttered Dougie, biting into an oatcake.

"Aye, but do you know what, young Dougie?"

"No."

"It only had one claw, and Donald says to Senga, 'This crab has only got one claw,' and Senga says, 'It has been in a fight,' and Donald says, 'well bring me the winner.'"

Donald jumped onto Hamish and the friends burst into fits of laughter.

They settled down to get some sleep, with someone always keeping watch. Alistair made Dougie go first and reminded him about the importance of staying alert and what had happened on the beach, north of Stranraer.

As Hamish's snoring filled the silence, the shepherd's thoughts went back to the Pictish camp. He had never seen so many people crammed together, except in battle, and he pictured the ship beside the quay with the three legs of Man on its sail.

"It must be the same ship we saw below the watchtower and that might mean it has been loaded with boxes of weapons."

He peered out through a window to check they were alone. All dark. All still. He went back to his thinking.

"The slaves, who are forced to make the light iron, must hate the way they are treated and Kenneth says they are a proud people."

He peered out again and could just make out the shadowy outline of another cottage. He shivered as he remembered the dead family they had discovered there.

"They must hate the Picts."

Somewhere in the distance an owl hooted. Somewhere in Dougie's mind, a small light grew brighter. Quietly, he woke Alistair and they talked for a long while about his plan.

***

Borak offered his brother a drink from his leather bottle.

"Another quiet night."

Tumora took it and smiled.

"Let's hope it stays like that. The Mac Mar wasn't happy about the boat Gath found."

"It was just washed up on the beach after a storm."

"Washed up with no crew."

Borak looked at the ship that had brought them to Man. He sat down on the sand and took his sandals off, and washed his feet in the sea.

"They are lost. Drowned, poor souls."

"I just don't like it. Something is wrong."

"We have the easiest of tasks, Tumora. Keeping watch with our enemies held prisoner in the stockade and any other enemies a long way away."

"I still think something is wrong."

Borak put his sandals back on and stood up.

"Come on then. Let's check the ship and the quay again."

***

A full moon, partly covered by cloud, shone down on the three clover leaves. The five friends, armed with claymore and dirk, descended bravely down the hill and moved as fast as they could to the beach. They kept their distance from the stockade to avoid being seen and hid, huddled close together, behind a line of rocks.

Alistair turned to them and whispered, "I can think of no other way to achieve our purpose."

Dougie wished he had kept his mouth shut.

"Hamish and Donald, you must break into the camp where the people of Man are held prisoner. When the moon touches the sea, you must hold the gate to their camp open."

"Aye," they said together.

"You must silently raise the prisoners and tell them about Dougie's plan."

"Aye."

"Kenneth, Dougie and I will take the ship. Then we will load two carts with weapons and bring them to the prisoners. Kenneth, you take the ship away from the shore. If we fail, you are to bring Malcolm to Man as quickly as you can."

Kenneth nodded.

"We attack just before dawn," said Alistair. "Good fortune to all of us."

Hamish and Donald disappeared into the night and Alistair

244

led the others across the shingle. At times, the cloud moved away from the face of the moon and they had to hide until the sky darkened. Kenneth believed that there were only two hours before the moon touched the sea. They quickened their pace.

The ship was linked to the shore by thick wooden planks and two guards guarded the quay, walking up and down and looking around for intruders.

"Stay here and be ready," hissed Kenneth and suddenly he began to sing.

He stood and stumbled, and waved cheerfully at the Picts. His song seemed to amuse the guards and one laughed when he swayed, and fell over. The Picts walked towards him. Kenneth tried to stand and fell backwards, somehow keeping his feet, stumbling past his friends in hiding. Then he fell again and sang some more.

The Picts marched right past Alistair and Dougie and were taken easily.

"Put on their kilts," ordered Alistair.

"I will not," replied Dougie indignantly.

"And how do you plan to get through the camp to the others?"

Reluctantly, Dougie wrapped the black kilt around his own. It smelled awful. They ran to the ship, crossed the gangplank and found hundreds of wooden boxes, stacked on the deck.

"Get them ashore," ordered Alistair.

When most of the boxes were ashore, Kenneth raised the sail and the wind took hold, and the ship drifted away from the shore. Alistair watched him steer a wavy course towards the open sea and marched around the stacked boxes, pretending to guard the empty quay.

Dougie went to find horses and a cart. In the dark, this was easier said than done and sometimes he stumbled as he ran up the wide lane, which led to the main fortress gates.

"If this is the way they bring the carts, then this must be the way to the horses," he said to himself, but it didn't sound too convincing.

In front of him, two long buildings stood outside the fort's sturdy, double gates. Two Picts lay knocked out beside the gates, which meant Hamish and Donald were already inside. Cautiously, Dougie slipped behind the back of the nearest hut and his shoulder blades brushed against the high fortress wall. In the shadow of the tall spikes of the fence, he put his ear to a plank with a crack running along it and listened, hoping to hear horses. He could hear something, but what? He listened again, but still wasn't sure. Dougie peered around the side of the hut and saw the moon. It was closer to the sea.

"Better get on with it."

As casually as he could manage, he walked to the front of the hut, put his hand on a latch and inched the door open. It was full of sleeping Picts and the smell of their unwashed clothes attacked his senses. One of them opened an eye and stared at him. Dougie froze.

"Get back to your post, you dog," the man mumbled, and then he shut his eye and went back to sleep.

Dougie ran to the next hut and noticed that its doors were three times as wide as the others.

"What a fool I am," thought Dougie. "No horse could have got through the other door."

Alistair's arms still ached from the effort of unloading the ship and he wondered how Hamish and Donald were getting on.

Hamish was sitting on the limp body of a Pict and Donald was wrestling with another, his hand clamped across the man's mouth. Hamish got up, smiled and thumped the man on the head.

"I could have managed," moaned Donald.

"Aye, but why should you have all the fun?"

They left the two bodies outside the fortress and stepped inside. Staying in shadow, they stared around this part of the clover leaf. It seemed deserted. Every twenty paces, in every direction, the dark silhouettes of round mounds showed the location of the clay furnaces. Each furnace was the height of a man and the smoky air around them reminded Donald of the Younger's Great Hall.

Hamish knelt down by a hole in the side of a furnace. A great heat came from the orange embers inside. He picked up a black rock and smelled it. It was light, like wood, but hard, like stone. He tossed it onto the fire and watched it burn. Donald tapped him on the shoulder and they ran along a path edged with furnaces, past a deep hole in the ground. Then they hid behind a furnace.

"Two Black Kilts," warned Donald.

"They guard the gate to the clover leaf where the men of Man are held prisoner."

Donald grinned. "Let's go and introduce ourselves."

With the guards dealt with, they pulled a thick wooden plank off the gate and went through. Beyond the gates were rows and rows of ramshackle wooden huts. Hamish ran to the nearest hut and popped his head inside.

"Hello," he said. "Anyone like to be rescued?"

***

Dougie's horse was lazy. It looked at him as if to say, "I have pulled carts about all day and I am not going to do it at night as well."

At last, he forced the beast into its harness and, with a second horse tied to the back of a wagon, he led them back to the quay. It seemed as though the steps of the horses and the creaking of the wheels would wake the dead, but no soldiers came out of the hut and the camp remained still. Dougie looked at the moon. It was nearly touching the sea and he began to run.

As quickly as they could, Alistair and Dougie loaded the boxes onto the cart. Then they walked the horses back up the wide lane and entered the camp. They passed the round furnaces and the great hole in the ground, and Dougie's stomach tightened into knots and he sweated with fear. Alistair looked as though he didn't have a care in the world.

As the moon touched the sea, they approached Donald and Hamish who stood, casually, beside the second gate.

"There is a bit of a problem with your plan, Dougie," said Donald.

Alistair raised an eyebrow and Dougie whispered, "How so?"

"We have raised the men of Man, but they say they are quite happy."

Alistair and Dougie looked aghast. Hamish pushed the gate open and they were looking at a huge crowd of silent people.

"Come on in. We are all ready," growled Hamish.

Two hundred warriors watched the cart enter and Dougie saw how thin they were. How gaunt their faces were. Without a word, the boxes were broken open and Alistair found himself at the head of an army.

One man stepped forward and the whispers of the crowd hushed. Gawain of Glamorgan, Lord of Man, and leader of his people was powerfully built. His red hair was cropped short and everything about his appearance spoke of authority. His smile was warm, but Dougie sensed this man would be a dangerous enemy.

"What do we do now?"

"I hadn't thought that far ahead," said Dougie.

Gawain nodded.

"Well, you had better get out of that black kilt, if you are not to be mistaken for the enemy."

"But you have not taken a sword," warned Dougie.

Gawain knelt and lifted a handful of soil from the ground.

"My sword is always with me."

Then he spoke ancient words, unknown to anyone except Tirani the Wise, and he let the soil fall between his fingers. Where it fell, the king carefully moved the earth aside to reveal a golden hilt.He stood to show the blade to his people, who silently raised their own swords made of the light iron.

"The Picts are sleeping and there is no better time to attack," urged Alistair.

"Hamish and Donald," said Alistair, "go and hold the main

entrance to the fortress. Dougie says there are guards asleep in a hut there. Gawain, may they take some of your warriors?"

"Take twenty. Go quietly. Let none of them live. Join us at the gates of the Pictish camp when you are done."

"What is to be done with the women and children?" asked Dougie.

Gawain smiled at him and walked over to a young boy, who held a sword that was nearly as tall as he was. His face was as black as pitch and when he grinned his teeth shone white.

"Ewan, gather the women and children from the huts and lead them in silence past the furnaces, and keep them safe by the quay. Kill anyone who threatens them. Tell the elders to prepare for the wounded."

Ewan bowed and skipped off.

"For freedom," said Gawain.

His men whispered, "Freedom."

***

As Donald ran back towards the main gates, past the beehive furnaces, he saw the outline of his big friend glow red, then return to black, then glow again. Behind them the sound of running feet grew louder from the warriors of Man and, when they overtook them, their bobbing, vengeful bodies glowed and darkened too. Then the warriors were through the gates and gone.

"Hope they leave some for us," panted Hamish.

From inside the mighty stockade a huge roar went up. Donald stopped to listen.

"Battle's started."

"Come on," urged Hamish. "Let's kill some Picts."

They ran towards the huts with claymores raised. A Manx warrior was leading horses out of one. The other hut shook. Muffled screams filled the hour before dawn. Suddenly the screams stopped. The door flew open and the men of Man came out and dashed back through the gates.

Hamish glanced inside. "All dead."

"They didn't stand a chance, did they?" said Donald and they began to run again.

***

Sprawled on shingle beside the quay, Borak opened his eyes and his first thought was for his brother. Tumora's crumpled body lay still and Borak leapt to his feet. Blood rushed to his head and an intense pain hit him behind the eyes. He staggered and fell.

Later, Tumora gently cradled his brother's head in his hands and tipped the leather bottle. Most of the water splashed away from the lips which opened a little. Borak coughed and spluttered, and looked up.

"I thought we were dead."

"So did I and whoever attacked us has our plaids."

Borak reached down and could only feel his shirt.

"Axes?"

"Taken too."

A distant roar went up from inside the stockade.

"Come on. Try and sit up. Let's get swords and go to Tella."

They stood, uneasily at first, and walked towards the quay. Offshore, the silhouette of a ship under full sail was lit by a low moon. Tumora grabbed his brother's shoulders and forced him down. A hundred paces away, warriors ran through the gates and entered the huts. A giant man and another half his size followed them.

"We can't go that way," whispered Borak.

"Let's go the long way and make the ship ready."

They crawled towards the high stockade fence and then followed it, walking as quickly as its shadow would allow, around the fort towards Tella's secret escape route. High above them, someone cried out in terror and they were drenched in blood. A Black Kilt's body thumped down beside them. His head followed.

Ewan kicked the door open and shouted out.

"Gawain orders that you follow me now."

Thirty heads peeked out of blankets. His mother stared at him.

"Why? Where are we going?"

The boy lifted a great sword and pointed it at her.

"This is not the time for questions. Gather everyone outside. NOW."

He ran to the next hut and the next. The women and children began to chatter in groups and some began to go back into the warm. Inside the Pictish camp, over the high walls that separated them from the other part of the clover leaf, a huge roar went up. Iron clashed on iron. Men screamed.

"You are all to follow me to the quay. Our people have been armed by the Scots. Gawain says we must prepare for the wounded. Follow me NOW."

Ewan led them out and along the lane that twisted through the furnaces.

"Stand aside," he commanded and the party stepped off the path.

Blood stained Manx warriors ran past them towards the Pictish camp. Hamish and Donald followed, panting with the effort.

"Follow me," repeated Ewan and they hurried on again, and were outside the stockade for the first time in an age.

"Mother, gather all the children together and hide them in the village, what is left of it."

Her face was a picture at being ordered about, but nodded.

"When this is over, young Ewan, I will be speaking to you."

His filthy black face and white teeth grinned back at her.

"And you will be taking a swim. You are filthy."

His grin disappeared. Behind her, in shadow, two Black Kilts were creeping away around the outer wall. He watched his mother lead the children off to safety. On the quay, old women tore cloth into strips, and laid out roots and herbs on blankets. Some lit fires and got ready to boil water. Ewan decided to follow the enemy.

***

With Hamish, Donald and Ewan away on their missions, the men of Man moved silently past a deep, black hole towards the Picts' enclosure. Dougie saw the outline of many ladders disappearing down into the hole and breathed in the smoky air. Alistair waited for a signal from Gawain.

"Stay beside me, Dougie," he whispered.

Dougie nodded. He had heard those words before.

Gawain crouched down behind a furnace and pointed his sword at a small door, cut into the thick, high tree trunks that were lashed together to form this part of the stockade. Two Black Kilts guarded it. Alistair and Dougie crouched next to him.

"Beyond the door, the Picts will be asleep in their tents."

"How many Picts?" asked Dougie.

"About two hundred," replied Gawain.

"How many are we?"

"Four hundred and, thanks to you, we are all well armed with the light iron."

Alistair nodded.

"So, all we have to do is move silently through the gate."

"Or hold the gate and take them prisoner," suggested Dougie.

The king's eyes flashed.

"I want this finished tonight."

The hairs on the shepherd's neck bristled.

"Stay here," commanded Gawain and he rose, and walked towards the guards.

In the dark, they couldn't make out who approached them. One called out something in a strange tongue. Gawain said something back and the other guard laughed, and lowered his spear. Twenty paces away, Gawain began to run.

Dougie stepped over their bodies and entered the third clover leaf, and stood next to Alistair, in shadow, with his back pressed against the fence. More warriors joined them and Gawain ordered total silence, and pointed his sword at the places he wanted each man to stand. In minutes, the round stockade was completely ringed by his men.

Tents, made from sail cloth, filled the enclosure and all the open spaces were lit by fires. At the centre was a tall and splendid tent with a flag of the black axe flying above it. A Pict came out of another tent and looked around. No one moved. He went across to a fire and warmed his hands. Then he went back inside. Dougie's pounding heart was in his mouth and he thought it was loud enough to wake the dead. Gawain stepped out of the shadow and raised his sword. His men did the same.

"Kill them!" he roared.

Tella kicked the furs from his bed and leapt up. He kicked Gath in the ribs.

"Fetch the horses," he growled.

Gath grabbed a spear and ran out of the tent. Around him the camp was full of a wild enemy who slashed out with swords at his people. Light iron crashed upon light iron and tiny white sparks surrounded him. A man came out of the darkness and brought his blade down at his head. Gath raised his spear and the sword cut through the shaft and twisted, and hit his helmet sideways on. Gath snarled and leapt at the shadow.

Dougie had never seen any warriors as fierce, or as desperate, as the men of Man. It was as if all the cruelty they had suffered was now released in terrible violence. Alistair fought beside Gawain, who cut the tent ropes and waited for the Picts to stagger out. In the small area of the stockade, escape from the carnage was impossible. Gawain's men hacked the Black Kilts down and if one of them did fall to an axe, another would roar with delight and take his place.

In the darkness before dawn, a blood stained Dougie saw Tella and ten of his chieftains mount horses and charge forward. The

Mac Mar screamed at his men to follow him. Their fierce war cries sent fear into the hearts of any who dared to stand against them. For a moment the line of half-starved slaves fell back.

A Black Kilt urged his steed forward, smashing his axe down onto one warrior and then another.

Gawain ran at the horse and his sword cut deep into the poor beast's neck. It fell and the rider was thrown. Immediately, swords flashed in the firelight and sliced his body to pieces. A huge Black Kilt ran at Dougie with axe and shield. He waved the axe at great speed above his head, and his blood-red eyes fixed angrily on the shepherd. Alistair raised his sword and brought it down onto the Pict's shield. It was sliced in two and his severed arm was trampled on as the king led his people forward.

***

"How far?" asked Tumora.

Borak glanced back along the line of the outer wall. He had a feeling they were being followed.

"Not far."

The screams from inside the stockade were louder here. The first rays of sun came over the sea from the east and lit the faint line of a path that ran right around the fortress. Tumora began to run.

"Come on, let's get the ship ready."

Borak dived behind a rock and watched his brother disappear around the curve in the wall. Light footsteps grew louder and he leapt out with a stone in his hand. A small boy ran at him and tried to lift a sword to make the first blow. Borak stepped forward and grabbed his wrist, and twisted.

The boy cried out in pain and dropped the sword. Borak slapped his face and knocked Ewan to the ground. Tumora ran back to join his brother, picked up the sword and placed it at the boy's throat.

Borak shook his head.

"Go home, brave warrior," he said and Ewan ran for all he was worth back to the quay.

***

"I bet I kill more Picts than you," boasted Donald.

Hamish growled and stepped inside the Pictish enclosure. There were dead Black Kilts everywhere and most of the tents were on fire. In seconds, they were surrounded by five of the enemy and they charged together, using claymore and dirk to fight their way out of trouble. On the other side of the stockade, the Pictish line held and slowly edged forward with grim determination, but they were swept back by an angry mob led by Gawain and Alistair.

Donald whirled round and stood, face to face, with a Pict of huge strength. The man held a flaming ball, an iron grate on a long chain, and whirled it around his head. The grate was full of fire and it swung, viciously, at Donald's head. Donald ducked and it singed his hair. Sparks flew from the burning weapon and they could feel its great heat.

"The man of fire!" said Donald, "better leave this one to me."

He threw his dirk into the man's chest.

Out of the corner of his eye, Dougie thought he saw a group of Pictish riders charge the stockade wall. He called out to Alistair.

"What are they doing?"

Alistair picked up a spear and threw it into a rider's back.

One of the Black Kilts cut a long rope that went up to the top of the wall and a huge stone fell. A gate in the fence appeared from nowhere and rose up too. Anyone who stood in the way of the horses were trampled to the ground. Then the riders were gone.

The Black Kilts, deserted by Tella, made a desperate attempt to escape the stockade. But there were so many of them that the gate became choked with bodies. Suddenly the gate crashed shut.

Gawain shouted above the noise of battle.

"Cut them down."

His men ran forward. Dougie followed them and found himself in the midst of the fighting. The cries of the warriors and the screams of the dying filled Dougie's mind. A spear was thrown at him by an angry Pict and he ducked. The spear went through the neck of the soldier behind him. Dougie lunged with his claymore and missed.

In that moment, Dougie thought of Mairi and his children. They were so clear in his mind and yet so very far away. A blow came crashing down and he remembered no more.

***

Gath's horse thundered through the gate and he stared down the path that led down to the secret mooring. Two of his people were guarding it and the sail was raised. He called back to his father.

"The ship is ready!"

Tella slashed out at one of his own soldiers and drove his horse through the gate. Three more riders and two of the enemy followed him. Borak and Tumora dashed forward. The men of Man aimed spears at the Mac Mar and the brothers let fly their axes. They hit the enemy at the same time and both fell.

Gath jumped down and ran at the gate, and cut another rope. The gate crashed down in front of the Black Kilts inside.

"Follow us, master," shouted Tumora and they ran alongside the king's horse to a wide gangplank which they had laid out as soon as they arrived.

Tella rode his horse onboard and his riders followed. Borak lifted the gangplank and tossed it aside. Tumora cut the mooring lines and the wind caught the sail.

Kenneth of Blacklock watched the distant sail tack and then run north. He pushed the tiller over and set a course back to the quay. He was in no position to follow them and needed to tell Alistair about the escaping Black Kilts. Now he knew that the men of Man were free and wondered what had happened during the Battle of the Foundry. Did his friends still live?

"Come here," growled Tella.

Fear gripped Borak and Tumora, but their leader said, "You did well. You are to be my envoys. Go to Patrick Three Eggs at Mountjoy. There were Scots leading the Manx people which means the Younger knows about our plans. He has no choice now but to win the Irish peoples as his allies."

Borak breathed a huge sigh of relief and looked to the southwest across an ocean alive with the reflection of an orange dawn sun. The ship lurched and Tumora caught his arm.

"Keep Patrick out of the fight."

The brothers bowed.

"We attack Scotland in two moons. Buy me that time."

"Yes, Master," they said together.

The Mac Mar walked over to the ship's rail, where his horse was tethered, and took something from a saddle bag.

"Take this as your reward."

Borak looked at the bag of coins. It was the same bag that Tella had gifted and taken back from Denbara the Scribe.

CHAPTER SEVENTEEN

THE RETURN OF THE HIGH TABLE

Alistair searched desperately amongst the bodies for his friend. The stench of death was overwhelming and his feet were covered in the blood that formed a red pool upon the grass. The wounded were carried on carts to the harbour, where the women did what they could to keep them alive. Tied to the quay was the ship with three legs on its sail and Kenneth stared down grimly at the horrendous aftermath of battle.

Hamish and Donald sat exhausted with a group of the Manx men, and looked out to sea. One of the soldiers lifted his hand wearily and pointed to a far headland.

"Look," he cried, and all eyes turned to see a black sail.

The Pictish ship was running north before the wind.

"So we did not get them all," growled Hamish.

"Wise words," agreed Donald.

Dougie's head was mighty sore. He touched it cautiously and found a throbbing lump underneath his thick hair. He felt sick.

A young woman sat beside him and took a cloth from a bucket of water. She wiped his face and Dougie looked worried when she dipped it back into the bucket. The water turned blood red.

She spoke gently, "Fear not, brave warrior."

"I am not a warrior," said Dougie, "I am a farmer."

She giggled, pulled an arrow from the fold in his tartan and ran off to tend another of the wounded.

"Hello, Dougie," came a relieved voice.

"Hello, Alistair," replied Dougie.

"I am very glad to find you still alive," and his friend smiled.

"Not as glad as I am."

The four friends got together and walked through the camp. In the sunshine, it seemed larger and more impregnable than it had in the hours of darkness. Gawain and his men were pulling the low, beehive furnaces to the ground. It was as if they were a symbol of all the terrible things that had happened to them and crowds cheered as one after another was turned to rubble.

Gawain saw them and came over to greet them.

"My men tell me that Tella the Mac Mar was here. He and his generals escaped at the height of the battle when they saw the way it was going. They will probably be back on Skye in two days, and no doubt think of more mischief to plague us with," he said bitterly.

The friends nodded and Alistair went to stand in front of Gawain.

"On behalf of Malcolm and the High Table, we offer you friendship and help in times of trouble."

"Thank you," said Gawain, "Malcolm is a good king, and in this dark age there are few of those." He looked around the camp. "Our first task will be to rebuild our village," and he looked at Dougie. "It was your plan that saved us, and the courage of all of you that freed us."

Dougie shuffled his feet, nervously.

"May we call our new village and home of my court after you?" asked the King.

"Would a true Manx name not be better for your people?" replied Dougie.

"If it were not for you, we would still be slaves."

Later, the Lord of Man called his people together.

"Tomorrow we rebuild our houses at this place," he said and paused. "We owe a great debt to these brave Scots and for all time they will be welcome amongst us."

The crowd cheered and waved their swords into the sky.

"What is your name?" asked Gawain.

"Dougie," said Dougie.

Gawain looked at the ground and whispered, "I don't think Dougie is a very good name for our village."

"Well you asked me what it was," replied Dougie in an indignant voice.

"His Sunday name is Douglas," added Alistair.

"Douglas," repeated Gawain, "yes, Douglas. From this day

the capital of Man shall be known as Douglas, and whenever it is spoken, we shall remember your help in our victory at the battle of the foundry."

The crowd cheered again.

The friends slept for much of the day on the deck of the Manx ship. Kenneth busied himself by arranging provisions for their journey home and clearly enjoyed giving orders to the local people who brought it on board. They woke late in the afternoon and ate a hearty meal fit for heroes. Dougie noticed that Hamish devoured many fish and a great loaf of bread that had been baked in the shape of a claymore.

After the feast they stood around the quay, with nothing to do, and looked back towards the stockade.

"We had better get some of that black rock for Archie," said Alistair and, grateful for something to do, they followed him to a massive hole in the ground with ladders descending into it.

Ewan's white teeth flashed in his grimy face. He couldn't have been more than twelve summers young and had been forced to work every daylight hour, digging the black rock from the depths of the Earth and carrying it back to the surface.

"I'll fetch some for you."

He grabbed a basket and his thin body disappeared down into the blackness. Then he emerged with the basket full of black rock. Its dark surface shone in the rays of the sun.

"It doesn't look like much," commented Dougie.

"It is the future," said Alistair, mimicking Archie's most serious voice.

Later, the friends talked to the men and children that had worked at the furnaces and discovered that burning the black rock was the secret of making light iron. They loaded many baskets of the black rock on board their ship. Gawain had agreed to let them sail home on the first tide in the morning. Their ship would be returned by the five Manx sailors who were to accompany them.

There was much excitement on the quayside and Kenneth came bounding up the gangplank.

"You had better follow me," he ordered, and he led them quickly through the camp.

They entered the clover leaf that held the remains of the tents of the Pictish army. Gawain came to greet them, but his manner was grave and the friends wondered what had happened. He led them past fallen canvas and the burning pyres of the dead. At last they came to a tent of great size and splendour. Above it flew a flag that had a black axe in its centre.

"This must be Tella's tent," said Dougie, and the others nodded.

The floor was covered in colourful rugs and sturdy oak chairs were placed in a circle. Dougie noticed that a single chair was larger than the others and its legs were carved in the shape of writhing serpents. On the tent wall behind Tella's throne was a fine tapestry. It showed a mountain that might have been one of the greatest of all mountains, Carn Liath.

Gawain beckoned them to sit and he walked to the tapestry. He tore it down, turned it over and rolled it onto the ground in front of them. The friends were looking at a map of Scotland. Dougie did not know this at first, for like so many people of that time he had never even seen a book. But he remembered the words of the "Watcher."

Alistair's face became grim.

"Malcolm suspected that there was much more to this than the new iron," he said.

Gawain looked at it too and added, "These are Pictish symbols, and though I am less familiar with them than others, this is what I think they mean. We are here to the south west of Scotland. Our island is clearly shown and this sword marks the place where the light iron is made."

Dougie stared at it and could not understand why such a big island was shown to be so small.

"These lines," continued Gawain, "show the way the ships go when taking the arms."

"One goes to the port of Stranraer?" asked Alistair.

"Yes," replied Gawain.

"And there are other lines," said Kenneth, who studied the map intently.

"Yes," agreed Gawain, "one goes to a place on the northern point of the land of the Welsh and another to Skye."

"So Tella is also giving arms to the Welsh King, Llewellyn," added Hamish sadly.

Gawain's finger followed a line from Man to Stranraer, and then through the borders to lands at the south eastern edge of Scotland.

"And to the Angles."

"So Cuthbert is in this too," muttered Alistair, and the king nodded.

"This map describes a dangerous alliance," said Gawain standing, "do you see how Scotland is divided into three colours."

Dougie had noticed it, but had not wanted to ask why it was so. The others had noticed it too, and in their hearts had known its terrible meaning.

"My guess is that Tella is in league with the Welsh and the Angles, and that they have come to an agreement about how to share out your lands." Gawain walked to the door of the tent. "You must reach Malcolm and warn him," he said, and left them all staring blankly at the map.

Under the cover of darkness, the fully laden ship slipped its ropes and left the safety of the harbour. The strong wind filled the sail and they made good speed. The island of Man was soon a small, dark line on the horizon and, like their memories, it faded away, and yet would never be forgotten. Kenneth seemed pleased with the hard work of the Manx sailors, although he rarely showed it with a kind word or a smile.

They had talked long about the map and the plans of the Picts and realised that the key thing they did not know was *when* Tella might invade.

"That might depend on when they think they have enough weapons," said Dougie.

"Aye, and Gawain told me that the foundries have been working since last summer, so we must assume that many swords have already been made," added Alistair.

"So it could be soon," said Hamish and Donald together.

"If it has not already begun," warned Alistair.

They kept watch night and day for enemy ships, but saw none, and yet Alistair believed Tella would do everything in his power to stop them reaching the mainland. The fine weather continued and, after two nights, Oban was sighted. Kenneth steered a course for the harbour and the white cottages of its seafaring folk came into full view. It was a beautiful morning and their spirits were high at the thought of standing again on their native soil.

A Manx sailor ran madly across the deck to Kenneth and pointed back out to sea. Behind them three black sails were chasing them into harbour.

"They will not catch us," said Alistair, and orders were urgently given to prepare to land.

The quay seemed deserted and Dougie could see that Kenneth was troubled by this.

"What is the matter?" asked Dougie.

Kenneth strained his eyes to catch any sign of movement.

"I do not know, but we should be seeing the fishing boats being made ready to leave and yet there is no sign of life at all."

Fifty paces from the shore, the skipper pulled the tiller around violently. The ship turned and the sail flapped as it emptied of wind. Running from their hiding places behind the cottages, were perhaps a hundred warriors in black kilts.

The ship rose and fell with each wave, but held its small distance from the quayside. Carrying a black axe and grinning at them was Gath. Dougie turned and saw the black sails getting closer. They seemed to completely fill the channel that led back to the open sea.

"Trapped," he said, and there was fear in his voice.

They lifted their claymores and watched the Picts. The enemy seemed content to wait and glared back at them, their mighty battle axes held ready. Some of them beckoned them ashore with a finger and shouted rude words. Gath just looked mean and nasty.

"What can we do?" asked Dougie.

"We cannot escape by sea," replied Kenneth, "the wind is against us and we would be an easy target for their ships to ram at full speed."

Dougie did not like the sound of being rammed at any speed and wondered how long they had left before capture and certain death. He looked across at Alistair and was taken aback. His friend was smiling. Hamish and Donald were smiling too. He followed their gaze away from the shore. The black sails of the ships were being lowered and new ones raised in their place. They were light brown, green and ochre, and at the bow of the leading ship was a tall, grim-faced man with a white beard.

And he wore the crown of the Scottish people.

***

The map of Denbara the scribe was laid out upon the long table in the Great Hall of the palace. Archie sat next to Malcolm with his back to them and Gangly made rude signs at Dougie. The alchemist gave his full attention to a piece of black rock that he turned over and over in his hand.

"Do you know what it is?" asked the king.

"Oh yes," replied Archie, "for I have looked into the Oracle of the Ancient Ones."

Gangly threw his eyes to the ceiling.

"Grumf."

"It is called *goal*, and in years to come it will be the reason for much *industrol production*," continued the alchemist importantly.

"*Industrol production*?" asked Malcolm, his eyes glazing over as he said it.

"Aye," added Archie, "and *goal*, when burnt, gives off more heat than charcoal, and that means you can make a lighter and stronger blade."

"So at last we know its secret," said Malcolm in a relieved voice.

"And not only that," continued Archie importantly, "the Oracle has shown me great crowds of people, thousands upon thousands of people, in a great temple called a *stay diom*."

He paused, and looked over his shoulder at the knights of the High Table. They were hanging on his every word.

"And in the *stay diom* they worship the black rock and cry out, *goal, goal, goal*!" shouted Archie.

The room went silent.

"Grumf," grunted Gangly.

"No I am not an idiot," replied Archie in an angry voice.

"But is that important?" asked Malcolm.

"All knowledge has a value, Your Majesty."

"But can you make light iron?" continued Malcolm in a slightly agitated voice.

"Oh, yes," said the alchemist.

"Well go and get on with it then," ordered Malcolm, and Archie walked backwards from the room with the long legged imp muttering curses in his ear.

Malcolm shook his head as though whenever he spoke with Archie he was left exhausted and not quite knowing what was going on.

The hall buzzed with excited talk about the discovery, and as Dougie looked round he saw faces he had not seen before. Only twenty knights had returned from the corners of the kingdom and new warriors had come to replace the fallen. Of the four parties that had embarked on the king's mission, only the Men of Tain had found anything of value.

Malcolm called the room to order and, glancing across at Alistair, spoke in a relieved voice.

"We feared you lost when we received no news from you. I led soldiers to Stranraer and saw the Picts heading north to Oban.

We followed, captured one of their number and learnt something of their plans."

Dougie nodded as he heard how the Scots had taken ships from Glasgow and sailed north to Oban under the pretence of Pict sails.

"And I am mighty glad that you are safe," continued Malcolm, and he smiled at them all.

Alistair told them about the stockade and its furnaces, and the battle to free the slaves. As the story unfolded, Dougie could feel people looking at him and went bright red.

"I see," commented Malcolm, nodding slowly, "and Gawain believes that Tella has supplied arms to the Welsh and the Angles."

"Many arms," replied Alistair, "and we believe that they have formed an alliance that will give them each a part of the land."

He pointed at the map of Scotland and the three colours that divided it. The knights became excited and scared as each realised the importance of what was being said. Malcolm sat down and put his head in his hands. The room fell silent. Hamish and Donald glanced at each other mischievously, but after Alistair shot them one of his looks, they remained respectfully silent as the king thought things through.

The fire that always blazed in the hall crackled and Dougie looked up at the carvings on the ceiling. In its very centre was a new painting. The thistle boasted a beautiful purple flower and the stem was covered in the sharp spines that had helped them forge the nation. He wondered what Malcolm was thinking and hoped that part of it might involve them going home, for a short while at least. His thoughts went out to his farm and his family, and as he lowered his head, he saw that Alistair was smiling kindly at him.

At last Malcolm rose.

"Men of Tain, you have done your country a great service and I beg you do me another."

Alistair, Hamish and Donald nodded. Malcolm looked at

Dougie who pointed at himself as if to say, "Me too?"

Malcolm nodded and so Dougie nodded back.

"Hamish and Donald," commanded Malcolm, and they sat upright in their seats, "will you take a fleet to Man and aid Gawain?"

"Aye, Your Majesty."

"And, Robert of Inverness, will you lead the fleet for me?"

Robert beamed and nodded eagerly.

Hamish and Donald glanced at each other again. Donald made a small squeak like a mouse. Then both grimaced as they remembered how Robert always liked to order them around. Hamish began to growl and Alistair shot them another look.

"There is a chance that The Mac Mar will try to take it back, for the foundry can be rebuilt and it is one source of his power," said Malcolm.

They nodded in obedience.

"Alistair and Dougie," continued the king, "go to Ireland and secure an alliance with Patrick Three Eggs. We shall need all the help we can get from our friends across the sea."

They nodded too, and once again Dougie's stomach started to tie up in knots.

"Knights of the High Table," said Malcolm impressively, "go back to your clans and raise them."

A loud cheer filled the hall.

The great king looked deep into the eyes of each man in turn and Dougie thought that he seemed both sad and determined. Malcolm took out his claymore and pointed it skyward to grace the thistle. His knights stood and raised theirs too and the court of the king became charged with energy. It was as though the very air around them was alive with their fears for the future.

"Let the defence of Scotland begin!" cried Malcolm.

CHAPTER EIGHTEEN

THE QUEST OF TIRANI THE WISE

Stoyalu was ten summers young and dying. He was close to losing consciousness as he drifted, from side to side, on the end of a long chain.

It was as though he was being rocked to sleep, an eternal sleep, in a giant hand. The metal creaked. All the cages creaked and Stoyalu stared up helplessly at the top of the wall, from which he hung. How far was he from the ramparts? Too far for his weak limbs to climb up and, anyway, he didn't care anymore. Through the bars of the iron cage he could see for miles. Below him were the dark and cold waters of the moat that surrounded Berwick Castle. In front of him, green fields stretched out to woodland. He had once played in those woods. He had once been happy.

Further beyond the trees, and hidden by them, was Stoyalu's village and he tried to remember his family and friends who still lived there. They would be coming home from the fields now and looking forward to supper.

It was hopeless. No matter where his mind wandered it always seemed to come back to food. Deep in dream, on the previous night, Stoyalu had imagined that he smelled, touched and ate fresh bread. It was warm, comforting, real. But, he awoke again to hunger and the pain of another day.

In the distance, clouds were gathering above the far hills and the low sun of day's end struggled to send a ray of comfort and warm the bodies of the shamed. Cateya began to moan again and Stoyalu reached out a thin arm to reassure his young sister. But her cage swung away from his and he called out to her.

"Hush now, wee one, hush now."

With a great effort, the girl raised her head to look at him. Stoyalu smiled and his heart went out to her as he saw how thin she had become. Without food for days, they had all become thin. But it was her eyes that hurt him. Cateya's eyes had always shone so brightly and now they were deep, hollow and empty.

The cries for mercy were long gone and even the tears and sadness had been replaced by a silence as each of the children prayed for death to claim them. Stoyalu put his head in his hands. They trembled and he wondered who might be the first victim of Cuthbert's cruelty.

He glanced along the cages of shame. On one side the bones and rotting flesh of Thomas Goodfellow. On the other side, Cateya was moaning quietly and her head rocked back and forth, as though she was in agreement in a conversation that had long lost its meaning. Beyond her, another girl was sleeping, her body at a sad angle and her thin legs dangling like twigs through the metal slats. At the other end was wee Sara. She was quiet now and had not spoken for two days. Stoyalu remembered how she had kicked and screamed, wildly, as soldiers forced her inside her cage. In full view of the villagers, they had been lowered over the side of the castle wall so all would know that disobedience to the baron would not be tolerated. They were Cuthbert's example.

Stoyalu's father had warned there would be trouble when they first heard about the escape of the prisoners from the castle. But no one in the village had imagined the cruelty which followed. Cuthbert believed the Scotsmen could not have achieved their freedom without help and would not be swayed by the pleas of the villagers. Mothers hid their children and lived in fear of their capture, but four were eventually taken and the baron's vengeance was complete.

Inside the castle, Tella the Mac Mar bit, greedily, into a chicken leg and smeared the grease across his thick, black beard.

"Cuthbert, I am truly impressed by your methods."

"There are times when a strong example must be made."

Tella belched loudly.

"You know, I think I might try it myself."

"Can we get back to the plan," interrupted Llewellyn, King of the Welsh peoples. "Does the Younger have a copy of the map?"

Tella's eyes narrowed. "He has a copy, I'm sure of it, and he has a small number of weapons made from light iron. But so what? He hasn't enough to equip an army."

"But he *knows*," said Llewellyn.

Cuthbert nodded. "He knows right enough, but what does it change?"

"We always believed that surprise was our greatest ally," said Llewellyn.

Tella held up a golden goblet.

"There is no need for second thoughts. The prize for each of us remains the same, a share in the rich lands of the north."

"And which of us does not want it, Llewellyn?" asked Cuthbert.

"Oh, I want it, but not at any price."

"What can he do?" asked Tella, "how can he fight three armies who carry the light iron?"

Cuthbert walked over to the window and watched a crowd of villagers walk towards his castle.

"We must not wait," he said calmly, "we planned to move in four moons and this gives the Scots time to prepare."

"Then let's attack now," said Tella, "I have given you all the arms you need to secure your part of the prize."

"Now is too soon," warned Llewellyn, and there was hesitancy in his voice.

Tella and Cuthbert glanced at each other.

"You aren't worried by the old stories about the stone are you?" asked Tella. "They are just stories and hold no threat to us."

"If they hold Amera's stone we have *every* reason to fear them," said Llewellyn.

Cuthbert smiled. "They are children's stories. True power comes from a blade which cannot be broken."

Llewellyn stared down at the map on the table. The lands to the north of his kingdom had been taken a generation ago, by the Elder, and now he had the chance to win them back. They were his by right but, like all of his royal line, he believed in the power of the Ancient Ones and knew in his heart that destiny would be shaped by more than armies. He stood up from the table and walked around, deep in thought.

Tella pulled a face at Cuthbert who raised an eyebrow.

"Very well," agreed Llewellyn, "we attack to the north on the next full moon. That gives Tirani the Wise twenty days to find the stone and steal it."

"And if he does not find the stone in twenty days?" asked Tella.

"Then we attack anyway," replied the Welsh King.

Cuthbert's thin lips curled into a greedy smile.

"Then we are agreed. The Alliance goes on."

The door to the chamber opened and a tall soldier entered. He bowed to Cuthbert, and to each of the guests, and with an irritated wave of his hand the baron allowed him to speak.

"The villagers are beyond the wall, as you commanded, Sire."

Tella laughed. "Entertainment?"

Cuthbert grinned and nodded. Llewellyn stared down at the floor and wondered why they gained pleasure from the misfortune of others.

Stoyalu saw his mother and tried to call out. But he was too weak and he raised a hand to show he still lived. There were many others below the cages too, perhaps two hundred, and he glanced from face to face to catch a glimpse of his father. There was a noise high above him and Stoyalu strained to see the soldiers, who gathered on the battlements, but all he could see was the tips of their spears. It began to rain and he shivered as much through fear as the cold.

"Cateya," he whispered, "there is something going on."

The little girl glanced across at him, for just a fleeting moment, and then her hollow eyes shut again.

"Cateya, look it is Mumma," but if she heard his words of hope, there was no sign of it.

Cuthbert and Tella climbed the stairs of the great tower. Llewellyn had already left them and rejoined his followers in the courtyard, as their horses were prepared for the long journey home. He didn't want any part of this.

Along the line of ramparts stood Cuthbert's bodyguard. Each looked down, grim-faced, at the villagers below and wondered what they might witness in the service of their master. Tella stepped over five chains, which ran from the wall to thick, stone pillars at the back of the high walkway. He noticed, keenly, that each chain was looped around a pillar and fastened by a single iron pin.

Cuthbert moved to the battlement and the Pict joined his new ally. They stared down into a sea of nervous faces.

"Which of you aided the Scotsmen?" called Cuthbert.

There was silence, at first, from the villagers and then a low murmur. Some of the women began to sob.

Tella saw two men walk through the crowd. Cuthbert noticed them too and they waited patiently for an answer. One of the men was old and carried a staff to support him. The other was Belus, Stoyalu's father.

"So, Cornicus, it is you who chooses to speak for your people," continued Cuthbert.

"It is," replied the old man.

"Well, if anyone knows who has wronged me, then it must be the village elder," mocked Cuthbert.

"I do know," called back Cornicus, and the crowd became restless.

"You say you *know*," said Cuthbert and he glanced across at Tella, triumphantly.

"Aye, I do," replied Cornicus, "I know in my heart that none in the village would dare to aid anyone who was your enemy. Indeed, have we not always obeyed your command?"

"But how did they escape?" demanded Cuthbert.

"We may never know, my Lord. Is it not enough to trust those who have followed you so loyally?"

The rain eased to a drizzle and the light faded, and the crowd became a dark mass below them.

Tella grinned. "He's got a bit of a point there, Cuthbert."

"One truth we all know," continued Cornicus, "is that

the children you torment were nothing to do with your misfortune."

"That's another good point," said Tella.

Cuthbert stared again at the dark mass and sensed a quiet anger amongst the villagers. At last he spoke.

"Let no man say that Cuthbert the Cautious is not without compassion for his people," and he ordered his men to pull up the two cages, which hung at the ends of the battlements.

"They shall be returned to you."

Several woman gasped and Stoyalu's mother fell to her knees, as if giving thanks for the deliverance she had prayed for and not believed.

"But you see, Cornicus, I can have no man saying I am easily swayed from dealing with those who oppose me."

Cuthbert walked back to a pillar and kicked out a metal pin. The crowd gasped as the chain flew, at great speed, through the gap in the stones at the top of the rampart. It gave off a high pitched shrill as it cut through the air and Cateya's cage plummeted down into the deep waters of the moat.

Cuthbert waved a hand, gracefully, at Tella. Inviting him to join in the fun. Stoyalu felt the world fall from under him.

***

After four days of hard riding and two changes of horses, Llewellyn and his guard came in sight of familiar hills. Again, he urged his men onward. He was counting the days and knew that he must speak with Tirani at the first opportunity.

Deep furrows cut across his brow as he thought about the task that lay ahead of his people. He had forged what he believed to be an uneasy, yet necessary, alliance. Tella and Cuthbert were as thick as thieves in the plot to unseat Malcolm the Younger, a king he had no real quarrel with, and he questioned his motives for joining them. Tirani would give him sound counsel.

They approached a tall, stone keep that stood proud above a

fast-flowing river. It was day's end and firelight could be seen through thin slots that marked out the windows. The path snaked down the hill towards it and was flanked by ancient standing stones, whose purpose and creators had long been forgotten by all but the Wise.

They rode silently until they reached the main gate of the fortress. Guards saw them and, like dancing shadows, moved swiftly to make a way through for their king. Llewellyn dismounted and hurried to the throne room. It was warm and richly furnished and smelled of apples. The chamber was empty except for a young boy who played silently on the floor with wooden toy soldiers. He glanced up at his master. His eyes were a deep blue and pierced deep into Llewellyn's soul.

Tirani smiled and said, "You want me to find the stone."

Llewellyn nodded at the boy.

"Of course, you shall take the northern lands, but you doubt the motives of the Picts."

Llewellyn nodded again.

"I can offer you no counsel about how things will be after the division," continued Tirani, "but Myroy knows that war is coming."

"Can he stop us?"

"I do not believe so. But he can make it more difficult by hiding the stone."

"The stone is lost then," mumbled Llewellyn.

The boy moved a soldier across the floor and studied it closely.

"Not lost, hidden. I have felt the presence of the stone and now I have no sense of it and that means it is below water."

Llewellyn walked across the chamber to his throne and slowly lowered himself down onto it. He remembered himself as a young boy, playing and learning with his closest friend. His father had played as a child with Tirani too, and his father's father.

"How old are you Tirani?" asked the king.

"Nearly as old as Myroy," and, as he often was, Llewellyn was left to wonder at his reply.

278

"You agreed a date with Tella and Cuthbert then."

It was a statement of fact rather than a question and Llewellyn stared at the fire.

"The next moon."

"So time is short," replied the boy.

"Will you find me the stone?" asked the king.

"But I do not know where it lies."

"But can you find it?"

The young boy glanced at his master and his face lit up.

"If you agree that the northern lands will need a prince to oversee its rule for you, then I can."

"Men and horses will be put at your command," replied Llewellyn, but the boy shot him a look of contempt.

"There is not enough time for that, for your intention is to march before an army that carries the stone. Go and prepare your warriors and leave the arrangements to me."

Llewellyn nodded and watched the boy rise and walk to a table at the side of the room. Tirani picked up a small leather pouch which he tied to his belt. He then lifted an old woollen cloak and threw it over his young shoulders. He looked like a poor urchin.

"If I do not return in ten days then you should believe that I have failed," said Tirani.

Llewellyn went across to the boy and hugged him. Side by side they walked to the castle gate and then out into the night. Neither spoke and Llewellyn tried to think if there was anything he might do to help his friend on the journey.

Tirani squeezed his master's hand and reassured him.

"It is better that I go alone."

In front of them stretched the path that Llewellyn had returned by. The standing stones formed a dark corridor and the sound of fast-flowing water grew louder.

"Did you know that all the things of the Earth have a power?" asked Tirani.

"You told me once when I was young," replied the king, "and

it is not by accident that the stones follow the river."

Like a pupil rushing to his lessons, Tirani skipped away down the path and called out, "I shall hurry back to you."

Llewellyn stared into the gloom and the outline of the Wise faded. The sound of the water grew louder still and a bitter wind blew through the stones and swept back the king's long hair. In that moment, all trace of the boy was gone.

***

Dougie of Dunfermline was thinking about his sheep. He could clearly picture himself resting against the standing stone that was his favourite resting place at day's end. The cold granite seemed to be shivering and hares, sensing an unknown danger, bolted for their burrows. A small boy in a ragged cloak walked from behind the standing stone, looked around and took no notice of Dougie. For a moment, they both gazed at the fine sheep that grazed on the rich pastures of Dougie's farm. The distant hills framed the landscape like a picture.

"Wonderful," thought Dougie as he sensed the power and beauty of the land.

A flash of sun on water caught their eyes and the boy made his way down the sandy path towards the loch. In the west, the morning sun was a salmon-pink. Dougie's thoughts were drawn down again to the calm waters of the loch and they seemed to be growing restless. Dougie could feel them boil with an intense anger.

Kenneth of Blacklock was staring down, grim-faced, from the top of the harbour wall.

"What a sight," he moaned and Dougie awoke from his daydream.

"Well, it's not the *Pride Of Tiree*," said Alistair.

"What a sight," repeated Kenneth and he shook his head.

The old seafarer climbed down onto the deck. He stumbled backwards over a small water barrel and cursed. Strewn all around him were the signs of decay and the lack of proper care. Oars, sail, leather buckets, tangled nets and empty cases formed an untidy mess across the wooden deck. Indeed, very little of the deck could be seen.

"You might have tidied her up a bit," teased Alistair.

Kenneth growled and began the long task of preparing for the voyage to Ireland. Dougie knew that this was a poor alternative to the fine lines of the ship his friend had loved and lost, but at least they had been assured that the timbers were sound and the lower part of the deck was dry.

The sailor barked instructions at the Men of Tain and, gradually, the chaos was replaced by order. Dougie was told to coil the ropes and he thought about their recent journey from the Palace to Oban. They had taken three days and ridden without incident to meet with Kenneth. Malcolm the Younger had provided them with thirty silver coins to help buy a new boat for their friend who had lost his in the service of the king.

The grumpy sailor had grunted, taken the money reluctantly and agreed to secure a new ship that would be capable of the long voyage across the Great Sea. Dougie was comforted because Kenneth would be their guide, but he still wished that he could return quickly to Mairi, the children and his farm. They all seemed such a long way away.

The *Leaping Salmon* was twenty-two paces long, with a single mast that was as wide as a man's hand at its base and as thin as a finger at its point. It creaked as it bobbed up and down and looked as though it needed a good lick of paint. But it was also the only ship that could be purchased immediately.

"He saw us coming," moaned Kenneth, remembering how he had bargained in the tavern for the *Leaping Salmon*.

He called for Alistair to help him carry the sail onto the quay. They manhandled the heavy cloth up the ladder and laid it out upon the ground. It was full of holes. Hugh and Rory, two brothers from the Black Isle, were sent to buy another and Kenneth started grunting angrily again.

"When might we leave?" asked Alistair.

Kenneth looked at the clouds on the horizon and then at his new ship.

"As soon as she is ready and we have tried her out in Oban Sound."

"And so it could be as soon as tomorrow," replied Alistair.

"If all goes well and we catch the morning tide," said Kenneth.

"And the journey to Mull?"

"With a fair wind, two days."

"And if, like last time, the wind is not fair?"

Kenneth walked to the ship's rail and pushed it. A length of wood broke off in his hand and the sailor shrugged his shoulders.

"Not good," thought Dougie and he busied himself to take his mind off their mission.

At the king's request, Archie had written a letter to Malcolm's brother Murdoch who was the Protector of the Outer Isles. Their plan was to secure an alliance with the Irish peoples through marriage. It was said that Murdoch's daughter was fair and of the right age for marriage. Alistair had told Dougie that Margaret was the bossiest and strongest willed woman he had ever met.

"The sooner we get going, the better, young Dougie," called out Alistair.

"Aye," replied Dougie.

Alistair's voice was grave.

"Malcolm may need help from Patrick sooner than we think. If only we knew when Tella the Mac Mar plans to invade."

"We may not know until it happens," said Dougie.

"Still, in some ways, it is not our concern for our task is clear."

"Clear, but not easy. What happens if Margaret does not wish to marry Patrick?"

"It is her royal duty and the fate of the Scottish people might hang on her decision," said Alistair.

"And yet you suspect trouble?"

Alistair nodded and, following a sharp word from Kenneth, returned to his work.

After an hour, the deck of the *Leaping Salmon* was neat and ship-shape. Hugh and Rory had returned and, with some difficulty, had rigged the new sail. They were the thinnest youths Dougie had ever seen, they seemed to be very eager to please and several times Kenneth nodded, approvingly, at the speed with which they tackled the tasks given to them. The Men of Tain were despatched to the village to buy provisions and Kenneth sailed out into the harbour with the two brothers acting as crew. The breeze was gentle and Dougie wondered if this would be a true test of the ship's mettle.

Alistair sensed his unease.

"Let's hope we have fair weather like this for the voyage."

"Or we might be meeting the sickness again," said Dougie.

"Aye laddie, aye," laughed his friend.

Next morning, Kenneth looked up at an autumnal, salmon-pink sky.

"Let go aft," he cried, and the *Leaping Salmon* drifted out into Oban Sound.

Dougie knew what was coming and tried to busy himself with even the smallest of jobs. But Hugh and Rory raced about the deck to complete any order that Kenneth barked to the crew and Dougie was left to stare back at the coast, disappearing quickly in their wake, and he tried to prepare himself for the first leg of their journey to Mull.

***

Prince Ranald of Scotland demanded that breakfast be brought to his chamber.

In the kitchens, in the depths of the Palace, a young and fresh-faced boy piled eggs and bacon high upon an oval platter. He returned the skillet to the old cook and beamed at her eagerly.

"May I take the tray for you, Eilidh?"

She smiled. "You're new here, are you not laddie?"

"I am new and I am very keen to help."

"You must learn that often a servant's tasks are not easy. Prince Ranald's tongue can be sharp."

The boy opened his eyes wide. They were a piercing blue and the cook felt as though she was seeing her own son as a youngster, so many years ago. In a strange way, he also reminded Eilidh of her grandfather, who had long since left the world.

"I would still like to try," he said and the cook felt as though she could not deny her new charge anything he asked for.

Having arranged the feast neatly on a tray, the servant climbed the kitchen stairs. At the door to Ranald's chamber, he stopped and knocked respectfully before entering.

"Put it down there," commanded Ranald, and the servant quickly placed the tray by the side of the bed.

"Will there be anything else, Sire?" asked the boy.

Ranald's face became angry and he pointed at the door.

"Aye, some peace."

"I did not think that that would be your reply,"

"And what reply would a dog like you expect?" barked the Prince.

"Why, *yes* of course," said the boy in a matter of fact voice.

The prince sat up in the bed and looked into two piercing eyes. Then he spoke more calmly.

"And what was the question?"

Tirani raised an eyebrow and grinned broadly.

"Would you like to be a king?"

***

The standing stone, Dougie's favourite resting place at day's end, shimmered and hares, sensing unknown danger, bolted to their burrows for safety. A small boy in a ragged cloak walked from behind it and glanced around. Many sheep grazed on the rich pastures and the distant hills framed the landscape like a picture.

"Beautiful," muttered Tirani and he too sensed the power of the land.

A flash of sun on water caught his eye and he made his way down a sandy path towards the loch. To the west the morning sun was a salmon-pink and the journey passed quickly as Tirani compared the scene to the lands with which he was familiar. Eventually, he stood where the path reached the shore. For a long time he thought about his quest and his agreement with Ranald.

As he had suspected, the prince had known where Amera's stone had been hidden and had wondered why a shepherd had been entrusted with it by the Younger. But why had Ranald been so easily persuaded? He might be a fickle ally, but the key to his allegiance was greed. He would see his own father destroyed if there was a chance of ruling the kingdom, even one part of it, and on behalf of Llewellyn.

Eventually, he knelt beside the cold waters and opened the leather pouch that hung from his belt. Tirani pulled out a silver whistle. It was short and thin and had only two holes on its top from which notes might be played. The boy edged closer to the water's edge and took a deep breath. He put the pipe to his lips and plunged his head below the water.

Gasping for breath, Tirani pulled himself backwards and sucked in the sweet air. He swept his wet hair from his face and carefully placed the whistle back into the pouch. He stared into the centre of the loch and the waters appeared to boil. A great osprey exploded from its depths and rose skyward. Then the bird hovered, seeking out those that had dared to disturb its peace. Tirani looked up at the bird.

"Very clever," he whispered.

The osprey's powerful eyes fixed on the boy and committed every detail to memory, for all might be important. Closing its wings the bird dived at a fantastic speed towards Tirani. A man's height above the ground its wings opened, like a huge cloak, and in seconds the osprey had begun its own journey to the south.

Tirani the Wise smiled and wondered how long he had before Myroy arrived.

It was two thousand summers since Tirani had last spoken to Amera, the King of the Sea People. They had played together as children and then the great warrior had grown old. But Tirani had not. He remembered being teased as others grew tall and strong, and he remained a child. It was Myroy who had helped him develop the wisdom he would need.

Tirani sighed. There were so few of his kind and much of their destiny was pre-ordained. It was as though his whole life, and the duty that had been promised to the line of kings, was laid out like a path before him. Still, the influence of the Ancient Ones would not last forever. The dark times of man would be replaced by a better future and then they could rest. Suddenly, Tirani felt tired and very old.

The boy closed his eyes and began to remember days of long ago. He stood beside Amera's death bed and sensed the king's followers preparing a cairn for the resting.

"You cannot hide the stone away," he had said.

"It is too powerful not to be hidden and we cannot destroy it," replied the dying warrior.

"Many will try to steal the stone and most will fail," continued Tirani.

"*Most* will fail, but not all."

Tirani smiled kindly at his friend.

"You do not really believe that burying the stone in a tomb will stop it calling out do you?"

The king's face was gnarled with age and his long hair, snow white. With a great effort, Amera shook his head.

"All you could ever do was to hold the stone for a short while and you should be proud that you have done that well," continued the boy.

"Would you not take it for me?" asked Amera hopefully.

"The stone was gifted to you and your people," replied Tirani, "and is not for the Ancient Ones."

"But it can be used for great evil," said the king.

"It will be used for evil, at times."

"Until *he* comes."

Tirani nodded, "Until the stone is destroyed by a boy with anger in his heart."

"Then bury it with me," commanded Amera.

His breathing was more shallow now, as though all life was leaving his body. The last act of the greatest king of the early peoples was to raise a hand and open his fingers to reveal a blood red ruby. He pressed it into the boy's small hand.

Tirani awoke and looked down at Amera's stone. It was beautiful and deadly. He rose quickly and skipped back down the path. He tossed the ruby in the air and caught it. The sun had reached its highest point in the sky and it was pleasantly warm. He noticed keenly that his shadow was longer than on a summer's day and knew that the winter months lay ahead.

"But not yet," he said and as he skipped he raised his young face to enjoy the sun's rays.

Tirani reached the standing stone quickly. He looked back at the loch and thought that he saw a large bird hover above it. On the other side of the hill, an old man placed a flower upon a mound of rocks.

The boy grinned and Myroy turned to talk to him.

"Be ready."

It was as though his brother was standing next to him.

The wind rose and it was bitterly cold. Tirani nodded, the standing stone shimmered and he skipped lightly into another place.

CHAPTER NINETEEN

MARGARET THE OBSTINATE

The Princess of the Islands stamped her feet and threw the parchment on the ground.

"Shan't," she yelled. "Why can't we marry *him* off to one of Patrick's daughters?"

"Because the Younger has chosen you, not Ranald. Patrick himself is the key to our fortunes," replied Murdoch.

"How can you do this?" screamed Margaret, "you have never been a good father, so selfish."

"Selfish?" asked Murdoch.

"It means always doing what *you* want to do."

"I know what it means," said Murdoch crossly.

The princess crossed her arms and bit her lip. She looked as though she was ready to fight an army.

"It is your duty," continued Murdoch in a soft voice, "and Matina will be with you,"

Margaret stamped her feet again.

"You can go and boil your head."

"Neither of us have much of a say in it for Malcolm is sure that war is coming and the whole kingdom may be lost if we stand alone."

"Shan't."

In the passage outside the Protector's chamber, Dougie, Alistair and Kenneth were grim.

"You said she might be difficult, Alistair," said Dougie.

"I think she has taken it rather well."

"Spoilt cub," muttered the old sailor as a plate broke into pieces on the door.

"But, my wee angel," said Murdoch.

"Don't you *wee angel* me!" screamed Margaret.

"I have heard that Patrick is wise and kind," persisted Murdoch.

"Old and ugly more like."

"And a king of great wealth."

Sensing defeat, Margaret dropped her head into her hands

and began to cry.

"But daddy," she said softly, "I love you and my home on the island."

The princess looked up with wide, pleading eyes into her father's. Murdoch felt torn between his duty to the Younger and his feelings as a loving parent.

"There are times when we all have to do things that we do not want to do."

"But this need not be one of them," begged Margaret.

"I am afraid that it is."

"But he already has six wives," snapped the princess as she threw her head back once more. "What kind of fool do you think I am?"

"The kind of fool who puts her king before herself," said Murdoch.

"Shan't," said Margaret.

Murdoch rose and walked to the window. He stared out at the Great Sea. "My mind is made up. You sail to Ireland on the first tide."

"You beast," screamed Margaret and she ran from the room.

The friends looked at each other as she swept defiantly past them. Then they glanced into the chamber at the Protector of the Outer Isles. He sat alone with his head in his hands and, without another word, they left Murdoch to his thoughts.

***

The *Leaping Salmon* bobbed against the harbour wall and was much improved by its new coat of varnish. Kenneth called out orders and Hugh and Rory raced busily around the deck. The sail had been hoisted to the top of the mast in readiness for their departure and it fluttered like an enormous butterfly. A fresh water barrel and crates of food were lowered down onto the deck and Dougie looked back up the path that led to the village.

"No sign of her Highness yet?" asked Alistair.

Dougie shook his head and looked again towards the cottages. Something seemed to be moving and then the quiet of early morning was broken by a single word.

"Shan't."

A small group of islanders was coming towards them. Murdoch seemed to be dragging something behind him. He looked exhausted.

"I shall marry Patrick and the first thing I will do is ask him to come and fight you, you bully," yelled Margaret.

"You do not mean that, my angel," said Murdoch.

"Don't I, you beast?" she screamed.

"Down you go," commanded Murdoch and the young princess was forced into the boat. Matina followed her loyally, head down and in silence. The ship rocked from side to side as the wind rose and drove rising waves against the quay.

"Stow your things over there," ordered Kenneth.

The princess stood tall and proud in the centre of the deck. Her long blonde hair was blown back to show a face that could be truly beautiful, but now it was shaped by a dark anger.

"You can go and boil your head," she screamed.

"Don't tell me to boil my head," said Kenneth angrily.

"Shan't."

Dougie glanced at Alistair and they both wondered what the skipper would do now that someone had so obviously refused his command. Kenneth hissed at Dougie through gritted teeth.

"We are going to have a real problem with this one."

The wind rose again and the ropes that held the mast snapped under the strain. The sail billowed out as the mast fell and it completely enveloped Margaret the Obstinate.

A muffled, "I suppose you think that's funny," came out from under its heavy folds.

"You know, Dougie," said Alistair, "there are times when you cannot help but believe in the power of the Ancient Ones."

Dougie laughed and went to help the others prepare for the passage to Ireland.

At the same time, the Scottish fleet was being provisioned at Glasgow. Eight fine ships were berthed beside a long quay and over a hundred warriors prepared themselves for the journey to Man. The largest and fastest vessel was the *Wave Rider* and Robert of Inverness was counting the last of the boxes that were being carried onboard.

"Job well done, everyone," he called out eagerly.

"Aye, jolly well done, everyone," mimicked Donald.

"Don't forget who is in charge," said Robert crossly and he marched up the gangplank to give Donald a dressing down. He wasn't going to let anyone talk to him like that in front of the crew.

Donald dropped the last of the crates on the deck.

"Careful with that," demanded Robert, "I won't have sloppy work on my ship."

"Sloppy work?" replied Donald slowly.

"I am going to give you a piece of my mind," said Robert.

"Can you spare it?" asked Donald.

Robert stepped up in front of Donald and prodded him roughly on the shoulder with an accusing finger. A shadow fell over them both and Robert turned to look into the chest of Big Hamish. It was the size of a barrel.

"Anyway, this is not helping the king's business," gasped Robert nervously and he went off to boss someone else about.

Donald was about to start squeaking like a mouse when he stared past his giant friend.

"She who must be obeyed is here," he whispered solemnly.

"Is it Senga?" asked Hamish.

Donald grinned and pointed at the path that wound its way down to the waters of the Clyde. A blue gypsy caravan was coming towards them.

"I think Babs has come to see you off."

Hamish's face lit up like a beacon. Then he looked at Donald and the other Men of Tain, sheepishly, for he knew what was coming.

"If she mentions a man of fire, tell her that we have already dealt with that one," called out Donald cheekily as his friend turned to meet his lady of the Union Of Souls.

Hamish stopped in his tracks and growled.

"Perhaps she has brought you a clean shirt, for you should never face an enemy when you are improperly dressed."

Hamish pretended to ignore his friend, who began to coo like a dove. His great weight made the gangplank bend like a bow and, as he glanced up, he noticed that Donald was ushering the Men of Tain to the ship's rail. They were watching him and Donald was grinning mischievously.

Babs brought the gypsy caravan to a stop at the end of a line of wagons which flanked the quay. She ran to her husband and threw her arms around him affectionately. A small ripple of applause came from the *Wave Rider*.

"My wee Hami," she said.

There was a slightly louder round of applause as they kissed.

Hamish picked her up, like a feather, and hugged her.

"I am so glad you could come."

"Jolly well done," called out Donald and there was more applause.

"Let's get away from here," growled Hamish and, hand in hand, they walked along the water's edge and the cooing of the crew faded away.

"How are the preparations going?" asked Babs.

"We sail on the tide," replied Hamish and he squeezed her hand gently.

"Take great care," said the gypsy girl in a mysterious voice.

"I will, my love."

"And beware the black and red sails."

"I know of no fleet that flies those colours," said Hamish.

"And yet I have seen them," she persisted.

"Then I shall watch for them, my love."

"And I shall wait for your return and count each day, my sweet."

Hamish sighed. "And so shall I."

They kissed once more, talked about the future and then slowly made their way back to the ships. They passed the caravan and Babs stopped to collect a leather bag. In front of the *Wave Rider* they kissed again and earned another round of applause.

"What is in the bag?" asked Hamish.

"Some extra food, my wee Hami," replied Babs.

"Lovely."

"And a clean shirt for the journey."

Hamish looked up at Donald. He had the biggest grin he had ever seen.

An hour later, the might of the Scottish fleet set sail for the west. It was a fine day and the spirits of the sailors and warriors were high. The quay was soon far behind them and the Great Sea beckoned. The ships formed a line along the Clyde, like the links in a closely woven chain. Then the river widened quickly and the banks, to the north and south, soon disappeared from view.

"Well, we're off," said Robert in his eager voice.

"Aye, well done, everyone," said Donald and Robert looked cross again.

Hamish leant against the ship's rail and stared, blankly, back up the valley.

"Sad to go?" asked Donald kindly.

"Aye," muttered Hamish, "Babs told me to beware the black and red sails."

"Och, don't you worry yourself about that," replied Donald, "no such sails exist, for the Picts have black sails with no red in them."

"Aye," agreed the big man, but he did not sound very convinced.

"You should worry about the sea sickness," joked Donald and they decided to get something to eat, so that they were primed and ready.

In his clean cloth shirt, Hamish lay snoring. Donald listened to the noise and tried to think of funny things to say about it when his friend woke and took over the tiller. It was a clear night with a gentle breeze, and the fleet had long turned away from its heading to the west. Donald kept the *Wave Rider* pointing straight at the southern stars and wondered how long it would be before they sighted the island of Man.

Theirs was a fast ship and, even under three-quarter sail, the rest of the fleet had become strung out behind them. Donald glanced back again to make sure that the last vessel could still be seen. Like demon shadows, the seven sails followed.

Everything was peaceful as timbers creaked, ropes tightened and slackened, and Hamish muttered unknown words in a never to be remembered dream. His head was tilted back at an unnatural angle, mouth open like a cavern.

Looking up at the half moon, Donald guessed that dawn would break soon. Even now, to the east, a pale rosy glow was appearing on an otherwise dark horizon. The bow of the ship had drifted from its course slightly and he gently moved the tiller to bring them back to the correct bearing.

He remembered the gathering of the High Table at the Palace and how determined Malcolm had been to provide help for Gawain.

"Go with all speed and ensure that the Picts do not make any more of the light iron," the Younger had commanded, but he and Hamish would rather have gone with their friends, Alistair and Dougie, to Ireland. In truth, they would rather have helped Malcolm raise the clans, at home, than set off on a journey that promised little adventure. In fact they would rather be anywhere than on a boat under the command of Robert of Inverness.

Archie was still trying to make the new blade and the few weapons they had captured on Man had been given out to the king's knights to aid their missions. Donald felt for the sword that hung through his belt and drew it out. It was perhaps half the weight of his trusty claymore and it looked a dull grey. Then the iron shone a weak orange as the first rays of sun burst above the waves to his left.

Donald did not feel the least bit tired and decided to wait a while before waking his friend. He plunged the sword into the deck by his side and it sliced its way deep into the wood. He watched it swing from side to side as the ship rocked. If their enemies were armed with these terrible weapons, then they had much to fear.

Donald thought that he heard someone call him. He glanced across the deck and everyone seemed to be fast asleep. He heard the voice again and this time he looked back over his shoulder towards the fleet. A bright light shone from the furthest boat and Donald guessed that a lantern had been lit and raised to the top of their mast.

"That's a signal," thought Donald and he listened intently.

A faint voice, from the nearest ship, came to him through the half light. It seemed to be urgent and he strained to hear the single word being shouted. A sailor seemed to be waving his arms frantically and Donald pushed the tiller round. The sail flapped as it emptied of wind and the *Wave Rider* slowed in the water. The fleet got nearer and then Donald heard it.

"Shails."

"Shails," thought Donald, "what is he on about?"

"Sails!" came the cry again.

He glanced around at the Great Sea, but saw none. The man shouted, "Sails!" once more and he followed his outstretched arm, which pointed along the line of the fleet. Lit by the dawn sun, the outline of a huge number of distant sails followed them. Donald called out urgently to the crew and, in a matter of moments, all eyes were strained to the north.

"How many?" asked Hamish and he yawned.

"I cannot tell," replied Donald, "but they are more than we."

"And their colour?" asked Robert.

"In this light we have no chance of knowing," said Donald, "but we can assume they are not friendly."

"Aye," growled Hamish and he cupped his great hands towards the nearest ship. "How many?" he bellowed.

"Twenty at least," came the faint reply.

"Twenty," gasped Robert, "so many. Surely the Picts do not have such a number."

"Well, all we can do is make a run for it," said Donald.

Hamish looked at him as though he would rather have some fun with them.

"Hamish," ordered Robert, "tell the next ship to make their own way to Man at the best speed they can manage. Ask them to pass this on to the others."

Hamish growled, but did as he was instructed.

"How far are we from the island?" asked Donald.

A short and weather-beaten sailor looked at him and shook his head.

"A day and a night, with a following wind, and not enough time to outrun a faster fleet."

"Better get ready for a fight then," muttered Hamish.

The sailors let out the sail so that it took all the power that it could from the wind. Their distance from the others grew by the hour and, when the sun was at its highest point in the sky, they looked back to see a single tower of black smoke. Six sails were now scattering in all directions, like pearls from a broken necklace.

"So their intentions *are* evil," said Robert bitterly.

"And they have overrun the slowest ship," growled Hamish.

Donald looked at the deck.

"And its crew lost."

"Aye," replied Hamish.

He had never felt so helpless for they could not come about and fight so many. Their distance grew from the towers of smoke that sprung up, one by one, on the horizon. By day's end they counted five fires that marked the fall of each ship and the death of their crews.

"Perhaps one was able to flee," said Donald.

"I hope so, laddie," lamented Hamish.

The sun was setting in the west and the base of the fiery globe touched faraway waters. Very little had been said that day and even now many eyes searched for the sails of their pursuers.

"There are two," yelled a voice and the friends leapt up from the deck to join the others.

"They must be their fastest ships," rued Donald.

"And what are their colours?" asked Hamish, but he already knew.

In the last rays of the sun, the enemy closed upon them at great speed. One sail was red and the other was as black as the *goal* they had first seen at the mines on Man. Donald looked at Hamish and Hamish looked at Donald. Both of them knew that the Welsh and Picts had combined in their intention to destroy the Scottish fleet and would be determined to complete the task given to them.

They walked back to their part of the deck, which had been home for such a short time.

"I could murder a dram of ale," muttered Hamish.

"Wise words," said Donald.

Then, in silence like the others, they began to sharpen their swords.

CHAPTER TWENTY

PATRICK THREE EGGS

Dougie went across to Margaret, and the sleeping Matina, with a peace offering and wondered how anyone could be so beautiful and obstinate. The ship lurched and some of the steaming broth he carried spilled onto the deck.

"Something to warm you through, My Lady," he said kindly.

Margaret turned her head away as though he did not exist.

"I am afraid it's not Mairi's lamb and barley broth, but it's the best we have."

A shoulder shrugged under her thick cloak. It was snow white and edged with a fine trim of silver weave, and the shepherd compared it to his own woollen plaid. "You could buy a hundred like mine for what it is worth," he thought.

"My Lady," persisted Dougie.

Margaret glared up at him and shivered with the cold.

"Leave me to my peace."

"Aye, I will lass, when you have warmed yourself with broth, for nights at sea bring a chill like none we feel on the farm."

"Are you a farmer?" asked Margaret.

Dougie's face showed a deep sadness.

"When I can be."

"I have heard my father speak of you, Dougie of Dunfermline. Are you not a great warrior?"

Dougie shook his head. "You know my name?" he asked at last.

"You carried the king's brooch when you first came to the island."

"That seems like a very long time ago," and he smiled.

"It was a long time ago and so much has changed for me since then."

Dougie passed her the broth.

"Aye, it has, lass."

"Who is Mairi?" asked Margaret.

Dougie looked at the floor and thought about his home.

"The woman I love."

"And you chose to marry her and were not forced into a union?"

"I wouldn't say *chose*. I think you just know."

"And if you don't know?"

"Then maybe choosing is the next best thing."

"But what if you cannot even choose?"

Dougie thought about his own daughter, Tanny, and knew in his heart how Murdoch must have felt as they sailed away from the quay on Mull.

"I do not know the answer."

The Lady of the Islands sipped her broth and looked up at the stars. There were so many and they shone brightly in the cloudless night.

"Kenneth says we should see Ireland after sunrise," whispered Dougie.

A flash of defiance shot across Margaret's face.

"I shan't marry Patrick," she said.

"We must all do what we believe is right," replied Dougie.

"And do you think it is right?"

"I am a farmer and know little of the dangers that Malcolm the Younger fears, but I do believe in him."

"But do you think it is right?"

Dougie stood and took off his shawl. He laid it gently across Matina's shoulders and turned to take his watch at the tiller.

"No," he said softly to himself.

***

"Land," yelled Kenneth and the *Leaping Salmon* listed to one side as the crew dashed to the ship's rail for a sight of it.

"It looks no different to Stranraer," said Dougie.

"Aye," said Alistair, "there are tales told that these lands were joined to Scotland in ancient times."

They stared at the far hills. They were very green and broken into small fields by low stone walls.

"Good country for sheep," said Dougie, approvingly, and Alistair smiled at his friend.

Carried by the turning tide, they made swift progress towards the village of Belfast. Dougie felt excited as they got closer and counted seven fishing boats, moored at the water's edge, in front of a row of brightly coloured cottages. It seemed busy and children ran to tell their parents about the approaching sail.

Alistair thought about Holke, and Kenneth barked orders for the sail to be lowered and for lines to be made fast to the shore. Horses were being led down the path towards them and Dougie saw Alistair searching the faces in the growing crowd.

"We are expected then," said Dougie.

"Aye, and by royalty, so tidy yourself up a bit, laddie," teased Alistair.

"But who will Patrick send to meet us?"

"Wait and see, young Dougie."

Dougie noticed that Margaret stood alone on the deck, staring back across the sea, and Dougie went over to comfort her.

"Home feels like a long way away," he whispered.

Margaret nodded and quickly wiped a tear from her cheek so that the others would not see it. She threw her head back and marched with dignity towards the gangplank. Before following, Matina gave Dougie back his shawl and smiled at him.

"How the devil are you, Alistair?" came a bright, cheerful voice.

"All the better for seeing you, Seamus," replied Alistair and the two men shook hands. "This is my friend, Dougie, and this is Kenneth of Blacklock."

"Welcome to Ireland," said Seamus, "I look forward to escorting you to the royal court at Mountjoy."

Dougie could not help but like this handsome man. He was tall and elegant, dressed in fine clothes and perhaps twenty summers young.

"Is it far?" he asked.

"Half a day's ride, so time enough to share tales about the wider world."

Then Seamus looked past them at Margaret.

"Are you not going to introduce me to the fair lady who graces our land with her beauty?"

His words were deliberately loud enough for her to hear and Margaret's sullen face changed in an instant.

"Margaret," said Alistair in a formal voice, "this is Seamus, Prince of all Ireland. Seamus, may I introduce you to Margaret, Lady of the Outer Islands and daughter of the Protector."

"That's a hell of a title," joked the prince, "and I hope you don't mind if we just call each other by our day names."

Margaret curtsied, nodded and gave him a smile. Her face seemed to light up.

"My, you are a fine woman," beamed Seamus, and Dougie thought she blushed a little.

Kenneth of Blacklock began to walk back to the *Leaping Salmon* and Alistair ran over to talk to him.

"Are you not coming with us to Mountjoy?"

The sailor stared past him at the open sea. It called to him.

"My work is done here."

Alistair knew that there were no words he could use to make him change his mind.

"Take Hugh and Rory with you, old friend," said Alistair.

Kenneth nodded, turned and walked back to his ship.

Within minutes the Scottish envoys were mounted upon strong white horses and Dougie held Matina in front of him, and felt her tremble. The stallions were truly magnificent creatures and forgiving to Dougie's inexperienced hands. The travellers' belongings were being loaded onto a wooden cart by two strong warriors. Dougie and Matina watched Seamus's bodyguards as they both hurried onto the ship to collect the last box onboard.

"I'll take that," said one.

"Oh no you won't," argued the other.

"And who's to say that I won't be the one to carry it to the wagon, certainly not you, Declan Finnegan."

"Oh! So you, Michael O'Mara, have become the chief box carrier in the kingdom now have you?" taunted Declan.

"I have always been better at it than you and most of your family have never lifted a finger, let alone a box."

"Oh! So the Finnegans are lazy now are they? It is only the O'Maras who would be experts in not lifting a finger."

"Your family are a bunch of good-for-nothings and I don't know why I have to work with any of them."

Dougie and Alistair sat, side by side, and watched, somewhat bewildered, as the two men began to fight. They punched and kicked each other ferociously, and traded more insults. Seamus saw them looking at the battle, that raged aboard the *Leaping Salmon*, and grinned.

"It is a bit of a peculiarity of the Irish people. They like to settle *little disagreements* this way."

Alistair grinned too and Dougie made up his mind not to have any sort of disagreement with anyone in these strange lands.

The ride to the palace at Mountjoy, on the western shores of Lough Neagh, was pleasant and free of trouble. Dougie held Matina and rode beside Alistair, and they talked about their mission. Matina just listened. Margaret and Seamus rode together and every now and then Dougie heard them laugh and it lifted his spirits to know that she would have at least one friend in her new home.

For part of the journey, Dougie talked with Declan and Michael about their life at the royal court.

It seemed that they were not to be the only envoys to seek Patrick's help, for parties from Tella the Mac Mar, and Cuthbert the Cautious, had already arrived.

"I am sure that Malcolm does not know that the Picts and Angles seek Patrick's favour," said Alistair, in a dark voice.

"Aye, and it can only make our task all the harder."

"But, succeed we must, Dougie. Even now I feel that time is against us."

"If only we knew when they plan to attack."

"It may be possible to find out if the enemy's envoys know the answer."

But Dougie could not see how they might find out the answer.

They stopped at the crest of a small hill overlooking grey water. Lough Neagh seemed as big as the Great Sea for the far shore could not be seen and its waters were many times bigger than the loch by Dougie's farm. A well worn path, rutted deeply by cart wheels, wound its way down to a castle with a huge central keep that stood proud above an outer defensive wall that itself must have been three men high. It looked impenetrable. The outer wall enclosed a wide area and within its protection were the roofs of many outbuildings. Seamus explained that these were available to visitors to the palace and that the largest of them was the banqueting hall.

"As you will find out, that gets the most use," said Seamus.

"Look, Matina, what a great place," said Dougie and she nodded.

They approached a huge stone gateway and many soldiers ran out to greet them. They were armed with sword and spear, and formed two orderly lines for them to ride through. With the smell of horse attacking their senses, they dismounted in a circular courtyard and their belongings were unloaded from the wagon. Dougie wondered if Declan and Michael would start fighting again.

Built into the high walls that surrounded them were perhaps a hundred stables. They looked back at the many horses which stared out at them, all magnificent creatures and of the same character, and quality, as those they had been lent for the journey. Declan led the way through a narrow stone passage and they had to bend double to get through.

Seamus held Margaret's hand.

"This is the main way to the palace," said the prince. "It can hold back the biggest and fiercest of armies."

"The smell of horse would do that too," added Alistair and Dougie grinned.

They walked for twenty paces, through the gloomy passage. It was damp and a poor entrance to the palace of a king. Then they were through and stepped out into bright sunshine. The castle rose majestically above them. A large, green open space, enclosed by a high stone wall, was full of richly dressed people who talked in small groups. Many were being waited upon by busy servants who laboured under trays piled high with food.

Children played games, like those played by Dougie's own children. Minstrels played a melodic tune and three girls, dressed in white robes, began to sing sweetly in an unknown tongue.

"Follow me," commanded Seamus.

He led them towards the banqueting hall. As they walked, Dougie was conscious of being stared at. He glanced to his left and noticed two warriors dressed in black kilts. They did not seem at all pleased to see the new arrivals. As they passed the Picts, Dougie could feel their eyes burn into the back of his head. They seemed to burn with a quiet hatred. He glanced at them again and the shorter one of the two spat on the ground.

"They are filthy Scots, Borak" he said loudly. His voice was cold and the words were fired out quickly, like a handful of gravel thrown onto water.

The inside of the hall was warm and smelled of bread. It must have been twice the height of the hall of Hamish's clan, but they shared the same raised platform at the far end. Along its length was a table and upon the table many candles burned.

"Father," said Seamus.

"Ah, Seamus you young rascal, want some food?" asked Patrick.

Standing in waiting behind the king was a short and elderly servant dressed entirely in green. He looked up at the ceiling as if thinking, "Not again."

Patrick turned on the servant.

"Time for dinner yet, yer whining ninny?"

"My name is Milligan, Sire, and I thought you might remember it, seeing as how I have served you since you were a baby."

"But is it time for food yet?" snapped Patrick.

"You have just eaten."

"Oh, so you're the king of bloody Ireland now are you?"

Milligan's face looked tortured.

"Your mother wouldn't like you eating one meal straight after another."

"Oh, so you're me bloody mother now as well are you?"

"And what will we be having this time?" asked the servant in a resigned voice.

Patrick rubbed his great barrel of a chest in anticipation.

"I fancy a half meal. How about a nice bit of chicken? What about you, Seamus?"

Seamus smiled and nodded to let Milligan know that chicken would do fine. Then he pointed at Dougie and the others, and held up six fingers.

Milligan mouthed the words, "Another six," and Seamus nodded.

"And will there be anything else, Sire?" asked Milligan, turning to face Patrick. "After all, I am only the busiest man in all Ireland."

"You'll be the worst suffering man in all Ireland in a minute," retorted the king.

"I am already the longest suffering. Will it be the usual?"

"Aye, I'd better have three eggs with that," he beamed.

"*Only* three eggs?" mocked the old servant, as he hobbled through a door behind them.

"I must do something about that whining ninny," groaned the king.

Seamus smiled at his father.

"You have been saying that since I was a boy."

"I don't know why I put up with him," said Patrick.

"Is it because you like him?"

"Like that whining ninny," boomed the King, "you are getting as soft in the head as he is."

Sensing another *little disagreement*, Dougie nudged Alistair who coughed politely.

The king looked at the party gathered before him.

"Is that you, Alistair?" asked Patrick.

Alistair bowed respectfully.

"At your service, My Lord."

"You know I hate all that bowing and snivelling," barked the king, "How is Malcolm, the old devil? Still worried about the Picts is he?"

"Worried in his heart," said Alistair.

"He has every right to be." Patrick raised a finger to his nose and tapped it twice. "This tells me they are up to their old tricks again."

Alistair nodded.

"I bring you greetings from the Scottish people. And we beg your council to discuss a matter of great urgency."

"Of great urgency to you maybe, but not to me."

Alistair passed a letter to the king, who read it slowly.

"So, you bring an offer of marriage," he said, "what the devil do I want with another wife, I have six already and a trouble they are to me too."

"It is more than a Union of Souls," persisted Alistair. "It is the bringing together of two royal households and two great peoples."

Patrick raised an eyebrow and passed the letter to Seamus.

"Fine words old friend, but what is she like?"

"She is as beautiful as a flower on a summer's day," mused Seamus.

Patrick pulled a face. Part grimace. Part disbelief.

"You like her then, do you?"

Seamus nodded and Dougie saw Margaret blush again.

"When you are king you can have as many wives as you like, but until then you will just have to do as you are told," barked Patrick. "Well, where is she?"

Margaret stepped forward, her long hair framing a defiant face.

"Do you like eggs?" asked Patrick.

"Hate them," lied Margaret.

"A girl with spirit, eh?"

Margaret glared at him and folded her arms.

"I shan't marry *you,* so you can go and boil your head," and then she smiled at Seamus.

"I can see I am going to have trouble with you, my *Lady*," roared the king.

Dougie could hear Kenneth's words in his mind, "We are going to have a real problem with this one."

At that moment, Milligan led a team of servants to the raised table.

"A half meal is served," croaked Milligan, and then under his breath, "again."

"Excellent," roared Patrick and he beckoned to the Scots to join him.

A young boy, of no more than nine summers, was bent under the weight of Dougie's platter. He helped him with it and looked down at two whole roast chickens and three eggs.

"Hamish would like this," said Dougie.

"Aye, he would that, laddie," agreed Alistair. "He should have reached Man by now."

Armed with knives, they began the first attack on the chicken and thought about their two missing friends.

***

The Welsh warrior snarled and hurled a three-pronged iron hook at the enemy ship. It caught on its wooden rail and he pulled hard so that they could board. Donald pulled the dirk from his belt and hacked desperately at the thick rope.

Big Hamish was fighting for his life. He lifted the Black Kilt above his head and tossed him, screaming, into another Pict and

311

the two of them fell into the sea. A flaming spear landed by his foot and Hamish grabbed it and threw it back into the mass of warriors on the enemy ship.

Robert stood by the tiller and watched the battle. The *Wave Rider* was hemmed in on both sides by warships. The Picts were scrambling on board despite the brave efforts of the Scots who formed a defensive line along the ship's rail. On the other side Donald, and a handful of sailors, were trying frantically to cut the many ropes that were being hurled from the Welsh ship. But as soon as one line was cut, two more hooks would bite into the deck, and the enemy inched closer.

He felt helpless. He could not turn the ship into free water and he knew that once the Welsh warriors boarded they would be lost. Robert pushed the tiller over and the *Wave Rider* lurched. Three Picts, who were jumping across from their ship, found a gap open up in front of them. Two fell in the sea and one dropped his axe and grabbed at the rail. Hamish picked him up by his neck, smiled at him, and pushed him backwards to join his friends.

The *Wave Rider* lurched towards the Welsh ship and their lines slackened. Donald unhooked one and pulled with all his might. A warrior at the other end of the line was caught off balance and fell overboard. The man was crushed as the two ships smashed together.

Hamish, like the others, was thrown to the ground by the impact. He stood and growled at Robert, who now threw the tiller over in the other direction. They crashed into the Pictish ship and Hamish fell over again. Donald grinned at him and the big man growled.

Another flaming spear came from the Black Kilts and it sliced through the *Wave Rider's* sail. It started to burn. Donald glanced at it and then over at the Pictish ship. Many of the enemy were placing spears into an iron brazier that burned on the deck. They lit quickly and were thrown with venom. Fires sprang up all around them and the *Wave Rider* lost speed as its sail burned away.

A hook from the Welsh ship landed behind him. Another caught in the shoulder of a sailor, who stood next to Donald, and the poor man was dragged over the side. Donald rushed across to Hamish.

"The ship is lost," he yelled.

"Well let's get another one then," boomed Hamish. "What do you fancy, black or red?"

"The Picts were the first to reach us, so their ship must be the faster."

"Wise words," chirped Donald.

As many iron hooks from the Welsh ship fell about them, the Men of Tain went on the attack.

"Follow me!" shouted Donald and the Scots drove the Picts back and swarmed onto their deck.

A great Black Kilt raised his battle axe and viciously brought it down. A young sailor, beside Hamish, fell and Donald drove his light blade into the enemy's stomach.

In the desperate and bloody fighting, claymores sang as they clashed on axes. Robert dashed from the tiller and leapt over the rails to join them. Bravely he fought two Picts and won control of the stern.

"That's the end of the mouse jokes then," said Hamish.

Donald dodged a spear and thrust his fist into a Pict's face.

Sensing defeat, many of the enemy jumped and escaped onto the *Wave Rider*. They stared with hatred at the Scots through the flames that were starting to consume its deck. They waited for the Welsh warriors to join them and heaved on the lines so that the three ships clung together as though they were one.

"We don't need this," boomed Hamish and Donald helped him lift the two poles on which the mighty brazier stood.

"Beware the man of fire?" joked Donald.

They threw the burning coals across onto the *Wave Rider*. Instantly, a carpet of immense flame and heat erupted upon its deck and a man screamed as his robes caught fire. He dived into the sea.

"Push us away," ordered Robert.

Donald grimaced.

"Shall I throw him overboard, or will you?"

The wind changed and great flames were blown their way. Hamish and Donald glanced at each other and obediently grabbed at stout oars that lay along the rail. They pushed with all their might, the black sail caught the wind and, slowly, they began to drift away from the burning hulk.

Behind them they could see the Picts clambering, for all they were worth, aboard the Welsh vessel. There were loud and urgent commands given in a strange tongue and many hands cut them adrift. In that moment, the *Wave Rider* listed and its fire was extinguished in a plume of black smoke. The ship hissed as it was claimed by the sea.

"I wonder what Babs will say?" teased Donald.

Hamish raised an eyebrow.

"About the danger from the black and red sails?"

"Och no," said Donald, "about your new clean shirt."

Hamish looked down at the tattered shreds of cloth, with ends that smouldered orange as the breeze caught it.

***

They made good speed before a following wind and Hamish hunted along the length of their new ship for food.

"Not a morsel. Do the Picts not eat?" he moaned, and looked north.

The ocean was empty and calm, and there was no sign of the enemy. The sun touched the western horizon and sent them its own red flames along a shimmering line on the sea.

"They will not follow us now," said Donald.

Hamish nodded and wondered how long it would take them to sight Man.

"Sails. I can see sails," shouted Robert.

Everyone's eyes followed the line of Robert's arm.

"How many this time?" asked Hamish.

"Just two," replied Donald, "the same odds as before."

Robert pulled hard on the tiller and the sail flapped angrily as they turned into the wind.

"What do we do now?" he shouted.

Hamish and Donald ran to join him and watched the ships tack, against the wind, towards them.

"They are definitely heading for us," said Hamish.

"Wise words," said Donald, "shall we have another good punch up?"

Hamish growled. "Our mission is to go to Man and we are in a fast ship. My vote goes to running straight past them under full sail."

Robert pulled the tiller back round.

"Just what I was thinking. Get ready everyone to make a run for it."

The gap between the men of Tain in the Pictish ship and the unknown sails closed quickly. With each rise and fall of the deck, waves of foam engulfed the bow and increased in height as they gathered speed. A worried sailor ran over to them.

"The sails are marked with the three legs of Man," he cried.

They all ran to the bow to get a closer look. The ship dived down and they were drenched.

"This is not good," said Donald.

"Better than a Pictish fleet," said Hamish.

"Aye, but they have no more love for the Picts than we do," and he pointed up at the black sail, billowing above their heads.

"And do you remember how they fought in the wooden stockade? They are a fierce enemy."

Five boat lengths from the sailors of Man, they could clearly see them preparing bows and sword.

"They mean to attack us," shouted Robert.

"Not if they know we are true Scots," replied Donald and he called for the sail to be lowered.

"I give the orders around here," said Robert. "Lower the sails."

Knots were untied and the canvas fell heavily on the deck. An arrow sliced into the canvas and everyone dived to find cover.

"Are you thinking what I am thinking?" asked Donald.

"Aye, and it is long overdue," growled Hamish.

Robert screamed indignantly as strong hands pinned him to the floor. In a matter of moments his plaid, of the finest king's own tartan, was raised high up the mast where it fluttered, ceremonially, on the breeze.

CHAPTER TWENTY ONE
INTRIGUE

The Prince of all Ireland smelled a small bouquet of blue lavender bound with gold lace. It reminded him of his mother and summer days in the meadows around Mountjoy. He knocked gently on Margaret's door.

"Go boil your head," said an annoyed voice.

He smiled and pictured the beautiful lady of the islands in his mind.

"It is I, Seamus," he whispered.

Something stirred inside the chamber, as though things were being hastily tidied away.

"Seamus, is that really you?" asked Margaret.

"Now, who else might you be expecting. Many men would be my guess seeing as you are the finest flower to grace our lands."

Margaret quickly ran a comb through her hair and opened the door. Seamus smiled again and handed her the flowers.

"Fancy a walk around the gardens? It is wonderful weather we are having."

"That would be lovely," she replied eagerly and, arm in arm, they descended the stone stairs.

Behind them, in the corridor, a grim-faced man stepped out of the shadows and followed quietly. He thought about Margaret's habits over the last three days and in particular the times when she was alone in her chamber, or with the mute serving girl.

"The best time would be after supper, as the guests slept, and it could be done quietly, without fuss." Tumora pulled a knife from inside his black kilt. "Now what if it was a Scottish dirk?"

He walked off to find Borak.

Dougie yawned contentedly.

"How can you eat so much?" he asked.

"So much?" bellowed Patrick, "it's noon and we've only had three meals today. You must be half starved up there in bloody Scotland. Doesn't Malcolm feed you lot?"

They lay in the sun on the green and Milligan stood to attention beside them, holding a tray of pastries. He tutted and stared up at the blue sky.

"Don't you tut at me, you old fool," spat Patrick.

"My name is Milligan, Sire, and I thought you might know ..."

"Not that old moan again," interrupted the king. "I've a good mind to set the dogs on you."

"Will that be all, sir?" replied Milligan calmly.

"No that's not bloody all, go get us a half meal."

Dougie groaned and felt his stomach. It seemed to have grown bigger than it had ever been these past four days.

"What would you say if we ran out of food?" complained Milligan.

"I'd say we need a new bloody servant, now clear off and get me something to see me through to supper."

Milligan tutted again and marched off to the keep.

"I don't know why I keep that ninny," complained Patrick, but he laughed as he said it.

"Daddy," cried a voice and three young girls in colourful dresses ran across the grass towards them.

Dougie thought the youngest was about four summers, and that the two girls who followed her were twins, and about the same age as wee Tanny.

"My buttons," said Patrick proudly as he was hit at full pace by the youngest girl, who leapt on his chest. "How are you today, mischief?" and he kissed her.

The twins leapt on him too and there was an almighty *woof*, and the king's face went white as he fought to sit up.

"You're not taking Murphy for his walk are you?"

The little girl nodded, giggled and stepped aside. Patrick tried to sit up.

"Oh no, bloody hell no," he said.

A great shape bounded out of the shadow of the curtain wall and moved at a fantastic speed towards them. The twins moved back, a mischievous look on their fair faces. Milligan, who had just stepped out of the door to the keep, turned gracefully on his heels and disappeared back inside with his tray.

Woof boomed the massive beast and, five paces from them, it leapt into the air. *Oooof* wheezed Patrick, as all the air was knocked out of him.

"So those naughty buttons have let you out have they?"

He rubbed the dog's belly.

"Meet Murphy-dog," said Alistair, "the finest wolfhound in all Ireland.

"Hello Murphy," said Dougie and he put out a hand.

The girls looked horrified and Patrick was just about to say, "Don't do that, whatever you do."

But, the dog gave another excited *woof* and trotted across to him. He licked his hand and Dougie tickled his ear. Contentedly, the great beast lay beside him and his tongue came out after his run in the heat.

"He likes you," exclaimed the twins, as though they did not quite believe it.

"I like dogs," replied Dougie and he rubbed Murphy's ear again.

The king looked at Dougie with a new respect.

"Well, would you know it, there are not many strangers that keep the flesh on their arms at a first meeting."

"He's a bit like my dog, Dog," whispered Dougie, "a big softie."

Murphy looked up at him as if to say, "Dog, dog? I am not deaf and so you only have to say it once."

They all laughed and Murphy spotted Milligan creeping across the green. He tore after him, followed by the girls who shouted at him to come back. But Murphy-dog knew that the king's servant was the best source of food and entertainment in the castle. Milligan spotted his tormentor. As the wolfhound leapt, he threw his tray skyward and, like a hare bolting across a field, he tried to scamper to safety.

"I'm bored now," moaned Patrick after a while.

Dougie opened an eye. "It can't be time for more food already."

"We need to build up an appetite," ordered the king.

Alistair winked at Dougie.

"I think you have killed mine off completely."

Ignoring him, Patrick stood up and stretched.

"Besides, I'll only get bothered by all the bloody children."

"How many children have you got?" asked Dougie.

"At the last count, thirty, and a trouble they are to me too."

"Thirty," exclaimed Dougie.

"You don't know what it is to be king, young Dougie, no peace and I can't even remember their names now, so let's go and organise a hunt."

Milligan returned at last. Part of his sleeve had been torn to shreds, but he proudly held aloft a tray that was full of ham and eggs. He staggered slightly and seemed out of breath.

"Well, you took your time," barked Patrick.

"A bit of trouble with wild beasts, Your Majesty, but a half meal is served."

"That's no good now," replied Patrick, "go tell Finn we may need him and prepare the horses, and ask the guests if they would like to join us on the hunt."

Milligan swayed on his feet and Dougie feared he might fall. But he turned, tutted, and walked with great dignity back to the keep.

"What do you fancy, Alistair?" asked Patrick, "wolves, deer, boar or bear?"

"Deer is good for the eating."

"Good thinking, so we will need the pack as well."

Dougie raised an eyebrow and the king saw it.

"You don't think that Murphy is the only one of his kind do you?"

Dougie shook his head and wondered how many he had.

Alistair looked at him knowingly.

"Fifty."

"That's not a pack," mumbled Dougie, "that's an army."

"And I know all their bloody names too," boasted Patrick.

"But not your own children," scolded Dougie.

Patrick shot Alistair a wicked grin.

"A man's got to get his priorities right."

The circular courtyard and stables still smelled of horse. Servants ran in all directions to make sure the king's guests were armed with spears. Provisions in small leather bags were quickly tied to their saddles. As Dougie was helped up onto a white steed he looked down at his bag and Alistair grinned at him.

"You never know when you might need a wee half meal."

Dougie's horse tossed its mane and snorted eagerly. As he sat, waiting for the main gate to open, he saw that the two Picts had mounted too. So had the Angle warriors and he began to feel scared.

Alistair and Patrick walked their steeds next to Dougie's and one of the Angles said something to his friend. The gate opened and, with the thunder of hooves, the hunting party galloped out into dazzling light.

The journey to the forest was short and Patrick led them into a clearing enclosed by mighty oak trees. In its centre was a hut and a fenced arena. The excited barks of many dogs came from behind the tall fence. They dismounted and a giant of a man walked over to meet them, looking intently at the riders in the party. His eyes moved from the Picts to the Angles and then settled on Dougie. Dougie smiled and the man smiled back.

"This is Finn McCool," said the king, "the strongest and bravest man in all Ireland and that is why he accompanies me on any journey outside of the kingdom. He also looks after the hounds, for no one else can control them."

Dougie thought that Finn must be a hand's length taller than big Hamish. He looked strong and had fine features, and it was clear that he enjoyed the respect of the Irishmen in the hunting party.

Finn nodded at the king's guests and remained silent.

"We wish to hunt the deer today, Finn," said Patrick.

It was more of a request than an order.

The giant strode over to the hut and returned with a side of venison. As he walked, he tied a thick rope around it. Without ceremony, Finn tossed the carcass over the gate into the fenced arena. He threw it as though it was a slice of bacon and kept hold of the rope. Instantly, the gate shook, as though a mighty wave had smashed against it. Angry growls and barks broke the silence. Finn pulled the frayed and empty rope back, and placed a hand on a wide, wooden beam that held back the ferocious tide.

"Better get on the horses," urged Patrick and he ran back to his steed.

Dougie and the others were not slow to follow his lead and as the last of the party mounted, Finn lifted the bar and nothing happened. Then he gave a low whistle and the pack was loose. It was an incredible sight. The wolfhounds charged out of the stockade, bounding like mad things across the clearing, and their barks quickly faded.

"Let's go," commanded Patrick and they galloped into the forest, hoping to reach their quarry before the angry pack.

They hunted for many hours and the time passed quickly. Two deer were laid across the back of a horse and another had been torn to shreds, before Finn could pull the dogs away. Dougie had seen it from a distance and felt sick.

Another deer was spotted, but the dogs barked and dashed off in another direction.

"There must be two, or more," yelled Patrick excitedly, "divide the party."

Dougie turned his horse and galloped away with some of the other riders, up a sandy path and through a dark stand of birch and ash, and then over a shallow stream. That was a mistake. A spear flew over his shoulder and he glanced back to see the two Angle warriors chasing him, and he realised too late that he was separated from his friends. The hunter had become the hunted.

He urged his horse to go faster than was safe when riding

through trees. He ducked under a branch that nearly took his head off. Then another spear glanced against the horse's flanks. In pain, it bucked and Dougie found himself hanging on sideways, his arms wrapped around the animal's neck and one foot clinging desperately over the beast's back. He bounced up and down and glanced ahead. They were galloping straight towards a tree. With a great heave he pulled himself back into the saddle. But a sharp branch cut deep into his leg and part of his plaid was torn away.

Behind him, the closest rider threw another spear. The second rider pulled up his horse and bent down to pick up the torn scrap of tartan. It was covered in blood.

Dougie was terrified and perhaps it was his fear that made him feel no pain from his wound. He urged his steed on, but sensed the enemy gaining on him. They rounded a sharp bend in the forest path and his poor horse stumbled. Dougie flew through the air and landed in a thick tangle of bramble. A thousand pins cut into his skin and thorns tore across his body. He tried to move, but the plant was wrapped tightly around him like a shroud.

Dougie stared out of the brambles and watched the Angle warrior dismount and run towards him. The man lifted his spear into the throwing position and grinned.

***

The thriving port of Douglas had been rebuilt and the two friends marvelled at its cottages, quay and outer defences.

"A lot has changed since our last visit," said Hamish.

"Wise words, but some things don't seem to have changed."

They looked at Robert. He was barking out instructions for the re-rigging of their ship. The Thane of Inverness saw them.

"Hey, you two, we need help to get this black sail down."

"Keep your plaid on," said Donald.

Robert stiffened, shook his head and marched off to find someone who would listen to his orders.

"I wonder if Gawain has a new palace?" said Donald.

"Gawain would see the homes of his people restored before he turned to his own needs."

"Aye, he seems like a just king. Let's hope he chooses to support us."

"We helped him."

"We did, but they may have had enough of fighting. Do not forget that they were treated very cruelly and will value the peace."

Hamish didn't want to think about the possibility of going back to Malcolm without the men of Man as allies. He stared out to sea and up at the darkening sky that signalled the end of another day.

"I'm hungry," he said at last.

"Och, you're always hungry. Why don't you take up something like basket weaving to take your mind off your stomach?"

Hamish lifted him up and glared at him. Donald grinned back.

A young girl, with wide eyes and short red hair, skipped along the waterfront, stopped and spoke urgently to them.

"Gawain of Glamorgan, Lord of Man, will see you now."

Hamish dropped Donald on the floor and they followed her up a narrow lane towards a long white cottage with a turf roof and only just big enough to be called a hall. As they waited outside its door, Donald remembered the commotion as they were escorted into the harbour and the angry faces of the warriors along the quayside. They would have met with a terrible death if they had turned out to be Picts.

"Not a place for Tella the Mac Mar to visit," he said.

Hamish said nothing, but remembered their gaunt faces when they had been enslaved and forced to make the light iron.

Gawain sat upon a plain oak seat, on a raised platform at the end of the smoky hall. The girl with short red hair ran to his side and Donald grinned as he spotted the family resemblance.

"I do not remember seeing your daughter when we were last

here," he said, "and what a credit she is to you and the line of Glamorgan."

The girl blushed and Gawain smiled, and placed his hand on her shoulder.

"Wise words," mimicked Hamish, and Donald looked at his friend with surprise.

Gawain gave them a warm welcome.

"You must have some story to tell, arriving here in an enemy ship and scaring the life out of the women folk. How about sharing the tale at a banquet to honour your return?"

Hamish rubbed his belly.

"And how is Malcolm?" Gawain continued.

"I think you know," said Donald.

The Lord of Man rose and shook hands with his guests.

"The word is that Tella, curse him, has led an army from Skye to Oban. I have no news of Llewellyn and Cuthbert, but the map tells us that they must surely be moving too."

"So soon," gasped Hamish.

"It is *too soon*, for you are here to ask for my help and I am not ready to give it to you yet."

Donald looked crestfallen.

"But you will help us, as we helped you."

In that moment Gawain's face changed. It looked dangerous.

"You do not need to remind me of the debt we owe you," he whispered.

Hamish glanced at Donald and they felt as though a spear had been run through their bodies.

"We are too small to play a part in this war," continued Gawain.

"We also were few and even one brave warrior will make a difference," said Hamish.

"I *will* consider your request, but do not expect me to risk the lives of my people without choosing the right moment."

"Alistair and Dougie have travelled to Ireland," persisted Hamish, "we hope to turn the tide with the aid of Patrick and so we do not ask you to risk your freedom alone."

Gawain looked at their eager faces and smiled.

"Very well," he said at last, "if Patrick leads his army to Scotland, then my fleet will attack the enemy."

"That is something, at least," thought Donald, "because Malcolm doesn't have a fleet any more."

Hamish stared at his feet and knew that so much now rested on Alistair's shoulders.

"Now come," and the Lord of Man led them down the length of the hall and into the fresh air.

He pointed up at a half moon that sat low in the sky.

"This is not yet *our* time, but do not fear."

"I am afraid," muttered Donald.

When Gawain spoke, his voice was warm.

"If Malcolm falls, we will all have much to fear, but Myroy has commanded me to wait for the right moment."

Hamish nodded and they walked down to the quay, talking about Tella's map and the growing troubles in the wider world.

***

Dougie dreamt that someone was cutting his leg off and he woke suddenly, and sat bolt upright.

His body shook and he gasped for air, like a drowning man who had reached the surface. He blinked in the bright light and looked around the chamber. A holy man, in a monk's habit, sat reading at a sturdy table. The sun streamed through a large window and its rays fell on the stranger and his book. Dougie's leg hurt and he glanced down to see that it was covered in bandages. Dried blood stained its edges.

"Hello," said Dougie politely.

Either the man did not hear him, or he ignored him, for he turned a page decorated with many colours and a fine script.

"Hello," said Dougie again and this time the man looked up and smiled at him.

The stranger had the kindest face Dougie had ever seen. He

was old, but his eyes sparkled with youth and any movements he made were deliberate, as though his entire being was shaped by a purpose. The man closed the book and nodded at Dougie. The crown of his head was shaved, his black hair forming a ring, and his dress was without adornment, except for a wooden cross hanging on a string around his neck.

"Now then, Dougie of Dunfermline, tell me how you feel."

"My leg hurts, but the rest of me seems to be working."

The monk rose and walked over to him, carrying a thin piece of wood about the length of an arm.

"You may wish to keep this as a memory token," he said, and he passed his patient the stick. "It went right through your thigh and took some time to pull out."

Dougie took it and wondered how big the hole in his leg was.

"Where am I?"

"In the rooms given to me by Patrick."

"And what happened? The last thing I remember was an Angle warrior trying to run me through with a spear."

"That must be when you fainted."

Dougie felt embarrassed.

"I am not very good at being a warrior, am I?"

"From what Alistair has told me, you are a great warrior and you have earned his friendship by the deeds you have done. It was Alistair who stayed with you, here, these past two days."

"Two days," gasped Dougie.

"And the fever seems to have gone completely. Your companions will be relieved to see you return, for we feared you lost."

"They will not be as relieved as I am," thought Dougie.

The man nodded and went back to study his book. Dougie raised an eyebrow and wondered if it would be alright to get up.

"Tomorrow," said Columba.

"What is it you read?" asked Dougie, some time later. He was full of broth that Matina had brought him, and bored.

"A story, a great story."

Dougie had never seen a book before, but he had seen words written on maps and the runes carved onto arrows.

"What is it called?"

"It has many names and it has a power that is greater than kings, or armies."

Dougie considered his words. Could its pages hold some of the old magic, like the stone Malcolm had given to him?

"May I see it?"

The man nodded and continued to read.

"A shepherd's work is never done," moaned Dougie, as he lifted himself off the bed and hobbled over to the desk.

"You are a shepherd too?" asked the monk, "I thought you were a warrior."

"Aye, I keep the flock and wish for no more than to share days with my family."

"Then why are you here?"

"I do not know," replied Dougie truthfully, "things just seem to happen to me."

"Well, the best thing for you to do now is to move around as much as you can. The leg will recover more quickly if you use it."

Dougie obeyed his instructions and, as he walked, Columba read him a story about a traveller who was robbed on the road. Many people ignored the poor soul until he was finally helped by a good Samaritan.

"Why did the others not help him?" asked Dougie.

"They were too concerned for themselves and sometimes the bravest heart beats inside the man who puts others before himself."

Dougie moved to the man's side and looked down at the book. The writing made no sense to him, but he could see that it was beautifully made. Certain letters were larger than the others and drawn with great skill. On another page was a colourful picture of the Samaritan, washing the traveller's feet.

The door to the chamber opened and Alistair entered.

"Hello, lazy bones. Good to see you up and about."

Dougie smiled and his curiosity got the better of him.

"What on earth has been going on?"

"You fell from your horse and two Angle warriors tried to kill you. Finn came to your rescue and speared one, the other is still at large in the king's forest."

"So I owe my life to Finn."

Alistair nodded. "And Patrick was furious at them for daring to kill someone under his protection. He will not ally with Cuthbert, that is for sure."

"But will he help Tella?"

"He may do, for Margaret is being as obstinate as ever. Their envoys are led by a man called Borak and he is brave and cunning. Patrick admires those qualities."

"He admires other qualities too," interrupted Columba, "for he has helped the followers of Christ to build churches and spread their word."

"Malcolm will help you too," smiled Alistair, "he will protect your people on Iona."

"And we value his help greatly. Even now I fear for our church and I can only pray to lead my people back there as soon as circumstances allow. War *is* coming and we will need to move with caution."

"Now, Columba, is the patient ready to face the wider world?" asked Alistair.

"The question is, whether the wider world is ready for young Dougie?"

The two friends laughed, thanked him for his kindness, and left the monk to his prayers.

***

In darkness, deep within the royal forest, Borak dismounted and led his horse through a corridor of ancient oaks. A single torch moved from side to side a hundred paces in front of him. He moved forward quietly and then called out.

"Mayalis, Mayalis are you there?"

The Angle warrior stepped forward and anxiously checked to see if his ally was followed.

"I am here and the moon is half full."

Borak handed him a bag stuffed full of food.

"Something to keep you going."

Mayalis took it gratefully.

"The armies will be on the move now, so what is to be done?"

"The Scottish envoys still live and we must ensure that Patrick joins with us."

"Curse that Finn McCool, I will see that he gets his just rewards."

"Later, perhaps," said Borak, "but tonight you must be ready, as we agreed."

"When you kill Seamus they are bound to suspect you."

"Not if they suspect Margaret's people and the Scot, the one they call Dougie of Dunfermline, is not able to voice his innocence," said Borak darkly. "You still have it?"

The man felt in the pocket of his cloak and smiled at the assassin.

CHAPTER TWENTY TWO

KILLER IN THE DARK

Dougie was fast asleep and dreaming again. Someone was lifting up his plaid and cutting his leg off. This time it was the other leg and he imagined that he might never walk home. The door to his chamber clicked shut and at once he was wide awake, trying to focus his eyes in the gloom.

He reached down to feel his leg and discovered that the dirk in his belt was gone.

He took a moment to remember where he was and then jumped out of bed, and ran to the door. Dougie stubbed his toe on a chair and hopped around in circles, clasping the foot tightly in his hand to take the pain away. He cursed and dashed out into the corridor. At the far end a dark figure in what looked like a black kilt turned the corner and seemed in a desperate hurry to get away. Dougie wondered if he should go and wake Alistair, and decided that if he did, he would lose sight of the thief.

Running as quickly and as quietly as he could, Dougie soon reached the turn and followed the figure down the cold stairs. His bare feet made little noise, but some way ahead came the sound of boots on stone. Then a door opened and the boots continued on gravel. Each step crunched and Dougie knew the man was in the garden.

A quarter moon shed some light onto the grass and fruit trees, and here the shadow moved more cautiously. Whoever it was stopped and crouched, as though preparing to leap. Then Dougie heard low voices. He could not hear what they said and so he moved closer, trying to make as little sound on the gravel as he could. He felt as though he was making enough noise to wake the dead, but the thief did not turn.

The Pict's eyes were fixed on a couple who sat together on a low trestle. They had their arms round each other.

"I am so glad you came," said the man.

The lady replied, "My life has had few pleasures of late, except when we have stolen the time to be alone."

"And what a beautiful night it is," continued the man in a soft voice, "but compared to you it is like a cup of water that dares to challenge the sea."

Margaret giggled.

"Oh, Seamus, you do say such lovely things."

Their heads moved closer, to kiss, and the shadow moved behind them. Dougie caught a glimpse of metal and began to run. The enemy turned with a look of complete surprise on his face. But he turned back in an instant and held his dagger aloft.

Dougie shouted.

"Look out, Seamus!" and the Prince of Ireland spun round on his seat.

Margaret screamed in terror as she saw the assassin. Dougie leapt at the man and knocked the dirk from his hand. It flew through the air, spinning wildly, before its sharp blade sliced into the grass at her feet. Margaret screamed again.

The enemy ran at great speed across the garden and Dougie gave chase. The man moved swiftly and the distance between them increased. He slowed as he rounded a bend in the curtain wall and then he was sprinting again, across the green in the direction of the stables. Dougie's injured leg began to scream with pain, but he kept going.

Dougie ducked his head as he limped through the low, damp tunnel. He glanced forward. The tunnel was empty and he guessed the man was already in the stable yard. The main gate to the castle stood open and a guard lay sprawled on the ground. Dougie raced past him and stopped to get his breath back. He stood outside the great defensive walls and, two hundred paces away, the shadow disappeared into the forest. The bandage on his thigh was now wet with blood.

"He must have hare's legs," thought Dougie, as he began the chase again.

Under the trees, all was black and eerie. The path that he had first taken on the hunt lay before him. It looked narrow and forbidding, and yet Dougie knew the horses had ridden two abreast down it. He ran as quickly as he dared, and as fast as his wound would allow, and came out into the clearing containing the stockade.

His eyes adjusted to the dark in the forest and gradually he could make out every detail. The man he had chased *was* a Black Kilt and he stood beside another man, the Angle who had tried to kill him.

The hounds barked like mad things, angry at those who dared to disturb their rest. And then a look of sheer terror appeared on Dougie's face. His body became cold, like ice, and he began to shake. The Angle warrior was running a piece of cloth along the cracks in the door and then he threw the scrap of bloodstained plaid over the top into the stockade. Its wooden fences shook as the pack leapt at it and took Dougie's scent. The shepherd started to run.

"Do you want the honour?" Mayalis asked

Tumora shook his head and edged backwards towards the hut. Mayalis smiled and opened the gate. The pack tore out into the forest and Dougie sensed them closing in on him. The barking of the beasts, hungry, vicious and deafening. Mayalis dived towards the hut to join Tumora and his cloak fell onto the ground.

After a few hundred paces, Dougie's leg gave way underneath him and he fell. His voice trembled.

"This is it."

The pack raced straight at him. The fastest dogs were only twenty paces away and saliva dripped from their fangs. A wolfhound leapt and Dougie shut his eyes. And then another leapt, but not at him. The giant beast snarled as it hit the killer hound in mid-air. They tumbled in a fierce struggle, but only one emerged as victor and leader. The giant hound trotted over and Dougie tickled Murphy-dog's ear.

After resting and wrapping strips of torn plaid around his leg, he limped back to the stockade, with Murphy-dog at his side, and the other wolfhounds following. Dougie thought they looked cheated and might turn on him at any moment before reaching the shadowy outline of the empty enclosure. The hut was empty now and Murphy began to bark. Along the path to the castle came a man, a giant man, and he strode with purpose.

"Finn," cried Dougie, "I am mighty glad you have come."

The hounds ran and cowered before their master.

"Who released the dogs?"

Dougie told his story. Finn's face became grim and he went over to Murphy-dog and stroked him.

"Would you see me back?" asked Dougie, "My leg is very sore and I don't want to meet up with those two again."

"Do not worry about them," growled Finn, "I passed a Black Kilt on the way here. He entered the castle."

"But what about the other one?"

Finn turned his back on him and picked something off the ground. Then he whistled, once, and instantly became surrounded by the animals he had raised as puppies. But as they took the scent from the cloak, they became wild and evil. The giant Irishman whistled once more and then the pack was gone.

Next day, the hall of the king was packed. Members of the court, royal guards, Seamus, Alistair and Borak all stood and waited in silence. Dougie looked across at Borak and realised he was not the man he had chased last night. This warrior was more heavily built and so it must have been his companion.

Finn McCool entered first and pulled the great throne out from behind a table. The chair might have weighed the same as a horse, but it did not trouble the king's bodyguard. Then Patrick entered, face like thunder.

"What the devil has been going on then?" he boomed and he sat down. "I let you stay under my roof and there has been nothing but trouble since the day you arrived."

Dougie winced. Patrick seemed to be looking at him.

"And you, Seamus, what were you doing in the garden in the middle of the night?"

Seamus seemed to wince as well.

The king stared at Alistair and Borak.

337

"You both want my help on the field of battle and I would just as well see you fight it out amongst your bloody selves."

Borak stepped forward and bowed.

"Your Majesty. I have been told the tale of last night's events and wish to assure you that we had no part in it."

"Oh, no bloody part in it. I wasn't born yesterday, you know."

Borak continued unconcerned. "We only have Dougie's word for it and he has everything to gain by trying to win your favour."

"As do you," said Alistair.

"By his own words he admits that it was dark and that he cannot be sure. Without surety there can be no justice and justice is something you stand for."

"Don't tell me what I bloody well stand for, Borak," barked Patrick, but the Pict had made his point.

Patrick nodded at Finn and the big man placed a cloth in front of his king. Patrick unfolded it and held up a leg bone. It was long, gnawed and devoid of flesh. Everyone in the hall gasped.

"Well," said Patrick, "the Angle won't be hiding in the woods anymore."

Alistair stepped forward beside Borak.

"It was a Black Kilt who tried to kill Margaret and your son, and it is known they are in league with Cuthbert."

"Oh, so Margaret is in this as well, is she?"

"They planned to kill them and then blame Dougie by stealing his dirk."

Patrick sat up on his throne.

"Seamus, did you see a Black Kilt in the garden?"

His son shook his head.

"It was too dark and it all happened so quickly."

"Did Margaret see one?"

Seamus shook his head again and stared down at his feet.

"So, my own bloody son is up to no good with a woman that is promised to me, in the middle of the night in my bloody garden."

Seamus nodded.

"Well, you can go to your room until I decide what to do with you."

Like a scolded child, the Prince of Ireland left the hall.

Finn towered above his king, motionless. Dougie glanced at him and smiled. He owed his life to this man and did not believe that he would urge Patrick to support the Picts. Finn smiled back at him. It was Alistair who broke the silence.

"We came here in friendship and ask for the help we would give you if the Irish people were threatened."

"The Irish people are not threatened," countered Borak, "and when Scotland falls, as it will do, there will be many opportunities for us all to trade and prosper."

Dougie's heart sank at his words.

"Scotland will *not* fall if it stands, shoulder to shoulder, with its friends," and Alistair pointed an accusing finger at Borak, "and the world will be a safer place for all the peoples who trade on the Great Sea if Tella is put in his place."

Patrick became deep in thought at these words. He had no intention of risking his kingdom, or the lives of his warriors, without good reason. He remembered the good relations he enjoyed with Malcolm and his many conversations with Alistair. The Scottish envoy had never lied to him. Indeed, Alistair had always given him sound advice whenever he had needed it. Patrick had only known Borak a short time, and that counted against him, but the Mac Mar would be a formidable enemy.

"We meet again in two days," he commanded, and Finn followed him from the hall.

The assembly bowed and then filed away. Dougie walked beside Alistair and, as they came out into sunshine, he saw that Borak was smiling.

"He seems happy enough," whispered Dougie.

"He has less to lose, Dougie," replied Alistair darkly, "as long as he can keep Patrick undecided, then the more chance the Picts have of succeeding with the invasion. If we do not convince

Patrick soon, then it may not matter if the Irish agree to come to our aid."

"How so?" asked Dougie, but he already knew why.

They stopped in the garden. Rosy apples clustered along the branches of the trees and bent them down. Dougie thought that Alistair looked like the branches, but weighed down by worry.

"Because if three armies take the land, then Patrick will have no choice but to accept things as they are."

They decided to talk with Margaret and try to convince her to marry Patrick, but in her chamber she was as obstinate as ever. Matina ignored them and poured water from a bucket into a jug.

"Shan't," yelled Margaret for the second time.

Dougie knew that the Lady of the Islands had been crying and put his arm around her shoulder.

"Seamus will be alright," he said, "Patrick shouts a lot, but he does love his son."

"As do I," she whispered.

"Even now," interrupted Alistair, "Malcolm and your father may be in terrible peril."

Margaret broke away from Dougie's arm and folded her arms defiantly.

"My father can look after himself."

"This is not about love, Margaret, it is about duty and saving our people."

"The future of Scotland should not rest on the shoulders of one person and if it does, then maybe it deserves to fall," said Margaret, but Dougie sensed she did not mean her words.
Outside the princess's chamber, Alistair spoke to Dougie.

"Kenneth warned us that she would be difficult and he was right."

"She is not difficult, Alistair, she is in love," and Dougie made up his mind to go and talk with Finn.

Murphy-dog was sprawled out enjoying the sunshine. He lay at Finn's feet, in front of the hut beside the stockade. Dougie had grown to fear this place and shuddered.

"Hello, Finn. I wanted to thank you for saving me."

The great warrior looked at him and seemed to be weighing something up in his mind.

"You have already done that," he said at last.

The shepherd nodded and went over to sit with them. Murphy's tail swished from side to side and Dougie grinned at him, and tickled his ear.

"Aye, Murphy, I need to thank you too," and as an afterthought, "they will be preparing for the harvest at home now."

"Tell me about your farm, young Dougie."

The shepherd told his friend about his flock, crops and family. Finn listened intently and Murphy-dog began to snore. They both talked about their homes and loved ones, and how Dougie wished more than anything to return to Mairi safely. At last Finn stood to leave.

"I must go now, for there are things to consider and do."

They shook hands and Dougie realised that he had not asked Finn for help to hurry Patrick's decision.

"But, Finn, I …."

"I know," interrupted Finn, "I guessed the moment I saw you here."

They smiled and, with Murphy bounding along beside them, walked back to the castle.

Borak stepped out from behind a great oak. He had heard every word they said and knew the Scots had an ally who was close to the Irish king, and who might sway things against Tella. He stood for some time wondering what to do and then made his way back into the forest. He searched amongst the trees and clearings and, at last, knelt beside a small stream. He pulled away some tall grasses and discarded them. Then his keen eyes settled on a plant with leggy green stems. Its fern-like leaves were crowned with small white flowers. A bit like wild carrot, or cow parsley.

He picked two handfuls and put the hemlock in his pocket.

***

"Where is that whining ninny?" demanded Patrick. "I fancy a half meal."

Alistair grinned and Dougie felt his expanding stomach. Milligan marched across the green with an empty tray.

"You called, Your Majesty."

"And where the devil have you been?"

"In the kitchens, Sire. It is where we prepare all the food you eat."

"Oh, so you're the bloody court jester now, are you?"

"I don't think there is anyone who could wait on you, Your Mighty Royalness, *and* have the time to entertain others. There are simply too many meals to fetch and carry."

"What's on the stove today then?" continued Patrick.

"Pheasant stew."

"Well tell the kitchen that if I am not fed soon it will be *peasant* stew."

Milligan groaned.

"Are you Scots hungry?" asked Patrick, and Alistair and Dougie were quick to shake their heads.

"Oh, I forgot," joked Patrick, "you won't be used to a decent amount of food if you have been served at Malcolm's table."

"And will there be anything else, Sire?" asked Milligan in his resigned voice.

"I'll just have three eggs with that."

"What a surprise," mumbled Milligan.

"What was that?" snapped the king.

"And I will bring you a nice surprise," promised the servant.

"Too bloody right you will, so go and get on with it."

Milligan turned on his heels and marched off towards the kitchen. When he had gone ten paces, Patrick called after him.

"And be quick about it, yer whining ninny."

Milligan stopped in his tracks, shook his head miserably and then, muttering to himself, continued on his way.

Borak waited for him in a dark corner of the great kitchen and studied two cauldrons that simmered above a raging fire. He watched the cook prepare the food and place the choicest cuts of meat into the larger of the two and he guessed this was reserved for Patrick and his court. The other cauldron would be for the servants. He chose his moment, sneaked over to the fire and poured a liquid into the stew, and retreated to his place of hiding.

Milligan entered with his tray and spoke urgently to the cook. The old woman looked as though she was worn down by her work and started to moan about the arrival of another order. But two bowls were prepared and, as he always did, Milligan tasted one. It was his duty to ensure that all food placed before the king was safe and of a high standard. It was the fourth time he had performed the duty that day. The stew did not taste like it normally did and he spoke to the cook.

"There is something different about this," and he ate some more.

The old woman nodded.

"I grated in some of the horseradish that has come into season."

Milligan pulled a face and swallowed another mouthful.

"Don't you pull a face like that at my cooking," she scolded.

"It is the same face that Patrick will pull at me if he eats it."

In his place of hiding, Borak stiffened.

"He loves the horseradish," defended the cook.

"He loves anything," sighed Milligan and he picked up the tray.

When the servant returned to the kitchen he staggered and fell.

"You had better … get … a guard," he moaned.

The cook reached him as he slumped on the floor. The pains in his chest felt as though someone was stabbing him with a knife and he rolled on his side in agony, and was sick. He found it hard to breathe and gasped for air. He grabbed at the old woman and pulled her to him.

"Get a guard … warn the king," he choked.

She ran from the kitchen and Borak followed her. Despite her years, the cook ran quickly up the narrow stairs. The Pict bounded after her and, half way up, called out to her to stop. She turned and Borak silenced her forever.

***

Patrick had eaten the lot. Wolfed it down like a hungry dog.

"Do you fancy another hunt?" he asked.

Dougie felt the bandage on his leg.

"Perhaps we could go for a nice walk along the river?"

"How about you, Alistair?"

"Anything, Your Majesty, as long as it doesn't involve eating."

"So a hunt it is."

He shouted at a young servant girl, who waited patiently for his next command.

"Marla, where is Milligan?" he asked.

Marla ran over to them and curtsied.

"In the kitchen, Sire."

"Well off you go then," said Patrick kindly, "get Milligan to ask Finn to prepare for the boar."

The girl smiled and turned to go. They stood and Patrick clasped his chest and fell back down. Marla screamed. Alistair tried to catch him, but the king's great weight meant that all he could do was cushion the fall.

"What is the matter, Patrick?" he asked anxiously.

The king gasped for air and struggled to speak.

"That … whining ninny said … he would … get me a surprise … and I think … he has."

The servant girl came sprinting back to them.

"Milligan is ill and lies upon the kitchen floor."

"The whining … ninny," coughed Patrick, and then he too was sick.

"Dougie," yelled Alistair, "fetch Columba," and Dougie raced away to fetch the man of healing.

All was chaos now. Guards ran to protect their king and commands were given so that no one might leave the castle. Seamus was sent for and took charge. He ordered that his father, and Milligan, be carried to Columba's chamber. He talked with Alistair, who confirmed that he suspected poison and that its effects had been obvious almost immediately. Strong hands lifted the king onto a stretcher and he was sick again. Sweat poured from his body, his face bright red as though on fire, and he writhed in pain.

Seamus was close to tears. Despite little disagreements, he loved his father deeply and he thought about all the things he had left unsaid.

"We shall find out who did this," promised Alistair.

Three girls in pretty dresses dashed across the green. They gasped as they saw their father and then, together, the twins began to cry. In that moment, Seamus's grief turned to anger.

"And why are you not ill?" he snapped at Alistair.

"We had already eaten our fill, when Patrick called for Milligan."

"That was convenient," and as he spoke, his body shook with rage.

"We were no part of this," replied Alistair in a soft voice.

Dougie ran over to them. "I have spoken with Columba and he is ready to do what he can."

"But did you do all that you could?" whispered Seamus, and Dougie looked at him with surprise.

"Guards!" shouted the prince. "In the name of the king, lock these Scots in a cell until we find some answers."

"You are looking in the wrong place," insisted Alistair, but rough hands seized them and they were led away in silence.

***

Borak moved quietly down the corridor. A guard, armed with a spear, came running and the Pict stepped into a dark corner. Borak held his breath and sweat ran down his back. If he was caught now, then all would be lost. He wondered how the Irish might deal with an enemy who had murdered their king.

The guard dashed past his place of hiding and Borak let out a low hiss as he began to breathe again. Further up the corridor, the soldier was searching for someone and Borak could hear doors open and then bang shut. Then all was quiet again and he crept across to Dougie's room. He moved quickly to the bed and lifted the blankets. Then he took the leaves of hemlock from his pocket and placed them underneath.

He bolted to the door and opened it a fraction. The hallway was deserted and he made his way down to the garden. He dared not run and tried to walk as calmly as he could across the gravel, but inside his heart raced and the fear of discovery nearly overwhelmed him. But, without incident, he made it to the trestle where he had left his brother.

"What a pleasant morning we have spent in the garden," he said.

Tumora nodded and knew the deed was done.

Borak reached over to a branch that bent close to the trestle. He picked an apple and bit into it. Then he wondered how long it would be before the guards came, but it didn't matter now. They had their story and *he* had won the time his master needed.

***

Malcolm the Younger's face was grim as he watched his men return.

They were weary and many carried wounds from the battle. Some limped and two warriors guided another man whose face was completely hidden by bandages. The king turned slowly and walked up the slope to the royal tent. He felt tired and each step was heavy, and more than once he lost his footing as he slipped on the mud that was a constant companion of their camp. They had marched and fought, and rested. Then they had marched and fought, and made camp again, and then again. Each time the result had been the same. More lands lost and fewer soldiers to continue the struggle for freedom.

Cameron Campbell stood, tall and fierce, at the entrance to the tent. The big bodyguard lifted his claymore, in respect, and the Younger nodded as he passed him. The map lay on a makeshift table and Malcolm went over to study it. Tella was moving east from Oban and back in control of the mountains that were the homeland of his followers. He had received word that Tella's army numbered nearly a thousand men. Worse still, they *all* carried the light iron.

Cuthbert was to the south at Melrose. His foot soldiers would be at the shores of the Forth in less than one week. His horsemen would be there even sooner.

But it was Llewellyn who he feared most. His massive army marched with the protection of Amera's stone and had already taken Glasgow. The Younger's riders had told him that the Welsh had slaughtered many. The clans in the south west of the kingdom were routed and Malcolm knew that this loss was only partly due to the light iron with which the Welsh were armed.

He felt alone. Even Arkinew was away and had his authority to do whatever was necessary to make new weapons from the *goal* that had been discovered in Fife. Yesterday, only one wagon of swords and spearheads had arrived. It was a pitiful supply when compared to the size of the Scottish army. Today, none had arrived.

"Where is Alistair?" muttered the king.

The floor shimmered and Malcolm stared at it. A head appeared and then the cloaked figure of Myroy was standing before him.

"You ask after Alistair," stated the ancient adviser of kings.

Relief flooded through Malcolm's veins.

"I do not know how long I can hold back the tide without Patrick."

"Patrick is dead and Alistair is imprisoned," replied Myroy, in a matter of fact voice.

Malcolm's head dropped into his hands.

"This is my darkest day."

"And Gawain will not aid you unless the Irish play a part in it."

The king groaned. "And my fleet is destroyed, and so the Picts and Welsh command the sea."

"They do."

Malcolm rose and looked into his friend's eyes.

"What shall I do?"

"There is nothing you can do, at the moment anyway," and Myroy smiled, as if reassuring an old friend. "Take your men into the lonely places and rest them. Keep them safe and ready. Let the enemy come and do not let fear overcome your judgement."

Malcolm nodded. "How is Dougie?"

"He is imprisoned with Alistair, because of a killer in the dark."

"But you believed he would play an important part in the war that was sure to come."

"You do not know it yet, but he has already played a part and will do so again."

"And Llewellyn has Amera's stone."

"He has," confirmed Myroy, "and you will come to be glad of it."

Malcolm raised an eyebrow.

"Oh, he is using it against you now, but that might not always be so."

"But how can I be sure?" asked the king.

Myroy drew a circle on the floor with his staff.

"You cannot be *sure*, you can only have hope."

"Ranald has fled. Was he a part of it?"

"It was as you suspected."

"My own son," gasped Malcolm.

"You are not the first king to have been betrayed by the ambition of his own kin."

"That is true and yet it does not make the knowledge any less painful for a father to hold in his heart."

"You knew when the Elder died that it would not be easy to wear the crown and yet you have reigned justly, and carried the burden well. Do not lose hope or faith in those that support and love you."

Malcolm felt strengthened by his friend's words and nodded.

"Your moment *will* come," said Myroy, "wait for it."

Then he disappeared into the ground.

The king gave instructions for eight riders to meet with him and for their steeds to be made ready. Cameron summoned them and before Malcolm had a chance to add his new knowledge to the map, he was told of their arrival. The warriors were mounted on tired, filthy horses and formed a semi-circle in front of his tent.

"I have a task of great importance for each of you," said Malcolm.

Some of the men loyally raised their swords and everyone felt the tension in the king's words. A cool breeze blew through the camp and one of the horses snorted, and reared up on its hind legs.

Malcolm pointed at five of them.

"I raise my standard at Glen Shee. Go to each corner of the kingdom and ask every man who can fight to bring food and claymore there."

The riders galloped away without a word, leaving three to learn of their mission. Malcolm looked into their eyes as if measuring the impact his words would have. At last he spoke to two of them.

"Go quickly to our armies who stand before the Picts and Welsh. Tell them to join me at Glen Shee. As they march they are to destroy everything that might give comfort to the enemy."

The two men nodded and left too.

Malcolm then spoke to the last messenger. Ancevo was young, tall, lean and eager, and, like Dougie, more used to life on the farm than the ways of the warrior.

"Go to Alistair at the Irish Court and tell him Scotland has fallen."

Ancevo's forehead creased with worry. You could have run a plough along its deep furrows and he wondered if the king believed there was really no hope of victory. Malcolm gestured to him to dismount and they walked alone, talking in secret, and the Younger gave him a parchment. Then they shook hands and the rider went west. His mission would prove to be more dangerous and vital than any of the missions of the other messengers.

"Cameron," called Malcolm, and his bodyguard came rushing to his side. "You fought with great courage today, but your reward is a poor one."

"I am pleased to help in any way."

"Choose two hundred men and go at once to reinforce the garrison at Stirling Castle. It is the key to the defence of our lands."

Cameron lifted his sword and kissed it.

"And take as much food as you can carry, for the armies of the enemy alliance will combine there in ten days."

A look of fear shot across Cameron's face.

"You expect the castle to be placed under siege."

"Aye, and it must not fall," and the king's voice became determined. "It must *not* fall."

"And apart from the soldiers I take, how many men are there?"

"The garrison is one hundred and twenty strong."

"And the enemy?"

"Four thousand."

They stood and stared at each other. Both men knew that the army that controlled Stirling would control the kingdom.

"I will go to choose the men," said Cameron bravely.

"And I will lead the camp to Glen Shee. Keep the castle safe in Scottish hands, until I arrive, and remember my promise. We *will* be coming to help you."

As the guard left him Malcolm added, "when the moment is right."

The king walked back into his tent and looked at the map. He was sure that Tella would expect him to turn his army towards the west and fight him. But the Younger knew he could not divide his army into three again and expect to win.

"But if we disappear it may keep them guessing, for a while at least."

At that moment, a new warrior burst into the tent.

"A rider with news, Sire."

Malcolm glanced up from the map.

"Good, or ill?"

The man did not reply, but his manner gave away the answer.

"Escort the messenger to me," said Malcolm weakly, and as he rose a feeling of dread swept over him.

The rider looked as though he had travelled far and suffered much to fulfil his mission. Kindly, the king beckoned him to sit and poured out some water. The man took it and drank thirstily.

"Enemy ships have landed on Mull and the flag of the Picts flies over the Outer Islands."

Malcolm's stomach tightened and he dared not ask the question that he feared more than any other question in the world. He thought about the boy he had grown up with and the man who was his closest friend.

"And Murdoch?"

The messenger stared at his hands and feared to give his king the answer. Then he shook his head sadly.

"Your brother died bravely on the field of battle."

Malcolm the Younger, King of the Scots and Protector of the Stone of Destiny, fell to his knees and sobbed like a child.

CHAPTER TWENTY THREE

RELEASE ME

"It's going to be quite a show," said Spiros.

Bernard took a handkerchief from his top pocket, wiped his brow and watched a crane lift a giant television screen into position on the busy quay. Their table overlooked the *Maid Of Norway* and a white marquee with WORLD PRESS written on the roof. Two big men in black T-shirts, black shorts and black baseball caps guarded the entrance to the marquee. A lorry stopped close to the giant screen. More men in black uniforms jumped out, and began to lay out chairs and music stands below the screen. A waiter came over.

"Beautiful afternoon, gentlemen. Coffee?"

"Coffee is good," said Spiros.

The waiter scribbled something on a pad and left them.

"Will Peter come?"

"If he chooses to come, there isn't a thing in the world that can stop him."

Spiros glanced at Bernard.

"And he is the last Keeper."

"He is."

Thorgood Firebrand appeared at a rail high up on the ship. His eyes fixed on Bernard and he nodded. Bernard nodded back.

"An old enemy?" asked Spiros.

"An ancient enemy."

Loud music sounded out from speakers along the quay and a flashing caption appeared on the giant screen. RELEASE ME. The waiter delivered coffee and they kept quiet until he had gone.

"Will the war begin today?"

Bernard shrugged his shoulders.

"We both know the Seekers will hold the stone one day. If Peter stays at the villa then Kylie will die and the war will be delayed. If Peter comes here to face Odin he will die before the sun sets."

"It is a terrible choice for one so young to have to make."

"It's a terrible choice for anyone to make."

Spiros put milk in his coffee.

"Does he know how to use the stone's power?"

"Some of it."

"And he is not armed with the whole story."

"No."

"What can we do?"

"Nothing. Just pray that the Seekers make a mistake."

***

Olaf Adanson walked from the bridge to the lift-tube and descended into the *Black Slug*.

"Is everything ready?"

A man lifted a flashing control panel off his lap, placed it back onto a magnetic strip on the wall and swivelled round in his chair.

"All ready, sir."

Olaf nodded and went to the cell at the back of the submarine. As he entered Kylie stared up at him.

"It's time, isn't it?"

He saw her shaking fingers and the look of absolute terror on her face, and wondered what to say.

"Follow me," he said at last.

On the aft deck of the *Maid Of Norway*, they waited for the Deep Sea Explorer to be lifted on a chain off a tubular storage-cradle, and lowered onto the deck. Guards in black uniforms swung the huge diving bell around so its small round door faced them. The awful picture of a purple face, with bulging eyes, fixed in Kylie's mind.

"You are going to kill me like you killed the man with the needle."

"It might not work out that way. You know what to do," said Olaf.

Kylie remembered Thorgood's precise instructions about how

to act out her triumphant release in the rehearsals. She had been filmed many times, being forced into the Explorer, gasping for air and then being rescued by divers.

"Where are the cameras this time?"

"A diver will film the whole thing."

"Why don't you just let me go?"

Olaf pointed at the round door, grabbed her arm and forced her inside. As he made the door watertight, by turning a wheel, he said to himself, "Because you are the bait."

A drum rotated and two yellow tubes unwound from around it. One providing the Explorer with power, the other with air. A metallic clanking noise started up as another much bigger drum turned, making the chain go tight, and the Deep Sea Explorer rose and swung out over the ship's rail with the guards feeding the tubes over the side. The clanking stopped, then began again as the drum rotated backwards and lowered Kylie into the sea.

Beneath the *Maid Of Norway*, the *Black Slug* disengaged from the mother ship and sank down to rest upon the seabed. As Kylie watched, the *Slug's* eyes glowed and powerful beams cut through the darkness, and bathed her in red light. A diver with an underwater camera rose out of a hatch and swam over. Ten metres from the Explorer he stopped to kneel on the sand, and a green light appeared on his camera. At the same moment, up on the bridge, Thorgood and Odin saw Kylie on a hand-held TV screen, her body framed by the *Explorer's* large round window.

From their seats in the café, Bernard and Spiros saw the fear in Kylie's eyes as she appeared on the giant screen which dominated the quay. Below them, members of the press began to arrive, to be searched by the two guards at the marquee's entrance.

"So, it is nearly time," said Spiros.

***

Peter lay on his bed, staring up at the ceiling. Bright sunshine streamed through the window and out in the garden Mr Agnedes was cutting the lawn. Peter felt sick with worry and kept asking himself the same question. Would Odin really kill Kylie? The answer was always the same. The Ancient One was driven by anger and greed, and would do anything to hold the stone again. If Peter gave it to him, what then? Would he let Kylie go? What kind of place would the world become? He remembered every word of Myroy's story, about how the Keepers had won the race to Amera's cairn, and how Odin had ordered Lars Stonehammer's death for making a simple joke. He had killed his own servant without a second thought.

"I have waited for century after long century and I missed the stone by one day," hissed Odin and he shook with rage. "Kill Lars, he has failed us."

As Thorfinn hurried up the passage a voice called after him.
"Tell him I have a way with people."

"You certainly do," thought Peter.

Odin was powerful and utterly ruthless, and in his heart Peter knew that he would have to stand up to him one day. He thought about Toady Thompson and Mac Mackinlay on the school bus. It had taken all his courage just to stand up to them. Down by the pool, Stefanos began to whistle his favourite tune and Peter guessed his friend had finished his jobs for the day. Why couldn't his life be as simple, as free, as Stefanos's life? He looked at his watch. 1400 hours. In one hour, Kylie would be dead just like his mother and father. Like James and Laura. He swung his legs off the bed, put his head in his hands and began to cry.

***

Thorgood Firebrand stepped inside the marquee and raised a hand.

"Welcome. Welcome to you all and thank you for being the guests of OASV. My name is Mr Brand and I am absolutely delighted that you have been able to give up some time, out of your very busy schedules, to join us on the beautiful island of Corfu for the launch of our new fragrance, Release Me. As you can see, most of the world's press have sent reporters and photographers here. Helped, perhaps, by OASV's financial assistance with flights and accommodation in Corfu's most luxurious hotel."

Some of the crowd laughed. Several flashes from phone cameras went off. Thorgood smiled.

"Please, help yourselves to Champagne and food. I hope you enjoy the show. Please join me in half an hour on the quay. Meanwhile …."

Thorgood clapped his hands and outside on the quay music began to play. A line of pretty, uniformed promotion girls filed into the marquee, handing out perfume gift boxes.

"A small token of our appreciation."

Thorgood stepped out of the marquee and glanced up at the giant screen, the orchestra playing below it, and the enemy who watched him from their seats at a café. At both ends of the quay, held back by small barriers, large crowds had gathered and more promotion girls handed out gift boxes to eager, outstretched arms. He took the hand-held TV from his pocket and switched it on. Kylie was staring out of the diving bell directly at the camera.

"I wonder when the Keeper will arrive?" he thought.

***

Peter listened to Stefanos whistle. The same four notes over and over again. Something deep inside snapped and anger pulsed through his veins.

"Stop that bloody whistling, will you."

In the pocket of his shorts, Amera's stone pulsed blood red. Peter imagined Stefanos rising up through the air and he looked out of the window. Stefanos was hanging in thin air, arms and legs flailing around, fear on his face.

"Stop that bloody whistling."

Peter nodded angrily and Stefanos flew away backwards, and a huge splash came from the pool.

The Keeper took the stone from his pocket and looked at the brooch. It was so small, but so powerful. He clasped it tightly in his hand and concentrated on a white paper bag on his bedside table. The bag rose up and came to him. He opened the bag and took out a pair of sunglasses.

"I am coming," he said.

On the bridge of the *Maid Of Norway*, Odin felt the stone's power. He glanced at Olaf Adanson.

"Go to Thorgood Firebrand. Tell him the Keeper comes."

"I obey, master."

"Begin the operation."

"I obey, master."

Inside the Deep Sea Explorer, Kylie watched the diver. He was still filming and she wondered what the pictures would be like with the red lights of the *Slug* shining so brightly onto the diving bell. Suddenly, the red eyes disappeared and all was darkness. Kylie's stomach tightened and she listened to her heartbeat, listened to the constant hiss of air as it was pumped down from the ship. A ring of white lights came on all around the Explorer. Then the hiss stopped.

With the stone in his hand, Peter strode to the door and tried to open it. Mrs Agnedes must have locked it and it refused to open. He nodded and the door fell down with a crash. Grandma came rushing up the stairs.

"Don't go, Peter. Please don't go."

"I have to go," said Peter quietly.

"You have to go," repeated Grandma.

"I will need a taxi."

"You will need a taxi."

"Tell Mr Minolas to hurry."

"He must hurry."

"Tell him it is an emergency."

"An emergency."

"Tell him it is for Bernard."

She hurried back down the stairs.

Peter waited on the drive, constantly checking his watch. It was two thirty and he realised he would not be able to get to Corfu Town for three. He smelled the newly cut grass and the heady perfume of the flowers. Every minute seemed like an age, but eventually a horn sounded and Mr Minolas shot through the automatic black metal gates, which only just opened in time for him. He was out of the car in a flash and staring at Peter.

"Where is Bernard?"

"You do not need Bernard."

"I do not need Bernard."

"We must go quickly to the quay at Corfu Town."

"We must go quickly."

The taxi's tyres screeched as they swerved around the tight bends going down the lower slopes of Pantekrator towards the coast road. Lime and olive groves flashed past and Peter began to question what he was doing. Then he thought about Kylie and decided that something good, something lucky, might just happen. Perhaps Myroy would save them?

The coast road was busy with traffic and Mr Minolas drove like a madman, overtaking and swerving back into the right hand lane to avoid oncoming traffic, ignoring the drivers who sounded their horns and shook their fists. The road followed the line of the beach, which curved inland and Peter could now look across the sea at the distant outline of Corfu Town. He glanced at his watch. Five to three. They weren't going to make it. Two hundred metres ahead, a campervan slowed, blocking the road. Peter gripped the stone and the taxi shot forward. Then it rose up into the air and flew over the campervan. Peter looked at Corfu Town and they headed directly for it.

"Faster," said Peter.

The taxi began to shake as they accelerated like a rocket. The windscreen wipers disappeared and Mr Minolas stared at the sea shooting by below them.

"Best taxi on the island," he muttered.

Peter tried to see the old fortress that overlooked the quay and the *Maid Of Norway*. Then he saw the ship and he gripped the stone harder. The taxi screamed forward and he got a clear view of the giant screen, orchestra and crowds. He willed the taxi to slow and they shot past the bridge of the *Maid Of Norway* and turned sharply to land heavily beside the marquee. Peter tried his door and it was stuck. He nodded at it and the wheels fell off. He nodded again and all the doors of the taxi flew outwards.

Mr Minolas stepped out and stared at the wreck of his taxi. Peter stepped out and the crowd gave him a tremendous cheer. Photographers surrounded them and the orchestra began to play, *Those Magnificent Men in their Flying Machines*.

Thorgood pushed his way through the press and forced the mini TV into Peter's free hand.

"Welcome, Keeper. I was beginning to think you were not going to join us." He pointed up at the giant screen. Kylie was pounding her fists onto the *Explorer's* window and gasping for air. Then he pointed at the mini TV. The same picture. "Hand me the stone and the girl will be released."

Peter pushed past him and ran towards the *Maid Of Norway*. The crowd gave out a huge, "Oooh," and he stopped in his tracks, and followed their gaze upwards. Small black dots jumped from a plane and plummeted towards the earth. Their parachutes opened and they steered themselves towards an orange buoy behind the aft deck of the great ship. The skydivers were wearing wetsuits, oxygen tanks and flippers, and ten metres above the sea, they released themselves from their harnesses and dropped into the water.

Peter glanced at the giant screen. A circle of white lights lit up the diving bell and the divers who swarmed around it. Then they were opening the small door and dragging a girl out. One diver placed an oxygen mask over her face. The crowd cheered. Then the camera followed them to the surface and Peter prayed that Kylie was safe. A ring of bubbles formed behind the ship and everyone strained to get a first sight of them. The crowd gave a tremendous cheer as their heads broke the surface. A girl with dark hair waved and was helped up a steep concrete slipway onto the quay. Somewhere above them fireworks exploded. Thorgood Firebrand's voice came over the speakers.

"Ladies and Gentlemen. I am sure you will agree with me that this has been one of the most breathtaking product launches of the twenty first century. Thank you for supporting us and buying RELEASE ME, the new fragrance from OASV Europe."

As the crowd went mad, Peter ran over to the slipway to hug Kylie, but when the girl turned it wasn't her. He looked at the giant screen. It showed a picture of a perfume bottle. He looked at his mini TV. Kylie's face was purple and she scratched like an animal at the glass. He threw the TV away and ran down the slipway into the water. When the water was up to his neck he squeezed the stone. As he forced himself down, a red bubble surrounded his body and he ran across the sandy sea bed towards the diving bell. A diver turned a camera on him and Peter thrust the stone forward. The man shot backwards out of sight. The eyes of the *Black Slug* shone out and bathed the Explorer with red light.

Odin appeared in front of Peter, standing tall inside a tower of bubbles.

"You have something that belongs to me."

"I want Kylie. Alive."

"You can have her. Give me the stone."

Peter watched Kylie collapse onto the floor of the diving bell.

"You will kill her anyway."

"I make you a promise, Keeper. Give me the stone and I will release her. She will be allowed to live."

Peter took a deep breath.

"I have no choice, do I?"

Odin stepped forward and took Amera's stone from Peter's hand.

"No. No choice at all."

Odin pointed the stone at the *Explorer.* The door opened and water rushed in. Then Odin was gone and through the sea his eternal voice sang out.

"Save her and remember my promise."

The red bubble around Peter disappeared and the sea engulfed him. Salt stung his eyes. He swam over to the diving bell and reached inside, took hold of Kylie and dragged her out. Then his arms were around her and he kicked for the surface, praying that she would live. Somehow, Peter got her head above water and she gasped for air. He swam on his back, still holding her limp body tightly, towards the concrete slipway.

On the top deck of the *Maid Of Norway*, Odin stepped out with Thorgood Firebrand. Odin held Amera's stone aloft and an intense red beam shot up into space. A red bubble, an impenetrable force-field centred upon Corfu Town, covered half of the world. Millions of people inside the bubble fell to their knees. Cars crashed and planes dived out of control as Odin's will took hold, and forced their drivers and pilots to their knees. The planet was now divided and Odin watched the crowd kneeling to his authority along the quay.

Then he saw Peter holding Kylie and swimming towards the slipway. He smiled at Thorgood.

"Kill him."

"I obey, master," and Thorgood ran off to join Mick Roberts on the aft deck.

Mick lifted the butt of the CAR to his shoulder and the green night sight lit up. He switched to daylight view and the green disappeared. He scanned the waters behind the ship and followed the slipway up to Peter. The sensors pinpointed him and small red letters appeared on the screen.

TARGET?

Mick squeezed the trigger and two hair-thin lines came in from the edges of the screen and centered on Peter's back as he helped his girlfriend out of the water and onto the slipway. More red words.

ADJUSTING FOR BREATHING

The information disappeared instantly and new words appeared.

ADJUSTING FOR WIND SPEED

Then –

READY TO FIRE

"What are Odin's orders?" asked Mick.

Thorgood thought about the new empire he would help to build.

"Make sure he suffers."

Mick centered the hair lines onto Kylie's back and squeezed the trigger. The gun spat and NO FURTHER SHOT REQUIRED appeared and disappeared.

"Now he will suffer forever," he said.

Thorgood saw the two bodies fall and turned to leave, and believed Peter to be dead.

Kylie and Peter were thrown forward by an invisible hammer blow. Stunned, he crawled over and threw his arms around the bloody body that lay in an unnatural heap on the concrete.

Through his tears he cried out.

"Don't leave me. Don't leave me. I don't want to be alone again."

He glanced back at the *Maid Of Norway*. It was already heading out of the harbour.

"You lied!" he screamed, but only Myroy heard him.

He stared up at the quay. Everyone was on their knees. He looked at Kylie and then at his hands. They were covered in her blood. Peter held her as tightly as he could and they rocked together, backwards and forwards, Peter sobbing and crying out over and over again.

"Don't leave me. Don't leave me. I don't want to be alone again."

The top of the old fortress, overlooking the seafront of Corfu Town, began to shimmer like moonlight on water and Myroy rose up like a ghost from the underworld. He stared down at the wake of the *Maid Of Norway* and up at the giant red bubble that covered the sky. Then he looked at the rocking bodies of two children on a slipway.

Again Myroy heard Peter say, "Don't leave me. Don't leave me."

The Ancient One smiled.

Dougie and Peter will return in their next thrilling adventure, *A Moment Comes*.

As Malcolm the Younger hides with his people in the lonely places and Dougie and Alistair await their fate in the dungeons of Mountjoy, Tella the Mac Mar orders the alliance to attack. In the north, Thorgood Firebrand rebuilds his army and waits for his own moment to come. As he watches the Picts, Welsh and Angles place Stirling Castle under siege, an unexpected ally, Prince Ranald, makes Thorgood a promise that changes the course of history.

In our time, Odin begins to build his empire and the world kneels to his power. Peter is consumed by grief, as he hugs Kylie's body, and Myroy helps him understand why he must be the last Keeper of Amera's stone.

In the passing of a single hour, on a concrete slipway, the world changes forever.

If you would like to read the start of the
next book then please visit -

www.myroybooks.com